BRIGHT IS THE DAWN

Meg watched. She didn't know what to do. Should she come out and offer to get old Mr Grizedale some butter and sugar and vinegar for his cough to make him better? Maybe he would look after her and Jonty, maybe he wouldn't let Jonty's da be cruel to him. She hovered undecided and in that moment saw Jonty's da pick up a pillow and hold it over the old man's face. Jonty's da was bending over the bed and holding the pillow down. Meg could see it plainly. Did he think that would make the old man better? For sure it had stopped him coughing. Behind her she could hear Jonty breathing. It was the only thing she could hear at all.

Jonty's da straightened up and put the pillow back under the others on the bed. She could see old Mr Grizedale now. He was lying quietly, peacefully, not coughing any more. Meg leaned forward, opening the door a little further the better to see what Jonty's da was doing. And the door swung open and she fell headlong out of the wardrobe and into the room with Jonty behind her.

Una Horne has lived in the Bishop Auckland area of Co. Durham for most of her life. Trained as a nurse, she gave up her career to raise a family but began writing ten years ago when her two children were grown up. After developing her writing skills on articles and short stories she published a couple of romantic novels under a pseudonym and began work on her first regional novel, *Lorinda Leigh*. *Bright is the Dawn* is her second novel; her third, *Come the Day*, is available in hardback.

Also by Una Horne

Lorinda Leigh*
Come the Day

* available in Mandarin

UNA HORNE

Bright is the Dawn

Mandarin

A Mandarin Paperback
BRIGHT IS THE DAWN

First published in Great Britain 1994
by Judy Piatkus (Publishers) Ltd
This edition published 1995
by Mandarin Paperbacks
an imprint of Reed Books Ltd
Michelin House, 81 Fulham Road, London SW3 6RB
and Auckland, Melbourne, Singapore and Toronto

Copyright © 1994 by Una Horne
The author has asserted her moral rights

A CIP catalogue record for this title
is available from the British Library

Phototypeset by Intype, London
Printed and bound in Great Britain by
Cox & Wyman Ltd, Reading, Berkshire

Glossary of Local Words
and Phrases

Bray: to beat

Candyman: bum bailiff

Canny: many meanings, none of them to do with the Scots word. Canny body means a nice person, gan canny means go carefully. A canny few means quite a lot. Can be used for every virtue. Canny is usually taken as a high compliment

Fettle: condition, of persons or things

Femmer: weak or ill. Can be used for something breakable

Gully: a bread knife or other kitchen knife

Howay: come on

Hadaway: go on

Hacky: filthy

Hunkers: haunches

In bye: away from the pit shaft bottom – the coal face

Out bye: the pit shaft bottom

Marra: corruption of the old English marrow or work mate

Ments: common sense

Pallatic: falling down drunk

Pan haggelty: dish peculiar to the north-east. Known as pan haggerty around Newcastle

Cracket: miner's stool

Skinch: used by children to mean pax in games

Satless: drunk to the point of being witless
Wot cheor: pitman's greeting to his fellows

N.B.: Most of these words are in direct descent from old English or Norse.

One

January 1878

It was cold in the lane behind Railway Cottages, so cold even the stink from the netties wasn't so bad today. But Meg and Jonty didn't feel the cold. Both were wrapped up warmly with mufflers tied round their heads and necks, criss-crossed around their chests and tied at the back. They were playing in the middle of the lane, they were playing house. Meg was standing inside a circle of stones which was the house, rocking the baby in her arms, and Jonty was striding down the lane with Uncle Jack's cap on his head. He was coming home from his work on the line.

'Now then, Meg,' he said as he stepped through the gap in the stones which was the doorway. 'Is the dinner ready? I'm starved.' He did his utmost to deepen his voice to sound like a man but at three years old, going on four, only succeeded in making himself cough.

Meg pursed her lip and shook her head in imitation of her mother.

'You'll be wanting some butter and sugar and vinegar the night, to cut that cough,' she said reprovingly.

'Meg! Jonty! Howay in now, I want you to get ready to go up to the Hall.'

The children dropped their make-believe and looked over the frost-covered lane to Meg's mam, standing in her back doorway. They moved close together. Meg took hold of Jonty's hand, feeling it tremble. She held the

1

baby, now just a peg dolly, by its head, dangling it by her side.

'We don't want to go to the Hall, Mam. Jonty doesn't like it,' said Meg, speaking for them both.

Hannah Maddison came out of the house and walked awkwardly towards them, the bulk of her late pregnancy lifting her apron high at the front.

'I know, pet, I know. But Jonty has to go, and you don't want him to go on his own, do you?' She put a gentle hand against each child's head, Meg's so fair and Jonty's so dark, caressing them both.

'Look, hinnies, it's Monday, I don't think Jonty's da will be there. You like Jonty's grandmother, don't you?'

'I don't think she *is* Jonty's grandmother,' Meg declared stoutly. 'If she is, why's she not mine an' all? Me and Jonty, we're twins.' Meg had heard Mrs Hart say they were just like twins so she had asked Da what twins meant, and he said it was when two bairns were born at the same time to one mam. So she knew she and Jonty were twins.

Hannah smiled, but still she led the children firmly into the house to clean them up for the visit to the Hall.

'No, Meg, you and Jonty are not twins, you're cousins.'

But Meg was not convinced. Later on as they walked over the fields to Grizedale Hall, Meg held on to Jonty. She was his twin and if Jonty's da was there she wouldn't let him touch Jonty, no, she wouldn't.

Jonty was quiet. He scuffed the frost with his boots, making long trailing marks, and Meg knew he was frightened, just in case his da was at home after all.

Mrs Grizedale, Jonty's grandmother, was waiting in the hall to greet them. She must have been watching out of the window. Meg rushed straight in but Jonty hung back, casting fearful glances around at the closed doors. Meg came straight to the point, even before saying hello nicely like Mam said she should.

2

'Is Mr Grizedale in?'

The old lady shook her head, smiling down at the little girl standing so fiercely before her cousin, ready to do battle for him.

'No, dear, John Thomas's father isn't in, he's gone to Darlington today on business.'

Meg relaxed and stood aside, allowing Jonty to move forward to be kissed by Mrs Grizedale. 'Hallo, Mrs Grizedale,' she said belatedly, 'are you well today?'

'Yes thank you, dear. Now, come into my sitting-room, both of you. I've ordered hot milk and Cook has baked some gingerbread men.'

Gingerbread men! Meg's eyes glowed in her rosy face. And it was weeks since Christmas. It must be somebody's birthday if they were to have gingerbread men. She waited impatiently while Mrs Grizedale loosed the knot in her muffler and unwound it, then did the same for Jonty.

Soon they were sitting before the fire in the sitting-room, drinking milk and eating the bicuits. Meg sat quietly, giving all her attention to picking out the currant eyes and eating them first then nibbling at the legs, bit by bit, making it last as long as possible. She was not really listening to Mrs Grizedale who was talking to Jonty, asking him questions. Was he well? Was his Auntie Hannah well? And Jonty was smiling and saying little, just keeping close to Meg and following what she was doing so that his biscuit wouldn't be finished before hers.

'Come, Jonty, talk to your grandmother,' Mrs Grizedale pleaded at last. Meg heard that all right and decided she would get this question settled once and for all.

'You're not Jonty's grandmother. How can you be his grandmother if you're not mine?' she demanded. 'She's not your grandmother, is she, Jonty?'

3

Jonty shook his head. He knew better than to disagree with anything Meg said.

'Oh, but I am, dear.' protested Mrs Grizedale.

'But me and Jonty, we're twins,' insisted Meg.

'No, dear, cousins, that's what you are. Your mother and Jonty's mother were sisters.' Mrs Grizedale looked at Meg's indignant little face, the biscuit poised in one hand, forgotten for the moment. 'Jonty's mother passed away, dear, so your mother took him to live with you. Then, when he's old enough for school, he will come back here to live.'

'He won't!' asserted Meg. 'Eeh, no, he won't. Jonty's going to live with us for ever and ever.'

Mrs Grizedale gave up the argument, there was plenty of time yet, Jonty was not yet of school age. She changed the subject.

'Hurry up and finish your gingerbread men,' she said, 'then you can go up to the old nursery and play with the rocking-horse. You won't make too much noise, will you? Grandfather is in bed today, he's not feeling well. Later on perhaps, you can go to see the horses in the stables. You'd like that, wouldn't you, Jonty?'

He smiled and carried on with his biscuit, carefully watching Meg, synchronizing his eating with hers so that they finished the last crumb together. Mrs Grizedale watched them, a faintly anxious expression on her face.

'Oh, I do hope I did the right thing taking you down to Hannah to nurse,' she murmured, almost to herself. 'I hope you won't find it too upsetting when you have to come here.' Luckily, her murmurs were too low even for Meg's acute hearing.

It didn't take Meg long to lose interest in the rocking-horse.

'Howay, Jonty,' she said, sliding down from the

4

painted wooden saddle. 'Let's go out to the stables and see the real galloways.'

'I haven't had a go yet,' he objected.

Meg sighed. 'All right. You get on the daft thing and then we'll go to the stables.' She went over to the nursery window and looked out between the bars, over the stables and outhouses and beyond to the frost-covered, sloping fields of Farmer Teasdale's farm. The rocking-horse squeaked and groaned as Jonty energetically rode it behind her.

'Howay, Jonty,' she said impatiently. 'Hurry up, man, I want—' Meg forgot what it was she wanted when out of the corner of her eye she saw a horseman emerge from the trees which lined the stream at the bottom of the slope. She clung to the bars and hauled herself up higher, the better to see. He was coming up to the Hall all right, up by Farmer Teasdale's hedge, but on the inside, not on the track which the hedge bordered.

'Jonty! Come and have a look.'

He slid down to the ground obediently and went over to the window.

'What is it?'

He climbed up beside Meg and peered out.

'What're you looking at, Meg?'

'Over there, by the hedge. Look, can you see?'

The horseman had dismounted and was leading his horse up the field, but the two children had no difficulty in recognizing him immediately.

'It's me da!'

Jonty's cry was panicky; he began to tremble all over. He dropped down from the window bars and turned to run.

'Howay, Meg, howay!'

But she was thinking hard. She knew they couldn't just run home, Mam would make them go back and say goodbye to Mrs Grizedale properly. No, the best thing

5

to do was find a safe place, somewhere Jonty's da wasn't likely to find them.

'We'll go to see your grandfather,' she decided, and led the way down a flight of stairs and along the upper hall to the door at the end which led to the master bedroom. She knocked hard on the door and Jonty knocked too, but no one said to come in and Jonty was getting more agitated by the minute. Meg reached up and turned the handle and went in.

It was a large room with tall windows which faced on to the rolling parkland at the front of the house. Meg found time to admire the lovely thick carpet on the floor and the gleaming wood of the furniture. By, she marvelled, it was grand. But the middle of the room was taken up by a large bed, an impressive four-poster, and in the bed, propped up on pillows, was Jonty's grandfather, dressed in a white nightshirt and covered with a huge, puffy eiderdown quilt. He had his eyes closed.

The children walked over to the bed and stood watching him gravely. He was breathing slowly and deeply and Meg stared, fascinated, at the tiny bubbles appearing at the corner of his mouth every time he breathed out.

'Go on, tell him good morning,' she urged Jonty. After all, it was Jonty who should wake him. He was Jonty's grandfather, wasn't he?

'Good morning, Grandfather,' said Jonty.

'You'll have to say it louder than that,' pointed out Meg, 'or he'll never hear you.'

'Good morning, Grandfather.' Jonty raised his voice almost to a shout and the old man stirred but did not wake. And in the silence they heard footsteps approaching along the upper hall, a man's footsteps, and the sound sent terror coursing through them both. If Jonty's da came in and his grandfather didn't wake up, Jonty would be in trouble. His da would hit him again.

He always hit him whenever he saw him and said nasty, nasty things to him. And it was too late now to seek out Jonty's grandmother for protection, she was downstairs somewhere.

Quick as a flash, Meg ran for the wardrobe, tugging Jonty after her. She thought she would never get the key turned in the lock but in the end she did and the door swung silently open. She pushed Jonty inside among the clothes and jumped in herself. She couldn't manage to close the door from the inside but she pulled it to and held it by the rail on the inside which held ties and things. Behind her, Jonty buried himself behind the clothes. Her poor Jonty! She wouldn't let his da get him. No, she wouldn't.

They heard the footsteps pause at the bedroom door and the door open. And Meg peered through the crack where the door wasn't quite to and saw Jonty's da walking over to the bed.

'Father?' he said.

Old Mr Grizedale stirred and opened his eyes, grunting when he saw his son. He pushed himself up against the pillows and as he did so began to cough, a harsh, dry coughing which seemed to catch his breath. His face coloured up with the effort of it.

'What do you want, sir?' he managed to say, between bouts of coughing. 'Didn't I make it plain you would get no more money from me until your next quarterly allowance?'

Meg watched. She didn't know what to do. Should she come out and offer to get old Mr Grizedale some butter and sugar and vinegar for his cough to make him better? Maybe he would look after her and Jonty, maybe he wouldn't let Jonty's da be cruel to him. She hovered undecided and in that moment saw Jonty's da pick up a pillow and hold it over the old man's face. Jonty's da was bending over the bed and holding the pillow down. Meg could see it plainly. Did he think that would make the old man better? For sure it had stopped him coughing. Behind her she could hear Jonty breathing. It was the only thing she could hear at all.

Jonty's da straightened up and put the pillow back under the others on the bed. She could see Mr Grizedale now. He was lying quietly, peacefully, not coughing any more. Meg leaned forward, opening the door a little further the better to see what Jonty's da was doing. And the door swung open and she fell headlong out of the wardrobe and into the room with Jonty behind her.

'What the devil!' cried Jonty's da, and his face went purple with rage as he saw the two children come out of nowhere. Meg didn't want to see what he would do, she had to save Jonty for it didn't look like old Mr Grizedale would wake up and stop Jonty's da hitting him. He must be having a really good sleep. She grabbed hold of Jonty yet again and fled out of the room and down the stairs to where Mrs Grizedale was just coming out of her sitting-room.

The two children paused. They had to say goodbye properly. Didn't Mam always say they had to?

'We have to go now, Mrs Grizedale,' said Meg, if a little breathlessly.

'Yes, we have to. Thank you very much for having us,' said Jonty, though he didn't take his eyes off the staircase. He was ready to fly the minute his da appeared at the head of the stairs, but they had to wait for Mrs Grizedale to answer them.

'Oh,' she said. 'I thought you wanted to look round the stables? It's early yet, you know, not twelve o'clock.'

'Aye, but me mam wants us to do the messages,' improvised Meg.

'Oh, yes, of course. I understand,' said Mrs Grizedale, and as she turned away she added in her undertone, 'Hannah must be near her time.'

8

Though she might as well have spoken out loud for neither Meg nor Jonty knew what she was talking about. And still Jonty's da hadn't appeared at the head of the stairs, even though they had to wait while Mrs Grizedale wound their mufflers round them and pinned them at the back, he didn't come.

The children ran down the drive and over the fields, racing each other like whippets let out of the cage to chase a hare.

'You're soon back, mind,' said Mam. She was kneading bread dough in the big earthenware dish, lifting the heavy dough from the outside and pressing it into the centre. The children watched fascinated by the rhythm.

'Da came back,' volunteered Jonty, and Hannah frowned and paused in her work to look closely at him.

'He didn't touch you, did he, pet?'

'We ran away,' said Meg. 'We said goodbye to Mrs Grizedale first, like.'

'Good lass,' said her mother. 'I'm going to put the stotty cake in now. I'll give you both a bit of dough and you can make little ones. Do you fancy doing that, then?'

The next half hour was spent happily, kneeling on the form at the table and moudling dough. Mam put the large bread cake on the bottom of the round oven and the slightly grey smaller ones beside it to cook, while the loaves were rising on the fender before the fire. And when the stotty cakes came out of the oven they ate them hot with treacle spread on them, soaking into the bread and oozing all over the place.

It was a lovely afternoon. Meg forgot all about Jonty's nasty da as they sat, one on either side of Mam, on the settle drawn up to the fire. And she told the story about how she took Jonty when he was a baby to love and bring up with Meg.

9

'Your mother was my sister,' Mam told Jonty. 'Eeh, she was a grand lass, she was. I married Uncle Jack and she married Ralph Grizedale. And when she died you were a tiny baby so you came to live with us.'

'Why did she marry Mr Grizedale, Mam? He's a nasty man.'

'Whisht, pet, don't say that,' said Hannah. 'Our poor Nell – she was your mam, Jonty – she must have loved him. And he is Jonty's da.'

'Mrs Grizedale's nice. She gave us gingerbread men,' said Meg. She wished with all her heart that Mr Grizedale wasn't Jonty's da.

'You won't die, will you, Auntie Hannah?' put in Jonty. He leaned against her and looked up into her face with anxious eyes. Meg hadn't thought of that and felt a tug of fear. They knew what dead was. Hadn't Mrs Hall in the end house died and they'd taken her away in a box and she'd never come back?

'Nay, lad, I'm not going to die,' said Mam, and Meg and Jonty sighed with relief.

At six o'clock Jack Maddison came home from his work on the line. He was a platelayer. Meg and Jonty both ran to him and he swung them up in the air and round and round before putting them down on the settle, breathless and laughing. But when he turned to face his wife he was no longer smiling. His face was grave.

'Old Mr Grizedale died today,' he said quietly. 'This morning sometime. He was in bed with a cold. The maid found him when she took him up a dish of tea. It must have turned to congestion or something.'

'Oh, poor man,' sighed Hannah. 'The bairns were up there today an' all, but they came home early. Jonty said his da had come home, that was what it must have been for.'

'Nay, lass,' said Jack, 'that cannot be right. Ralph Grizedale was away in Darlington all day.'

10

'But – well, mebbe Mrs Grizedale just told them Ralph had come back so they would come straight home.'

'Aye.' Jack sat down by the fire and unlaced his boots. 'The old man'll be missed, he was a good man. At the chapel an' all, he was a good preacher.'

Meg had been listening and understanding far more than her parents thought.

'Jonty's grandmother didn't tell us, we saw him,' she asserted, and Jonty nodded agreement.

'Yes. Well, I think it's time you two were in bed,' said her mother, and Meg knew she thought she was making it up.

'But it's not time yet,' she objected.

'It'll be nice and warm in bed. I've put the oven shelf in.'

Hannah was brooking no arguments and in no time Meg and Jonty were tucked into bed, their feet cosily on the towel-covered oven shelf and a new clippie mat over the blanket for extra warmth. And it was nice to cuddle down in the bed with only their noses out in the cold air. They were almost asleep when they heard a great commotion as someone came in.

'I've come for the boy.'

The words and the voice speaking then sent terror coursing through Meg's veins. Her eyes flew open and Jonty clung tightly to her, already beginning to tremble.

'Get under the bed,' she said urgently, but Jonty could do nothing but cling to her. She listened hard to what was going on downstairs. Da would stop him taking Jonty, wouldn't he?

'Why, man, the bairns are in bed,' said Hannah. 'You can't take him now. Whatever for would you do that?' Her voice was rising, she sounded panicky, thought Meg, not like her mam at all.

11

'I can do what the hell I like, Hannah Hope. Haven't you heard I'm master now?'

'Not in my house, you cannot,' said Da. 'And my wife's name is Hannah Maddison.'

Jonty's da laughed and the sound of it gave Meg a horrible feeling in her stomach. She felt sick.

'Your house, is it? This hovel doesn't belong to you, Jack Maddison, it's railway property. And now I'll be on the board, think of that.'

The sound of his footsteps as he bounded up the stairs galvanized Meg into action. She jumped from the bed, pulling Jonty after her, and for the second time that day she tried to hide them both from Ralph Grizedale. But it was no good, he saw them straight away, they hadn't time to get under the bed. He caught hold of Jonty and even though Meg clung on he managed to separate them, knocking her down with a backhanded blow across her head.

'Don't you touch my bairn!' cried Jack. He had followed Ralph up the stairs and just reached the small landing to see Meg go flying across the room. She lay for a moment, dazed, and saw Ralph give Da a great kick in the stomach which sent him flying, head over heels, to the bottom of the stairs. She screamed, and Mam screamed. But Jonty's da tucked Jonty under his arm, though Jonty was kicking and yelling too, and took him down the stairs and out into the bitter cold night dressed only in his nightshirt.

He shoved his way contemptuously through the group of neighbours gathered to see what it was all about, climbed on his horse and galloped off.

'Jack! Jack!'

Meg heard Mam cry as she got to her feet and ran down the stairs. Mam was there at the bottom, lifting Da and cradling his head in her arms. Now Da was stirring. He got to his feet and lifted Mam up with him.

12

'I'm all right, Hannah,' he said. 'Oh God, Hannah, I'm sorry, I'm sorry, I couldn't do anything.'

Meg clung to them both, hanging on to Hannah's skirt with one hand and Jack's trousers with the other.

'He took Jonty, Da,' she sobbed. 'He took Jonty.'

Jack bent and lifted his daughter up into his arms. 'Whisht now, petal,' he said softly. 'Whisht now. He was Jonty's father, we couldn't help it. I'm sorry, I'm that sorry.' He carried Meg back to bed and lay down with her until she fell asleep.

Meg woke next morning and turned over on to her back, putting a hand out for Jonty before remembering what had happened last night. She got out of bed and pushed her feet into her boots and walked over to the window, shivering.

The world was white. During the night snow had fallen and everything was covered with it: the coalhouse roof and the nettie, the fields behind and the trees. Almost, she called for Jonty to come and see, before remembering numbly that he wasn't there. She could hear Da moving about downstairs; she would go down and ask him if he could get Jonty back.

Da was standing by the fire, cooking strips of bacon in the iron frying pan.

'Morning, petal,' he said as he turned and smiled at her. He looked tired out, she thought, had he not been to bed? Why was Mam not frying the bacon?

'Da, where's me mam? Can you go up to the Hall and get Jonty back?'

Jack shook his head. 'I cannot, Meg. I cannot, bairn. But your mam's in the room, go away in and see her. She's got something special to show you.'

'But Da, I want you to—'

'Go on now. Go and see your mam.'

Meg reluctantly went through the connecting door to

13

the front room and over to the brass bed in the corner. Hannah was sitting up with a bundle in her arms.

'Mam, why can't we get Jonty back?' asked Meg. All she could think about was him. It left no room in her mind for questions such as why Hannah was still in bed or what she was holding in her arms.

'Jonty's me brother, Mam,' she said vehemently.

'I've got a new little brother for you, Meg,' said Hannah, and Meg stared.

'Howay, hinnie, come and see your new baby brother.'

Meg clambered on to the high bed and peered at the bundle in her mam's arms. She looked at the tiny nose and the fair downy hair on its head.

'That's not a proper brother,' she said stoutly, 'not like Jonty. That's just a babby.'

Two

May 1878

'The candymen! The candymen are coming!'

Mrs Hart's warning cry rang through the houses, bouncing down the short street and reverberating off the middens across the back lane. Meg jumped up from the back step where she had been playing house with the peg dollie Mam had made for her, her heart beating wildly, responding to the alarm in Mrs Hart's voice and increasing at the sight of Mam flying out of the house. Mam had a look on her face such as Meg had never seen before. It was enough to send fright racing through the little girl.

'See to the bairn,' her mother called over her shoulder, and Meg, peeking out of the front door before she obediently turned back to watch little Jack in his cradle, saw her joining the other women of the street and forming a line, a thin barrier against the half-dozen or so strange men marching on them.

Jack Boy, disturbed by the noise, began a fretful crying and Meg rocked the wooden cradle with her foot as she had seen Mam do while clutching her dollie to her and staring out of the door with round blue eyes.

'Whisht, whisht,' she said softly, her voice trembling. Where was Da? He'd been around the house for days and days, getting under Mam's feet till she scolded him and, muttering, he would fling himself out of the door and go for a walk, calling to Meg to go with him if she wanted to. And she usually did want to now, for Mr

Grizedale had taken Jonty away and stopped him coming to play with her and Meg didn't know why that was. Her heart hammered as the shouting outside increased. By! She wanted Da to be here, she wanted him more than anything, and he'd gone out somewhere and this time hadn't even asked her to go with him. Jack Boy snuffled and his eyes closed again so Meg stopped rocking the cradle.

There was a great commotion on the old line, there was. A lot of people were shouting and a woman was screaming. That was Mrs Hart, Meg knew her voice well. The ball of fear in the little girl's stomach grew larger and larger. The screaming wakened the baby again but he didn't whinge, he was just staring up at Meg with wide open eyes as blue as her own.

'Whisht now, Babby,' said Meg, as much to reassure herself as her baby brother. If only Mam would come back in. Fearfully, Meg went to the door and peeped round to see what was happening.

Mam was glaring angrily at the hefty Irishman confronting her, her anger heightened by her despair. It was hopeless, even little Meg knew it was, the women couldn't hold out against men.

'What did we do to you?' Mam demanded. 'Aren't you ashamed, throwing women and bairns out of their homes?'

'Just doing the work I'm paid to do, Missus,' the man answered casually. At least that was what Meg thought he said, his speech was so thick she had trouble understanding him. Leaning over, he pushed Mam out of his way as easily as if she'd been a straw. Meg gasped as Mam staggered and would have fallen but for Mrs Hart, who held on to her arm.

'Mind, Hannah!' she cried.

Mam found her feet and would have fought back but

16

just then a cry went up which sent her fleeing for the house.

'The Bobbies! The rotten sods have sent the polis an' all.'

Most of the women turned with her, they knew the day was lost. All they could do was get the bairns out of the houses before the candymen got in. They had to save what bits of furniture they had. Mam reached the door barely in front of a burly bully-boy. She rushed in and snatched the baby from his cradle, thrusting him into Meg's small arms. She picked up the cradle as the grinning candyman reached for it. Shrugging, he picked up her two good chairs and flung them out of the house.

'You didn't have to be so rough,' Mam cried, but his grin grew wider as he picked up the rocker, the old rocker that had been Gran's, and threw it after the chairs to the ominous sound of breaking wood.

'Now, Missus, out,' he said, and started towards her. 'Or I can always carry you out.'

Meg edged to the door whimpering softly as her mother took the cradle outside and put it down beside the broken chairs before going back in for Meg and little Jack.

'Away wi' you then. Go out, pet,' Mam said quietly as she folded the baby in her shawl. As Meg, crying softly but steadily now, went out of the door, Hannah Maddison gathered the spittle in her mouth and spat full in the face of the candyman. Then, quick as a flash, she turned and ran. Meg grabbed a hold of her mother's skirts almost by instinct as she went, the angry roar of the candyman close behind them as they fled.

Meg's terror flared. She ran as fast as her four-year-old legs would carry her, clinging on to Mam's skirts for dear life, stumbling and falling over the uneven ground of the old railway track, past Mrs Hart's door which was already being nailed up by the men, stubbing her toes

17

on the stones through her thin boots, choking on her sobs.

'Da! Da!' she cried, for the Irish would catch them, and then what? Her young mind couldn't imagine what would happen then.

But Mam was slowing to a walk. She was looking over the field by the side of the old railway, the very first railway in the world, Da had said proudly, the irrelevant thought running through Meg's head even as she gasped for breath.

'I dropped me dollie!'

Meg rubbed her eyes with the back of her hand and looked fearfully over her shoulder. The candyman had stopped too. He was watching them though. Meg followed Mam's gaze. A man was sitting on a great grey horse in the field, just sitting there quietly, watching them, his face blank. A big man with a florid face, bigger even than the candyman who had been chasing them. Meg knew him all right, it was Jonty's da. Maybe the sight of him had put off their pursuer for now she saw the Irishman go back to the little row of cottages.

'You did this.'

Meg stopped sobbing altogether and looked up at Mam, surprised. Mam was talking to Jonty's da. Was he a candyman then? Meg stared at him. He was way up in the sky on his big horse. Cal. Short for California, Jonty had told her, but she didn't know what California was any road. And then, Jonty's da didn't like her, Meg knew. He had yelled at her that time in the Hall and then he'd taken Jonty.

Mr Grizedale was staring at her now. Meg moved in even closer to her mother.

'Not at all, my dear Hannah.' He smiled, and his voice was patronizingly pleasant. 'It was the board's decision. I'm only one man, what could I do? No, if you want someone to blame then go no further than Jack

Maddison, the man you married, the man who led the men into this folly. The brave champion of the people.' He glanced around him and shrugged. 'But where is he when you need him?'

'You know well where he is. You knew the men were at a union meeting in Shildon. That's why you brought in the bully-boys from Hartlepool.'

'Well, my point is proven then. Why couldn't he see that this would happen? No, Hannah Hope, you married the wrong man, a man who can't protect his own—'

'My name is Hannah Maddison!'

'Oh, so it is. Hannah Maddison. Well, you are Hannah Hope to me and always will be. Maybe now you wish you'd married me and saved all this trouble?'

'God damn you to Hell, Ralph Grizedale! The biggest bloody candyman of the lot, that's what you are! I hope your soul rots in—'

Meg turned to see Mrs Hart, all four feet ten inches of her, dancing with rage as she screamed abuse at Jonty's da. It was true then, Jonty's da was a candyman, Mrs Hart said so. But there was a polis close behind the little woman and he was putting out a hand to her.

'Now then, Missus, that's enough of that.' The polis took a firm grip on the woman's arm and nodded respectfully at Jonty's da.

Mr Grizedale acknowledged the salute before shortening the reins and wheeling Cal round. Without another word he galloped over the fields in the direction of Grizedale Hall. Meg watched him ride over the hill and out of sight before turning back to her mother.

'Mam, where's me da?'

'Eeh, never you mind, pet, don't be frightened.' The hard, set look left Hannah's face as she bent down, lifting a corner of her apron to wipe the tears away from Meg's rosy face. She hoisted Jack Boy into a more comfortable

19

position under her shawl. 'Howay, we'll walk up the line and find him, eh?'

'I'm frightened of the candymen,' Meg admitted.

'Aye. Well, they won't hurt you, petal, they just wanted us out of the houses.'

A small group of women, some of them with babies in their arms and other children around them, had gathered around Hannah. All of them had a defeated look about them, their anger drained away, all except Mrs Hart.

'Bloody hell! Can you believe it, Hannah? I'm summonsed. Causing an affray, the polis said. Obstructing the bobbies as they escorted the candymen. Eeh, man, lass, it'll be Durham Gaol for me.'

'Aye, an' me an' all,' cut in Hannah's next-door neighbour, a widow of forty who looked all of sixty. Her husband had been killed in an accident in Shildon Railway Works but she was allowed to keep a railway house because she had two sons platelayers on the line. Keep her house until now, that is. None of them had anywhere to sleep tonight.

'My God,' a woman wailed suddenly, 'what are we going to do?'

'Bear up, lass,' urged Mrs Hart, 'talking like that will get us nowhere.'

'We'll go up to meet the men for a start,' suggested Hannah, and the small group of women, trailed by their children, tramped up the black, rutted road which had been built in the time of their parents to carry coals from the Black Boy colliery to Shildon and on to Darlington, Stockton-on-Tees and the coast.

'They broke our chairs, Da! The candymen did it. Da, they were chasing us—'

At last the men had come. Jack Maddison reached the side of his little family and swung Meg up in his arms, holding her tight. His eyes were black with despair as he looked over her head at his wife.

'I shouldn't have gone, Hannah. Oh, God, I'm sorry, I knew this might happen.'

'What could you do? You had to go to the meeting, you're their union man,' said Hannah. 'You couldn't just let them cut the pay like that, you had to try.'

'Aye, but I knew it wasn't any good. And now we haven't even got anywhere to sleep tonight, and you with the babby an' all. Eeh, they didn't give us much time, did they?'

'Aw, man, we'll get by, lad, you'll see.'

'Were they chasing you? Did they hurt you, Hannah?'

'No, no, they just wanted to frighten us away, they weren't chasing us really. But Meg took fright.'

'Mam spit at them! Didn't you, Mam, you spit at them?' Sitting in her father's arms, Meg was brave enough to feel pride in her mother's defiance.

'Spat at them? By, if I'd been here I'd have done a lot more than spit at them.' Jack let some of his anger and frustration burst through.

Hannah looked up at him glumly. Though Jack Maddison was no more than average height he was well-built and strong, tanned and healthy-looking, showing his farm upbringing in this area where the men were often short and stockily-muscled, but pale from working underground.

'Aye,' she said. 'Well, mebbe it's as well you weren't here. You might have been on your way to the polis cells in Auckland by now, or even Durham Gaol.'

The rest of the people were beginning to drift back to the cottages to pick over the piles of their belongings before each front door. There was no sign of the candymen, just a lone policeman, there to make sure no one tried to get back in the houses.

'What are we going to do, Jack?'

One of the younger lads, a boy of sixteen but head of the family now his father was dead, fell into line beside Jack and Hannah as they approached the row. Jack shifted Meg's weight from one arm to the other and smiled encouragingly at the boy.

'Why, Albert,' he said, 'you'll manage. It's only May yet, the summer's afore us. At least it's not snowing.'

Albert failed to return his smile, his face woebegone.

'Haven't you any family, like? Somewhere you can stay for a while?' Hannah suggested. The lad's mother answered for him.

'Why aye, we have that. I have a sister up at Coundon and another in Shildon. It would be no good going to Shildon, though, her man works on the line and if they took us in his job would go, likely.' She turned to her son. 'Nay, lad, we must go to Coundon. Our Betty's man works in the pit. Howay, thou must be a man.'

Albert, who'd been told he must be a man over and over since the death of his father, sighed. 'Aye.' He regarded the pile of furniture which was theirs. 'The thing is, what are we going to do about this lot?' He picked up a chair with a broken leg, looked around and found the leg and tried fitting it together, dispiritedly.

'You can use my handcart,' offered Jack. 'We'll get your stuff shifted this morning then I can use it this afternoon.' He put Meg down and walked over the line to where a small wooden cart was resting in the grass. Hannah followed him, speaking in an undertone.

'What about us, Jack? We have nowhere. Now my mother's gone, like.' For Mrs Hope had not lived long after Nell died, she had lost any will to live.

'I've been thinking.' He paused and looked at her with a question in his eyes. 'Grizedale might be your brother-in-law, but he's not going to let us take shelter anywhere near the Hall. He'll hound us out. But mebbe you and the bairns can sleep in one of his barns, just for a night or two? Then I can go and look for a place.'

Hannah shook her head in emphatic denial. 'No, Jack, we can't do that. I'd rather sleep in the open, any road. It's May, the weather's warm, we'll take no hurt.'

Jack sighed heavily. 'Aye. And then, if I was away for long and you had to apply to the Guardians – well, the way things are now, I could be taken up by the polis if I left you and the bairns to be a charge on the rates. No, we have to go together or all go into the workhouse.'

Hannah shivered. 'Eeh, no, Jack, not that. We'll sleep under a hedge first.'

'Well, we won't be the first ones to camp out on the fell. There'll be more than us doing it this night.' Jack patted her clumsily on the shoulder. 'Don't worry, lass. You'll see, I'll find something, see if I don't. An' it won't be for want of trying if I don't.'

Hannah nodded and managed to summon up a smile but in truth her hopes were not high. Jack was a leader and union man and would be blacklisted by the railways and banned from carrying on his trade as a platelayer. Even if the Board didn't do it straight away, Ralph Grizedale would see to it that they did eventually.

'Where are we going, Da?'

Meg, from her seat in the middle of the cart, asked the questions as Jack turned left at Eldon and took the track which led to the Great North Road. It would lead them north and east and away from the Auckland district of south-west Durham. Until now, Meg had been quiet, staring around her with wide open eyes, awed by the events of the day.

The little girl had never in her life been this far away from the row of cottages on the old line which had always been her home. They had passed Grizedale Hall, glimpsed only fleetingly through the trees of the park

23

created by Ralph's father from farmland in imitation of the wealthy landowners surrounding him. Landowners made even wealthier by the coal under their land. She had looked and looked, hoping to see Jonty, but there was no sign of him, none at all.

At last Meg gave up staring as the tall chimneys of the Hall disappeared from view. Her father began to pant a little as he drew the cart up the steep hill. He had no breath to answer Meg for a while. Hannah, walking beside the cart with the baby slung in her shawl, shifted little Jack to her hip and lent a hand by pushing until at last they crested the rise.

Meg gazed round in surprise and pleasure at the rolling hills in the distance, one crowned by an ancient church. Everything was so green and fresh and glowing in the late-evening sun. By, she thought, it's grand.

Jack halted to take a breather and looked round at Meg, summoning up an encouraging smile. 'We'll see, pet, we'll see. But I don't think we can go much further tonight. Mebbe as far as Old Eldon.' Taking hold of the handle of the cart again, he walked up the lane.

The sight of the village, the first one Meg had seen which was untouched by industry, made her gasp with delight. Here there were no slag-heaps, no smell of coal and coke ovens, just farms and little cottages. Under the hedge, primroses reflected the sun and in the field beyond, daisies and dandelions grew. Were they going to live here? She watched in fascination as a farmer herded a small group of cows up the lane and in to a field gate.

'Cush, cush,' he said quietly as they turned, followed by a bright-eyed collie. Meg looked at her father, wanting to share the moment with him, but he was looking at Mam, concern for her on his face. Mam was weary, Meg could see it in the way her body slumped as she leaned against the cart.

Propping the handles of the cart against the fence so that it remained approximately upright, Jack lifted Meg down and walked over to speak to the farmer. Meg went to her mother and stood watching quietly as the two men talked. Her thumb went to her mouth as the man looked over at the woman with a child in her arms and a small girl hanging on to her skirts. He nodded briefly.

'Aye, all right, so long as you're not tinkers. I can't abide tinkers, thieving rascals.' He clanged the gate shut after the cows and turned back to Jack. 'You can sleep in the barn round the back. Keep out of the way, mind. There's fresh milk you can have for the little 'uns but don't light a fire, there's still some winter feed in there.' He frowned as Jack Boy woke up and started to cry fretfully. 'I suppose you've been turned out? I heard of such goings-on today when I took the milk down to Eldon. I don't like it, I don't, turning women and bairns out of their homes. But mind, I'm only a tenant here. You'll keep out of sight of the road and be gone first thing in the morning, will you. All right?'

Hannah and Jack hastened to reassure him that it was indeed all right and they were very grateful. So soon they were ensconced in the barn where the baby's cradle was taken down from the cart and little Jack fed and put to bed. Meg, after a piece of bread and dripping and a drink of milk supplied by the farmer, was also put to bed in the hay.

Wearily, Jack and Hannah sat down, talking in hushed tones together. Jack sprang to his feet as the barn door opened and a middle-aged woman, obviously the farmer's wife, came in with a tray which she put down at their feet. There was a pot of strong black tea and a piece of cold bacon together with fresh bread and home-made pickle. Hannah, who had not cried or complained all day throughout their misfortunes, felt her eyes fill with tears at this evidence of the innate kindness of folk. The woman understood, however.

'Don't thank me, Missus, it's nowt, we had it to spare,' she said, and hurriedly left the barn.

Meg watched as her parents ate their meal in the doorway so that they could take advantage of the waning light. Even though she was not yet four, she knew the food was especially welcome. They had brought some with them but their supplies were meagre. No money had been coming in because of the strike. And she had often heard Mam say she had to eat or she would lose her milk and then what would the babby do?

'I'll get up early and help the farmer, we're not taking any charity,' Jack remarked, half to himself.

'Aye,' said Hannah. 'By, I'm tired though. I don't know where we'll go either. I've got no one, not since me mam died. Just Cousin Phoebe, like, over in Haswell.'

'Me neither, just me brother in Australia and we can't go there,' said Jack.

Meg could hear every sound made by the animals in the farmyard until at last she fell asleep through sheer exhaustion, as a cock crowed in the hen-house across from the barn and grey streaks of dawn slid in through the cracks in the barn door.

'Cousin Phoebe might help,' Mam was saying as she fell asleep, 'we can ask. What else can we do? And Haswell is far enough away from Shildon for you to look for work, Jack.'

The day dawned clear and cold with a light frost covering the ground. Meg shivered as Hannah washed her hands and face and neck under the tap by the horse trough. She stamped her feet in their shabby, black boots to warm them up. But she forgot about the cold when she ran away into the field, watching the geese as they trooped out to go down to the pond at the bottom, scurrying away as the gander raised his wings and quacked angrily at her as he shepherded his family. She came back to Hannah with a bunch of wild flowers, primroses and dandelions, daisies and sweet violets, which she handed proudly to her mother, her blue eyes sparkling and her cheeks rosy fresh with the sharp air.

'Where've you been?' demanded a harassed Hannah. She was busy removing all traces of their occupancy from the barn, determined that their hosts should not think they were like the tinkers. She didn't see the posy in her haste. The baby was wailing fretfully, something Mam couldn't abide, Meg knew. It always made Mam anxious when Jack Boy cried; anxious and bad-tempered. Now she looked up angrily at Meg from her kneeling position by the cradle.

'I wanted you to see to Jack Boy, maybe he's getting a tooth already. You could keep his chin dry. He's dribbling all over and his skin will get sore.' Then she saw the proffered posy in Meg's hand and the smile fading from her daughter's face. She got to her feet and took the posy, burying her nose in its fragrance.

'Eeh, I'm sorry, petal, I am. I didn't mean to shout. By, they're lovely, they are. I just didn't feel very well, I'm badly like. Now howay, honey, we have to pack up and be on our way. Your da must be nearly finished his jobs by now.'

By ten o'clock, the family was once more on its way, making for the Great North Road then travelling slowly up to Thinford where they would branch off for East Durham and the smoky colliery village of Haswell. Hannah could only hope that Cousin Phoebe still lived there, along with her miner husband, Thomas. She was very thankful indeed when, after making a few enquiries, she knocked on a cottage door and it was Cousin Phoebe who opened it, a Phoebe Hannah would have recognized anywhere from her likeness to her mother.

'Eeh, our Hannah, I can't believe it's you!' she said when Hannah told her who they were. 'By, I haven't seen you since you were little more than a bairn. Howay in then, don't just stand there on the step, like.' Phoebe peered over Hannah's shoulder at Jack who was carrying Meg in his arms. 'Eeh, what's the matter?' Phoebe's welcoming smile became a little concerned as she stood back to let them in.

Meg heard Mam going into lengthy explanations punctuated by Phoebe's exclamations but she was more interested in the man who had been sitting in a rocking chair before a blazing coal fire. He had risen to his feet as Jack carried her in and put her down on the floor. He had red cheeks, a bristling walrus moustache, and his eyes twinkled in welcome. Eeh, Meg thought, he was just like her friend Molly's granda who lived on the end of the row at home; he even smiled like Molly's granda did.

'Are your my granda?' she asked, hope shining out of her blue eyes. She'd always wanted a granda like Molly's.

The man chuckled. 'No, pet, I'm not your granda. I'm not anybody's granda. But I'm your Uncle Tot and that's pratically the same thing. You can pretend I'm your granda if you like.'

Meg swelled with happiness, Uncle Tot was a grand man, he was. The grown-ups were bustling about, Mam explaining why they'd come and Da and Uncle Tot were shaking hands while everybody talked at once.

'Well!' Auntie Phoebe said. 'Mind, what a surprise! Not but what you're not welcome – you are. Eeh, it's lovely to see you. Me poor old mother was always talking about you and wondering how you got on, your man and you.' She shook her head sadly. 'Things were bad then, they were, after the men were killed in the explosion.

28

You were all the family we had left and you had to move away.' All the time she talked she was filling the kettle and settling it on the coals and going to and from the pantry to the table. 'It's a good thing I made a pie the day – it was for the journey tomorrow but we can eat it tonight. I can do sandwiches for the morn.'

'Tomorrow?' Hannah asked, latching on to the important fact that Phoebe was talking about a journey.

She stopped setting the table and turned to look at her cousin. 'Aye,' she said. 'I'm sorry, Hannah, you know we would've took you in, but Tot's got a new job to go to. He's to be fore shift overman at Black Boy. We're moving tomorrow.' Even through her concern at telling Hannah they would be unable to take in the family, her pride in Tot's new job shone through. But she saw the despair on her cousin's face. 'Eeh Hannah, you can come with us for a week or two. You know we won't leave you with nowhere to stay. We're kin. No pit folk would leave kin with nowhere to stay.'

'We can't go to Black Boy,' Hannah said hopelessly, 'it's too near Shildon.'

Meg heard the silence which fell on the grown-ups; saw the dismay on their faces. They sat round the table and looked at each other. Suddenly little Jack began to cry, a hungry insistent sound. But for once Hannah didn't jump up and go to him immediately; she didn't seem to hear him.

'Mam, the baby's crying,' Meg said, and when her mother didn't answer she went to the cradle herself and rocked it gently with her foot. 'Whisht, babby,' she said.

Uncle Tot watched her a moment then cleared his throat. 'Mebbe it's not so bad,' he said. 'You can camp out in here till Saturday, the key's not due to be given up till then. You have some furniture. An' then mebbe Jack can find a job. There's the pit . . .' He faltered, knowing Jack was no pitman. But then Tot remembered something else. 'Hang on, wait a minute, I heard today that there were jobs going in the quarries up Marsden way. What about that, Jack?'

Three

Ralph Grizedale rode over the fields to Grizedale Hall and trotted California straight round to the stables at the back of the house. A young groom came running as he yelled imperiously and Ralph flung himself off the horse and threw the reins to the boy.

'Give him a proper rub down – I'll have no skimping, mind. And when you've done that, take a broom to this yard, it's filthy.'

'Yes, sir.' The boy's voice trembled as he answered, he had a healthy fear of Ralph. Taking the reins, he led Cal over the already spotless yard. Hadn't he been up at five that morning to clean the stables and sweep the yard? But if Master wanted it swept again, well then, that's what he would do. He needed to keep this job.

Ralph strode into the house and across the hall to his study, feeling decidedly out of temper though he didn't know why. Shouldn't he be feeling better now that Hannah, that thorn in his side for so many years, had gone and taken that prying brat of hers with her? If he didn't see Hannah he would forget about her, he would find a wife among his own kind and put her out of his mind altogether. Striding over to the bell-pull by the fireplace, he jerked it a couple of times and when his man appeared, ordered whisky and water. Something he hadn't been able to do when his father was alive, he thought, feeling amused for a moment. What the old man would have said if he'd heard the order. When the drink came Ralph threw himself into a great leather armchair by the ornate fireplace and sipped from the brimming glass.

In spite of himself, he couldn't keep his mind off Hannah and her brat. He could still see the two pairs of eyes staring up at him after the eviction – eyes so alike, so intensely blue, emphasized by the milky white complexions and fair, almost corn-coloured hair glinting in the sun. The familiar ache of longing rose in him and turned to the usual bitterness. She had chosen to marry a common railway worker, let her take the consequences. And her child . . . too sharp for her own good, that one. He remembered the way she'd lifted her chin and glared at him. So like her mother she was. Well, she had to be separated from Jonty, there was danger there.

Ralph frowned heavily as he heard a child's voice in the hall. Handn't he told Jonty to keep away from the front of the house? Mouthing an oath, he stalked to the door and flung it open.

'Look at me, Grandmother, look at me!' Jonty was at the foot of the stairs, standing on his head and with his face red from the effort of holding his balance, his legs wavering in the air before he toppled over. Mrs Grizedale was in the doorway of her sitting-room, clapping her lace-mittened hands gently and smiling at the child.

'Oh, clever boy, clever,' she was saying, and Jonty giggled as he jumped to his feet. But then he saw his father, face black with rage, striding over towards him and his face went from red to white and his eyes widened in terror.

'Don't—' Mrs Grizedale stepped forward to put herself between her son and grandson, but she was too late. Ralph held Jonty by the scruff of the neck and was holding him off the ground and shaking him.

'How many times do I have to tell you not to make a

noise in the house? And to use the back stairs, not to come into the front hall at all.'

'Ralph! Ralph!' Mrs Grizedale caught hold of the boy and held him to her, shaking along with him until Ralph let go his hold and Jonty collapsed into a sobbing heap.

'It was my fault, Ralph, not the boy's. He was with me, we were going to have tea together in my room. I didn't know you were back from your ride,' cried Mrs Grizedale. She bent protectively over the child, while looking up at his father beseechingly.

'Ah, he's not fit to have tea in a lady's room, Mother. Look at him, he doesn't know how to behave, racketing on in the hall and then not man enough to take his punishment, sobbing and crying. Look at him, he's as weak as his mother was!'

'Ralph! Do not talk like that in front of the child.' Mrs Grizedale didn't often face up to her son but when she did it was usually in defence of Jonty. Now she lifted the child to his feet and wiped his eyes with a wisp of lacy handkerchief.

'Now go up and wash your hands and face, Jonty, and when you come down again we will have tea. Go on.'

The boy glanced at his father and turned to the stairs.

'The back stairs! How many times have I told you? The back stairs for you, servant's brat that you are.'

'Ralph!' cried Mrs Grizedale, but Jonty turned and ran to the back of the hall to the baize door which led to the kitchens and the back stairs. He was only glad to get away from his father without a beating. As he climbed the stairs he thought about Meg and her da. Meg loved her da and he loved her. Why wasn't his da like his Uncle Jack? Jonty sighed and shook his head. He couldn't understand why his da was always in such a rage with him.

Now Jonty had gone, Mrs Grizedale reverted to her

normal hesitancy when dealing with Ralph. He was so short with her sometimes. It was her fault usually, she knew she irritated him. She still mourned his father, her dear George. A tear rolled down her cheek as she thought of him, wondering why Ralph was so different. She dabbed at the tear with the lace handkerchief, still wet from Jonty's tears, before tucking it back into the wrist of her black lace mittens. She looked at Ralph, hoping for a sympathetic word, but he had turned back into his study. Poor boy, she thought, he must be missing his father too, that was what made him short with his own son. She walked to the open door of the room and peered anxiously in.

'Did you meet any of your friends, dear? On your ride, I mean?' Oh, she did hope he hadn't been drinking so early in the day.

'What do you mean, meet any of my friends? What friends do I have in this hole? Do you never listen to anything I say? I have been to Shildon, to a meeting. I told you I was going, only this morning.'

'Oh, yes, of course, dear,' Mrs Grizedale said faintly. Why did she always say the wrong thing?

Ralph stared at her. 'You just stop spoiling that boy. It was a mistake letting you give him to that woman to wet-nurse when Nell died, though I was glad to get the sickly, puling brat out of the house at the time. If it hadn't been for that strait-laced father of mine he would never have been here in the first place. Forcing me, his own son and a gentleman born, to marry a pitman's daughter. Nell . . . common name for a stupid common girl. Just a pale imitation of her sister, too.'

Mrs Grizedale stepped back, gasping in horror, and perhaps Ralph realized he had gone too far for he strode from the room without a backward glance.

'I'm off to Darlington for the evening. Maybe I'll get some better company there,' he snarled, and a moment later she could hear his raised voice shouting for the stable boy.

'Has Da gone?' The small voice from the hall made Mrs Grizedale turn and cover up her shock and upset with a smile.

'Yes, dear, he's gone. We'll have a nice time together now, won't we? Cook has made scones, I know, and there's strawberry jam.' She hesitated, biting her lip. Maybe she had been wrong in giving him to Hannah to wet-nurse. He'd picked up some bad habits of speech.

'It would be better if you didn't call your father Da, dear. You must call him Father, that's his proper name.'

Jonty nodded his head slowly. His father wasn't a da, any road, he thought, not like Meg's. He took his grandmother's hand and they went into her sitting-room. His normally sunny nature was reasserting itself; his father was gone out and Jonty didn't have to worry about offending him for a while.

'Strawberry jam?' he cried, and smiled in delight as he ran into his grandmother's room. Auntie Hannah had made jam once, from the wild raspberries growing alongside the lane, and sometimes she made rhubarb jam. But Jonty had never tasted strawberry jam until he came to live with Da and Grandmother, and by, it was lovely! Maybe he would be able to save a little from his tea and take it down to Meg's house for her to taste, he thought happily, but then his brow creased with anxiety. If he did and his father found out, Da would hit him with his riding crop, he knew. That was what he had done last time Jonty sneaked out to see Meg. But he would sneak off, he vowed. Da was out and might not catch him. And Jonty's heart ached from the pain of not seeing Meg and Auntie Hannah and the baby.

After tea, when Grandmother said he could go out and play in the shrubbery, as soon as he was out of sight from her window, Jonty tiptoed along the side of the

35

hedges until he was away from the Hall and then flew down the bank to the little row of cottages by the old line, clutching a scone liberally spread with strawberry jam for Meg. But when he arrived, Meg wasn't there. No one was. No children playing in the back lane, no smoke from the chimneys. Jonty walked round and round the row, and peered in the cracks between the planks of wood which were nailed to Auntie Hannah's kitchen window. The kitchen was empty: no table, no chairs, not even Grannie's rocking chair. Out front again he found Meg's peg doll lying on the path. He picked it up and looked around.

'Meg?' he called. 'Auntie?' But he knew it was hopeless. He walked back to the Hall carrying the doll, his eyes full of tears, not even caring if Da saw him and whipped him for going down there. They had gone away and left him, they didn't care about him, they'd gone without even telling him, abandoning him, they didn't care what his father did to him. Not Auntie Hannah or Uncle Jack, not even Meg.

Arriving back at the house, Jonty went in the front door and climbed the main staircase, not bothered if Da saw him. The way he felt, he would almost welcome a beating. Maybe it would take away the awful emptiness which was there right in his middle. But Da wasn't there, only Grandmother, who came into his room to hear his prayers.

'I'm not saying prayers tonight,' Jonty said firmly, and climbed into bed and turned his face to the wall.

'Is something the matter, dear?' Mrs Grizedale hovered anxiously but Jonty refused to say another word. After a moment she went to the door, closing it quietly after her.

'Poor boy,' she said, 'your short life hasn't been easy. One night without praying won't hurt.'

36

And Jonty put his hand under his pillow and felt Meg's dollie there and clutched it tightly to his chest.

Meg helped Hannah and Jack load up the hand cart for the journey to Marsden. She was bubbling over with excitement as she gathered Jack Boy's clean clouts into a bundle and wrapped them in a blanket. It was a lovely day and they were going to live by the seaside, Da had told her. And hadn't he got a fine new job, working in a quarry?

It was Saturday morning and Da had been gone two days when he came home last night. Her mam had been worried he wouldn't get a job, Meg knew it. She had been so upset she had sicked up all her breakfast in the sink in the yard. But that was yesterday. Today Hannah was bustling about piling things on the handcart while Jack Boy lay in his cradle by the gate.

'Da, Da,' said Meg, 'tell us again about the sea and the rocks an' all.'

Jack laughed. 'Wait till we get going, pet, then I'll tell you all about it. By, it's going to be grand. We'll be living right on the cliff top, and further down there's the sands and you can plodge in the water and look for shrimps.'

'Eeh, Jack,' said Hannah. 'I hope it's not too near the edge, mind. What about the bairn, is it safe?'

'It'll be all right, man,' Jack avowed. 'We'll just have to watch until Meg gets used to it. She's not daft, like.'

At last they had finished loading the cart and were on their way, calling at the colliery offices for Jack to leave the key to the house they had only been in for a few days.

Meg had got used to the travelling now. She thought they were going all the way with the handcart and maybe they would be able to sleep in a farmer's barn again and she would see ducks and hens and cows. So she was a bit disappointed when their next stop was the

37

railway station and she and Mam and Jack Boy got on a train for Sunderland, and then another smaller train for Marsden. But still it was nice on the train, too, they went so fast, and before teatime came they had arrived and were getting down at the station at Whitburn Colliery.

And there was the sea, miles and miles of water. Meg had never seen anything like it. Her eyes widened with the wonder of it. Even though Da had told her about it, she had never thought it would be like that.

'Eeh, Mam,' she said, as they walked up the path past the tall building which Mam said was a lighthouse and on towards the rows of houses which made up the pit village of Marsden. 'Eeh, Mam, wouldn't it be lovely if Jonty could come? By, wouldn't he be surprised if he saw the sea?'

'You forget about Jonty,' said Hannah. 'Jonty won't be coming here, there's nowt so sure. Now stop chattering, do.'

Mam sounded tired and cross and Meg's excitement dimmed a little. Mam didn't mean it. Jonty would come sometime, Meg knew he would. But she obediently stopped talking and contented herself with watching the birds wheeling over the rocks and calling loudly to one another, great big birds like she had never seen before. Why, they were nearly as big as ducks!

Four

Meg loved the sea. She loved the sound of waves breaking on the rocks below the cliffs, loved to lie in bed at night and listen to it. After her day at school Meg liked to lie on the cliff top near Souter Lighthouse and watch the seabirds feeding their young in the nests on the sides of the sea stacks and down the steep-sided cliffs. And she would talk in her head to Jonty, telling him about the cormorants and the kittiwakes flying about their business and taking no notice of the people living on the cliff top. But only when she was not needed at home, for there was a new baby soon after they moved to Marsden, and then another. And Mam wasn't as strong as she used to be, always weary and tired.

Meg was plagued by a nightmare, always the same one, where she and Mam and the babby were running up an uneven road black with coal dust and someone was chasing them. Meg knew it was the Candyman and he was catching up with them, no matter how hard they ran, and she would wake up screaming, just as the Candyman put out a hand to get her.

And then, the next day, the nightmare would put her in mind of Jonty, her lost brother Jonty, and she would ask Mam about him.

'Forget about Jonty. He's your cousin, not your brother, any road.' Mam would say every time she asked. But Meg didn't want to forget Jonty. She would go over in her mind the last time she had seen him. He had come back to see her. Jonty's da had come to their house then and dragged him away. But first Jonty had stood up straight and defied him, and his father had cuffed him and Jonty had gone flying into the wall. Jonty had gone very white and Meg had run to him but she had been pushed roughly out of the way.

'I told you not to come here!' Jonty's da had roared, and tucking his son under his arm like a bundle of rags, had flung him over Cal's saddle.

Hannah had stood by quietly after her first shocked protest. She had clutched the baby to her and Meg had gone to her and held on to her skirt for comfort.

'Mam!' she had whimpered, and Hannah had put down a hand and pressed her daughter's head to her, clucking her tongue in automatic shushing. 'It's no good, Meg, I can't do anything about it,' she'd said.

That was all Meg could remember of Jonty and even that was fading from her mind. So she made up conversations with him when she was on her own, and a little glow would rise in her.

Meg was nine years old when she began working. She was by Souter Lighthouse one day with her little sister Alice on one hand and two-year-old Miles on the other. Meg was keeping them out of Mam's way for a while so she could get the baking done. Miles was gurgling and laughing, tugging at Meg's hand because he wanted to go to the edge of the cliff after a seabird.

'No, Miley, no. You have to be a good lad and stay with me or we'll have to go back home.' Meg pulled him back and his chuckles threatened to turn into tears. 'Look how good Alice is, pet,' urged Meg. 'Alice keeps hold of me.' And it was true. Alice was standing quietly, watching Miles with the superior expression of a three-year-old for a baby of only two.

'Aren't you at school today?'

Meg looked round to see the head keeper of the lighthouse on the other side of the wall. Meg knew all the keepers by sight, this was a favourite haunt of hers, and they all knew her.

'I've left school now,' she confided. 'I'm going to get work.'

The head keeper looked at her speculatively. 'Why, I might be able to put you in the way of a position,' he said thoughtfully. He liked the little lass and she might just do. 'Our step scrubber's leaving on Friday. How would you like to take on the work? There's a lot of steps, mind.'

Meg looked up at the lighthouse. It was tall, she thought, she'd not been inside it before. And no doubt there were a lot of steps, there would be in a building like that. But she wasn't afraid of work, she was used to it, being the eldest.

'I'll have to ask me da,' she said.

'Gan on then, ask him,' said the lighthouse keeper, well pleased that he had found a new steps scrubber so quickly.

So Meg came to the lighthouse every morning and scrubbed down the steps with hot water and soda to keep them free from any grease and dirt which might cause the keepers to slip in their frequent journeys up and down to the light. And she got paid, two shillings a week, which she proudly took home to her mother. For not only did her leaving school and finding a job so soon mean there was an extra two shillings in the house, it also meant that the threepence a week she'd had to pay for her schooling was saved too.

Working on the steps was lonely work, though the keepers usually had a word with her as they passed. But Meg had a lively imagination and she would amuse herself with day-dreams. Most of her dreams were about Jonty – not a Jonty she remembered, not really. It was so

41

long since she had seen him that his image was blurred as she tried to picture him in her mind. But she knew more about who he was now. Mam would sometimes pause in what she was doing and look pensive, and when Meg asked what she was thinking about, she would say, 'I wonder how Jonty's getting on? Eeh, my own sister's lad and I can't get to see the bairn.'

Or Meg would hear Mam and Da talking about days gone by and Da would say, 'If it weren't for Ralph Grizedale ...' and the name would strike terror into Meg's heart for she knew he was Jonty's da and the Candyman and maybe she would have the nasty dream again.

But Jonty, Jonty had become her knight, the man who would find her one day, perhaps as she emptied her bucket over the rocks and paused for a moment, letting the fresh sea breeze off the North Sea lift her hair away from her damp forehead, cooling and soothing. He would ride up on a big grey horse and lift her up in front of him. And he would look after her so that she didn't have to go back in the lighthouse and start scrubbing yet another flight of steps.

Usually at this stage her day-dream would falter for there was a shadowy figure behind Jonty, large and black and menacing. And Meg would plunge her brush into the water and go on scrubbing the everlasting steps.

Meg was walking along the shoreline one day after her work was done, her shrimping pail in her hand. By, she thought, with the uplift to her spirits she always felt when she gazed out to sea and saw the birds wheeling above the collier boats heading into the mouth of the river Wear to Shields, free as air, birds are. Plenty to eat and no one to bother them. It must be grand to be a bird. She grinned to herself. It was grand to be Meg Maddison, though. She was lucky to be living here by the rocks where she could gather shrimps and maybe a crab to take home to tea. And the feel of the wet sand between her toes was grand, and even the shock of the icy waves breaking over her feet. And she was never bad with the cough like Alice, she was never ill.

So why, she pondered, had she had the nightmare last night? Why did she have this feeling that something was going to happen? She shook her head. Mebbe she was just being daft and fanciful. Mam said she often was.

Meg found her question answered when she arrived at the back door with her pail of shrimps.

'Howay in, pet, I'm glad you're back. We have a lot to do tonight,' Hannah greeted her. She was on the floor packing a box with the children's clothes and Meg stared in surprise as she dropped the latch behind her.

'A lot to do? Why, like?'

'We're moving.'

Hannah saw the stricken look on Meg's face and rushed into explanations. 'Now, don't take on, there's nowt we can do about it. Your da's had a bit of bad luck, he's got turned off, and we can't live on air. So we're going over to Cousin Phoebe's. She'll put us up till we find a place. There's work going down the pit.'

'Da's going down the pit? But he hates the pit. He won't be able to stand it down there!'

'Aye, well, hate it or not, he'll just have to get used to it,' Hannah said flatly. 'There's nowt else for it.'

'But . . .'

'Aw, stop standing there with your mouth open and come and give us a hand. The bairn's crawling into everything.'

Numbly, Meg did as she was told, scooping up baby Miles from under the table where he was sucking a lump of coal purloined from the coal bucket by the fire, his face as black as any pitman's. With the child on one hip, she filled the iron pan with water from the bucket in the

43

pantry and put it on the fire to boil the shrimps. Then gently she took the coal away from her brother and, to still his protests, gave him the bleached bone which was doing duty as a teething ring.

'Where's Da?' Meg asked at last, thinking how he would hate the pit. He was even nervous of being in the pantry if the door was shut. Poor Da didn't like to be shut in.

'He's gone to see the carrier. He can't go traipsing about the country with a handcart nowadays, there's too much stuff for that. And your da and you can ride with the carrier. That'll save the fares on the train, any road.'

'We're not going tonight?' Alarm rose in Meg. 'What about my job at the lighthouse?'

'Oh, aye, you'll have to run along and tell them. You'll mebbe lose a day's pay, but it can't be helped. If we go, you have to come with us.'

'We're going tonight!' Meg couldn't believe it. 'Why didn't you tell me before? Are we doing a flit?'

'No, we're not going tonight – tomorrow we're going. An' we'll pay the rent an' all, we'll leave no debt behind us. Not like that lot down the street who did a flit. Now, hadaway with you to the lighthouse and take the bairn with you. It'll keep him out of my feet.'

'But why didn't you tell me?'

Hannah bit her lip. 'Eeh, lass, we didn't want to upset you, not till we heard from our Phoebe that it was all right. But mind, you'll like it there. Phoebe says she's got us a grand house with a backyard and a garden. Howay now, there's a lot to do, I'm telling you.'

Meg wiped most of the coal dust from Miley's chubby cheeks and settled him on her hip. Then she walked along to the lighthouse, to see the keeper. At least he was understanding when she stood before him and told him she was leaving.

'Me da's got a job inland,' she mumbled, still hardly believing it herself yet. 'Can I have the day's pay?'

The lighthouse keeper regarded the sturdy young girl with her brother straddling one hip and sighed regretfully.

'Aye, well, if you have to go, you have to,' he said philosophically. And he handed her the day's pay she was owed. After all, there were plenty of young lasses who would jump at the work. But would he find another worker like Meg?

She loitered a little on her way home with the pennies clutched in her hand. By, Mam would be pleased she'd got her money after all. She felt a rush of affection for the kindly lighthouse keeper. He didn't have to pay her, she knew, not when he'd had no notice.

Walking slowly home, with Miles holding on to her hand and toddling unsteadily beside her, Meg took a good look round at the place where she'd been happy. The bright sea now shimmered in the evening sunlight, calmly rolled in on the soft sands, made the barest splashing on the rocks. She passed the school where she had learned to write in an elegant copperplate and read the religious primers, all for threepence a week. The money had been hard to find but Hannah, who could neither read nor write, was determined that her children would get the chance.

Meg stared up at the grim stone building, remembering the rapped knuckles she had often received from the master, mostly for talking and laughing in class; the list of rules pinned up in the entrance.

'Children must be punctual and attend some place of worship on the Lord's day,' had been the first and most important.

So Meg and Jack Boy and later Alice had attended the Wesleyan Methodist Sunday School every Sunday morning, promptly at ten o'clock. She would miss the friends she'd made there, Meg thought sadly. But never mind, she would make new friends at Winton Colliery. For that was where Uncle Tot and Auntie Phoebe were living now, Uncle Tot with a grand job in the pit there.

Miles started to whimper for his tea and Meg lifted him up and settled him on her hip again. 'Whisht, babby,' she said, and dropped a kiss on the fine, baby hair on top of his head. 'We'll soon be home now.'

In the overcrowded kitchen of the cottage which had been the family home for the last five years, she found the meal was already begun. The shrimps were cooked and piled on a plate in the middle of the table, liberally seasoned with salt and vinegar. For Da there was a slice of cod, bought from the fisher boats at South Bents and fried over the open fire so that the smell filled the room and spilled over into the rest of the house.

'I got paid, Mam.'

Meg grinned in triumph as she handed over the money to her mother before sitting down at the table with Miles still on her lap. She began spooning shrimps on to her plate. Hannah was cutting thick wedges of bread. Meg watched as she buttered the loaf before holding it to her clean apron to cut it. There was a mug of milk for Miles, and for the other children weak tea with a spoonful of condensed milk stirred into it.

'Thank God for that any road,' said Hannah wearily, slumping down into her chair. She looked tired, thought Meg, and there was still a lot of work to be done and the tiring journey tomorrow.

'Here, I'll take the bairn.' Hannah held out her arms for Miles. 'You get your tea, Meg, I'm not very hungry.' She thickened a crust with butter and put it in the child's hands. He sucked it, absorbed in the taste.

Meg stared at her mother in quick concern. Hannah's not being hungry meant only one thing, she had

46

discovered very early in her young life. Oh, she had guessed that there was a new baby on the way, but usually the sickness and lack of appetite had gone after the first few weeks. Except those times when Mam had lost a baby . . . Eeh, she thought, feeling a little fluttering of fear for her mother, why do mothers have to be always having bairns?

Meg looked across the table at Da who was quietly eating his meal, sitting with them but somehow apart from them, taking little notice of the others. Jack Maddison had aged in the last five years. There was a defeated look about him too. Lines had appeared on his forehead and down his cheeks, and he had developed a stoop.

Poor Da! He would hate it down the pit. He must have felt her eyes on him for he looked up and half-smiled at her.

'Well, pet, we're on our way again. You'll have to help your mam as much as you can. But there, I know you will, you're a good bairn.'

'I will an'all, Da, I will,' put in Jack Boy. At six years old he was a thin, wiry boy with an open, freckled face and hair so fair it was almost white.

Jack smiled at them both, feeling impelled to lighten their earnest sympathy. 'It'll be all right, it will, I'm telling you. An' plenty of lads have had to go down the pit whether they wanted to or not, let alone a man grown like me. I'm not the first by a long chalk. Now eat your tea and get the little 'uns to bed, we have a lot on the night. The carrier's coming at eight the morn.'

At eight o'clock sharp the carrier was indeed by the door and by nine the cart was loaded and on its way. Meg and her father were riding with the carrier but Hannah and the younger children caught the Marsden Flyer to Sunderland, where they changed for Bishop Auckland.

47

Hannah should be at the new house fairly fresh from the train ride rather than bumping along in the cart. A letter had come just before they left Marsden, reassuring them that a job was waiting for Jack and a house, right next-door to Auntie Phoebe's.

'A good house, it is, Hannah,' she wrote, 'two bedrooms and a room besides the kitchen downstairs. And a copper setpot in the yard, and a good garden at the front.'

Jack had read it out to them all to cheer everyone up. And it did, so that the children were happy and excited, looking forward to going on the train, and not just one train, but two.

Meg had mixed feelings, though, as she and Da set out on the carrier's cart. Jack sat in front with the driver, a garrulous man who spoke continually around his clay pipe which he never seemed to take out of his mouth. Meg was fascinated but couldn't understand a word he said though Da seemed to make sense of it which was just as well. It was a good long journey to have to go trying to answer someone when you hadn't understood the question, she thought.

She herself was sitting behind, snug between boxes of clothes and Grannie's rocking-chair. She'd wanted to sit in the chair but Da said it wasn't safe, she might fall off, and if they were travelling at any speed she would hurt herself and how would he face Mam if she did that? Meg had looked doubtfully at the placid cart-horse. He wasn't going to travel very fast, she thought, but she knew better than to argue with Da and so had climbed into her niche obediently.

They soon left the coast behind and were travelling across country to Winton Colliery. The way was hilly and often Meg and the two men had to climb down and walk

48

beside the cart while the driver talked encouragingly to the horse.

'Howay then, lad, giddy up, giddy up. Come away then, Benny, we'll have a bit of a blow when we get up t'd top and then there's a nice easy road down. Howay, Benny lad, I've a bag of oats ready for thoo, just keep on, lad.' And he would take his pipe out of his mouth to talk to the horse as they both puffed and panted up the hill.

True to his word, he would slip the nosebag on Benny for a while when the top was crested and they would all have a rest and a bit of bait to eat and cold water out of a lemonade bottle.

It was already evening and the light beginning to fade when Da shook Meg gently to waken her from her tired dozing so that she could get off the cart and begin the walk up the last hill.

'Will we be long now, Da?' she asked as she plodded up the steep gradient to the accompaniment of the carrier's soft voice as he talked to his horse. Her feet felt like lead weights and it was getting more difficult to put one foot in front of the other all the time.

Jack glanced at her. Her face was pale and drawn and there were dark patches under her eyes. She shivered as they passed under the shadow of a great winding wheel, briskly turning as it brought its load to the surface. It was no different to many another they had passed on the way but Meg was sensitive to her da's feelings and saw when his glance slid from her to the pithead buildings. She tucked her small hand in his with an instinctive need to comfort him and he squeezed it with his own, the skin rough and dry with working the magnesium limestone of Marsden Quarry.

'No lass,' he said, 'just up this bank and down the other side. We'll be home before dark.'

Home! How could this place ever be home? They

49

reached the top and gazed down at the straggling pit village with its pit yard at one end. An aerial flight was strung out across the field to a towering mountain of a slag heap and the air was heavy with coal dust. There was coal dust in the air at Marsden but not like this. A sad longing for the tang of sea air beset her, or maybe the sight of the kittiwakes wheeling over the cliffs.

A cold wind rattled round the houses as they reached the colliery rows. They were all recently built with dirt roads bare of tarmac but footpaths paved with flagstones and yards opening on to the back lanes. They turned into the last row, the only one with gardens to the front, a row with a larger house on the end where Uncle Tot and Auntie Phoebe lived, for he was a colliery overman.

'Eeh, there you are, we were wondering where you'd got to.'

Auntie Phoebe must have been on the look-out for them for she came rushing out of the house and down the garden path to the road. 'An' this is our Meg. By, what a big lass you are now. An' I bet you're a good girl an' help your mam? Eeh, it's good to see you, Jack, an' all. Howay in then, I've got a nice knuckle of ham and fresh pot of pease pudding all ready for you. An' you an' all, Mr Carrier, I know you'll be ready for it.'

Meg was dazed by this time, what with tiredness and Auntie Phoebe's overwhelming questions which didn't seem to need any answers. She mumbled a greeting and followed her aunt up the path.

'I've put the bairns to bed upstairs for now, Jack, that'll give you a chance to see to things next-door. Howay in then, what're you waiting for?' This last was addressed to the carrier who was quietly unharnessing his horse.

'Oh, aye, the galloway. You can stake him out in the garden next-door, man, it's not turned over yet and he'll find a bit of grazing there. He'll be right as rain. No need to pay livery stables, there's not.'

50

Jack breathed a sigh of relief when the carrier agreed to this. That would be a sizeable chunk off the bill and the horse would be fine, the grass was fresh and the night mild enough.

'Run round next-door for your mam. She's been scrubbing the floors before the furniture came,' Phoebe said to Meg, and obediently she went and there was Hannah, just throwing a bucket of dirty water out into the garden. She looked up when Meg came through the gate and the girl was shocked to see the violet shadows under her eyes and the weariness etched into her face. Her own tiredness was forgotten.

'Have you finished, Mam? Auntie Phoebe said to go for our supper. I can finish for you if you like?'

Hannah smiled wanly and put down her bucket and brush. 'Aye, I'm coming, pet,' she said. 'There's no need for you to do anything, I'm about done. Howay, I'm fair clemmed and you must be famished an' all.'

She put an arm around Meg's shoulders. 'It'll be grand here, pet, see if it's not. Look, a good flagged floor in here and a wooden one in the other room. And two big bedrooms – we've plenty of room. An' we can grow a few taties and leeks in the garden, mebbe a few flowers. I mind the smell of the stocks and roses at the Hall, they were grand of an evening. Oh, aye, we'll be fine.'

She looked down at Meg and saw the doubt in her eyes. 'You'll be thinking about your da. He'll be fine an' all, you'll see. When he gets used to it, like.'

'Aye, Mam, he will,' said Meg, but in her heart she wondered. They closed the door behind them and went down the path by the quietly munching horse to the gate, and turned in to Auntie Phoebe's garden. And the thought ran through both their minds, at least they had kin near now. Phoebe might just be a cousin but she was kin, and kin was security.

* * *

As they went into the kitchen, the smell of boiled bacon and pease pudding and fresh-baked bread filled the air, and Meg felt her stomach rumble. By, she was starved. Even though it was a warm summer's evening the fire was lit and a large black iron kettle simmered on the hob. The men were already sitting round the table and Phoebe was standing with a loaf in her hand, cutting thick slices of bread and butter. Meg watched as she spread the thick, creamy butter and cut, spread and cut, spread and cut. Her mouth watered as she watched.

'Howay in an' sit you down. I was only waiting for you before I mashed the tea. Now don't be shy, help yourselves, there's plenty.'

Auntie Phoebe, plumper and older then Meg remembered her, picked up a large tea caddy with a picture of Whitley Bay on the lid and spooned the tea into the large brown pot warming on the fender. She looked happy and excited as though she was enjoying herself hugely. She paid special attention to Meg, filling up her plate and giving her real milk in her tea. Meg didn't like to say she didn't care for it, she'd got used to condensed milk.

'Tot's on the night shift, filling in like, he won't be back before midnight. But he's looking forward to meeting you all, aye he is.'

The bread was crispy on the outside and still warm on the inside so that the butter melted into it, and Auntie Phoebe was liberal with the butter. And the milk. 'Farm milk, fresh from the farm like the butter,' she said. Luxury to the family from the coast.

Meg tucked in, relishing the taste of the hot pease pudding and ham and swallowing the milky tea manfully. But her head began to droop after a while and she could hardly lift the food from her plate to her mouth. Dimly, she heard the chatter of the grown-ups but everything was fading from her consciousness.

52

'Will you look at the bairn!' Auntie Phoebe cried suddenly. 'She's already asleep, poor pet. Will I take her up and put her in with the little 'uns?'

'I'll do it,' said Jack, and picked Meg up bodily. Though she protested sleepily she really enjoyed being treated like a child again. Even though she was nearly ten and old enough to earn a living.

'It's up the loft for you, my bairn,' said Jack, and pushed aside the curtain which cloaked the bottom of the stairs and took her up and laid her on the shakey-down bed which already held Jack Boy and Alice and Miles. Meg woke up enough to slip out of her dress but she went to sleep in her petticoat to the sound of Auntie Phoebe's voice floating up the stairs.

'Did I tell you about Ralph Grizedale? Eeh, what goings-on there is! Well—'

Ralph Grizedale, Meg thought as she drifted on the edge of the sleep. She knew him, didn't she?

Five

In the kitchen, Phoebe was continuing her tale without noticing that both Hannah and Jack had taken on guarded expressions when she spoke of Ralph Grizedale.

Hannah did not in fact hear what was being said at first. At the mention of her hated brother-in-law's name she was lost in bitter memories. The day of the evictions at Eldon, the look of terror in Meg's eyes that day, a look a mother could never forget. But worse there was the memory of the cruel pain Ralph had inflicted on her sister Nell.

Poor Nell. She had been so determined to marry him, she could hardly believe her good fortune when she did so. Anything Hannah said to discourage her was discounted as merely envy at a younger sister netting a rich husband. Hannah still blamed herself for not being more convincing in her arguments. And so Nell had suffered years of pain and degradation at the hands of Ralph, for her first two babies were stillborn. And then there was that terrible day he had beaten her half to death when she was seven months pregnant. Jonty had come soon because of it and Nell had died. Her lovely, lovely Nell.

Dragging her thoughts back to the reality of sitting round the supper table in Cousin Phoebe's house, Hannah pushed back her bitter feelings before they could engulf her. She lifted her eyes from her plate and saw that Phoebe and Jack were looking at her expectantly as though they were waiting for her to answer a question.

'I'm sorry.' She looked at Jack and then at Phoebe, not even sure which one had been speaking to her. 'What was that? I was dreaming. Tired, I think.'

'Not very nice dreams an' all,' commented Phoebe. 'Not judging by the look on your face. No, I was telling you about Ralph Grizedale, your poor Nell's man. Eeh, if anybody deserves their come-uppance it's that one. Why, man, there's poor little Jenny Mitchell, her from the bottom row. She went to the Hall to work six months since and now she's back with a big belly. An' she's not the first. Jenny wouldn't have gone there else, but her mam needed the money, she was desperate.' Phoebe pursed her lips in disapproval and sat back in her chair with her arms folded over her ample bosom.

'I tried to warn them, you know, but folk'll never listen to good advice, will they? An' there's no one to put a bridle on him at the Hall now, not now his da's gone. Not like when it was with your poor Nell.'

'It would have been better if his da hadn't made him marry Nell,' put in Jack.

'Eeh, but Jack, the bairn would have been born out of wedlock then,' Phoebe said, before reflecting, 'Aye, well, mebbe it would have been better. Some things are worse than being an orphan an' all.' She paused to catch her breath before launching into the story of Ralph's latest iniquity, the one she had been leading up to. 'I didn't tell you about the little lad, did I? Your nephew he'll be, an' didn't you nurse him when he was a babby an' your Nell died, poor thing? What's his name now?'

'Jonty? What about Jonty?' Hannah sat up straight in her chair, anxiety coursing through her veins. 'Has something happened to Jonty?'

'Well, man, it depends on what you mean by

happened,' Phoebe said judiciously, and picked up her tea cup and drained it. She didn't go on until she had placed the cup back in its saucer and she had sat back again. Hannah could have screamed at her.

'It's like this, Hannah. Grizedale's Master of the Hunt now – oh, aye, he's proper in with the County set. Or some of them, I should say – the wild young ones. By, things have changed since old Grizedale's day! They don't usually come over here, like, but there they were that day, riding all over the place. The farmers round about were up in arms. Last February it was, aye, and fences got broken down, and stock got out. Why, that farmer on the Auckland road out had a gander killed by a horse. You know what ganders are like for defending their own. An' then they even went through the pit yard and the fore shift just turning out! I tell you, there was war on, there was.'

'But what about our Jonty?' Hannah said softly, evenly, her nerves at screaming pitch, she was holding her temper on a tight rein.

'Oh, aye, Jonty.' Phoebe reluctantly shortened her story and came to what Hannah wanted to know. 'Well, they rode through the village, the hounds baying and the horses galloping after them with no thought for the folks running out of the road.' Indignantly, she shook her head from side to side. 'They can't get away with that sort of thing nowadays, you know. Not in 1884, they can't. They might have done once upon a time . . .'

'Aye, but what about Jonty?'

Phoebe halted abruptly as she saw the impatience in Hannah's face. 'Eeh, sorry. But I get so flaming . . .' She composed herself and leaned over the table before going on.

'Well, as I was saying, along come little Jonty. I looked for him most particular, him being kin, like. Riding a proper horse he was, an' all, not a little galloway. Eeh, he looked ever so little perched up there but he trotted on grand, he wasn't a bit frightened of the horse nor nowt. But he was being careful, you know? Didn't want to hurt anybody, I reckon. But, by, his da, he turned and yelled at the bairn to get on, an' then he came back himself and slashed at him with his whip, and what with that and Jonty's horse getting upset, like—' Phoebe paused and cast a pitying glance at her cousin. 'Jonty fell off.'

'Was he all right?'

It was Jack who asked the question for Hannah found herself unable to.

'Well ... he would have been, but his da's horse kicked him on the thigh. The bairn's right leg was broken. I don't think there was much else, though he was stunned and bruised. They took him to Doctor Brown's surgery an' he set the leg. But they shouldn't have moved him, the doctor said. We tried to tell them that. Why, us pit folk know what to do about broken bones, if we don't we ought to, we see plenty. But no, they were gentry and they don't take any notice of us. The lad cried out when they took him up, it was a bad break like. He'll always have a limp now, Doctor Brown says.' Phoebe shrugged. 'Could have been worse, like. That Ralph Grizedale, though, callous sod.'

Hannah was weeping tears inside for her dead sister's son. Hadn't she promised Nell she would look out for him when her sister was dying, her face all bruised from a blow from Ralph, and the baby coming early through it? Oh, it was all her fault, it was. She should have realized what was going on before Nell fell wrong with Jonty. And if she hadn't told Ralph's father when Nell told her, and if Mr Grizedale hadn't ...

If. There had been so many ifs and might have beens. She had promised Nell she would watch over Jonty, but what could she have done? She and Jack had had to move away, they'd had to live, hadn't they? At least, she had told herself, Jonty wouldn't starve, not as the heir to Grizedale Hall.

Conversation at the table flagged, even Phoebe's tongue quietened as she saw how stricken Hannah was. She cast about in her mind for something cheerful to say, something to lighten the atmosphere. She wished she hadn't mentioned Jonty. In the end, she simply stood up and began collecting the dishes together.

'I'll give you a hand,' said Hannah dully, but Phoebe shook her head vigorously.

'Nay, nay, you go your bed. You must be fair worn out what with the new babby coming an' all. No, I'll stack the dishes in the pantry an' have them washed in a couple of shakes come the morn. I'll just leave a place for Tot when he comes in. He's fond of a bit of ham an' pease pudding an' all.'

'I can wash up . . .' began Hannah, but Phoebe shooed her and Jack out of the door.

'Away to your bed, the pair of you. I won't wash the pots up tonight. Tot'll need the hot water that's in the set pot, he'll be coming in black. I'll soon get a bucket in from the pump in the street come the morning.'

'We'll say goodnight then,' said Jack, and taking Hannah's arm he led her out and into the house next-door. He and the carrier had erected the brass bed earlier so it wasn't long before Jack was drifting off to sleep in it, the silence disturbed only by the carrier's snores coming up the stairs from his shakey-down in the kitchen.

'I'll have to go and see him, Jack,' Hannah whispered. 'Eeh, I'm not sure we did right now. Coming here, I mean. I wasn't thinking it was so near to Grizedale Hall.'

Jack turned over and slipped his arm around the swollen body of his wife, feeling the kick of new life within her. 'It's not so close,' he said, 'he'll never think of us being here, pet. But I don't think you should try to see Jonty. What if Ralph catches you?'

Hannah didn't answer. If she went to see Jonty and Ralph saw her, would he make trouble for Jack at the pit? They had their own bairns to consider and the new one coming, one more to feed. She lay awake long after Jack fell asleep. She heard the night shift come out, the colliery whistle calling the fore shift in. And later she head the soft, 'Goodnight, then,' as Tot left his marra to walk up the short garden path, and the soft scuffling noises as he opened the door of his house and pushed the bolt in after him. Then at last she slept.

Meg was up at six o'clock next day. She rushed into her dress and went outside into the street to fetch water from the pump for her wash. At least it wasn't far, she thought, right outside Auntie Phoebe's house. She considered getting Jack Boy up to carry water in to Mam's house, but he was still fast asleep, along with Alice and Miles. There was no sign of Auntie Phoebe and Uncle Tot, either, but then Uncle Tot wasn't going to work until after dinner, she knew, they would be having a lie in. Softly, Meg closed the door behind her and went next-door where she found Hannah and Jack already up. They were breakfasting on bread and jam washed down by hot black tea, for Jack had to be at the colliery offices by eight o'clock, and before then he was going to put up the children's bed. The carrier had taken his fifteen shillings promised for the job and was already on his way back to the coast.

'Morning, pet.' Hannah looked up as she lifted the sneck of the door and Meg was struck by how pale and wan she was, with great dark circles under her eyes.

'Morning, Mam, Da.'

She gave them both a peck on the cheek and helped herself to a cup of tea from the large brown pot with its

59

mismatched lid. The lid was willow-patterned and pretty against the brown. Meg couldn't remember when the true lid of the tea pot had been broken or where the pot of the willow-patterned lid had got to. The lid had been with the pot for so long they seemed like a pair to her.

Sitting down at the table, she added a dollop of condensed milk and took a long swallow. By! It was lovely after that wishy-washy stuff of Auntie Phoebe's.

'You mam's a bit tired,' Jack said to her. 'Try to do your best for her today, will you, lass? An' keep the bairns out of her way.'

'Aye, Da, I will.'

Meg spread plum jam over a thick slice of bread and took a bite, savouring the sweetness of the jam against the nutty flavour of bread made from unbleached flour.

'Aye. I know you will, lass.' Jack rose and patted her head. 'I'll away and get the bed up then.'

The day was filled with putting the house to rights. The floors had been scrubbed the day before, but the doors and windows had to be scrubbed too with washing soda to remove the greasy finger marks. Then there were the curtains to hang at the front window and the furniture to be pushed into position. The bricked yard had to be swilled and the steps scrubbed with sandstone. After all, they couldn't let the neighbours think it was a family of tinkers come to live alongside them.

They were just about done when it happened. Hannah was unrolling the clippie mat before the fireplace in the kitchen, bending down to straighten a corner, when she suddenly gave a cry and fell full-length on the mat.

'Mam!'

Meg practically tumbled from the chair where she had been fixing the heavy cotton-net half-curtain to the window, and the chair fell over with her unheeded. Dropping the curtain, she ran to her mother and turned her over on to her back, screaming as she saw the deathly pallor of Hannah's face.

'Mam, Mam!' she cried, picking up one cold hand and holding it to her own warm face. Was her mam dead?

'What's the matter, our Meg?'

Jack Boy came in from the yard where he had been told to keep the little ones amused until the house was ready. He stood in the doorway uncertainly, little Miles peeping round the leg of his raggy-edged short trousers. His hand went to his mouth and he stared, horror-stricken, at the sight of Hannah on the floor, lying so still.

'Go and get Auntie Phoebe!' Meg shouted at him, and still he stood, as though rooted to the ground. 'Go on, now!'

But there was no need to go for Auntie Phoebe. She had heard the commotion through the thin wall which connected the houses and was already bustling up the garden path to the front door. She fairly ran through the front room to the kitchen, and at the sight of Meg kneeling on the floor beside her prostrate mother, she took charge at once.

'Jack Boy, go on, lad, take the bairns out somewhere.' Jack Boy hesitated and she took him by the shoulder and turned him round bodily. 'Hadaway, lad, this is no place for you. Take them down to the pit head and wait for your da. He won't be long now, back shift must be loosing. Don't fret, son, you mam'll be fine, you'll see.' Firmly, Auntie Phoebe closed the back door on him and only then did she turn her attention to Hannah.

'Is she dead?' whispered Meg.

'Nay, lass, of course she isn't. It'll be the babby, I should think. Look, she's coming round already.'

And indeed Hannah was moaning slightly and turning her head from side to side. Suddenly her eyes flew open and she looked about her, at Meg's tear-stained face and

61

from there to Auntie Phoebe's kindly one. She struggled to sit up, mumbling incoherently, but Phoebe took hold of her shoulders and prevented her.

'Lie still a minute, pet, pull yourself together, that'll be best. Then me and Meg will get you up to bed. I'll put the kettle on and make you a nice cup of tea. You've been doing over much, that's what. Is the babby coming, do you think?'

'Eeh, no, it can't be the babby coming yet. I reckoned another month or six weeks.' But even as she spoke, a spasm of pain crossed her back, radiated round her side and gripped her. She cried out with the shock of it and Phoebe pursed her lips.

'Aye, well, another month or not, we'll be better off with you upstairs and abed. Then Meg can run for the midwife.'

Hannah had no option but to agree. Slowly the older woman and the young girl managed to get Hannah up the bare wooden staircase to the bed, though not without a few stops on the way while she gasped at the severity of the pains gripping her. Meg was frantic with the worry of it. Her mother's hair was sticking to her forehead and the sweat was running down her neck in tiny rivulets. For Meg it was the longest journey of her life.

'Hadaway then, Meg,' Phoebe said as soon as they had rolled Hannah into the bed.

'But I don't know where—'

'Oh, aye, you don't know where to go, do you?' Quickly, she gave Meg directions to the midwife's house before turning back to her patient. 'Where's your clean nightie?' she was asking when Hannah gave an involuntary scream and Meg stared at her, horrified. Her mother's teeth were clenched over her lower lip where a droplet of blood was slowly forming; her eyelids were closed, their blue veins standing out against the stark

62

white of her face. Meg paused long enough to take out the clean nightie from a drawer and drop it on the upturned tea chest which, covered by a cloth, did duty for a bedside table. Then she fled down the stairs.

'Turn left at the other end of the street, along the top of the colliery rows, left up Simpson Street, to Short Street, and the second house along.'

Meg was repeating the directions aloud as she ran for the midwife, fairly sprinting in her anxiety to get there. It seemed an age before her frantic knocking and crying were answered. Then it was the midwife's husband who opened the door, an unshaven individual in dangling braces and collarless shirt. He listened to her appeal and scratched his head as he stood aside of her, unspeaking.

The midwife was sitting by the kitchen fire drinking tea from a pint pot, stretching bootless feet along the length of the steel fender. She sighed impatiently when she saw the girl, her face all blotched and crying.

'Please!' sobbed Meg, hardly able to get her words out in her urgency. 'You'll have to come now. Mam's awful bad, and the babby's too soon.'

'Eeh, I can't even get a sip of tea now an' I've been up all night. What's your name, lass, any road? I don't think I know you. Incomers, are you? You're supposed to book me, you know.' She took another sip of tea, making no effort to respond to Meg's plea.

'We've just come, yesterday. I'm called Meg Maddison.'

'Maddison? I haven't got a Maddison booked. Where do you live?'

Meg was frantic now as the midwife showed no inclination to hurry and put on her boots but simply sat, calmly drinking tea from the pot.

'We live in the rows, Pasture Row, the end one, next to Phoebe Lowther. Auntie Phoebe said to hurry.' Meg's nerves were stretched to breaking. Why didn't she come, the silly woman?

'Why, man, there can't be that much of a hurry. I'd think she's just a bit shook up if she was journeying yesterday. But I'd better have a look for myself. Phoebe Lowther's had none of her own, she won't know. When did she start the pains?'

'She swooned half an hour since. Then she was bad, she's awful bad.'

The woman took a long swallow of tea and put the pot down on the fender before reaching for her boots. 'So you're kin to Phoebe Lowther, are you? Aye, well, she's a nice body. A bit of a gossip though.' She stood up and smoothed down her black serge skirt before picking up her capacious black holdall from the table.

'Eeh, who would have my job, I ask you? I'm at it night and day the way people around this place breed.'

The midwife walked at such a leisurely pace that Meg felt like getting behind her and pushing her. But at last they were there.

'An' you took your time!' Auntie Phoebe was at the front door when they came up the path. 'Didn't the lass tell you it was a rush job, Mrs Hall?' All Phoebe's self-assurance had deserted her, she was white and strained-looking. Catching hold of Meg before she entered the house, she drew her aside.

'You go down to the other bairns, pet. This is no place for you, not now. And when your da comes out of the pit tell him to take the bairns next-door to our house. That'll be the best.'

Turning swiftly, Phoebe shut the door in Meg's face and the girl was left staring at the wooden boards, an un-named dread rising in her.

Meg could hear Mrs Hall's voice as she climbed the stairs to the bedroom. 'Now, Phoebe, I know it's because

64

you've had none of your own, but don't panic, lass . . .'
The voice broke off abruptly, the only other sound a
muffled exclamation. Meg turned and ran off blindly.
Suddenly she didn't want to be told that the midwife had
found anything wrong. Mam was just having a bairn, a
babby. She'd had a babby before, hadn't she? Why
should it be different this time?

There was the day little Alice was born. She'd thought
Mam was dying then but she didn't, it was all right. It
would be all right this time an' all, Meg said to herself.
Deliberately she slowed to a walk and wiped her face
with the corner of her apron. She would go down to the
pit yard. Da would be coming up now and it was best if
she was there to warn him before he went home. Besides
there was Jack Boy and the little 'uns to think about.
Miles was likely crying for his mam by now.

The mine hooter was blowing as Meg reached the
yard. Men were already streaming from it, brushing past
the children standing by the gates, the boy holding Miles
against his hip. Miles had his face buried in Jack Boy's
neck. He seemed to have cried himself to sleep. Alice
was huddling close to him and watching the men, black
with coal dust, some of them stopping to light the first
cigarette in nine or ten hours. They drew the smoke into
thier lungs and it made them cough and gather up the
phlegm in their mouths so they could spit out the coal
and the stone dust, clearing their tubes. Meg watched
too, anxious now about Da. Had he managed not to
panic in the cage?

'Here, give us the bairn.' She leaned over and took the
sleeping Miles, holding him up to her shoulder, cradling
him in her arms.

'Eeh, Meg, I can't see me da at all.' Jack Boy, relieved
of his burden, looked anxiously at his elder sister. His
eyes asked the question he was too shy to put into words.

'Mam has the midwife,' was all Meg said, and they turned to scan the men once again.

'Da! I can see Da.' Alice was diving between the men, running towards her father. 'Da! Mam's took bad,' she cried, before Meg could stop her.

How Alice could recognize Da, Meg couldn't think. To her the man coming towards them, holding on to a grinning, skipping Alice, was like a stranger. He was covered in coal dust from head to toe, her fastidious da, who was always clean, no matter what. His hair was encrusted with it, his clothes stiff with it, only his eyes were the same, an intense blue staring out of a black, streaked face. The bait tin hanging by his side which had held his sandwiches clanked against the gate as he came through and his pit boots rang on the stones.

'What it is, what's the matter?' he asked, ignoring the younger ones clamouring to be noticed and turning all his attention on Meg.

'Mam. The bairn's coming.'

'Nay, it can't be, there's a while to go yet,' Jack Maddison objected.

'I know, I know, Da, but that's what Auntie Phoebe says. And I had to go for the midwife, and when we get back we have to go in Auntie Phoebe's house. That's what she said, any road.'

Jack Maddison grabbed the sleeping Miles from Meg, ignoring her protests about getting the bairn all black from the coal dust, and set off at a run for the colliery rows. He far outstripped his family so that when Meg got back to the house with her brothers and sisters in tow, he had already disappeared inside. Slowly, she went up the garden path to number one. The kitchen was empty, the fire dying in the grate. Uncle Tot had gone to the pit.

'Watch them for a minute, Jack,' she commanded, deciding to brave whatever was going on next-door. At the very least she could bring little Miles out of the way. She could hear his fretful crying.

'Aw, man, our Meg, I wanted to play cricket.' Jack Boy was mutinous, hadn't he minded the bairns all day? And it was lass's work.

Meg turned on him furiously, venting her worry and frustration.

'You do as I tell you or I'll tell Da! Then he'll bray you, an' if he doesn't, I will.' She stopped as she saw the stricken look in his eyes. He was hardly seven, after all.

'All right, all right, our Meg. I never said I wouldn't,' he muttered.

She crept out of the back door. As she walked up their own yard, which was still glistening wetly from the swilling it had had earlier in the day, she could see through the kitchen window that there was no one about, only Miles sitting on the mat, newly wakened from sleep and sobbing as he looked round his unfamiliar surroundings. Meg rushed in and picked up the child, holding him against her shoulder and rocking gently.

'There, there, me bairn. Meggie's here, she's got you now. Be a good lad and I'll give you a nice buttered crust to suck. Whisht now, whisht, me pet.'

Gradually, Miles's sobs lessened and Meg strained to hear what was going on upstairs. She looked up at the brown boards which made up the ceiling of the kitchen and the floor of the bedroom above. There was much creaking of wood, the sound of footsteps going backwards and forwards, hushed whispers. A man's voice, Scottish, said something and the midwife answered.

'Yes, Doctor.'

Doctor? They'd had to get the doctor! They never did that just for a baby coming. Mam had never had a doctor

67

before. Meg's heart thumped in her breast. She strained to hear more.

But there was silence. Miles whimpered suddenly in her arms, sensing the anxious turmoil going on in Meg. And there came a sound Meg had never heard before in her life, great racking sobs in an unfamiliar voice which it took Meg a minute or two to realize was Da's. And Auntie Phoebe began talking in a funny sort of voice too, softly, coaxing, as to a feverish child.

'Howay, now, Jack, there's nothing you can do now. Best go downstairs and let us get on here, this is no place for you now. You have to hold up for the sake of those poor bairns.'

And a new sound was added, the weak wailing of a baby.

Six

Meg sat beside Alice and Jack Boy on the wooden form along the back wall in the kitchen. She was cradling the sleeping Miles in her arms. He'd cried and cried for his mam but in the end fallen asleep, exhausted. Alice was swinging her legs backwards and forwards, nursing her own baby, a peg dollie wrapped in a bit of clout for a shawl. Meg looked at her younger sister. Alice hadn't cried when Auntie Phoebe told her that her mam had gone to heaven, she'd simply picked up her doll and hugged it. And now she was sitting quietly, still hugging it.

Auntie Phoebe and Uncle Tot were sitting at the table with Da. They were talking earnestly together. At least, Auntie Phoebe and Uncle Tot were talking, Da gave no sign that he was even listening.

'I asked the minister to come, Jack,' said Auntie Phoebe. 'It'd be best if we have the funeral on Wednesday morning, Tot'll be able to come then.' As she spoke, Auntie Phoebe was rocking the cradle with her foot, the wooden cradle which had been taken from Eldon to Marsden on the coast and back inland to Winton Colliery. Meg watched her. There wasn't any need to rock the cradle, she was thinking. The baby, Bella was sound asleep. In spite of the violence of her arrival, Bella slept most of the time.

But Auntie Phoebe had taken over the new baby already. She couldn't bear to be away from Bella at all.

She even wanted to take the baby next-door the night, thought Meg, sudden resentment overlaying her numb misery. She knew she wasn't old enough herself to have proper charge of Bella. But the baby was a Maddison, she thought, not a Lowther. Families had to stay together. Da would see that if he was more like himself.

Jack Maddison was sitting quietly, giving no sign that he even heard Auntie Phoebe. Miles woke up and struggled to be down from Meg's lap. He toddled over to his father and tried to climb on his knee, but Jack made no move to help him. A strained, white Jack Boy went to him without being told and picked him up in his skinny arms, leaning backwards to take the weight.

'Howay, Miles,' he said softly. 'We'll go and pick some daisies and cowslips, and mebbe Alice'll give us a hand, eh?'

The room was quiet after the younger children left. Meg glanced through the connecting door to the front room. Already the coffin was laid out on two trestles supplied by the undertaker. The top was left off until the actual 'lifting' so friends and kin could view Hannah for the last time. It was the custom, Meg knew, only there wouldn't be any friends and relatives, not for her mam. There weren't any left, just Auntie Phoebe and Uncle Tot. Meg looked at her uncle who was sitting in his shirtsleeves next to Da, his face solemn.

'I shouldn't have gone down the pit, I knew I shouldn't,' Jack said suddenly.

'Eeh, Jack, man, you going down the pit didn't do anything,' protested Uncle Tot.

'It was another worry for Hannah, it was, it upset her,' said Jack.

Meg watched him from her seat by the back wall, it was the first time she had heard Da say anything since Mam died.

'I'm not going down any more,' he added now.

70

Uncle Tot started to argue but broke off in mid-sentence as he saw he was getting nowhere. 'Aye then, Jack,' he said. 'I tell you what, I'll see about a job on bank for you. It'll be less money, but if you mean it . . .'

'I do.'

Auntie Phoebe looked at Meg and sighed. 'Howay then, Meg, there's a lot to be done if we're to be ready for Wednesday. It's up to thee and me now, lass.' And somehow the awful day passed, full of work for Meg and her aunt.

The funeral was held on Wednesday at eleven in the morning. Auntie Phoebe and Meg had scrubbed the house out from top to bottom yet again, to make it decent for the funeral meal afterwards. And Meg had bathed the little ones in the tin bath which hung on a nail in the back yard when not in use. But Auntie Phoebe bathed the baby.

'You're not big enough to do the babby, pet,' she said to Meg, who was watching her and thinking that Mam had done it differently. Mam had held a baby easily, but Auntie Phoebe was awkward and she used too much soap an' all. And Meg rebelled in her heart. Hadn't she been big enough to do little Miles? But she said nothing, just got on with dressing Alice and Miles in the clothes normally reserved for Sunday School.

The day was wet and dismal. Meg had been up early, helping Auntie Phoebe boil the ham and ox tongue and pease pudding and slice the pickled beetroot which was to go with it. And all the time they had to skirt round Da who was in the rocking chair by the kitchen range, just sitting there.

'Well,' said Auntie Phoebe, 'no matter how hard up we are, we have to have a decent tea to offer anyone who comes back to the house after, we couldn't not give Hannah a decent send off.' And Meg knew she meant anything less was too much akin to that thing dreaded above all, a Parish burial.

'Eeh, Auntie Phoebe!' Meg exclaimed when she saw the size of the ham and beheld the tray of cakes which Phoebe had brought round from her own house. 'Eeh, Auntie Phoebe, we can't pay for all this.' She cast a quick glance at Da to see if he knew anything about it. She knew all their meagre savings had gone on the move from Marsden. And Da hadn't been to work since Mam died, he'd only been down the pit that one day.

But Jack Maddison didn't even look up.

Auntie Phoebe looked guardedly at Da too before she answered. 'Dinna worry, pet,' she said. 'Your Uncle Tot has seen to it. An' mebbe your mam carried a bit of insurance?'

Meg looked doubtful. Da might know but they couldn't ask him now. She couldn't remember the insurance man calling at all when he was on his weekly rounds, though.

'Well, never mind, pet. It'll be fine, you'll see. Everything will get paid for, things turn up.' With a touch of surprise, Meg realised that Auntie Phoebe was embarrassed about something. Her face was all red and she kept darting funny looks at Da.

'There now, I think it's all ready. Now, I'll just go round and change into my black.' Auntie Phoebe changed the subject with obvious relief. 'They'll be here in half an hour.'

The hearse, when it came, was pulled by two black-plumed horses and the undertaker and his boy were wearing top hats in a shining black silk with trailing ribbons. That would all be extra, Meg knew. Worry niggled at her as she picked up Miles and followed the minister and Da out to the hearse, Jack Boy and Alice by her side and Auntie Phoebe carrying Bella.

'I'll take Miles,' whispered Uncle Tot, and Meg

gratefully released her burden to him. She couldn't think about money now; she could still hear in her mind the sound of them nailing down the coffin lid.

Mr Barton, the young minister barely out of his training, looked down on the family from his place in the pulpit, hardly knowing what to say to them. Distress surged through him as he saw the stooped shoulders of the husband, covered by a threadbare suit, and the group of children round him, the youngest girl looking bewildered by it all.

His attention was drawn to the eldest girl who looked to be nine or ten years old. She had an air of vitality and strength with her springing fair hair and bright blue eyes, even though these were now red with weeping. Already she was acting as mother to the younger ones, a role he realized she would have to fill in earnest now. His heart filled with pity for her.

The minister sighed. He had never met the family before the day the mother died, but there were so many others like this one. He thought about his own comfortable middle-class home in Surrey; how he had been fired with enthusiasm when he had heard about the surge of revivalism in the northern pit villages. And he remembered the shock it had been when he had seen for himself the dirt and poverty and downright human misery here. Though there was another side to life in the pit village, too, a side he found himself quite unable to do anything about. There was a wild side, a drinking, gambling fraternity as well as their more pious chapel neighbours. The drinkers and gamblers were catered for by the beer houses and inns like the Pit Laddie which stood right next-door to the chapel. And on a Sunday night at service they were sometimes put to it to hear themselves sing the hymns for the roistering and shouting going on. Abruptly the minister recollected himself and controlled his wandering thoughts, announcing the last hymn and bringing the service to a close.

'You will take a bite of tea with us, won't you, Mr Barton? You'd be welcome, I'm sure,' said Auntie Phoebe as they left the graveside. She looked across at Jack for him to endorse the invitation. Jack was not listening.

But nor was he sunk in the stupor which had affected him since the death of his wife. He was staring at a man standing apart from the other mourners. Meg followed his gaze. It was a gentleman who stood there, his top hat in his hand. She looked at his fine grey suit and the snowy linen showing at collar and cuffs. He was a proper toff with his silver-topped cane in one hand. Then Meg looked closer. What was it about him, did she know him?

His cheeks were coarse with tiny red veins showing on the skin and deep lines around his eyes, but yes, she thought she knew him. And the knowledge filled her with a sickening terror.

Candyman! That was who he was. She remembered him, oh, she did, she did. She remembered that day when she and her mam and the babby had run from the candymen, and he was on a great, grey horse, and he was the biggest bloody candyman of them all, Mrs Hart had said so. And hadn't she seen him since, time and time again, in her nightmare?

There was something else, an' all, something her mind shied away from. What was it? But search her mind as she might, she couldn't remember what it was. She only knew it was something to do with him.

'That's very kind of you, Mrs Lowther,' the minister was saying in that plummy, flat voice he had, 'but really, I think I'd better not.'

Auntie Phoebe bridled. The minister always came

back for the funeral tea, it was expected. Mr Barton saw he'd offended her and began again.

'Well, perhaps I can—'

He was saved from his embarrassment by the sound of a low growl of anger. He and Phoebe both turned in surprise to see what it was.

'You bloody, filthy cur!' Jack had roused himself all right. The stream of oaths which he uttered startled everyone and shocked the minister to the core. He saw Jack fling himself headlong at the gentleman, Mr Grizedale, for that was who it was, everyone knew well. 'You killed her,' Jack yelled.

The force of his rush and the suddenness of it took Ralph off balance and he stumbled and fell beneath the flailing onslaught, his cane rolling from his hand. It took the combined strength of all the men present, including the shocked minister, to drag Jack Maddison off his quarry. Tot had to hang on to his arms and Auntie Phoebe step between him and Ralph before Jack would stop straining to get at him.

'Jack! Jack, man, remember where you are, lad. Think of the bairns, will you?'

Meg watched, shrinking back into the hedge with Alice and Miles whimpering in terror as Uncle Tot held on to Da, remonstrating. She cast a fearful look at the candyman, Mr Grizedale. Eeh, what would he do to her da for this? Ralph was climbing to his feet, his face flushed to an angry hue of purple; he was shaking with rage, she could see, as he brushed the soil from his fine coat, leaving dark brown stains on the elbows.

'It was all his fault! All his. My Hannah would be alive today but for him. I'll—' Jack began to choke and his words faded into incoherence. Tears coursed down his cheeks.

'Come now, Mr Maddison, you are overwrought,' put

in the minister, trying to reason with Jack before turning to Mr Grizedale.

'I'm sure you will forgive him, sir, he's not himself. His wife, you know.'

Ralph brushed Mr Barton aside contemptuously and strode up to Jack, towering over him, his face only inches away. Meg moaned and took a step forward, sure he was going to kill her da. Little Alice started to scream; a thin, high, terrified shrieking.

'I killed her, did I?' shouted Ralph. He laughed, a hard, mirthless sound. 'Why, you bare-arsed animal, you excuse for a man! Was it me who filled her with babies until they killed her? Was it me who couldn't even feed her right? Why, man, you couldn't pay for a decent burial for Hannah. Who do you think paid for this lot? Certainly not any of this gaggle of paupers!'

He turned on his heel and strode from the churchyard. Mounting his horse which had been left tied to a tree in the hedge, he rode off without a backward glance.

Clumsily, hampered by the weight of Miles, Meg ran to her father. All she could see was that Da hadn't been murdered and the candyman was gone. A glad thankfulness filled her heart and lighted her eyes.

'Da! Eeh, Da, I was that worried,' she cried.

But Jack didn't seem to hear her. He didn't watch Ralph ride away either. He was staring at Auntie Phoebe and Uncle Tot, his face so white and set that Meg felt a terrible fear growing in her yet again and her arm trembled as she took hold of Alice's hand and drew her back from the grown-ups.

'Eeh Jack, what could I do?' Auntie Phoebe quavered. Her voice was all different, subdued, her confidence gone. 'He offered, man, an' well, me an' Tot thought . . .' She floundered to a stop and looked at her husband for support.

'Aye, Jack. After all's said and done, he is your brother-in-law, man.'

'How did he know? You told him?'

'Eeh, no, we didn't, Jack. He found out somehow,' said Phoebe.

They had forgotten all about the minister who came forward now.

'I'm sorry, I forgot, a pressing engagement . . .' he said. His face was still white with shock. 'I have to go.'

He was unheeded by Jack and the Lowthers, though the few curious funeral followers who were hoping to sit down to the funeral tea fell back respectfully as he left the churchyard. Meg looked at them. Their faces were agog with excitement. Why didn't folk mind their own business? she thought bitterly.

Jack stared at Auntie Phoebe and Uncle Tot, his face showing conflicting emotions. Suddenly he wheeled about and walked away, taking the Auckland road out of the village. Galvanized into action, Meg dragged little Miles after him, terrified he was going to leave them, and if Da took off now, what would they do?

'Da! Da!' she cried, and Miles tripped but didn't fall for Meg had such a hold on him she simply carried him along by his arm in her determination to get to her father.

The panic and despair in the girl's voice somehow penetrated the fog in Jack Maddison's brain for he hesitated long enough for Meg to catch up with him, Miles sobbing and panting by her side. She caught hold of him with her free hand, and gazed up into his face.

'Da, Da, howay home with us now. Come on, Da. Howay now. We need you, Da. You can't go off, what'll we do?' She scarcely knew what she said, she only knew she had to stop him from walking away. If he carried on walking he wouldn't come back, oh, she was sure of it!

Jack looked down at her tear-stained face, unseeing at

77

first, then gradually his eyes focused and he took in what he saw, he heard the fretful sobbing of little Miles as he rubbed his wrist where Meg had held him too tightly as she pulled him along.

The father in him responded to the distress he saw and Jack's face softened. He stooped and picked the tiny boy up in his arms to soothe him.

'Whisht now, bairn, whisht,' he said, 'Da'll kiss it better.' And his voice was almost back to normal. Meg breathed a long sigh, letting the tension fall from her. Mebbe Da was going to be all right now, mebbe it wouldn't be so bad. She looked around for Jack Boy and Alice. They were standing just outside the churchyard, Jack Boy holding Alice's shoulder. The little girl was clinging tightly to her dolly with one hand, and the thumb of the other was stuck far into her mouth.

Behind them, Auntie Phoebe and Uncle Tot were standing, uncertain what to do, and behind them again, the few funeral followers who were thick-skinned or perhaps just hungry enough to remain.

'Howay, then.' Meg called her brother and sister to her, and Jack Boy's face cleared. He took hold of Alice's hand, pulling her thumb firmly out of her mouth, and brought her to his father and his sister Meg and his little brother Miles. The family turned for Pasture Row and home, and after a moment, Uncle Tot and Auntie Phoebe followed them with baby Bella.

Seven

Jonty heard his father ride into the stable yard, Cal's hooves clattering against the cobble stones, and swiftly the boy ducked behind the half-door of the tack-room. Jonty was almost ten years old now and had learned that the best way to avoid a whipping was to keep out of his father's way. He waited, heart beating uncomfortably as he listened to his father talking to the stable lad. Father didn't usually enter the stable at all. Usually when he came home he threw the reins at the lad and stumped off into the house. But this time he came to the door, only a few feet away from Jonty's hiding place, and he shrank down further and tried to keep his breathing quiet.

'Where's John Thomas? That brat's never there when I want him. I thought he was working in here today?' Father was asking the stable lad, Bob. He had only been with them for a week. Lads were always coming and going at the Hall, every hiring day there was a new one. Jonty trembled. Would Bob tell Father where he was?

'Sorry, sir, I've not seen the young master,' said Bob and Jonty breathed easier.

Ralph laughed, shortly. 'Young master, eh? That's what he is, is it? Aye, well, if you do see him, *if the young master* deigns to come back, you tell him I want to see him, in my study.'

'Aye, sir,' mumbled the lad.

Jonty's left foot was going into cramp. He tried to ease

it, carefully moving it forward, his toecap making a small sound against the flagstone. He froze, the pain running up his leg as he watched the grotesque shadow of his father against the far wall of the tack-room and the smaller shadow of the stable lad. But Father hadn't heard the noise.

'Aye,' he was saying, and now he sounded really amused and that made Jonty even more fearful – he knew the sort of thing that amused his father. There was the time the servant girl, Jenny her name was, had told Father she was having a baby and he had toyed with her, making her think he might look after her, maybe even marry her. He'd had Jenny doing awful things, degrading herself for him. Jonty's thoughts shied away from the memory. And then, when she got too far gone in pregnancy for Father's tastes, he had thrown her out. Oh, aye, Father'd thought it all a great joke.

And there was the queen cat, Smoky, who had scratched Father's hand when he bent to pick up her babies. Father had hung Smoky on a tree and made Jonty watch her death struggles. He shuddered and came back to the present as something his father said caught his attention.

'I have some bad news for the precious young master, I have. I've been to a funeral today, the funeral of his aunt.'

My aunt? I don't have an aunt, thought Jonty, startled. Not a Grizedale aunt, at least. There was only Auntie Hannah. Meg's mam. Auntie Hannah who had gone away and left him to his father's mercy.

Jonty clung to the memory of Auntie Hannah. Why had she gone like that, why? He thought of the row of houses down by the old line. They all had new tenants in them now; he'd gone down there once but Auntie Hannah and Uncle Jack and Meg hadn't come back. Suddenly a picture flashed into Jonty's mind, a picture

80

of Meg and her mam, both with bright curling hair and shining blue eyes, and both smiling at him. He forgot his fear of his father and slowly got to his feet.

'My aunt?' he asked.

Ralph Grizedale laughed cruelly. 'So you were there, listening all the time, were you? Sneaking around in corners, hiding away, eavesdropping on folk. Well, you've heard some bad news this time, haven't you?' Ralph's voice hardened and he rounded on the stable lad, still standing holding on to Cal's reins. 'You knew he was there, didn't you?' he shouted. 'You can get your—'

'He didn't know, Father, I've just got here,' butted in Jonty, and Ralph forgot about Bob and leaned over the half-door to haul his son up and over. Dragging the boy behind him, he strode into the house and headed for his study. Bob cast a thankful glance after Jonty as he took Cal into the stable. He rubbed him down, talking quietly to the horse all the while. He wouldn't stay past next hiring day, he resolved. Then he would try to get work with the pit ponies in Winton.

Ralph dumped Jonty unceremoniously on the floor and closed the door of his study, checking first that his mother was not about. If the old witch heard what was going on she would try to interfere. That one never learned her lesson. And besides, she might not be so happy to turn over to him the shares he wanted if he upset her.

Jonty picked himself up and faced his father. All he wanted to know was if anything had happened to Auntie Hannah. He didn't care if he was whipped.

'Auntie Hannah?' he asked.

Ralph took his time, settling himself in his armchair, selecting a cigar from the side table and lighting it. Jonty watched as the smoke rose in the air towards the ornate ceiling, already stained a dull brown with tobacco. At last Ralph sat back, crossed his legs before him and smiled at Jonty. But not with his eyes. His eyes were like hard, black pieces of coal sunk into the fleshy folds of his face.

'I wondered if you remembered Hannah,' he said pleasantly. 'Yes, I meant her. I've been to her funeral today.'

Jonty stared at his father. Dimly, he remembered the feelings of love and tenderness which had wrapped him round when he went to Auntie Hannah's house; even though he hadn't seen her for so long he felt an acute sense of loss to learn she was dead. When things were bad, when his father was worse to him than usual, he would go to his room afterwards and comfort himself with the thought that one day, when he was big enough, he would find them. Meg and Uncle Jack and Auntie Hannah. He would find out if what his father said was true, if they had just abandoned him because they didn't want him. His expression didn't change. He couldn't let his father see that Hannah still meant something to him.

'I had to pay for it too, they were destitute. Jack Maddison couldn't even pay the undertaker.' Ralph was watching Jonty carefully, a small smile hovering round his mouth. When still there was no obvious response, he went on, 'Half-starved they looked. It would have been a pauper's burial but for me.'

Jonty turned his face away. He wanted to ask all the questions which were clamouring in his mind. Where was it, was Meg there, was she all right, was Uncle Jack there, was he all right, what did Auntie Hannah die of? But he knew Father was waiting for him to ask and he wasn't going to. Indeed he would not. Jonty lifted his chin in the air and closed his mouth firmly.

In the end Ralph lost his temper. There was no point in teasing the brat. Stubborn as a mule he was, like the pitmen he'd sprung from. He rose to his feet and fetched the lad a great swipe across the ear, knocking him half across the room.

'Get out of my sight and don't let me see your measly face again today!' he snarled, and went over to the whisky tray in the corner. Suddenly it wasn't so funny to him either. He couldn't get used to the idea that Hannah wasn't there somewhere, that the day would never dawn now when she would come to him on her knees. He poured himself a tumbler of neat whisky and tossed it off in one gulp, unheeding of Jonty who picked himself up yet again and limped from the room.

Upstairs in his room he ignored the ringing in his ear, though the skin was tingling from the heat of the blow. He went to the drawer of his bedside table and took out a little peg doll wrapped in a bit of cloth, yellow from being shut away, and ragged. He stared at it until his vision blurred with tears and he crept on to his bed and curled up in a tight ball, hugging the doll to him.

The morning after the funeral, Meg prepared Da's sandwiches and put them in his bait tin and filled his water bottle in time for him to go down the pit with the fore shift. Da had changed his mind about the pit. He was going down, had told Uncle Tot not to worry about getting him a job on bank.

'Well, there's more money to be earned down the pit than on the top,' was all Uncle Tot had said.

Meg was worried about Da, though. He was different somehow, kind enough with the bairns and he always answered when he was spoken to, but he was different.

Auntie Phoebe bustled in after Da had gone to work and Jack Boy to school. She went straight to the cradle, to where the baby was sleeping by the side of the fire, leaning down and peering under the covers at Bella before straightening up and speaking to Meg, who was washing up the breakfast pots in an enamel bowl and putting them to drain on a tin tray.

'I'll bath the babby now.'

'I was going to do her in a minute, when I've finished this,' Meg objected, but she was overruled and had to watch helplessly as Phoebe took over the baby. Alice and Miles were under the table, Miles chewing on his bleached bone and Alice rocking backwards and fowards, nursing her dollie. They were very quiet. Sighing, Meg got on with the housework, sweeping and dusting and scrubbing in the neverending job of keeping the place free from dust and smuts which were carried down in the soot-laden air.

'I'll just take the babby round our house,' said Auntie Phoebe, 'keep her out of your road.'

'What about her tittie bottle?' Meg asked, going to the pantry for the bottle and the jug of milk.

'I've got one round home. I got one in, thought it would come in.'

There seemed to be nothing Meg could do. Auntie Phoebe had been so good to them an' all, she couldn't say something to affront her. Best let it go for now. When Da was feeling better she would ask him what to do. Though she hadn't much hope of help from Da, he hadn't looked at the babby even.

'Will you take Alice and Miles with you, Auntie Phoebe?' she asked. 'I have to get the messages and I want to—' She had been going to say she wanted to go to Mam's grave to put a posy on it, but found herself unable to say the words.

'Well, I'll take Alice,' said Auntie Phoebe, not noticing there was anything amiss with Meg. 'You can take the lad with you, can't you? Do him good, a bit of fresh air, like.' She lifted the cradle with the baby in it into her arms. 'Howay, Alice, come along of me and Bella, petal.'

It was clear to Meg that Auntie Phoebe was only really

84

interested in the baby, she didn't want the bother of Miles. Oh, well, she had been going to run to the shop and then pick some wild flowers from the bunny banks up by Old Pit. Mam liked the bluebells the best. And good bluebells grew under the trees by the bunny banks. She could mebbe do that after dinner, take Alice and Miles with her.

The days seemed to be galloping by, faster and faster, Meg was thinking, one Sunday morning when for once the family were all breakfasting together before Sunday School. She looked at the young ones, the three of them sitting on the form along one side of the table. Alice was telling Miles a story and they were giggling together. Alice was always telling stories. In school she was forever getting slapped by the teacher for talking and laughing in class. Jack Boy was sitting right on the end of the form, quietly eating porridge with a large dollop of treacle in it to sweeten it.

Jack Boy was like Da, Meg thought, quiet. Da was a silent man now. He seemed to have lost his fear of being underground and never missed a shift. At weekends he worked hard in the garden, filled with restless, neverending energy. He never smiled, though.

Meg's thoughts were distracted by shrieks of mirth from Alice and Miles. They had waited until Jack Boy sat back on the form, having finished his porridge, then, working together, the two younger ones stood up. Of course Jack's weight tipped the form and he went sprawling on the flags. Screaming with glee, Alice and Miles fled the kitchen, with Jack Boy not far behind.

Smiling, Meg poured another mug of tea for her da. It was grand to see the bairns getting over Mam, she'd been worried about Alice at first. But now she wanted to talk to Da about Bella. She looked at him as he sipped his tea, his face expressionless.

'Da,' she began, and he looked up at her. He always replied when she spoke to him, just didn't speak first himself. 'Da, I'm worried about the babby.'

'Bella?' he said. 'She's all right with your Auntie Phoebe, isn't she?'

'Yes. But, Da, I don't like it. Auntie Phoebe wants Bella to live with them altogether. And, Da, I think we should be together, I do. Bella's one of us. She's a Maddison, not a Lowther.'

Jack stared at her. 'Bella's lucky to have Phoebe.'

'Aye, I know, Da, but I could see to her, I could. Auntie Phoebe wants to be her mam.'

Jack rose to his feet and walked to the door without answering.

'Da?'

'Leave things be, Meg, you're only a bairn yourself,' he said, not turning round. 'Our Bella likely needs a mother.'

Only a bairn, thought Meg rebelliously as she cleared the breakfast table and washed up the pots. Only a bairn when it comes to the baby, but a woman when it comes to the work. She worked on, furiously, cleaning the kitchen before washing and changing herself and seeing that the other three were clean and decent enough to join the trickle of children walking through the village to the plain, stone buildings of the Wesleyan Chapel and Sunday School.

Inside, the Sunday School was full of children, boys on one side and girls on the other. The under-fives were all together at the front with kindly Miss Gunner, their plump, grey-haired teacher, in charge of them. Meg saw Miles and Alice settled on the front row and went to join her own class farther back. Jack Boy headed for the boys' rows.

Meg was lost in her own thoughts and hardly heard the first hymn or the prayers that followed. She simply

86

stood up when her neighbours stood up and sat down when they sat down.

It was during the prayers that it happened. All of a sudden there was a loud bump followed by a wailing which completely filled the hall, rising to the rafters, louder even than the combined Sunday School reciting 'Gentle Jesus, meek and mild, look upon a little child', louder than the singing of the hymn which had gone before.

Mr Roberts, the superintendent, stepped forward and picked up a squirming, struggling Miles. The boy's face was red with anger, his fat little three-year-old legs kicking poor Mr Roberts in the stomach.

'Meg! Our Meg!' screamed Miles. 'I want our Meg!' Alice stood by, looking innocently on.

Meg pushed past her classmates and went down to the front, her face rosy red with embarrassment; the whole Sunday School was looking on, she could feel every eye on her. She reached Mr Roberts and held out her arms for Miles who cuddled into her neck, sobbing.

'You're a bad girl, Alice,' said Miss Gunner mildly, 'pushing Miles off the seat like that, and so hard he's hurt himself.'

'I never,' asserted Alice. 'I never pushed him. An' any road, he's not hurt. He's just a big babby, that's what.'

'Alice!' Meg said sharply.

'Do you know what happens to little lasses who don't tell the truth?' queried Mr Roberts, his face sternly. 'And in God's house an' all, *and* during a prayer. Jesus won't love you any more, Alice.'

'I don't care,' she said, defiant now, though her eyes were suspiciously bright. The Sunday School waited, hardly daring to breathe for fear of missing anything. This was better than boring old prayers, any time.

'Alice,' said Meg urgently. 'Howay. Be a good girl, say you're sorry.'

'Nay, I'll not,' said Alice. 'I never did nothing.'

'*And* bad girls who push their little brothers off the seat and then tell lies about it don't get to go on the Sunday School trip to the seaside.' Mr Roberts gave the ultimate threat. He cast a quelling glance over all the scholars as they gasped and murmured to each other.

'I don't want to go to the seaside. We lived at the sea, it's nowt so special,' Alice declared stoutly.

But Meg had had enough. Holding Miles under one arm, she grabbed Alice and pulled her on to the seat beside her, holding her tight so that she couldn't move.

'Whisht!' she whispered fiercely in her sister's ear. 'Whisht or I'll tell Da and he'll bray the life out of you. Do you hear me, Alice?'

Alice looked at Meg, and from her to Mr Roberts, and suddenly her defiance left her. She sat still on the seat and cried softly to herself. There was silence for a minute while the superintendent watched. Satisfied that his authority was no longer under threat from the little girl, he went back to the business in hand.

'Now, children, we'll begin again. Hands together now, close your eyes. "Gentle Jesus, meek and mild—'

'By, I thought our Alice was for it there,' said Jack Boy as they went out into the sunshine after class. 'Eeh, Mr Roberts was fair frothing, he was.'

'I never did anything,' Alice said, 'our Miles pushed me an' I pushed him back, that's all, it wasn't my fault.'

'I fell off the seat,' said Miles, 'I hurt me leg.'

'Let's have a look, our Miles. There's nothing there to see, you big babby, that's—'

Meg grabbed hold of them both, keeping them by her. Mr Roberts was talking to another teacher by the gate and she wanted to get past them without attracting their attention. She managed it. The two men were deep in conversation and ignoring the children sidling by them. But Meg heard what they were saying.

'That little Maddison lad's too young to be coming to Sunday School any road,' the younger man said.

'Aye, but they're motherless, poor bairns. That eldest girl is all they've got but for their father,' answered Mr Roberts.

'They'll be growing up wild, you mark my words, causing a ruckus like that, and during prayertime an' all. What'll they be like when they're older? Why, when we were bairns—'

Meg didn't hear the rest. She was hurrying the children away, burning with humiliation. If Mam was alive they wouldn't talk like that. They'd all gone to Sunday School by Miles's age, hadn't they? Wild! Growing up wild, he'd said. Why, they were doing nowt of the sort! She'd never let Jack Boy or Miles hang about on street corners like that Wesley Cornish and that lot, swaggering about like grown men, shouting after the lasses and drinking beer an' all. She'd seen them herself. Only about twelve they were, or maybe thirteen; they were going down the pit now and they couldn't do that until they were twelve at least. Now Wesley Cornish was wild all right, and his mam was alive, a chapel woman herself. It had nowt to do with whether you had a mam.

'Howay in here, lass, I've made the dinner for all of us.' Her aunt's voice broke into her indignant thoughts.

Auntie Phoebe was standing by the gate, Bella in her arms, waiting for them. Bella lay gurgling happily, looking up at Auntie Phoebe, making no effort to sit up though she was nearly a year old now. The smell of roasting meat and Yorkshire pudding wafted out of the open door of Auntie Phoebe's house. She stood aside as Alice and Miles, their dispute forgotten, whooped with glee and raced up the path, then followed them into the house.

'Go and get your da, Meg,' she called over her shoulder, 'he's in the garden. I saw him digging over that patch where the taties were.'

'I was going to do the dinner, like,' said Meg, thinking of the scrag end of mutton waiting in the pantry, cooked with barley and all ready to warm up. But what could she do? Auntie Phoebe was so kind. She was good to the bairns, helped out all the time. And she had no bairns of her own. Meg watched her now, gazing fondly down at the baby, cooing and talking baby talk to her. And Meg could see that the baby was happy, anybody could see that. She went to call Da in for the meal, and realized she was going to have to let Bella go to Auntie Phoebe. Her feelings were still raw from the trouble in Sunday School. By, if it was the last thing she did, she'd see that her brothers didn't grow up wild. Nor Alice, neither.

Uncle Tot was talking quietly to Auntie Phoebe when Meg got back to the door. She paused for a moment, realizing he was talking about Da.

'He's a loner, Phoebe, he is, I get a bit worried about him down the pit. A good worker mind, his marras say that of him, but he never has a bit of a crack wi' them at bait time. I've seen him going off into a corner on his own, eating his bread and jam and swilling it down with water, then going back to the face straight away. Why, man, the other's haven't time to get started on their bait. An' he's got no friends, like, never goes for a drink with his marras. A man needs a drink. You have to get rid of the coal dust, like, haven't you?'

'Aye, well, it's better than going the other way,' declared Auntie Phoebe. 'There's many a poor body in the rows would wish her man never took a drink of ale.'

'Aye, but Phoebe . . .' Uncle Tot, sitting by the fire with his feet on the fender, moved out of the way as his wife leaned over and opened the door, letting out a blast of hot air. She took out the pudding tins with the

90

Yorkshires risen way over the rims, rich with the browning from the meat. As she turned to put them on the table, she saw Meg hovering in the door.

'Howay, lass, give us a hand with this lot,' she said loudly.

'Aye.' Uncle Tot got to his feet, and pulled his dangling braces into position. 'Aye, lass, howay in, don't hang about there,' he said. 'Is your da coming?' He glanced sheepishly at Auntie Phoebe.

I'll not let on I heard anything, decided Meg to herself. But she knew why Tot was worried about Da. She'd lived among the pitmen long enough now to know that a gang of men working a seam together had to be friends in and out of the pit. They had to be able to depend on each other. The work was dangerous, it could mean their lives. If Da was a chapel man, why then his marras would understand if he didn't go in the pubs. But he wasn't, never went inside a chapel. Not since Mam died. Eeh, she wished he'd be more friendly, joke on a bit like the others. There was always a group of men squatting on their hunkers at the corner, off shift and enjoying a crack together. But Da was never with them. That was something else to worry about.

In the summer of 1887, Jack Boy left school. He was to work at the pit head with the old men and widows and other young boys, screening the coal as it came out of the pit. He was nine years old and thought himself well able to do a man's job.

Meg sent him off on the Monday after the school closed for the summer holiday, her heart heavy. But Jack Boy was excited. This was his big day. He grinned happily as he set off to meet his old school mate. They were starting together.

'Where's me bait tin, our Meg?' he asked importantly. 'Howay, man, I can't be late on me first day.'

91

Meg handed the shiny new tin over along with the water bottle.

'An' you be careful, our Jack Boy,' she said. 'Keep out of the road of the coal tubs when they come up.'

'Aw, our Meg, don't be so daft,' scoffed Jack Boy, but Meg felt on edge all day. There were dangers on the screens, she knew there were. Hadn't there been a lad crushed between two tubs only last month? Well, at least the lads didn't go down the pits nowadays, not till they were twelve. Another three years for that, thank God.

Going into the yard for the tin bath, Meg brought it into the kitchen and placed it before the black-leaded range. Da would be in in a minute and would be wanting his bath as soon as he'd eaten. Then there would be pit clothes to dash against the wall in the back yard to get rid of the coal dust and the washing to start. By, she thought as she worked, I don't want Alice to leave school when she's nine, I want her to stay on. She's clever, our Alice. I want her to get a good job, mebbe with the Cooperative Society, the store in Bishop Auckland. Eeh, wouldn't that be lovely?

Eight

'Does your da know you're out?'

Meg didn't look round to see which one of the lads on the corner was tormenting her, she knew it was that Wesley Cornish. Holding her head high and gripping her shopping basket tightly in both hands, she went on her way to the store for the messages. The jeering and giggling of the lads rang in her ears which flushed as pink as her cheeks.

By! I hate them lads, she said to herself. Can't leave a body alone. They come off shift and have nothing to do but pester folk. Why don't they get away to bed, like Da and Jack Boy when they come in?

Meg became aware that someone had fallen into step beside her, one of the lads; she turned a furious face to him.

'Get away!' she hissed. 'You leave me alone, Wesley Cornish, or I'll call the polis.'

Wesley Cornish grinned, an open, cheerful grin which lit up his light brown eyes and showed his strong white teeth. He backed off, raising a hand in self-defence.

'Eeh, Margaret Anne Maddison,' he said, giving her her full name as she had him, 'give us a chance. By, you're bonny when you're mad, you are.'

Meg turned on her heel and walked rapidly away. Why couldn't she think of a quick retort, like Alice? Alice was only nine now, but she was never short of an answer, not to anyone. And here was Meg, sixteen years old all but, and blushing and tongue-tied when a lad made up to her. She got to the end of the row before realizing that Wesley had stopped following her. In spite of herself she couldn't help glancing over her shoulder before rounding the corner. And could have kicked herself, for there he was, not ten yards back, laughing and waving.

'Ta ra, Margaret Anne Maddison. I'll be seeing you.'

Meg seethed. A group of women were standing by the end gate gossiping and all of them turned and craned their necks to see who it was calling after her. Meg stomped on her way. Next time, she thought, I'll send Alice for the messages. Wesley did that on purpose, he did. Now everybody'll think me and Wesley Cornish are going with each other.

Thinking of Alice brought a touch of pride. She was nine years old coming up ten and she wasn't going to leave school, Da had agreed that she could stay on at least for a year or two.

'It'd be a shame for our Alice to leave school,' Meg had said persuasively. 'She's clever, always top of the class.'

Da was nodding his head in agreement. After all, with Jack Boy earning and almost old enough to go down the pit, not just work on the screens, they didn't actually need Alice to earn.

'Well, I don't see what she needs with all that book learning,' Auntie Phoebe had put in. 'I never went to school at all and I've got by, haven't I? She'd pursed her lips and stared at Meg, defying her to contradict.

'Things are different now, Auntie Phoebe,' Meg had said mildly. 'You didn't have the chance to go to school.'

All the while Alice had been sitting on the form in the corner anxiously listening to her elders debating her future. For once she was quiet and solemn but Meg had known Alice desperately wanted to stay on at school,

94

not just for a year or two but to become a pupil teacher. Alice wanted it passionately. But Meg had thought that if she told Da that now, he would think it an impossible ambition. Best get him to agree to one extra year at a time.

'Aye. All right,' he'd said. 'So long as you can manage, Meg.'

'I don't think it's fair on the other bairns,' Auntie Phoebe had said, and gone out of the door and stumped off down the path.

'Da! Thank you, Da, I'll work in the house and help our Meg, I will. I'll do anything!'

Meg smiled now at the memory of Alice dancing round Da in the kitchen. Carrying her basket home from the shop, she was almost dancing herself. Eeh, life was grand.

'Is that smile for me, Margaret Anne Maddison?'

Meg sighed. She'd completely forgotten about Wesley and the other lads. Determinedly she didn't look at him nor speak to him, but rushed down the row to her gate and up the path to the house. What was she going to do about Wesley Cornish?

'You doing the washing the day, Meg?'

Jack was sitting at the kitchen table eating his bacon and black pudding. He was still black from the fore shift at the pit, though he had shed his jacket and shirt, both stiff with coal dust, and was sitting in his undershirt. Even that was stiff with the all-pervading dust and the hair on his forearms stood up stiffly with it. He looked at his daughter with that dead expression in his eyes which had been there since the death of his wife.

Meg paused in her journey from the back yard with the tin bath which she was getting ready for her father. She was surprised. He spoke so little to her or the other children that if he started a conversation it was always something strictly necessary.

'Aye,' she answered, standing up straight and stretching her spine unconsciously. Bending over the poss tub so often made her back ache.

'But you were washing yesterday.'

Meg bit her lip. It was true she had been washing yesterday but that had been Mrs Brown's. For a year or two now, Meg had been working 'monthlys'. That was, going out to women who were laid up in bed after having a baby, cleaning up a bit for them, maybe making a pot pie for the man coming off shift and bringing dirty clothes home to wash and dry and iron. She'd not told Da. He never noticed, not usually, what she was doing. But it earned an extra two or three shillings a week.

'Aye,' she said at last, 'but I was helping out . . .' She looked at her da and broke off what she was saying. He seemed to have forgotten about it and went on with his breakfast. Meg filled the set pot and lit the fire under it, sighing. Not at the work she had to do. Work didn't bother her, she usually hummed as she worked, it was no trouble. But she felt unsettled today, unhappy somehow. She'd thought she'd got used to Da's ways, but today she found his indifference bothering her. He hadn't even been interested enough to ask her why she had to wash clothes two days in a row.

Da went up to bed and Meg cleared the table for she would need it later on to hold the steaming piles of washing. Da was a funny one all right, she mused, mechanically sorting the white or delicate articles from the heavy cottons, keeping the pit clothes well away from them on the floor. If she didn't get the first lot of possings done and the whites into the boiler before dinner time, she would not be finished before Alice and Miles came in from school. In spite of all her resolutions to the contrary, Meg had got out of the habit of including

Bella when she thought of the younger ones. Bella would go next-door straight away; she thought of herself as Auntie Phoebe's bairn.

Dragging the large poss tub and possing stick out of the outhouse in the yard, Meg set it up near the set pot boiler. Soon she was working steadily, rhythmically, up and down with the weighted stick, forcing the dirt out of the clothes, watching the water bubbling up through them and singing to herself in time to the rhythm of her arms. Her vaguely troubled thoughts disappeared with the work. She had a lot to be thankful for, she knew.

By the time Jack Boy came in from his shift at the pit, most of the clothes were waving in the wind in the front garden and Meg was just finishing off the last possing of pit clothes, lifting them to the heavy wooden rollers and threading them through. Alice was drying out the set pot, leaning over the edge to reach the bottom, in serious danger of toppling in altogether.

'Your dinner's ready,' Meg said swiftly, on the defensive. Jack Boy hated her taking on outside work and he wasn't like Da, he noticed straight away if she did.

'Why do you do it?' he asked now, rubbing the back of his hand wearily across his brow and smearing the black, sweaty smuts. 'It was washing day yesterday. I mean, it won't be long before our Miles is on the screens, we can do without it. You've plenty to do here.'

Meg smiled placatingly. It was true, Miles would be working in a few months, he wanted to, he was no scholar like Alice. But it had started with Mam's funeral and Da's determination to pay back every penny it had cost Mr Grizedale. It had taken a long time, and then Alice had been poorly with a bout of fever and medicine cost money. The money was repaid now to Mr Grizedale, but Meg liked to keep a few shillings in hand. And then there had been union meetings. There was unrest in the

97

air. Suppose there was a strike? Best have a bit put away, it didn't hurt.

'I've got a nice pot pie on the fire,' she said. 'I'll leave this and put it out for you.'

'I'm not hungry, our Meg.'

Meg looked at Jack Boy in quick concern. He was short for his age, going on thirteen, but was already developing the strong shoulders and arms of the miner. It was impossible to tell if he was pale because of the coal dust. She put a hand to feel his forehead to see if he was sickening for something but he knocked it impatiently away.

'Aw, give over, our Meg, I'm all right. I'm just not hungry. I'll have a wash and go for a walk out. I'll eat me dinner after.'

Reassured, Meg called to Alice: 'Get the bath in. I've saved some hot water in the buckets, they're by the fire. Then call Da and tell him the dinner's ready.'

As soon as the meal was over and the pots washed, Meg took off her sacking apron and combed back her hair, securing it into a knot at the nape of her neck with hairpins.

'I'm just going for a walk myself,' she said. Alice looked up hopefully, and Meg hesitated. She still worried about Alice's health; her winter cough had lasted well into summer this year. Usually Meg kept her indoors in the evenings. But though it was September already, the day had been very warm. In fact, it was still warm, it could almost have been an evening in early August. The fresh air might do Alice good. There was no stink from the coke ovens at the minute.

'Howay, then. Put your shawl on mind, I mean it.'

Alice had started to protest that it was too warm for a shawl but shut up at Meg's last words. When Meg said she meant it, nothing would change her mind.

The sisters walked slowly past the colliery rows and

into the older part of the village where there was a remnant of village green, much trodden and blackened. Meg was carrying a parcel of clean clothes. She had been careful not to let Jack Boy see it, even though it was not paid work. It was just a small bundle of clothes she had done for a widow who lived on her own outside the village on the Shildon road. The widow would have been doing it herself but for the fact that she was wheelchair-bound with arthritis.

Meg was enjoying the relaxation of the walk. Being able to stand up straight after stooping for so long at the tub was grand. A cool breeze sprang up and Alice shivered slightly, clutching her shawl to her. Meg looked down at her. The lass was so thin and pasty-looking, what would this winter do to her? Eeh, it was a good thing she didn't have to go out to work, it was that. At least she could stay in the warmth of the schoolroom.

'We'll soon be sheltered from the wind,' Meg said, 'it always seems to blow along here. When we get over the hill and down the road a bit we'll be sheltered.'

Indeed, leaving the village they soon took a right-hand fork with a high hedge to one side, shielding them from the wind. The sun shone low on the horizon as the scene changed; the smoking chimney and winding wheel of the pit village were left behind them and there were long fields sweeping down the hill. Meg smiled. She loved this view, it was her favourite walk.

The harvest was in progress and the sweet smell of ripe corn lay heavy on the air. Behind the hedges they could hear the harvesters talking among themselves and further down the slope, nearer the farm buildings, they could see the cows and hear them lowing as they were driven out of the byres after milking. The farming world seemed so clean and peaceful to the sisters after the muck and bustle of the colliery, though they were not unaware that life was hard on the farms and the wages very low. Which was the reason so many young lads left the farms and ended up in the pits where, so long as there was work, the wages were better.

'Meg! Meg! Where are you going?'

She was brought out of her reverie by Alice who had stopped by a small cottage, the end of a row. This was Old Pit, named after the long defunct mine at the other end of the row, the wooden structure over the shaft green with age and mould and some of it fallen down. Only two of the cottages in Old Pit were occupied now, and those by miners' widows. The others were boarded up, the slates on the roofs sliding and leaving gaping holes, the gardens overgrown. Even the slag heap was greened over with weeds and there were swathes of rosebay willow herb all over the place.

When Meg was smaller, she and Jack Boy had lain on the stony ground around the shaft and thrown pebbles down, counting to see how far they would fall before hearing the splash of the pebble hitting the water. They would stare at the iron ladder going down, imagining the pit lads climbing up all those rungs with wicker baskets full of coal on their backs. Jack had even climbed down once and found a wicker basket floating in the water at the bottom, but when he brought it up into the light it crumbled to bits. Meg shuddered. By, she'd been frightened that day, frightened Jack Boy would fall.

'Eeh, our Alice, I was miles away.' She smiled at her young sister, and lifted the knocker of the unpainted batten door.

'Howay in, lass, don't bother knocking, I'm right glad to see you.' The quavering voice belonged to Mrs Dobbs, the owner of the clothes. The sisters went in and had a few words with the lonely old woman. Meg diplomatically refused payment for the washing and looked round the threadbare kitchen to see if there was any other pressing job.

100

'Can I get you a bucket of coal in while I'm here, Mrs Dobbs? It'll be no trouble, like.'

'I'd be right glad o' that,' she said simply. 'The nights are drawing in now, there's a nip in the air.'

'I'll get it, if you like,' offered Alice.

'No, you sit and talk to Mrs Dobbs, I won't be a minute.'

Meg went round the back of the cottage to the coal house, taking the bucket with her. She bit her lip as she saw the meagre store of coal inside. Being a miner's daughter, she was used to having plenty of coal to go at in winter. She resolved to get Jack Boy to fetch a barrow full from Da's allowance next time it was delivered. He was good-hearted enough was Jack Boy, he would do it.

As they walked back to the village, the sun had gone down and the evening was indeed chilly. But Alice was happily sucking a black bullet given to her by the old lady and didn't seem to notice the chill. They reached the old village quickly and turned to go down to the colliery rows.

'Margaret Anne Maddison, does your da know you're out in the dark?'

The voice came from a group of young miners who were lounging against the wall of the Black Boy, a pub on the green. Meg's heart sank. Not Wesley Cornish again. He always seemed to be off shift. The lads were grinning and nudging each other knowingly, looking not at all like the little lad depicted on the inn sign swaying above their heads.

It was a painting of a young trapper boy of forty or fifty years ago, little and thin and dressed in raggy moleskin trousers, with a candle in his hat brim casting a halo over his black streaked face. Meg always looked up at it. She liked to see the little black boy swaying in the wind and think how good it was that her brothers hadn't had to go down the pit when they were only six.

101

Though for the lads lounging about the Black Boy, maybe it would have done some of them a bit of good, she thought. Catching hold of Alice's arm, she pulled her closer.

'Take no notice, Alice, don't answer them,' she whispered fiercely, and strode rapidly on to the rows. But Wesley Cornish stood in her path, hands on hips, his handsome head cocked to one side, the picture of male arrogance. Alice's hand tightened on Meg's. She was unsure what to make of him. Hadn't the minister thundered against the ways of Satan taking hold of the wild lads of the village only last Sunday?

There had been a lot of trouble in the village lately, gangs of young miners spending their pay in the Black Boy or the Rising Sun, and coming out satless drunk and spoiling for mischief. One night they'd taken the gates off the farmers' fields all the way along the Aukland road and the sheep and the cows had got out and into folks' gardens. And another time, when one of the farmers had gone into the Rising Sun, leaving his horse and trap outside, they'd uncoupled the horse and put him on the other side of the fence and fastened him to the trap again. The farmer had come out pallatic drunk, got in the trap and shouted 'Giddyup' till he was blue in the face. The horse had strained and strained. But of course they hadn't got anywhere, for the fence between them. Alice had been much struck by the picture painted by the minister as he described the scene and even more so by that of a horned man with a forked beard and long tail catching the lads and leading them down to the fires of Hell.

'Get out of my way, Wesley Cornish,' she snapped, and moved to go round the man who anticipated it and moved with her. Her face was flushed and she was staring straight ahead at some point over his shoulder.

'I'll do more than that, lass.' Wesley flashed a winning

smile. 'I'll walk you home, if you like? You and Alice. It's getting dark and you never know who you might meet after dark.'

Alice gasped as Meg darted by Wesley, perforce taking her sister with her as she was holding her arm. They fairly flew down the colliery rows to the end of Pasture Row, then Meg stopped and looked back.

'I'm sick to death of you pestering me!' she screamed at the top of her voice. 'An' I'm sick of that lot an' all, daft as goats, laughing and gawping.'

Wesley, undaunted, was already halfway down towards them. He grinned in amusement at Meg's outburst.

'Hadaway, Meg, you know you like me really,' he said. Then turned on his heel and walked back to his friends.

'Wesley Cornish is sweet on our Meg!'

Meg was mortified as Alice ran into the kitchen where her brothers were playing cards, bursting with her news.

Jack Boy looked up and frowned heavily. 'Aye, I know,' he said. 'When he sees me down the pit he asks me where you are. You haven't been walking with him, have you, our Meg?'

'What do you think I am, like?' she retorted.

But in bed later that night she thought about walking out with a boy, wondering what it would be like to have a lads's arms round her, to kiss a lad who wasn't her little brother. The thought made her feel strangely hot and uncomfortable. You haven't time for lads, Meg Maddison, she told herself, and turned over on to her side. Thumping her pillow into shape, she settled herself for sleep. There was too much to do at home.

As she drifted off to sleep she remembered, half-dreaming, her old fancies about Jonty, the knight on a big grey horse who had been looking for her all these years, searching till he must surely find her. And he would find her and lift her up and take her with him to his big house. But she'd forgotten his face. Instead she kept seeing the mocking features of Wesley Cornish, grinning cheekily at her, his light brown eyes running up and down her body, his hands reaching out to her. And she woke up in a sweat. She didn't want Wesley Cornish, she wanted . . . oh, she wanted the old lovely feeling she'd had when she was a bairn and made up stories about her and Jonty.

She tried to settle down to sleep again but it was early yet. The fore shift hadn't even gone in. But there was a lot to do tomorrow, the ironing and the bread to bake, and she wanted to go up to tidy Mam's grave, and then look for brambles for a boiled pudding for a treat for the bairns. Aye, she thought, she had to get some sleep.

Nine

Jonty limped across the yard from the stables to the kitchen. There was no welcoming smell of a meal cooking, he realized, and sighed, remembering the lovely smell emanating from the Home Farm kitchen when he went past. His stomach rumbled. Bread and cheese again, he supposed.

Since the cook had walked out the previous month because she hadn't been paid, there was only a young maid of all work and the manservant who had served his grandfather. Johnson was old now and Jonty supposed he had nowhere to go or he would have been gone by now too. He limped through the kitchen and out into the hall.

'Is that you, Jonty?'

The thin voice of his grandmother made him turn and look up to the head of the stairs. Mrs Grizedale was frail now and rarely came out of her room; she shook a lot and leaned heavily on her stick. Now she swayed on her feet and Jonty started in alarm and rushed up the stairs to her.

'Grandmother!' he cried, taking hold of her arm and leading her back along the upstairs hallway to her room. 'What are you doing out here?'

'I was cold,' she answered tremulously, and he felt the quivering of her arm as he held it. In her room, he saw the fire had gone out and there was no coal in the scuttle.

There was a damp and musty chill in the air. The fire must have been out for hours.

'Why didn't you ring?' he asked her gently. 'You should have got the girl to fetch coal up and mend the fire long since.'

'I did, Jonty, I did, but no one came. I rang and rang.'

That girl! Jonty seethed, but covering up his anger, he smiled at his grandmother. 'Well, never you mind. Come and sit down and I'll get a warm shawl for your shoulders. I'll have a fire going in a couple of ticks, I'll see to it now.'

He picked up the coal scuttle and went out and down the stairs. There was no sign of Sally, the maid, so he went out of the kitchen door himself and filled the scuttle with coal. In the kitchen he found newspaper and kindling sticks and piled them on top of the coal. In the process, he got a smear of coal dust across his already dirty riding breeches and even a streak on his cheek.

Jonty was going across the hall towards the stairs when he heard a loud giggle from his father's study, a feminine giggle. His mouth tightened and he paused for a moment. Should he go in and get Sally and make her see to Grandmother's fire? The stupid girl was flattered by his father's attentions, just like so many before her had been. Sally had some ridiculous idea he would marry her though, she thought she was different. And already she thought herself too good to do the menial work of the house. The place was a pigsty, he thought, his anger mounting.

Putting down the coal scuttle, Jonty strode over to the study and flung open the door.

Sally was leaning over his father's chair, wiggling and squealing. Her bodice was open, displaying young half-ripe breasts, and his father had a hand inside, squeezing and tugging to the accompaniment of her squeals. She heard Jonty enter the room but didn't even move or try

106

to cover herself. No more than fifteen years old either, Jonty knew.

'Well, what do you want?' Ralph glanced up lazily, his lip curling into the usual look of contempt as he saw Jonty's dirty face and the smears on his riding breeches. 'I see you're your usual smart self. My God, lad, anyone would think you'd been down the pit!' Ralph grinned slowly. 'Still, I suppose you're happy looking like that. It was all pitmen on your mother's side of the family.'

Jonty's face tightened and his eyes went cold. If his father started on again with his ranting about his mother and her family, he swore he would go for him. He'd taken it all his life but now he was seventeen and a man grown, he'd take no more of it. First he had to make Sally see to his grandmother's fire. He would be better facing up to his father if the two of them were alone in any case.

'Sally, there's a scuttle full of coal and kindling at the bottom of the stairs. Grandmother's fire is out. I've told you time and time again that she needs to be kept warm. Old people can't stand the cold.'

'Light it yourself then!' Sally exclaimed, not bothering to disguise her disrespect for him. She was confident that Ralph would simply laugh at her spirit, but in this she was mistaken. Roughly drawing his hand from her bodice, he shoved her off his knee so that she ended up sprawling on the worn carpet.

'You mind yourself, girl!' he roared, and springing up, stood over her threateningly. 'You'll get out and do as you are told, this minute!' His face was screwed up in anger so that the lines of dissipation which had appeared these last years deepened into channels which ran all the way down his face. His colour heightened until he was a deep bright red.

Sally, suddenly transformed into a frightened little

girl, whimpered and fled for the door, tears of mortification starting into her eyes.

Ralph watched her out then gave his attention to his son, his gaze raking him from head to foot.

'And you, you misbegotten whelp,' he said venomously, 'look at you! Is it any wonder the maids cheek you? You look as though you sleep in the stables. For God's sake, go and wash the coal dust from your face and change into some clean clothes.'

Jonty lifted his chin and stared his father in the eye. 'If I'm a stable lad, then you made me one,' he stated flatly. 'And if we had proper staff in the house, I wouldn't have to bring in coal for Grandmother's fire.'

Ralph's mouth fell open. He was taken aback by Jonty's standing up for himself. His son limped over to stand directly before him.

'I want to talk to you about Grandmother,' he said, 'she has to have proper care.'

'The old hag! Always whining and moaning around the place.'

'Yes, she's old.' Jonty kept his voice level as he struggled to control his rising temper. 'She's old and needs a woman to look after her all the time. And not someone like Sally either.'

'And where do you think the money will come from? She's the only one with anything left and she has that tied up in shares. Women these days aren't content with a roof over their heads and food in their bellies, they have to be paid. If you want her watched over then you'd better do it yourself, it's about all you're good for.'

Jonty stepped forward until his face was but an inch from his father's. Ralph eyes widened in shock.

'And who was it went through the money, not only your own inheritance but most of Grandmother's too?' Jonty could feel himself losing control. He stared into

Ralph's bulging eyes, bloodshot with rage and alcohol. 'If we paid our servants, we'd be able to keep them.'

Ralph mouthed an oath and raised his fist to punch Jonty over the ear as he had done so many times before. But this time Jonty caught his wrist and contemptuously flung the older man back into his chair.

'Don't you raise your hand to me, Father, never again. Not ever again or I won't be responsible for what might happen to you.' Turning on his heel he strode from the room, leaving his father, for once, quite speechless.

Upstairs he found a cheerful fire in his grandmother's room and she was sipping tea from a delicate china cup brought up on a tray by Sally. That's better, he thought, and a good thing too.

'How are you, Grandmother, warm again?' he asked, walking over to her and taking her hand. Indeed the hot tea and the fire seemed to have worked wonders with her, she already had a little colour in her cheeks and her fingers felt quite warm.

'I'm fine and dandy, really I am, Jonty. Come and have a cup of tea with me, the girl will fetch another cup.'

'Oh, I'll have to clean myself up.' He laughed. 'I shouldn't be here at all, reeking of the stables as I do.'

'I don't care about that,' declared the old lady 'just so long as you come to see me, I don't care at all.' She smiled wistfully and Jonty knew she was thinking of her son. Ralph avoided visiting her and frowned blackly if he saw her venturing out of her room. Jonty stooped and dropped a kiss on her cheek, thinking that her skin felt as thin and dry as tissue paper. She was getting old, his grandmother, the only person in the world who cared a damn for him. The thought saddened him.

'I'll come to see you again this evening, Grandmother,' he said. 'Now, I think you should drink that tea before it gets cold.'

After Jonty had bathed, he dressed in his one decent suit. It was short in the arms and legs and threadbare at the elbows, but it was the only one he had which was fairly presentable. He combed his dark hair before the looking glass and paused to feel his chin for stubble. It was still fairly smooth, he'd shaved that morning. Jonty had only recently started to shave and was quite proud of the fact. He was becoming a man now. Hadn't he faced up to his father? His dark brown eyes mirrored in the glass showed his satisfaction; he was elated that at last he would be his own man, no longer frightened of his father.

Walking down the staircase, not the narrow, steep stairs at the back of the house but the broad, sweeping staircase leading directly into the hall, he told himself he would never use the back stairs again, except for his own convenience. Snores were emanating from the study and Jonty rightly surmised that Ralph had drunk himself into a stupor.

At least he would have no more trouble that evening, Jonty thought grimly, and opened the heavy front door to let himself out into the cool twilight. He was going to visit the people of the estate, though perhaps 'estate' was a grandiose term for the lone farm and few broken-down cottages left. And even they and the land farmed by the tenants was mortgaged up to the hilt.

As Jonty walked along the farm track, he pondered on what he was going to do about his future. His education was sketchy to say the least, for Ralph had not allowed him to attend school along with other sons of the gentry.

'I'm not paying any school fees for that brat,' his father had said shortly when Grandmother raised the subject. 'Teach him yourself, if you want him taught, or send him to the National School.'

Grandmother wouldn't think of letting him attend the

National School, so she had taught him herself. She had managed to teach him reading and writing and simple arithmetic, but after that her own education had been confined to embroidery and home crafts. So, secretly, she had sent Jonty to the parson every Monday for further tuition.

Monday was market day in Darlington and she could rely on Ralph's being safely out of the way then. He did not frequent the market, of course, he wouldn't bother himself with that. No, it was because he had cronies there and they would meet in an inn there and spend the day and half the night.

Later, when Mrs Grizedale found it too difficult to raise even the small sum required by the parson for Jonty's lessons, he was older and his own natural intelligence won through. He was diligent, he would work on his own, driven by an innate curiosity about the world around him. He borrowed books from the parson and also subscribed to the Lending Library in Bishop Auckland.

'You're so like your grandfather, my dear husband,' Mrs Grizedale would say. 'Oh, if only Ralph . . .' and she would stop, unable to continue, and her eyes would fill with tears.

'Don't worry, Grandmother, I can teach myself now,' he would answer. But he knew there were still gaps in his education and his speech was sometimes rough and ready, mixing as he did with stable lads and farm-hands.

Jonty was approaching the farm now and his heart sank as he saw that the hole in the roof of the barn was bigger. It was gaping now and tiles had slid down to the ground in an untidy broken heap. No doubt a result of the recent gale. Farmer Teasdale would be asking for the repairs to be done as he had a perfect right to. After all he had paid his rent in full, last quarter day. And Father had taken the money and gone into Darlington and

111

neither Jonty nor his grandmother had seen him for a week.

I should take off, thought Jonty, biting his lip in his vexation. Make my own way in life. He had a good head on his shoulders and a will to work. Wildly he thought of emigrating to Australia, America even. Oh, he had great ambitions. But as always his dreams of a brilliant future came up against the reality of his grandmother and how she would fare if left to the mercies of his father. He could not leave until Grandmother passed away, and there was nothing he could do about his father's headlong rush into bankruptcy, nothing at all.

There was still the two thousand pounds his grandfather had left him. Oh, yes, there was that. But it was in trust until he reached the age of twenty-one and firmly tied up so that his father could not get at it. In fact, Father didn't even know about it, Grandfather had known Ralph so well that he had put the money aside for Jonty long before he died and only Grandmother and her solicitor knew about it. If she had not shown Jonty where the document was hidden in her room, he would not have known either.

'Your grandfather,' she had said softly in Jonty's ear, looking over her shoulder to make sure her son was nowhere near, 'saw to it that you would be looked after. The day after you were born, he rode into Auckland and got Mr Whitehead to draw it all up. You know, Mr Whitehead, the solicitor, dear.' She shook her head regretfully, 'Maybe if he had trusted Ralph more when he was a boy, not been so harsh with him . . .'

Jonty thought about the money he had coming to him now. He could do so much with it, make repairs, get the mortgage paid off. He would be able to hold his head up in the county. But it was four years before he would be twenty-one. Would they be able to last out until then? Had his father nothing left? Jonty was pessimistic about it. He knew his father's railway shares were long gone, along with anything else which was saleable.

He saw Farmer Teasdale standing by the farm gate as he neared the farm. The farmer was watching him as he walked up the lane and his expression was sombre.

'Evening, Master John,' he called. 'Come to tell me when the tiler's coming then?' Jonty knew the farmer didn't really think that was why he had come. The man was in a bad humour and the remark meant to be sarcastic.

Jonty flushed a bright red. 'I'm trying to see to it for you,' he said diffidently. 'I asked Father to see him when he went into Auckland but I'm afraid he must have forgotten.'

'Aye. Forgotten. Just like all the other times. An' leaving me to shift for myself and make the repairs if I'm to save the hay.'

Jonty was beginning to wish he hadn't come out this evening. It was pointless, in any case, visiting the tenants and pretending everything was normal up at the Hall. He felt a proper fool.

Farmer Teasdale saw his discomfiture and relented. 'Nay, it's not your fault, lad, none of this.' He eyed his visitor up and down, and Jonty knew he was noticing that the elbows were practically out of his coat and the edges of his trousers halfway up his calves.

'We'll say no more, Master John. Howay into the kitchen and the wife'll give you a glass of fresh milk. There's nowt like it for a growing lad and you are that, all gangly legs and arms, not a picking on you.'

Jonty flushed an even brighter red but thanked him politely.

'It's very good of you to offer me your hospitality,' he said formally, 'but I'm afraid I must be on my way.' For he had recognized only too well the element of pity in the farmer's offer and was mortified; he marched off

113

down the lane with his head held high though his stomach rumbled. He would get that bread and cheese, he thought, and afterwards he would have to check that Grandmother had been served some supper.

Next morning Jonty was up with the sun, completing his work in the stables in record time. Then he saddled his mare, Nancy, a not very well-bred Dales pony, but sturdy and dependable. Jonty felt he had to get right away, anywhere, so long as it was miles away from his father and Grizedale Hall.

He rode in the direction of Bishop Auckland then changed his mind and took one of the old bridle-ways and donkey paths which riddled the local countryside. Along these paths there used to be strings of donkeys with their side panniers of coal, transporting it to the mills of the industrial towns. Before the days of the railway, that is, thought Jonty, even before the days when there was a railway with the wagons pulled by donkeys and horses.

He glanced over at a hill on his left, remembering a story his grandmother had told him. In those days, she had said, there were donkeys pulling the wagons up that hill, and they pulled them willingly once they knew there was a dandy cart on the end of the line of wagons. At the top of the hill the donkey would be uncoupled and the train of coal wagons would go rumbling down the other side and gravity would take it all the way to Aycliffe. And the donkeys grew adept at waiting for the low-slung dandy cart and jumping aboard, holding their heads up high as they faced into the wind, enjoying the ride as any human would. And of course, at Aycliffe, they were ready to take an empty train back again, up the hill to Brusselton and down again on the other side.

Jonty smiled. How he had loved Grandmother's stories! Often after a beating from his father, when he

114

was curled up in a ball on his bed, she would creep in and take him in her arms and cuddle him and tell him stories to take his mind off the smarting pain.

He rode on now, thinking of nothing in particular, just enjoying the freedom riding gave to him, freedom from his hated limping.

The morning was dull and grey with rain clouds threatening from the west, but Jonty didn't notice the weather. So it was that he came near to the miners' rows by Winton Colliery, just as the first large raindrops fell. They rapidly became a deluge and soon Jonty was soaked to the skin.

Lord, what a fool I am! he told himself angrily. Now he would have to seek shelter. He looked around. There was no barn in sight at this end of the village, only the colliery rows and the huts and pigeon crees across the road and in the gardens of the end row. He eyed the first house. It had a chimney which was throwing out smoke, denoting a good fire, and brightly clean lace curtains at the windows. Perhaps the miner's wife inside would give him shelter? He could ask at any rate. Dismounting, he led Nancy to the front gate and tethered the reins loosely over it.

He was not prepared for his reception. The woman who came to the door was middle-aged and motherly. He was sure he hadn't met her before. But she peered closely at him for a minute before opening her eyes wide.

'Jonty! Eeh, it's Jonty Grizedale! Tot, come here, lad, you'll never guess who's come to see us.' Phoebe Lowther was fairly gasping in excitement. 'Howay in then, lad, come by the fire. Eeh, I never did.'

Ten

Meg was at the bottom of the stairs calling her da down from his afternoon's sleep when Auntie Phoebe rushed in, her face flushed with the importance of what she had to tell.

'Is your da up? Eeh, Meg, where've you been? You'd never guess who I've just had in the house, aye, standing in my kitchen and drinking tea from our Tot's pint pot.'

'I'm just calling him, Auntie Phoebe. He's on nights the night. As to where I've been, I went out for the messages and then when the rain came on I waited in the shop 'til it cleared up.'

Meg walked into the kitchen and raked some small coal from the shelf at the back of the fire down on to the flames.

'The days are getting colder now, aren't they, Auntie Phoebe?' She smiled to herself, teasing her aunt who was expecting eager questions on who her mysterious visitor was. Meg was not disappointed in Auntie Phoebe's reaction.

'Are you not going to ask me who it was, then?' she demanded, placing her hands on her ample hips and glaring at Meg.

Her grin widened. 'Oh, aye, you said you'd had someone in, didn't you?' Calmly she settled the kettle on the coals before reaching up to the high mantelshelf, taking down the tin tea caddy and spooning tea into the

116

pot. But she was all attention when she finally heard the name.

'John Thomas Grizedale, that's who. Standing in my kitchen, sheltering from the rain.' Auntie Phoebe stood back and nodded her head importantly.

'Who?' asked Alice, who had just come in with little Bella.

Auntie Phoebe sighed. 'Oh, aye, you two bairns won't know who I mean, but I thought Meg might remember. You know, our Meg, Jonty, your cousin Jonty.'

'Jonty?'

'Aye, Jonty.' Auntie Phoebe's news was not being received in the way she had expected it to be and she was becoming impatient. Meg stared at her. Surely she had made a mistake?

'Surely you remember Jonty? You were brought up with him until you moved to Marsden.'

'Oh, Jonty,' Meg said wonderingly, memories crowding in on her. Warm memories. Jonty. Mam used to say that it was the first word Meg had uttered. Jonty. The son of her dead Aunt Nell. How Mam had gone on about her sister Nell, and the way she and Nell and their mother had come across the county after the explosion in Haswell pit which had killed their da.

'Meg!'

She dragged her thoughts back to the present, Auntie Phoebe was talking to her.

'Yes, I'm sorry, Auntie.'

'Aye, well.' Auntie Phoebe looked a bit put out but she carried on with what she was saying. Bella had gone over to her and Phoebe was stroking her head as she talked.

'Aye, I was telling you, there he was standing at the front door and asking if he could shelter from the storm. Why, I knew him straight away from that time he fell off his horse and broke his leg. He's the spit of his da to look

117

at, like. 'It's perfectly all right,' he said, 'I'm John Thomas Grizedale from Grizedale Hall. I've foolishly allowed myself to get caught in the rain. It's a distance back home and I thought . . .' Eeh, an' do you know, he speaks just like us. Well, mebbe not just like us, but he's no side to him, no side at all. Not like his high and mighty father. And when I told him who I was, well, he was flabbergasted, he was.'

'Who was?'

Unnoticed by Auntie Phoebe, Jack had come downstairs and was putting his slippers before the fire.

'Why, Jonty Grizedale, you know . . .'

'Rain's cleared up any road,' he said calmly, and the girls looked at him in astonishment. He had ignored what Auntie Phoebe was saying altogether. Getting to his feet, he walked to the window and looked out. 'Blue sky again.'

'Eeh, but Jack, did you not hear us, man? Jonty it was, but he's gone now. You know, Nell's Jonty, Jonty Grizedale.'

'Look, Phoebe,' said Jack flatly, 'I don't want to hear the name of Grizedale in this house ever again. Not now, not ever. I don't want to hear about Jonty and I don't want to hear about his father. Now, is that plain enough for you?'

'But, Jack, he's kin after all's said and done. And Hannah thought the world of the lad.'

'He's no kin of mine,' Jack snapped, and turned deliberately away from her and spoke to Meg. 'Now then, lass, what're we having for tea?'

'But Jack, man—'

'Phoebe, I'm sorry to have to say it but if you've come to talk about any Grizedale, any one of them at all, you're not welcome in my house.'

There was a universal gasp at this and little Bella,

118

who hated any sort of trouble and was sensitive to the heightened tension in the room, began to sob.

'Howay, pet, we'll be going, before something's said that cannot be taken back.' Auntie Phoebe took Bella's hand and went out of the door, even her back bristling with the affront.

Meg carried on making the meal, buttering bread and slicing the brawn she'd brought from the store, her emotions churning inside. By, she thought, Da was bitter. None of it had been Jonty's fault, had it?

'Aye, well, it's all right him saying,' Auntie Phoebe stated a day or two later as Meg helped her fold sheets and put them through the mangle. They were in Auntie Phoebe's back yard and nobody was going to tell Phoebe Lowther she couldn't talk or not talk about whoever she wanted to in her own back yard.

She put the last sheet into the bath tin which did duty as a clothes basket, just one of its many uses. Straightening up, she rubbed her back.

'It's all right him saying, I said, but Jonty is kin and the poor lad looked like he needed his kin. Why, his suit was miles too small for him and his elbows were fair out of the sleeves. And then there's that limp he has, and it's not getting any better . . .'

'I'll hang these out for you if you like, Auntie.' Meg interrupted the flow of words.

It was Monday morning and there was a stiff breeze, the clothes would dry well. Besides, Meg wanted to get back to her own washing. At this end of the year it was best to have it out on the line early as the days were getting shorter and otherwise there wouldn't be time for them to dry.

'Eeh, would you, lass?' Auntie Phoebe rubbed her back again. 'My back's giving me some stick today.'

As Meg picked up the peg bag and the bath full

of sheets to take through to the front garden, Phoebe continued her monologue, shuffling after the young girl as she talked.

'If you'd seen his face when I told him. Anyone would think I'd given him a hundred pounds. Guineas even. 'I never knew what happened to Aunt Hannah's family,' he says. Would you believe it? That wicked man, that Ralph Grizedale, he never told him. But you would have thought the old lady, you know, Ralph's mother, would have said something, wouldn't you?'

Meg finished pegging out the sheets and turned to go back into the house. She wished Auntie Phoebe would stop talking about Jonty, it made her feel churned up inside, bringing her dreams and nightmares that much more into reality. And Meg wasn't sure if she wanted Jonty to be real.

'I'll have to go, Auntie Phoebe, I've a lot to do.'

'Aye, well, I know that an' all.' Auntie Phoebe was indignant, wasn't there always a lot to do on washday? 'But I thought you would be interested in hearing about him. Why, you two were like brother and sister, once, I remember your mam telling me.'

'Oh, Auntie, it was so long ago. And you know what Da's like when any of the Grizedales are mentioned, I think it's best we just forget all about them.'

'Aye, but you can't. He's coming here next weekend. Sunday, in fact.'

'Auntie Phoebe! After all Da said.'

'I dinna care. I asked him before your da ever said that.' Phoebe folded her arms across her bosom and lifted her chin in the air. 'An' I have a perfect right to ask anybody I want, any time I want. I asked Jonty to *my* house for a dish of tea.'

She stared at Meg, daring her to argue, but Meg simply lifted the bath tin and put the peg bag in it, deliberately

120

keeping her expression impassive. Auntie Phoebe softened and tried a more persuasive line.

'Mind, pet, I did think you would come in to meet him. I know he's really wanting to meet you all. Eeh, he'll be that disappointed if he doesn't see you.'

Meg sighed. If she was honest to herself she knew she wanted to see Jonty too. But there was Da. Da was so bitter, and he was never bitter about anybody else except the Grizedales. And Da had been through so much, how could she hurt him by going against him?

'I don't know, Auntie, I don't. I might have a talk with Da but if he's still dead against it, well, I'll do what he wants.'

Auntie Phoebe looked as though she was prepared to continue the argument but Meg left and went back to her own work. But she couldn't help her mind wandering, imagining what it would be like to meet Jonty.

She would have to do something about her blue dress, she mused, she couldn't afford a new one. Though Auntie Phoebe would lend her the sewing machine and maybe she could get an off-cut at the store. If she was going to meet Jonty, that is. She didn't really need a frock else.

The rest of the morning Meg was occupied rubbing and scrubbing and mangling while her mind ranged over the possibilities of making a new dress. She would have to look her best, just in case she was to meet Jonty. After all, he was gentry.

When Meg did bring up the subject with her father, she received a very unpleasant shock. He became so angry and upset that she gave up the idea of meeting her cousin. Jack Maddison, the quiet, gentle man who hardly ever spoke to anyone, who never lifted a hand to the bairns or anyone else for that matter, mouthed an oath and flung his arm across the table, scattering pots and plates to land in a broken heap in the corner of the kitchen with butter thrown out of the butter dish and oozing down the white-washed wall.

'I'll not have it! Do you hear me, Meg?' he shouted, his voice loud and harsh, and he leaned over her and raised his fist to her so that she cowered back from him. And then he stormed out of the house, leaving his daughter to stare after him as he banged the gate shut and disappeared up the row. Her blood pounded loudly in her ears as she looked at the yellow stain running down the wall and mingling with the brown tea leaves at the bottom. The teapot, Mam's brown teapot with the old willow-patterned lid, was on its side with the spout knocked clean off and the lid broken in half. Meg's mind went numb. All she could think of was clearing up the mess.

She went outside for the coal shovel and sweeping brush and cleared up the broken bits of pottery. She'd never get the stain off the wall, she knew she wouldn't, and what were they going to do for pots? There were only two cups left whole in the house and she couldn't go to the store for more, it wasn't payday this week. The miners were paid out last Friday and the money was about gone. It was only payday once a fortnight at the pit. Whatever had Da done that for?

'Our Meg!'

Meg looked round to see Alice had come in and was staring in astonishment at the sticky mess in the corner.

'Da did it.'

'Da?' Alice was incredulous. 'Did he have an accident like?'

'No, he did it on purpose,' said Meg. 'He was in a temper.'

'A temper?' Alice showed her disbelief. 'Da's never in a temper.'

Meg's control snapped and she shouted at Alice,

122

'Well, he was in a temper the day. Now stop asking so many questions and give us a hand here, will you?'

'But what're we going to use for our tea the night?' continued Alice, though she fetched a cloth and some soda water and tried to clean the stains from the wall.

Meg had been wondering the same thing and all she could come up with was that she and Alice could drink out of jam jars, Jack Boy and Miles could use the two remaining cups, and Da would have to use the earthenware jug.

'I'll go next-door and see if Auntie Phoebe has a spare teapot,' she said when at last the mess was cleaned up and the broken pots tipped into the ash closet. And while she was round there she would have a serious talk to her aunt, she determined.

'But where's he at now?' Auntie Phoebe asked after Meg had told her what had happened.

'I don't know, I suppose he's just walking it off,' said Meg. 'But I want you to promise me, Auntie Phoebe, not to mention Jonty or Mr Grizedale in front of Da again. And you can tell Jonty that when he comes. Tell him we don't want to see him. Tell him what you like but don't let him try to see us.' Meg was earnest and trembling with the need to impress on Auntie Phoebe how important it was to her and her father.

Auntie Phoebe was wide-eyed and solemn as she saw the unshed tears in Meg's eyes. 'He didn't hit you, did he, lass? Your da I mean? By, I cannot abide violence, there's no need for it, no need at all. Why, I would have done what Jack said any road. He just had to say.' She nodded her head to emphasize her words and Meg forebore to remind her that was not what she had said earlier in the day. She was only grateful that her aunt was agreed to it now. Thanking her, Meg hurried back to her own kitchen to wait for the return of her father.

Jack was on fore shift, going out just before midnight, so she cut his jam sandwiches and put them in his bait tin and filled his water bottle fresh from the pump on the end of the row. But she waited and waited. The house grew quiet and Da did not return. The pit whistle sounded to signal the night shift coming to bank and to warn the fore shift men it was nearly time for them to go down. And still he didn't come.

It was two o'clock in the morning before Jack Maddison made his unsteady way up the garden path and when Meg opened the door for him he practically fell into the house. For the first time she could remember her father was rolling drunk, too drunk to go to work. It was the first shift he had missed since the death of her mother.

Next morning, Jack had reverted to his normal self, silent and impassive. He didn't say anything about where he had been or what has been said the day before. After breakfast when Alice and Miles went out to school he took his spade into the garden and dug over the potato patch so that the frost would break the soil down over the winter, staying out for most of the day.

Meg said nothing either, simply going about her work, heating the flat iron by the fire and ironing the clothes over a blanket laid on the kitchen table. She called Jack Boy up for his night shift at the pit and made suet pastry to line a basin for the meat pudding she intended for the meal. But though the work was the same, she herself felt different, Da had changed everything. No longer could she dream her lovely dreams about Jonty as her shining hero and the absence of them would leave a gaping hole in her life, impossible though she knew they had been really. Da was what mattered to her, Da and the bairns, and she would never chance doing anything to hurt any of them.

When Sunday came, cold and dreary with a bitter

124

north-easter blowing with a foretaste of winter, she hurried the children home from Sunday School and kept them shut up inside for the rest of the day playing games in the front room. The worsening of the weather made a very good excuse. Though Miles and Alice both argued about it, Meg was adamant.

Eleven

'There'll be trouble for you, Jack, I'm telling you.' Uncle Tot was sitting at the opposite side of the fireplace to Meg's father. He was sucking deeply on his clay pipe and swirls of smoke were wreathing around him before being drawn up into the chimney over the brightly burning fire in the grate.

Meg watched the two men, her father and Uncle Tot, foreboding welling up inside her. In spite of the heat of the fire she shivered. Uncle Tot looked so grave, leaning forward in his chair and pointing with the stem of his pipe to get across the seriousness of what he was saying. Meg looked from him to her father. Da was sitting there quietly, courteously listening to the older man, but his expression remained calm.

'You're in the union, aren't you? Aye, of course you are. Your marras wouldn't work with you if you weren't. The union'll make it official, Jack man. You don't want a cut in your pay, do you lad?'

'I'll not go on strike,' he said mildly.

'Why, man, you mean you'll just let them cut the pay ten per cent without making a fight for it?' Tot was growing exasperated, Meg could see his face getting redder and redder.

'It didn't get us anywhere when we struck on the railways, did it, Tot?'

'The pits are not the railways,' said Uncle Tot. 'And have you thought what it will be like after, when the pits

126

get back to normal? Pitmen stick together, Jack, they won't forget a blackleg. You won't remember what happened after they brought in the Welsh in the seventies. If it's the pay you're thinking about, you'll be worse off in the long run. When the men got back to work, the Welsh had a hard time of it all right.'

'I can look after meself.'

'Aye, mebbe you can. But there was many a blackleg in those days found there was no pay on payday no matter how hard he worked in the pit after the rest of the men were back at work. The tally discs off the tubs would go missing before the coal reached bank so the coal wasn't credited to them.'

Jack paused and Meg could see the indecision on his face. But in the end he stuck to his resolve.

'I'm not joining any strike.'

Meg listened unhappily. Oh, she'd known it was coming ever since last year when the owners wanted the men to take a fifteen per cent cut. The dispute had rumbled on 'til the year turned and now it was 1892 and the owners were insisting on ten per cent. And the miners were going on strike.

'We'll stick together, lads, they'll have to give in,' was the cry Meg heard whenever she passed a group of miners in the village or squatting on their hunkers at the end of the pit rows.

Uncle Tot rose to his feet and knocked the dottle from his pipe into the fire before going to the door.

'I promised Phoebe I'd try to change your mind, Jack,' he said, 'but I can see I'm not going to. I don't know what the railway bosses did to you, lad, but you've no fight left in you.'

It wasn't the railway bosses, thought Meg, just one of them. Ralph Grizedale. It was him who'd broken her da. And the memory came back to her: running up the old

127

line, with Mam and the baby, the terror she'd felt, the candyman running after them . . .

Meg shook her head to rid it of the old nightmare so vividly recaptured in her dreams and always when something bad was going to happen. Hadn't she had it only last night?

'I'll make a cup of tea, Da,' she said, and filled the kettle from the water bucket and placed it on the glowing coals. Jack nodded absently, lost in a dark world of his own.

> Oh, early in the evening, just after dark,
> The Blackleg miners creep te wark,
> Wi' their moleskin trousers an' dorty short,
> There go the blackleg miners!

Meg held on to Miles and Alice, keeping them close to her side as the children clustered at the end of the row saw them coming back from the store.

'Take no notice, Miles,' she hissed. 'I told you you shouldn't have come with us.'

Miles, a sturdy twelve-year-old now, squared his shoulders.

'They might have tipped your basket if I hadn't come,' he said grimly. 'With three of us they won't be so brave.'

The children were forming a ring round them, holding hands and skipping to the old Tyneside song. Miles carried on walking, looking straight ahead as they were forced to move their circle ahead of him.

> They'll take your tools an' duds as well,
> And hoy then doon the pit of hell,
> It's doon ye go an' fare ye well,
> Ye dorty blackleg miners!

128

So join the union while ye may,
    Don't wait until your dying day,
For that may not be far away . . .

The song was interrupted as one of the little girls stumbled and fell, taking some of the others with her.

'He pushed me!' she screamed, and angry growls came from the row as a couple of burly miners rushed out to avenge the girl. It was Albert Pierce and his younger brother Henry, Meg saw, both of them stocky, broad-built men, though only of average height. They were in an ugly mood and Miles was seized and flung down the back street to land sprawling in the central gutter, banging his head against a brick. He lay there, dazed, while the miners turned their attention to the two girls. Meg held on to Alice as they were shoved roughly down the row before the two men.

'Leave us alone!' she cried, standing over Miles who was slowly getting to his feet. 'You're just a load of bully-boys, that's what you are. Hitting a young lad like that, you should be ashamed.'

'Nay, lass, it's the other way round. It's you Maddisons that should be ashamed. Dirty blacklegs, bloody scabs.'

'Howay, Meg, howay home.' Alice was white and terrified. 'Take no notice, that's what you said.'

'Aye, that's right, run away home, you're not fit to be among decent folk,' Albert Pierce snarled.

'What did you say?' Miles was on his feet by now, his temple already showing a red bump from its contact with the gutter. His fists were up and he was fairly dancing with rage as he pushed his sisters behind him.

'You run home, Alice,' hissed Meg, 'get Da.' What had started out as a game on the part of the youngsters was turning into a nasty fight now that two of the fathers had taken over. Miles was only twelve, he'd get a hiding. He couldn't defend himself, not against two men.

129

'Aye, fetch your da. We'll give him what for, an' all.'

The men grinned at each other and allowed Alice to escape down the row. Miles lunged out at the nearest one and was knocked flat on his back for his pains. Meg screamed and ran to him but Miles was already getting to his feet again. She looked round wildly. Where was everybody? Usually there were women in the yards, gossiping over the walls to each other, but not one was in sight. The back doors were all firmly closed. Oh God, where was Da? Where were Jack Boy and Uncle Tot?

'Leave the lass alone! And the lad an' all.'

A man was coming down the row. Meg was practically weeping in relief as the miners turned away to see who it was.

'Fighting with lasses now, are we?' asked Wesley Cornish.

'It's the blackleg, man, we weren't hurting the lass,' Albert Pierce said, though his brother looked sheepish. He was a marra of Wesley's and Wesley was something of a leader among the younger pitmen.

'He's only a lad, he's had enough,' Wesley growled. He stood by Miles and Meg with his legs apart and his hands on his hips, outstaring the Pierce brothers. Meg felt a rush of gratitude to him, already he had made her feel safe. Wesley was tall and strong and as hardened in the pit as the Pierce lads. The brothers were turning away now, muttering to themselves, it was true, but no longer threatening them.

'Get away in the house!' Albert Pierce shouted to his children, venting his anger on them. The youngsters scattered.

'Did they hurt you, lass?' asked Jack Maddison who came running up at that moment. 'I was out the front talking to Tot, I didn't hear what was going on 'til Alice came and told me.'

'I'm all right, Da,' said Meg, 'Wesley stopped them doing anything much. But our Miles is a bit battered.'

'Aye. Well, he shouldn't be a blackleg, he's too young to stick up for himself,' said Wesley. 'But don't think I'm on your side, 'cos I'm not. Blacklegs is scum.' He glowered at Jack. 'An' you want to look after your lot a bit better an' all.'

Jack stared at him. 'Aye. Well, I suppose I have you to thank. But it doesn't matter much any more, the owners have padlocked the gates. The gallowers are up on bank an' all. It's a lockout, an' it looks like they're not in a hurry to open the pit up again. Tot Lowther's just told me, he was up at the pit when they put the padlock on.'

'We're going to join the strike, Da,' Jack Boy was standing before the kitchen fire shoulder to shoulder with Miles. 'You can stay at work if you like, but me and Miles, we're joining the men.'

Meg, following her father into the house, looked fearfully at Da. He was so dead against the strike. Why were men so stubborn? she wondered wearily. There was Miles, a great purple bruise disfiguring his head. She'd have to get some cold cloths on that the day. At least she was thankful for one thing: if there was a lockout, Da couldn't go down the pit, he'd have to join the men.

'Aye, well, it's matterless now,' he said. 'It's a lockout, we couldn't go inbye if we wanted to. Do what you want, it won't get you any strike pay, you're too late.'

Meg hadn't thought of that. What were they going to live on? Alice was still a pupil teacher, and brought nothing in. And there was no one among the miners' wives lying in, no babies due. There'd be nothing there for her to earn herself. There was a bit put by but not much. Black despair engulfed Meg. How long would it last? And coal . . . the coal would stop too. It was only the end of February, how could they keep warm and cook without coal? Meg's thoughts raced round and round, looking for answers. She was eighteen years old now. She'd thought that with the bairns grown, all except Bella, that is and she was living with Auntie Phoebe and Uncle Tot, things would be easier. But instead they were worse. Sighing she fetched a bowl of cold water in from the pump and got a flannel.

'I'll bathe that bruise for you, Miles,' she said, but the boy shrugged her off impatiently.

'Leave us alone, our Meg,' he said, 'I'm not a babby.'

She looked at him in surprise. It was the first time he had challenged her authority. He really was grown up, she thought, even if he was only twelve years old. Ah, well, no doubt the bruise would go down of its own accord in a day or two.

'Look what we've got, our Meg.'

She was on her knees by the kitchen fire, trying to coax enough heat from a few broken branches of wood to boil the pan of soup she had made from the last of the potatoes and carrots and onions. She gasped with surprise when she saw inside the sack which Jack Boy and Miles had brought in. Round black balls of pitch were there, about half a hundredweight.

Jack Boy grinned in delight when he saw her face. 'They'll soon get the fire going,' he said.

'Where did you get them?' Meg scrambled to her feet and pushed back a lock of fair hair which had fallen over her eyes.

'Down by the coke ovens,' Miles answered, grinning, his teeth showing white against a face as black as the balls of pitch.

'You might have got caught!'

Meg was horrified. They could be jailed for that, she knew they could.

'We didn't, though,' Jack Boy pointed out. 'Howay, let's get some on the fire, I'm fair starved.'

The fire did give out a lovely, satisfying heat, thought Meg half an hour later, and it had cooked the broth grand. She'd had a bit of dripping with browning left in the fat pot and had added that to the vegetables. It gave the broth a bit of taste. And Auntie Phoebe had given her a loaf of bread from her baking, it went lovely with the broth. Though it was the end of March the winter showed no sign of lifting. The weather was wet and windy and penetratingly cold so the warmth was heavensent.

The Maddisons had no strike pay. The rest of the men had five shillings a week from the union, but Jack and his sons didn't qualify.

'Is there any more?' Miles asked hopefully as Meg dragged the iron pan on to the hob after she had served the boys. He was already mopping up the last of his broth with a slice of bread.

'I want to save it for Da and Alice.'

Meg bit her lip as she saw his eager face. He was a growing lad and wasn't getting enough food, she knew.

'You can have mine, I'm not that hungry,' she offered.

'Don't you touch that!' snapped Jack Boy. 'Don't be so greedy, our Miles.'

'I wasn't going to take Meg's,' he said, sitting back in his chair, his face red.

Jack Boy looked at his younger brother. He was well aware that there hadn't been enough for Miles just as there hadn't been enough for himself. He got to his feet and reached for his jacket.

'Howay, Miles,' he said. 'Let's away up the bunny banks. Mebbe we can snare a rabbit. A bit of rabbit stew would be grand, wouldn't it?'

'Just you be careful,' said Meg as the two boys went out. 'Watch out you don't get caught.'

133

The miners often caught rabbits to supplement their diet in ordinary times, but the local tenant farmer had strict instructions from the owners to prosecute any pitmen seen rabbiting during the lockout. Nevertheless, sometimes the farmers pretended not to see and it was a chance most of the miners took. But Meg was uneasy about the boys going to the rabbit warren,

She decided to wait and have her broth with Alice when she came in. She sat down in Da's chair and stretched her toes across the steel fender, delighting in the warmth from the burning pitch balls. By, Da's coal allowance was a big loss, it was, she mused. There wasn't a nut left in the coal house. It had all been swept clean by the beginning of the week before.

The owners wouldn't give in, why should they? her restless thoughts ran on. They would keep the men locked out, they could afford to. Coal was stockpiled still in the pit yard. Oh, they'd planned this all right, hanging on 'til the stocks were high, judging the right time to provoke a strike. The lockout would go on now 'til the men were on their knees and had to go back on the owners' terms.

Meg jumped to her feet, forgetting about the strike as her father opened the door. She pushed the pan of broth back on to the fire to heat up for him. He must be cold and hungry, he'd been out all day. Jack Maddison didn't speak as he hung his jacket on the hook behind the door, simply nodded to her as he approached the fire, but Meg was accustomed to his silence. She waited for him to ask who had got the pitch balls for the fire but though they provided the first real heat they had had for days, he didn't question them or even seem to notice them.

'I've got some broth saved for you, Da,' she said, stirring the soup as it began to bubble in the pot.

'I'm not hungry,' he answered, sitting down in his chair and starting to unlace his boots.

'But, Da—'

Meg was going to say he must be hungry, but seeing the dead look in his eyes, she stopped. She knew he had been out tramping the roads all day. That was all he seemed to do nowadays, walking restlessly on from one place to another, wearing out his shoe leather.

Da was a truly broken man now. She worried about him all the time. When Uncle Tot had offered him seed potatoes and cabbage plants from his greenhouse, Da hadn't even dug over the ground in the garden to take them. In the end it had been Jack Boy who took over the gardening just as he was taking over all the other tasks which needed a man's strength. Da had refused to join the strike and in the end it did him no good at all. He was locked out of the pit as effectively as any of the strikers. Meg sighed as she pulled the pan back from the flames and lifted it down to the hearth. Poor Da, he was never on the right side.

'Meg, I'm going to place.'

Meg hadn't noticed Alice's approach up the yard and she looked up in surprise as her sister swung the door closed and fairly danced into the kitchen, her eyes bright in a face flushed both with cold and excitement.

'What?'

Straightening up, Meg looked at Alice. What on earth was she talking about?

'I've got work!' Alice cried triumphantly. 'I'm going to place in Manchester.'

'Don't talk soft, our Alice,' Meg snapped, 'you've got work, you're a pupil teacher.'

Alice shook her head. 'Not after the end of the month, I'm not,' she declared. 'I've got proper work, six pounds a year and all found. I'm to look after children and do light housework, that was what the letter said.'

'The letter? What letter? There's been no letters here.'

'Well, our Meg, I knew you wouldn't like it so me and

135

Jane Thompson, you know, the other pupil teacher, we wrote from her house. The agency advertised in the *Northern Echo* and we wrote to it. And we've both to go, we've got jobs in the same street in Salford. I'll be working for a Mr and Mrs Rutherford, looking after the bairns, like.'

'You can't go!'

'I can, our Meg, I can. You can't stop me. It's a good chance, I'll be earning money, be able to send some home for you. I'm fourteen, I'm old enough to go if I want to.'

Black despair filled Meg's heart as she gazed at Alice's excited face.

'But you wanted to be a teacher,' she blurted.

Alice shrugged impatiently. 'Aye. Well, that's all right for folk as can afford it. But we can't, can we? I need to earn a bit of silver, our Meg, I do. Me and Jane are going together. We'll be fine, we will.'

'But are there no young lasses in Manchester, then? Why do they want to 'tice ours away for?' Meg's voice was bitter. Manchester was the other side of the country. She remembered the map on the wall at school in Marsden. Manchester was over the fell tops past Weardale, and halfway down the country an' all. It was miles and miles, she knew it was.

'They all work in the cotton mills, Jane says. They make more money.'

'Da!' In a last desperate attempt to stop Alice she appealed to her father for support.

Jack had been sitting staring into the fire, oblivious to the conversation going on over his head.

'What?'

'Our Alice wants to go to Manchester. She wants to go to place. Work as a servant in somebody else's house. Da, she was going to be a teacher!'

Jack Maddison looked gravely at his eldest daughter,

seeing the appeal in her blue eyes which were full of tears ready to shed; he had been letting the argument go over his head as though it had nothing to do with him. His face still expressed no interest.

'Da?'

Jack shook his head. 'If she wants to go, she'll go,' he said, and turned his eyes back to the fire.

Alice knew she had won and tried to be conciliatory.

'You won't have to feed me, Meg,' she pointed out. 'You know it would be a long time yet before I got a proper teacher's wage. And this lockout, it could go on for ages yet. Once the summer comes and the warm weather, the coal trade'll slacken.'

'Not from this pit, it won't.' Jack Boy had returned with Miles. Triumphantly he handed a couple of rabbits to Meg. 'This is coking coal for the iron mills, you know it is, our Alice. What's this all about then?'

'She'll tell you,' said Meg shortly, and picked up the rabbits. One was quite small and thin but the other seemed plump.

'I'd better get these gutted and skinned then.' She walked to the pantry door, her shoulders slumped and her head down. Picking up a knife, she felt the edge to see how sharp it was. The rest of the family watched her. Her lower lip was trembling, and her eyes bright with tears. She looked defeated. The boys glanced at each other unhappily.

'I'll sharpen the gully on the step for you, Meg,' offered Miles.

'I'll do it meself,' she snapped, and took the knife to the front step and ran it backwards and forwards with swift, savage strokes, as though venting her anger at the world. She couldn't hear what was being said in the kitchen, she couldn't bear to hear Alice talking about her new job again. Slap, scrape, slap, scrape, she went with the gully knife along the step, her vision blurred so that she could scarely see what she was doing, spending a long time on it, until the knife was as sharp as a razor.

When she went back in the kitchen Alice and Jack Boy were gone, the pan of broth forgotten on the hearth.

'Can I have the broth that's left?' asked Miles eagerly. 'Our Alice didn't eat it.'

'Aye, go on then.'

Meg stuck the knife in the largest rabbit, slitting it from breast bone to tail. And out tumbled tiny, blind, baby rabbits, bloody and slimey. Something snapped within her.

'Did you have to catch a rabbit with babies inside her?' she yelled at the startled Miles, who turned from the fire, pan in hand.

'We didn't know . . .' he began, his eyes opening wide with shock at the sight of his sister, bloody knife in hand and tears streaming down her face.

'Well, you damn' well should have done! What do you expect at this time of the year? Aren't they breeding?' she screamed, her whole body shaking.

Miles turned back to the fire and carefully put the pan back on to the hearth before running to the back door and down the yard, his lips clamped tightly together, his face white and set.

Da looked across at her. 'Don't shout, our Meg.'

Meg stared at him but he had already forgotten about her and was once more gazing at the fire. She stopped crying abruptly and returned to her task of getting the rabbits ready for the pot, forcing her emotions back under control, making herself think about the job she was doing. Best make the stew tonight, while they had some fuel to cook it with, she thought dimly.

Meg and Bella went to the station with Alice to see her off on her journey to Manchester. Meg helped her carry her straw box with her spare clothes in it and Bella skipped along beside them.

'Where are you going, Alice?' she asked.

'Manchester, I'm going to place,' said Alice patiently, though she had told Bella a dozen times before.

Meg watched her sister closely. Alice looked white and strained now the time had come. She had clung to Jack Boy and Miles at the door of the house, though Miles had uttered an embarrassed, 'Give over, our Alice!' and walked out of the door.

'You could still change your mind,' she suggested.

'I'm not going to though,' said Alice quickly, casting a sideways glance at Meg. There was silence as they trudged along the path, a shortcut through Badger Wood.

They emerged into the town but a short walk from the station at Bishop Auckland, and there, already on the platform when they arrived, was Jane and her parents. Alice brightened up immediately as though the presence of her friend lent her courage.

'Eeh, I thought you weren't going to make it,' greeted Jane.

'There's five minutes yet,' Alice retorted. 'We've plenty of time.' But the train was already drawing in to the station.

'You'll write, won't you, Alice?' Meg hugged her sister, feeling her thin frame. A spasm of anxiety went through Meg.

'Alice, you'll be careful of your chest? Wrap up warm and keep out of the wind?'

'Oh, Meg, I'm not a babby,' she said, but she didn't snap impatiently as she sometimes did if she thought Meg was fussing over much. She climbed on to the train and Meg handed her box up after her. Meg and Bella stood together and watched as the train began to move.

'Our Alice is going to place,' Bella said importantly to Mrs Thompson.

'Aye, pet, I know,' she answered, while she waved vigorously with her handkerchief.

Meg ran after the carriage a few steps. 'Alice! Alice! You'll come home if they make you do too much, won't you? Alice, if you don't like it . . .'

But the train was gone, steaming round the bend of Shildon. Meg took hold of Bella's hand and led her out of the station. She felt a foreboding. The family was breaking up, she knew it. Oh, she was used now to Bella living next-door at Auntie Phoebe's, but Alice wasn't next-door. Soon she would be hundreds of miles away.

Twelve

'I chased them, I did,' Auntie Phoebe declared as she came into Meg's kitchen, Bella sobbing and crying in tow.

'You chased who, Auntie Phoebe?'

Meg looked up from her ironing. She was still doing the washing and ironing for old Mrs Dobbs and wanted to take it to the old lady that evening. It was a lovely June day and she was looking forward to the walk.

'Those ragamuffins from up the rows. Yelling at our Bella, they were, calling her dummy.' Phoebe took Bella, big as she was, into her arms. 'There, petal, never you mind, I'll bray their backsides for them if I catch them. You're no dummy, you're not. You're just a bit slow with having to miss so much school with your weak chest.'

Meg watched them, the nine-year-old girl cuddled into Auntie Phoebe's arms like a baby. She bit her lip. There was no denying Bella was a bit slow but she was a lovely bairn for all that, pretty and biddable and usually smiling. But not now. Now she was clinging to Auntie Phoebe, sobbing her heart out.

'I've made some biscuits the day, Bella,' she said. Bella loved her food and sweet biscuits in particular. But the child only clung the tighter to Auntie Phoebe.

'Howay now, Bella, ginger biscuits they are. You like ginger biscuits, don't you?'

Bella's sobs lessened. She lifted her head and watched

as Meg brought the biscuit tin out of the pantry. Sitting up, she accepted the ginger biscuit offered by her sister.

'What do you say, pet?' asked Auntie Phoebe.

'Thank you,' Bella mumbled, through a mouthful of biscuit crumbs.

'That's a good lass.' Auntie Phoebe rocked the little girl to and fro, her face troubled. 'I think I'll have a word with their mothers,' she said, but without much hope that it would do any good.

'We'll have a cup of tea,' suggested Meg, 'these biscuits are nice when they're fresh.' The kettle was simmering on the fire and it wasn't long before they were sipping tea and nibbling at biscuits.

'It's funny, isn't it?' said Meg. 'Only last month there wasn't even enough bread, never mind biscuits.'

'Aye,' answered Phoebe, but neither of them looked happy about the change in their fortunes.

The miners had been forced back to work in May; they had had no option but to go back at the reduced rates proposed by the owners. Still, it was no good dwelling on it, Meg thought, it was easy to become bitter.

Da and Jack Boy and Miles were working now, and luckily the other miners seemed to have forgotten that the Maddisons hadn't joined the strike at first. The lockout had been worse for them even than the other pitmen as they had had no strike pay, but at least it was over now. Everything was getting back to normal in Winton Colliery though the families had to live on reduced wages.

Meg sipped her tea. She was filled with an uneasy restlessness. For the first time she was dissatisfied with her life, looking after Da and the boys, spending most of her time in the house working by herself or chatting with Auntie Phoebe. She was eighteen going on nineteen, and had her hair up now. And the only time she went out was when she went to the store for the messages or worked in other womens' houses when they were having babies. There were no bairns in her house now. The only really bright spots in her life were the days a letter came from Alice and they didn't come round very often. For a lass who had been wanting to be a teacher, Alice wasn't a great letter writer.

Auntie Phoebe took Bella home and Meg finished her ironing and started to prepare the meal for the menfolk coming home. Mooning about didn't do any good, she told herself, she just had to get on with it.

After tea, Meg set out on her visit to Old Pit Cottages and Mrs Dobbs. She had combed her hair and piled it on top of her head with pins so that only the shorter curls nestled at the nape of her neck and at her temples. The southerly breeze was warm and yet refreshing. She relished the feel of it on her neck and face. Her dress was a simple black serge but she had added a touch of crocheted lace at the collar and cuffs. Now she loosed the top button at her collar the better to enjoy the breeze.

The months of the lockout had taken their toll and Meg was thinner by pounds than she had been at Christmas, but her slimmer shape suited her. She had a fine strong body, heavy-breasted and slim-hipped, and as she walked into the centre of the village and down the road by the Black Boy, there was many a head turned to watch her go.

And one of them was the head of Wesley Cornish. She saw him have a quick word with his marras and fall into step behind her. Meg felt her colour rising. She tried to ignore him but was feeling so mixed up today. Wesley Cornish had always been sweet on her and suddenly she was thinking of him in a new light. He quickened his steps and jumped in front of her as she took the lane leading to Old Pit.

143

'Get out of my way, Wesley Cornish,' she said, as she had said often in the past when he was pestering her. But if Alice had been there she would have noticed that Meg didn't use her, 'I mean it' voice, nor did she make a great deal of effort to get round him. Meg's face was flushed as she stared ahead at some point over his shoulder.

'I'll do more than that, lass,' Wes said, flashing a smile, and Meg noticed for the first time that he had really deep dimples, not only in his cheeks but one in his chin too. Though, of course, she wasn't looking at his face. Not really.

'I'll come with you. You never know who you might meet on a country road these days.'

'No, you won't, Wes Cornish,' she answered.

'Well, then, how about taking a walk on Sunday?' he ventured, adding hastily as he saw her objection before she could voice it, 'After chapel, I mean.'

'I have the dinner to get,' Meg said, implying that though he might have all the time in the world for walks on Sundays, some folk didn't.

'Oh, aye, I know,' Wes said hastily, 'but after, then?'

'Then there's tea and evening chapel.'

'Why, Meg, we could go in the afternoon. We'd be back for chapel, like.'

'Aye,' she conceded, though she frowned consideringly, adding, 'Are you going to chapel, like?' This being courted by a lad was all new to her. It was all she could think of to say, though she had not seen Wesley in chapel for years. But she had never let a conversation with him go this far before. It was a bit fast and she couldn't seem to get her breath. She had to think a bit, and any road, what would Da say? Well, maybe not Da, but Auntie Phoebe? Da didn't say anything about anything these days.

But Meg forgot what people might say as she stared

into Wesley Cornish's hazel eyes. They looked almost green as he gazed earnestly down at her and, by, hadn't he lovely fair hair? Not this wishy-washy straw colour like hers, but with reddish tints. He was so good-looking, and not all wild and bad either, in spite of what the minister said about him and his marras. Hadn't he sided with Jack Boy and Miles when those pitmen went for the lads during the strike?

'I might go to chapel,' said Wesley. 'Well, what do you say?'

'I said yes,' said Meg. 'Two o'clock then? At the end of the rows?'

For she wasn't going to have the lads gawping at him if he called for her at her house. Neither was she ready for him to meet her da, not like he was in the house. Before Meg could guess his intentions and move out of his reach, Wesley dropped a kiss lightly on her brow.

'Well then, I'll see you on Sunday.'

Turning on his heel, he swung jauntily down the row, whistling a tune as he went. Meg went on her way to Old Pit Cottages, not sure how she felt. Her feelings were all mixed up, she had a trembling inside of her and her cheeks remained flushed a rosy pink.

After delivering her parcel of clothes to Mrs Dobbs and doing one or two odd jobs for the old lady, Meg decided to walk on for a short distance along the lane which meandered between fields green with young wheat and barley. The cow parsley, or black man's baccy as it was known locally, was coming into bloom along the hedgerows and that, combined with may blossom, gave the air a sweet, pleasant scent, so different from the stink from the coke ovens. She remembered Uncle Tot laughing at her when she wrinkled her nose at the smell when the ovens were going full blast.

'It's a good smell, lass, it cleans the air and it's good for you,' he'd said. But she was not convinced.

Meg wandered along the road under the evening sun, enjoying the unaccustomed leisure and feeling unwilling to go home. But the shadows were lengthening and the sun dipping below the horizon and in the end she decided she must go if she wanted to be back before dark. Reluctantly she retraced her steps. It was later than she'd thought. As she climbed a small rise in the road and looked down over the fields and woods to Winton Colliery, she saw that already there was a mist drifting along the valley of the Gaunless River.

I'll cut across, she thought. If I hurry I'll be through the woods and out on the village road before it's completely dark. Finding a gate in the hedge she climbed over it and set off across the field to the woods which lay beyond. She hadn't been that way before but had a good sense of direction and felt confident she would find her way through the trees.

She was almost to the hedge which bounded the wood when she suddenly heard galloping hooves. They were almost upon her before she realized, having been masked by the soft marshy ground of the pasture. She cast a quick, startled glance behind her, seeing the horseman almost on top of her, and jumped for her life into the hedge, falling into the ditch, still with water in the bottom from the spring rains.

'What the hell are you doing on my land?' demanded the horseman, struggling to control his mount, pulling on the reins as the frightened animal pranced about, neighing and rolling his eyes. He managed to quieten the horse but did not dismount to help the girl out of the ditch. She had to scramble up the bank herself, dishevelled and with the hem of her good skirt muddied and wet.

'Answer me, girl. I'll have you in front of the bench

146

tomorrow for trespassing, damn me if I don't! After something, I've no doubt. You'd better tell me, girl, have you no tongue? I'll have you locked up tonight, see if I don't!'

But Meg was mute with terror, staring up at him with wide blue eyes, her colour coming and going, panic rising in her heaving breast. She hardly heard the threat, wasn't frightened of the lock-up, no. It was because she knew him. After all these years, she knew him, though the last time she had seen him was at her mother's funeral when she was still a child.

Ralph Grizedale, the candyman!

The candyman, the candyman ... the name beat through her head, over and over. She was frozen with fear, forgetting the trees and fields around her, forgetting the approaching dark, forgetting everything and seeing nothing, nothing but the face of the man who was now dismounting from his horse and walking over to her. Ralph Grizedale, the candyman.

His mood had changed, he no longer looked angry. Instead, he was watching her with a peculiar, intense look in his eyes, looking from her face to the swell of her breasts against the rough serge of her dress, the white vee at her neck where the button of her collar was undone.

Meg knew why he was looking at her like that, she knew she should run before he got to her, but she couldn't. She could only stare at him dumbly.

And she saw he could see her fear. When he put an arm around her shoulders she knew he could feel her trembling and she knew he found her fear exciting.

'And who are you, little maid?' he asked softly, and his hand slid from her shoulder to her breast and she could feel the heat from it as he pressed the softness under the serge and his other hand circled her waist and drew her to him. And still she stared at him, held captive more by her terror than that man's arms.

Ralph was encouraged, and laughed softly.

'All the same, you pitmen's lasses, aren't you? I suppose you think I'll let you off the lock-up. Well, I might just do that, if you are good enough.'

He was leading her to the gate in the hedge, his arm still an iron band about her waist, his other hand still clamped on her breast. Under the trees there lay a bed of last year's leaves, rustling and brown. Ralph led her there, leaning her against the trunk of a great oak, and began unbuttoning her dress, feeling underneath and pushing aside the thin shift to grasp the nipples. As his excitement mounted he pulled the undergarment roughly aside, tearing it. And all the while he held her gaze, enjoying her numb terror. He kneaded her breasts with his fingers, pulling at the nipples cruelly and pushing himself hard up against her, so that the bark at her back was pushed painfully into her.

Pulling her down on to the bed of leaves beneath the tree, Ralph scrabbled with his own clothing. It was time to enjoy this unexpectedly docile girl to the full.

But that gave Meg her chance. His own buttons were proving stubborn and Ralph had to take his eyes off her to see to them. In that moment she was galvanized into action and, taking him completely by surprise, flung him away from her, strength returning to her arms and legs as she jumped to her feet. Leaving the candyman gaping after her, flat on his back with his clothes half undone, she ran through the woods in the gathering darkness, instinctively heading in the right direction though she stumbled once or twice over bushes and fallen logs.

He hadn't known her, thank God he hadn't known her, she thought wildly, sobbing now, her breath coming in gasping, painful pants. Oh, thank God he hadn't known her! She could see the edge of the wood now and

148

trees were thinning out. She stood by the hedge getting her bearings as the moon came out, a full moon which cast a bright white glow over the landscape. And there, in the distance, only a mile or two away, she could see the pitheap and winding engine of Winton Colliery and the sparks coming out of the colliery chimney. She could even hear, though faintly it was true, the whistle blowing from the engine pulling the coal trucks along the line.

Meg was still fearful as she ran along the hedge, making for the lane. No more walking in the fields for her, she vowed. And she didn't even feel safe in the lane; she wouldn't be safe until she got to Winton Colliery, she knew. At least the lads off shift in the village wouldn't go for her, they wouldn't attack her. They had some decency, she told herself, not like that man. And she jumped back in renewed terror as a figure on horseback turned off the main road into the lane.

'What is it? Are you all right?'

The figure had dismounted. He had a lantern and was holding it high in the air as he looked down at her, concern showing in his face.

'Look,' said Jonty, 'I'm sorry if I startled you, I didn't see you at first. Are you all right?'

There was something familiar about him to Meg, though she didn't know who he was. There was a familiar air about him, a reassuring air. She remembered how disordered her clothes were and hurried to cover herself up, blushing furiously as she did so.

'I'm sorry,' she said softly, still trembling. 'I'm sorry, it was my fault.' She looked from him to the welcoming sight of the pit and its colliery rows beside it, and began backing away along the road.

'I'm in a hurry, I must get home, it's late . . .'

She fairly raced up the road, lifting her muddied skirts in one hand and flying over the stones, hardly feeling them though the leather of her boots was worn paper

149

thin. Jonty gazed after her, wondering, but the moon went behind a cloud and soon she was lost from sight. Gathering the reins of his horse, he remounted and jogged slowly up the lane and across the fields to where he could pick up the track which led to Grizedale Hall. What on earth had the girl been doing out here on her own? It was almost eleven o'clock. Where on earth had she been and why was she so agitated? And why did he feel that he knew her from somewhere, somewhere else and long ago?

The puzzle was resolved for him when he came to the edge of the wood and saw his father's horse, reins dangling as he cropped the lush grass of the pasture. Just emerging through the gate which led into the wood was his father, a black scowl on his face.

'What have you been doing?' asked Jonty grimly.

'What the hell business is it of yours?' Ralph blustered, grabbing his horse's reins and pulling them savagely before climbing into the saddle.

Jonty leaned over and caught hold of the bridle of his father's horse.

'What the hell are you doing?' roared Ralph, jerking the reins so that his horse danced and neighed as the bit sawed against his mouth.

'You accosted that girl, didn't you?' demanded Jonty, his face grim. 'What sort of a name do you think you're giving the family?'

'What girl? I've seen no girl. Now will you let go of my horse and let me get on my way?'

Jonty released his grip on the reins and allowed his father to gallop away. He realized they were only hurting the horse. But he followed close behind. Ralph was just dismounting as Jonty rode into the yard and jumped down to the ground.

'Father—' he began, but Ralph was already striding away, leaving the stabling of the horses to his son. There had been no stable hand at Grizedale Hall for a couple of years now and no money to pay a lad even if they could prevail on one to come.

Jonty unsaddled the horses and let them into the stalls. He rubbed them both down and piled fresh hay in the boxes, leaving them contentedly chewing before he doused the lantern and closed the stable door behind him. He leaned against the door, looking up at the house. There was only one light which beamed thinly through the curtains of his father's study. Good, thought Jonty, I'm not finished with him yet, I'll have it out with him now. Striding into the Hall, he paused only to remove his riding boots and find his indoor shoes before going to the study door. Not bothering to knock, he flung the door open and went in.

Ralph lay sprawled in his usual place in the armchair before the fireplace, though the fire in the grate was quite dead and filled with only grey ash which had built up and spilled out on to the hearth. The whole room had a neglected air about it, the leather of the armchairs worn thin and even showing holes in places with the horsehair stuffing springing out. Ralph had poured himself a liberal whisky and was tipping it down his throat as though he hadn't had a drink in days. He paused and looked sourly at Jonty.

'Don't knock,' he said with heavy sarcasm.

Jonty ignored this. He strode over the the fireplace and glared down at his father, a heavy bloated man now with a large belly spilling over his trousers and the red mottled nose of the habitual drinker. He hadn't even bothered to remove his riding boots.

'What did you do to that girl? I met her at the end of the lane. She was in a distressed state and her clothing looked to be torn. She ran off up the road to Winton Colliery, but I saw enough to know something had happened to her. And then there you were, coming out of the wood. What were you doing there at that time of night?'

'I was having a pee, what do you think?' snapped Ralph, and took another gulp of whisky.

'You wouldn't have bothered to go into the wood, I know you better than that,' Jonty said. 'You molested that girl, didn't you? Did you violate her? By God—'

Ralph flung his empty whisky glass into the fireplace and the glass shattered and flew out over the hearth and on to the carpet. He sat up in his chair, his face a deep purple.

'No, I did not violate her, as you put it. And even if I did, what is it to you? She was only a pitman's daughter, I found her trespassing in the fields. She should have been glad I didn't haul her in front of the bench. I should have taken her to the lock-up . . .'

'Then you *did* see her. Heaven's alive, Father, don't you know what will happen to you if you rape a girl from the pit villages? The miners look after their own, don't you know that? You've lived among them long enough. If she tells what happened there'll be a gang out after you tonight.'

Ralph laughed shortly. 'Aw, stuff and nonsense,' he said. 'She won't tell them. There was nothing *to* tell. The little bitch led me on to think she was willing and then took fright and ran off. No doubt she thought she heard someone coming. They're all the same these pitmen's brats – wanton little whores until they think they've been found out. There'll be no gang after me, not tonight or any night.'

'Are you sure you didn't hurt her?'

'Man, haven't I told you? And anyway, even if I did, it's none of your damn' business. Though I suppose it's the common blood coming out in you. Your mother was a wanton little whore—'

But Jonty was not prepared to listen to this. It was a

long time since Ralph had talked like this about his mother, he'd been a bit more careful since Jonty had grown up, but tonight whisky had loosened his tongue and his voice had taken on the contemptuous tone which had burned itself into Jonty's mind as a boy. He was not going to listen to his father calling his dead mother names again, he was not.

Leaning forward, he grabbed hold of his father's shirt front and hauled him to his feet.

'What the hell!' ejaculated Ralph.

Jonty brought up his fist and hit his father full in the face, sending him sprawling on the carpet. Ralph lay for a moment, dazed, before lifting his head and shaking it carefully. A trickle of blood ran down his upper lip from his nose and he wiped the back of his hand across and inspected the blood which came away on his fingers, hardly believing what he saw.

'What . . . what . . .?' he said, looking up at Jonty who was towering over him, waiting for him to retaliate. Jonty's blood was up. He felt that if only his father got to his feet and hit him back, he could carry on giving the older man a thrashing he would never forget.

'Stand up,' he said hoarsely, 'stand up and fight.'

But Ralph was not so drunk as that, he still retained some instincts for self-preservation. He stayed where he was, looking up at his son.

'I'm your father, boy!' he snarled. 'Don't you think you owe me some respect?'

'A pity you didn't act like a father when I was young. Respect? You want me to show respect for a drunken wastrel like you? I had to hide out of your way when I was a boy, I feared for my life.'

Jonty laughed, but without humour as the rage in him died away, leaving only a grim, black contempt for the man still lying on the floor.

'Oh, get to your feet,' he said, 'I'm not going to hit you

again. The fact is, you're just not worth it.' He strode to the window and stared out into the blackness of the park, bitterness welling up in him, poisoning him. If it wasn't for his grandmother, lying asleep in her room upstairs, he would go away from Grizedale Hall. He was sick of it and all it stood for. But the fact remained, his grandmother was there, old and frail. And he could not leave her to the mercies of her son, he could never do that.

Ralph had crawled to his feet and poured himself out a fresh glass of whisky. He stood before the fire and downed the spirit in one gulp before taking out his handkerchief and dabbing his upper lip.

'You'll pay for this,' he said savagely, but Jonty merely grunted disparagingly and strode from the room.

Thirteen

Meg took off the all-enveloping apron which covered her Sunday dress of blue cotton. Going over to the mahogany-framed looking-glass which hung over the fireplace in the front room, she stared at her reflection. She ran her hands down her body, smoothing the thin cotton, wincing only slightly as they passed over her breasts, still a little sore from her encounter with Ralph Grizedale.

Shivering slightly at the memory, she tried to forget the way she hadn't even fought him at first, not even protested when he unbuttoned her dress. Why had she been such a rabbit? She'd felt dirty when she'd come home that night. She'd drawn fresh water from the pump and washed herself all over in its icy coldness before letting down the chiffonier bed in the corner of the front room where she slept alone now that Alice was gone. Now that they were grown, the two boys had one of the bedrooms upstairs and Da the other. But at least Meg had the downstairs front room to herself.

Frowning, she gazed into the looking-glass. The colour in her cheeks was far too high and wisps of hair had fallen over her white forehead. Why couldn't she have been born with a pale, interesting complexion and manageable hair? Nicely copper-tinted hair like Wesley's, or dark hair like . . . like whose?

Impatiently she took the brush from the mantelpiece and brushed vigorously at her hair, succeeding only in making it stand up in a thick halo around her head. She pulled it into place and pinned it tightly on top of her head, though even then tendrils escaped and hung down by her ears.

There was nothing she could do about her cheeks, she decided, inspecting the offending colour critically. It was the heat from the oven and the exertions of getting the meal on the table in time for the boys, who wanted to go off somewhere with their marras. And Father too. He wanted to have his usual Sunday afternoon in bed.

Meg was nervous, apprehension rising in her throat. Which was daft. After all, it was just a Sunday afternoon's walk, wasn't it? They weren't courting, Wesley and her, not courting or even walking out properly. Oh no, she wasn't ready to go courting yet. She turned away from the looking-glass. She wasn't satisfied with how she looked but short of putting powdered chalk on her cheeks there was nothing she could do. And beady-eyed Jack Boy was still in the kitchen, she daren't get the chalk out.

In fact, the kitchen was deserted, Jack Boy and Miles had already gone and Da had disappeared upstairs. Meg went through to the back yard and called softly over the wall.

'Bella!'

Auntie Phoebe and Uncle Tot were also having their Sunday afternoon lie-down as Meg had known they would be, but Bella was sitting on a chair in the yard, hopelessly trying to spell out a page in a book. She lifted her head. The book was *The Water Babies*, and she was aware it was a religious book, the sort it was all right to read on Sundays. But Bella wanted to be able to read it when it was her turn to stand up in class on Monday. The book belonged to the Wesleyan School library and she had promised Miss Atherton faithfully she would have it back by Tuesday.

Bella tried to read, she was desperate to read, just once she wanted to stand up in class and not have the others sniggering and laughing at her attempts.

'Bella!' Meg said again, but Bella could see that she was not annoyed, she was smiling, 'Bella, pet, will you see the kettle is boiling for the tea for me? I've already set the table and everything is ready. Only I might be a bit late meself.'

'Aye,' said Bella eagerly, always pleased to help. 'I mean, yes, Meg, I will.'

Bella lived in fear of Miss Atherton who was trying to get the children to speak properly. Miss Atherton spoke lovely though sometimes she sounded as though she had a mouthful of pop alleys.

'You won't forget?'

'No, no, Meg, I won't forget.' For the minute, Bella had forgotten the book though. 'I have nothing else to do.' She looked hopefully up, wanting Meg to say, 'Come along of me.'

Meg knew very well what was in Bella's mind but she didn't let on. 'You could learn your lesson, that's what you should be doing,' she said sternly. 'I heard you had to be prompted this morning.'

'Who said that?' wailed Bella, red-faced. 'I bet it was our Miley.'

'Never mind who said it, just try to learn it this week, pet, try harder for me.' But Meg knew that Bella did try hard, her whole life was trying hard to be as good as the other children, but no matter how hard she tried she never managed to rise beyond the bottom section in weekday or Sunday school. Meg felt mean for saying it as she let herself out of the house and walked down to the corner of the rows.

Wesley was there waiting for her, lounging against a wall and whistling quietly through his teeth. He fell into step beside her wordlessly and they walked side by side, not touching, leaving at least a yard between them.

Meg glanced sideways at him. He was different somehow, without the other lads to back him up; quieter, not so brash. Was he a bit bashful? She noticed his arms and shoulders, bursting out of his Sunday suit. They were powerful-looking, the shoulders of a mature man, like all shoulders of lads who swung a pick down the pit, often in seams less than three feet high.

How did he manage those long legs when he was working in such cramped conditions? she wondered. His legs were gangling, there was an air of coltishness about the way he walked. He caught her eye and looked quickly away, and Meg felt an impulse to giggle which she quickly suppressed.

There was no one on the road they took out of the village which led to the track winding over the fields to the wild area of scrubland known locally as the bunny banks for the profusion of rabbits which occupied it. Fleetingly, Meg remembered the rabbit which Miles and Jack Boy had brought in during the lockout, the blind helpless babies inside it. She looked about to distract her thoughts. There were gorse bushes and whinney and dark green shoots of broom growing in uneven disorder. The grass beneath the bushes had that close-cropped, velvety texture which always shows where the land is being grazed by rabbits.

Wesley stopped on the side of a small hillock and looked at her fully for the first time.

'We'll sit here?' he asked. They were the only words he had said since his muttered greeting at the end of the rows.

'I thought we were going for a walk,' she objected.

'Oh, howay man, we can have a rest, can't we? We'll go for a walk after.'

'I'll get my dress stained,' said Meg, eyeing the grass.

It was quite dry but grass stains were murder to get off clothes and this was her good dress.

Wesley sighed. Reaching into his pocket he drew out a large red and white spotted handkerchief and spread it on the ground, sitting down beside it himself.

'There now.'

Meg sat on the handkerchief, careful to keep her dress over her ankles and knees together. A warning was sounding in her head. But after all, she was just sitting beside him and the soft green turf was pleasant to sit on and the view was grand too. There was nothing wrong in sitting and enjoying the view. Carefully Meg eased her feet forward and folded her dress decorously around her knees.

'Just for a minute, mind,' she said primly. 'And only because I like the view from here. It's grand.'

She stared out over the familiar countryside, the rolling hills with their crowns of green trees. There wasn't a pitheap in sight, she thought dreamily, not even tell-tale columns of smoke in the air for it was Sunday.

Wesley, sitting beside her, edged closer a little at a time and she pretended not to notice, though she could feel her cheeks getting warmer with hot colour. Meg felt strange, a little light-headed, and somewhere in the pit of her stomach there was a funny ache.

'Am I going to get a kiss, then?'

His voice was so soft and close to her ear that Meg started and turned to him, ready with a denial, but somehow it didn't happen like that. He brought his lips to hers and brushed them together, light as featherdown. Her own parted in surprise. Her eyes widened as she looked up into his. They were almost green, she thought, and there were tiny gold flecks in them, sparkling brightly. He was staring at her intently and she found herself watching the gold flecks glinting and glowing.

Meg sat perfectly still, not even moving when she felt his arms go round her waist as he leaned over her.

This time his kiss was different. He brought his mouth down on hers and at the same time bore her down on the ground so that she could feel the bumps in the grass beneath her head. Her eyes closed, instinctively hiding the rush of feeling, the tremulous delight, which was coursing through her in waves. She was lost to everything but the delightful sensations he was giving her with his lips and his tongue, his hand running up and down her arm, her shoulder, her breast.

'Margaret Anne,' he said softly, and she opened her eyes in shock at the upsurge of feeling within her as he buried his face in the nape of her neck. One hand cupped a breast and he brushed the upright nipple under the thin cotton with his thumb.

Suddenly she began to struggle. The nipple was painful still, and it reminded her of how dirty she had felt when Ralph Grizedale did this. She took Wesley completely off guard as she threw him from her and scrambled to her feet, brushing her hair from her eyes and smoothing down her dress, trying desperately to get her feelings under control. He lay on his back, a lazy smile on his face.

'Did you not like it, then?'

Meg turned her face away. She felt shaken because she had liked it – until it reminded her of the candyman, that is. She was as bad as those women who hung about one or two of the beer houses in Bishop Auckland. How easy it would have been to carry on, to find out for herself what the women were talking about when they gathered round the street tap at the end of the rows, making obscure jokes about men. No, she told herself, if it was that easy to fall she'd best keep away from it, not let men touch her at all.

'Aw, howay, lass.'

Meg jumped as Wesley crept up behind her and put his arm around her, whispering softly in her ear, cajoling, 'ticing.

'No,' she said, 'I'm going home.'

But she had taken only a few steps before he ran in front of her, walking backwards as he talked, his smile beguilingly innocent.

'Margaret Anne ... Meggie! It's all right. It is, really. I'm sorry, I won't touch you again, I promise I won't. Not if you don't want me to, that is. Howay, we'll go for that walk, eh? What do you say?'

Meg hesitated but only for a moment, trying to decide if she trusted him. What if someone had come out of the village and seen them like that on the ground? She'd never be able to hold her head up again. She walked on.

'Meg!'

His appeal was cut off suddenly as he caught his foot in a rabbit hole and went head over heels on the grass. Meg's innate sense of the ridiculous got the better of her and she burst out laughing to see the expression of surprise on his face as he lay there, winded. Her blue eyes twinkled with merriment and for a moment she thought he was going to take offence for he scowled. But the expression was only momentary. His smile was soon back and he was on his feet, ready to take advantage of her change of mood.

Getting to his feet, groaning loudly, he hopped about on one foot, holding the ankle of the other with both hands.

'Eeh, did you hurt yourself?' she asked.

'I did, I did!'

Meg quickly controlled her laughter as she sat down on the grass again and loosed his boot and held up his foot – which showed no sign of injury as far as she could see.

'It doesn't look bad,' she said.

161

'Oh, aye, but it is. It doesn't always show right away, you know.'

Meg knelt by his side and took the offending foot in her capable hands, taking off his thick wool stocking and gently massaging the ankle.

'I bet it will be twice the size in a minute,' declared Wesley, enjoying the change in his fortunes. 'I won't get my boot back on. Then what will I do? You'll have to carry me home, that's all. Do you think you're strong enough?'

'Well, I don't know, I don't think—' she began gravely, then looking up at him, saw the merriment in his eyes. He was having a hard time not to laugh openly.

'Wesley Cornish!' she snapped, intending to be stern, but his grin was so infectious she couldn't help the corners of her mouth lifting and soon they were grinning at each other, sharing a joke.

Wesley leaped to his feet and demonstrated how strong his ankle was by doing a little jig before sitting down again and putting on his stocking and boot. He offered her a hand to help her up, and after a moment she put her hand in his and allowed him to pull her to her feet.

Somehow the incident had changed the atmosphere between them altogether and they continued their walk hand in hand. Her own fingers were work-roughened and the nails, though possessing a natural shapeliness, broken and brittle owing to their constant immersion in hot, soapy water. But her hand felt soft and smooth compared to his. His was a real man's hand. She was supremely conscious of the feel of it as they strolled over the hill and down the other side to a grove of trees at the bottom. There was a pond they had to skirt before they got to the trees, and as they watched a pair of ducks flew in and landed on the water, quacking loudly and paddling around busily.

162

They stood there watching the ducks: the drake with its brightly coloured wings and the female a dowdy brown. And Meg looked up at Wesley and thought that that was what they were like, she and Wes, he so good-looking and she so commonplace. No wonder he was a bit full of himself among his marras in the village. He could have plenty of girls, she knew that. Wesley glanced down and caught her look and she noticed his eyes crinkled when he smiled.

'Nice, aren't they? The ducks, I mean?'

'Yes, bonny,' agreed Meg, and shivered suddenly as a cool wind sprang up and clouds gathered in the sky.

Wesley slipped an arm round her shoulders. 'Cold? Did you not bring a shawl?'

She didn't say she didn't bring her shawl because it was only a workaday grey wool and the fringe was getting a bit raggy.

'I didn't think it would turn cold.'

'Howay then, we'll get back.' Wesley kissed the tip of her nose before she could protest, and then they went running back up the hill like two children.

The rain began before they reached the village so that by the time they arrived at the pit rows Meg's blue cotton dress was soaked and her hair was stuck to her head.

'I'll see you next week, Meg?' Wesley stopped at the corner, not coming down to her end of the street. He sounded a little unsure of himself and Meg was struck once again by how different he was on his own, away from his marras. When he was with them he swaggered, they all seemed to compete with each other in being outrageous, but when he was with her, he was nice.

'Aye,' she murmured, and slipped away, running through the rain to the back door.

'Eeh, our Meg, you're wet through, man.'

163

Bella looked at Meg in astonishment as she saw her come in. She herself wasn't allowed to get wet, Auntie Phoebe said it was bad for her. Meg's thin cotton dress was clinging to her and her boots were soaked through.

'You'll catch your death,' Bella said primly as she pulled a towel from the brass rail under the mantelpiece and handed it to her sister. It was nice to get back at an older sister who was almost as bossy as Auntie Phoebe.

Meg went up to the black-leaded range, feeling the heat coming from the fire gratefully. She took the towel and wiped her face before taking the pins from her hair and towelling it briskly.

'Did you not take your shawl, you daft happorth?' Bella was still being self-righteous. She pressed her lips together in imitation of Auntie Phoebe and shook her head reprovingly. 'I came in to put the kettle on like you said, but I didn't go back when it started to rain, I thought I'd better wait.'

'I'm all right. We got caught in the rain, that's all, we had to run back,' Meg said absently. She stared into the fire and rubbed at her hair dreamily.

'Well,' said Bella, 'you'd better get yourself changed. The steam's coming off you like a fog. And just look at your boots.' She sighed and shook her head as though she couldn't get over the folly of some folks. 'Any road, you go and get changed, man, the tea will be ready in a minute if you let me get to the fire and see to it.'

Meg took the towel to the front room-cum-bedroom and stripped off her clothes, rubbing hard with the rough towel until she felt glowing and dry. When she came back into the kitchen ten minutes later she was wearing her everyday black serge skirt and shirtwaister.

'You can't wear that for chapel,' said Bella.

'I'm not going tonight.'

'Eeh, but you have to go!' said Bella, scandalized at the idea. Meg always went to evening chapel besides morning service. Then her voice took on a note of concern. 'Are you feeling out of fettle, like?'

'Just a bit tired.' Meg seized on the excuse. 'I thought I'll stay in the dry after that soaking.'

Bella tutted and Meg had to repress a grin, her sister sounded so like Auntie Phoebe.

'Are you having your tea in here then, Bella?'

As if on cue Auntie Phoebe had come in, looking a little affronted as she saw Bella place the shiny new tin teapot on the table.

Bella looked at her, and from her to Meg. She didn't want to upset Auntie Phoebe and hurried to deny that she had thought of doing just that.

'Eeh, no, Auntie Phoebe, I was just helping our Meg out. I said I would boil the kettle for her. And then it started to rain and you always say I shouldn't get wet, it's bad for me chest . . .'

'All right, pet,' said Auntie Phoebe, mollified. 'Run around home now and call up your Uncle Tot, I've some nice scones warming in the oven.'

She watched as Bella went down the yard before turning back to Meg.

'Where've you been?' she said baldly.

'I went for a walk, that's all,' said Meg, on the defensive.

'With a lad?' demanded Auntie Phoebe. 'Oh, it's no good denying it, I saw you go past the end of the rows with that Wesley Cornish. I was looking out of the bedroom window at the time.'

'Well, I am eighteen, Auntie Phoebe,' said Meg. 'Nearly nineteen now. I can go out with a lad if I want to.'

Auntie Phoebe bridled. 'Aye. Well, you just want to be careful who you go with. He's got a name for himself has that one, an' you'll be getting a bad name an' all if you

165

go out with him. There was talk about him once with a lass in Auckland, didn't you hear about it? Like I say—'

'I don't want to hear it,' said Meg, surprising herself, let alone Auntie Phoebe. 'Any road, here's Da coming down the stairs for his tea. The lads'll be in in a minute.'

Auntie Phoebe leaned forward and whispered fiercely, 'You watch what you're doing, our Meg. You don't want to be bringing any trouble home, now do you?' And with that, she marched out of the door.

Meg seethed. Who did her aunt think she was? If she went out with any lad, even Wesley Cornish, why should that mean she would bring trouble back to the house? But then her brothers came in and Da was wanting his tea and Meg had to forget about it all until she had finished the meal and washed up. Da went out on one of his solitary walks and Jack Boy and Miles went off behind the pitheaps where they were meeting their marras for a game of cricket. At last Meg was alone to think about Wesley and her meeting with him that afternoon.

And she had to be honest with herself. The way her feelings had been roused when Wes took her in his arms and kissed her, Auntie Phoebe could have been right.

Fourteen

'You don't want your name bandied about, our Meg,' said Jack Boy. It was Monday evening and he was still black from the pit. He was on day shift and hadn't been long in the house.

'What do you mean?' she demanded.

'Going up to the bunny banks with Wesley Cornish, that's what I mean.'

Meg was on the defensive. Jack Boy had come in from the pit and she could tell straight away that he was worried about something. Now he had followed her into the front room so that he could speak to her on her own.

'How did you know where we went?' she said helplessly.

'Wes is always boasting about the lasses he takes up there, didn't you know that?'

'He wouldn't tell anybody about me.'

'Aw, no, not about you, he hasn't said anything about you,' her brother admitted. He gazed earnestly at her, his blue eyes solemn in his black-streaked face.

'I knew it,' Meg said, but all the same, relief flooded through her.

'But any road, you listen to what I'm telling you. He's bad news for a decent lass, he is.'

Meg tossed her head, the colour flaming in her cheeks now. She wasn't going to let her brother tell her what to do nor who she could go out with. Why, Jack Boy was just a bairn. She had practically brought him up, hadn't she?

'It's none of your business,' she snapped. She had her dander up all right. 'If I want to walk out with Wesley Cornish, I will.'

Jack Boy looked as though he was going to protest further but Meg jumped in first.

'Remember he was the one who helped you and Miles when you needed it,' she said hotly. 'You know what I mean, when the pit was on strike.'

Jack Boy shrugged and turned away. He'd put in his word of warning, there was nothing more he could do. Da wasn't interested enough to do anything about it.

Meg had been unsure of her feelings towards Wesley Cornish, and as the week progressed became more so. She might have wavered, she even thought about telling Wes she had changed her mind, she didn't want to meet him again. But Jack Boy's opposition stopped her. She couldn't let her brother think he had influenced her. She was going out with Wesley Cornish on Sunday afternoon even if it snowed. She liked him, she told herself, he was a good-looking lad, wasn't he? What was wrong with him any road? Nothing was going to happen. She was in control of her emotions, and would stop anything happening. He had shown respect for her last Sunday, hadn't he? And he was so exciting . . .

Sunday afternoon came round soon enough and Meg, dressed in her blue cotton frock which she had managed to press into fairly good shape, though it no longer had that pristine freshness it had had the Sunday before, set out to meet Wesley again. She had made the usual arrangements for the household to go on without her for an hour or two and this time brought her old shawl for there was a cool wind blowing from the moors.

Auntie Phoebe came to the door as she went out, she must have been watching for her.

'You're not meeting that Wesley Cornish again, are you, Meg?' she asked.

'I am, Auntie,' she said firmly.

'If your da was himself, he wouldn't want you to.'

Meg lifted her chin and walked rapidly up the row, not deigning to reply. Auntie Phoebe was not even her real aunt, she told herself, she couldn't tell her what to do. Her real aunt was dead. She had been Nell, Jonty's mother. Hadn't her mam told her about Aunt Nell often enough? The thought unsettled her and she was filled with vague regrets as she saw Wes in the distance waiting for her. Her footsteps slowed.

From out of nowhere a memory popped into her head of being in Grizedale Hall, playing with Jonty. He was hiding and she was looking for him, feeling a little nervous and frightened because she was upstairs in the big house and might meet Jonty's da. And she had been in a bedroom, and she had been ... he had been ... What had Jonty's da been doing? The wisp of memory slipped away, leaving her puzzled.

'Whot cheor,' Wesley came to meet her and fell into step behind her. 'You look as though you'd lost a shilling and found a ha'penny.'

She looked up into his merry twinkling eyes and the puzzled frown left her face and she smiled up at him, the memory forgotten. By, Wesley was a handsome lad, she thought happily. He looked so open and fresh-faced, there just couldn't be any real bad in him. He had been a bit wild growing up, that's all it was. The old wives in this place would call anybody names, nothing else to do all day.

'Good afternoon,' she said primly.

They walked out of the village taking the same road they had the Sunday before and in the same fashion.

There was a gap of a few feet between them and they were awkward, hardly acknowledging they were together until they were clear of the last straggling houses. But when Wesley would have turned and taken the track up through the bunny banks, Meg demurred.

'I don't want to go there.'

Welsey lifted his eyebrows in surprise but halted nevertheless.

'Where to then?'

'Oh, I don't know, let's just walk along the road a bit.'

Meg, in spite of herself, couldn't put out of her mind what Jack Boy had told her about Wesley taking all his girlfriends up to the bunny banks. It had turned her completely off the place.

They wandered silently along the road for a mile or two and Wesley began whistling tunelessly through his teeth. He looked round at the countryside and scuffed at last year's dead leaves with his feet, looking bored. But when they came up to a footpath which led over the fields to Old Eldon, he brightened up. Pausing by the stile, he looked at Meg.

'We'll go off here then?'

He didn't wait for her answer but climbed over the stile and waited for her on the other side. After a minute's hesitation, Meg followed, tentatively taking his hand when he offered it to help her down. His grasp was warm and firm and her hand tingled after she let go.

They wandered up the path by a hedge bright with wild pink roses nestling among shiny green leaves. At the top of the bank the path branched and Wesley drew Meg along the smaller path which led not to the pretty farming village of Old Eldon but to Old Pit, though a different path from the one Meg took to visit Mrs Dobbs. The gap between the hedges widened and on one side there was a broad grassy bank, covered with wild strawberries.

'Oh! I wish I'd brought something to put them in, I could have taken some home for tea.'

'Will my handkerchief do? It's clean. Me mam just put it in my pocket.'

Wesley took out the large red and white spotted handkerchief from his jacket pocket and tied the four corners into a knot, making a sort of bag with it. Soon they were picking the tiny, juicy fruit, filling the handkerchief in minutes even though Wesley was eating as many as he put in. Their fingers were soon red and sticky with juice and Meg sighed as she sat back and tried to lick them clean, to no avail whatsoever for they were well and truly stained.

Laughing, she looked up at Wesley. He had a glistening red mark on his chin where juice had run down and there was a further stain on his white shirt.

'Eeh, Welsey, your mam'll kill you,' she laughed. 'She'll have a job getting that back to white.'

'I don't care, it was worth it. Am I going to get to have some of those strawberries for me tea, then?' He caught hold of her hand and they resumed their walk along the path, Wesley swinging the bag of strawberries by his side.

Meg was speechless. She felt confused. This was going too quickly for her. For Wes to ask that question even casually meant he was asking to come to her house for his tea, which meant he was intending for them to be officially walking out together, which meant he was serious.

'Well?'

'I don't know, Wes, really I don't.'

'You like me, don't you?'

Meg felt his hand tighten on hers, and peeped up at him. By, he was a handsome lad, she thought. And Jack Boy was wrong about him. He might have been wild before but he meant to do the right thing by her. The trouble was, she still didn't know if that was what she wanted. Panic rose up in her and threatened to choke her.

'I like you, Wes,' she said at last. 'But I don't know if I'm ready for anything else, not yet.'

Wesley stopped walking and turned to face her. He put up a hand and circled the back of her neck and his fingers were hard and rough against the soft skin of her nape. They had reached another fork in the path. Around the bend on their right was Old Pit and on their left a broader track with an iron 'cowcatcher' gate. Beyond loomed a dark, dense wood and to one side farm buildings appeared, or rather the chimneys of a house and a roof of a barn, surrounded by a high stone wall. Gently, Wesley pulled her towards the trees.

'Not ready?' He laughed softly, 'Eeh, lass, you're ready, you're ripe for the plucking. I've been watching you these last weeks and I can see it in you, the way you look at me when you think I'm not looking, the way you swing your hips. Oh, aye, you're ready right enough. An' you know I've had a soft spot for you for a long time.'

They reached the wood and he leaned her up against the trunk of an oak tree and brought his mouth down on hers, gently at first, then with increasing passion.

In the beginning, Meg felt herself responding to him. Strange feelings, strong, secret feelings, clamoured for release in her body. Her mouth opened under his and she kissed him back with a fervour which surprised her. She who had never kissed a boy before last Sunday, except for her father and brothers, found her natural modesty being overwhelmed in the sweetness of her desire.

She could taste the strawberries on his tongue as he thrust it between her lips, she made no resistance when he slowly pulled her down on to the layer of leaves

172

beneath the tree. Alarm bells did ring in her mind when he began touching her more intimate places, pushing up her skirt and moving on top of her. She struggled but it was too late. He had her completely in his grip now and brushed her objections aside impatiently.

Meg fought still but Wesley was strong from hewing coal underground, his arms were immovable, his eyes glazed as he held her down easily and used her. All she could see was his face, red with exertion, almost inhuman as he panted at the end. And when it was over, all she could think about was the pain and soreness he had caused her, how shamed she was, how dirty she felt.

Wesley rolled off her and lay on his back, panting, and to her at that moment he was the same as Ralph Grizedale, the candyman. She couldn't bear to look at him, lying there, smugly satisfied. Hurriedly, though her mind was numb with what had happened, Meg rearranged her clothing, pulling her torn and bloodied cotton drawers together, trying to make herself decent.

I'll never be decent again, she thought dully with a sense of the irrevocable. She scrambled to her feet and pulled her shawl round her shoulders, turning her back on him. Would he boast about this to his marras in the pub tonight? she thought, feeling nauseous.

'Meg! Meg, where are you off to?'

She didn't answer. Instead she started to walk away back down to the path and on to the road, not even noticing the large red stain on her dress where the discarded strawberries had been crushed beneath her.

'Meg!' Wesley came after her and caught her elbow and she wrenched it away, her lips pressed tightly together to stop herself from screaming at him.

'Meg, what ails you? You're my girl now, it's all right, I promise you.'

His girl? Meg shuddered at the thought of that awful thing happening to her again. No. Her face blushed a bright red and her eyes stung with the passion of her denial.

'That's the wrong way, Meg,' she heard him call. He had stopped following her and she was thankful for that, but she halted and looked around her.

It was true, she was walking towards Old Eldon, not back to Winton Colliery. She bit her lip. She could see Wesley standing on the path grinning at her. He looked arrogantly pleased with himself, sure he was dealing with some feminine whim. She would come right in the end. She could see that that was what he was thinking. It was written on his face. Now she would have to walk past him to get on to the right road.

He waited for her, arms folded. By, she hated the grin on his face. She loathed and detested him. And he was so sure of his charms he couldn't even see it.

As she came abreast of him she skirted the path so that she didn't have to go near him. She was uncaring about the mud she got on her boots, wasn't going to give him the chance to touch her again. Wesley, of course, had other ideas. As she drew closer he stepped forward and caught hold of her by the upper arms, holding her in a firm, steady grip.

'Meg, hinny, what's the matter with you? What did you expect was going to happen between a lad and a lass? You've come walking wi' me twice, I thought you liked me.

Meg shuddered, she couldn't bear his hands on her arms. Loathing showed in her face and Wesley stepped back in surprise. Even he could not fail to see that. He dropped his arms abruptly and his grin faded, his expression hardening.

'Hadaway then,' he snapped grimly. 'If that's how you feel, why the hell did you come out with me in the first place?'

Meg didn't answer, simply turned on her heel and

174

walked on rapidly down the path. Why *had* she come out with him? She didn't know, she couldn't remember. His words rang in her ears: 'What did you expect?' She didn't know what she had expected but she knew it wasn't what had happened. Surely a lass should have some say in how far to go? Why did it have to be so brutish? Why did Wesley take no notice of her protests and struggles? Maybe it had all been her own fault, maybe she had led him to believe she wanted it to happen. She vowed she would never, never, let it happen again.

All the bones in her body ached and she felt as though a great bruise was covering her from the waist down. She stumbled slightly and a great weariness overtook her. She was aware that Wesley was following only a few steps behind her but didn't look back. Her pace quickened. She walked blindly on, longing only to get home.

'Hey, I say! Watch where you're going. Whoa! Whoa!'

The voice startled her out of her misery. She had reached the end of the path and had almost walked into a man leading a stocky Dales pony. He had been busy opening the stock gate by the stile to let himself and his pony on to the path.

The horse nickered and pranced a little but settled down immediately when the man spoke to him, obediently going through the gate and standing patiently while he spoke to Meg.

'Can't you look where you're going?'

'I – I'm sorry,' she muttered, her face flushing even redder than it had been. She looked up at him desperately, wanting the incident to be over and him to go so that she could be on her way before Wesley reached them. Dully, she took in the fact that he was more of a boy than a man, somewhere near her own age. And he was obviously gentry though his suit was threadbare.

'Do I know you?'

Startled, her eyes opened wide at the query. He did look familiar but she couldn't put a name to him. He frowned down at her, his face looking puzzled. She knew he was looking curiously at her face, could tell she had been weeping. She was embarrassed and looked quickly down to the ground.

Wesley caught up with her and she saw the gentleman's lip curl slightly as he properly took in their dishevelled appearances and saw the red strawberry stains on their clothes. He mounted his horse and rode on up the path without waiting for her to answer his question. Gathering her skirt in one hand, Meg hurried over the stile and ran down the road to the village.

Jonty rode on and branched out over the fields for Grizedale Hall, but as he rode the image of her tearstained face and flushed cheeks rose up in front of him. There was something about her: her fair, curly hair and her blue eyes fringed with thick lashes, bright and attractive in spite of being damp and reddened with weeping. Obviously he had interrupted a lovers' quarrel. He rode on to the drive leading to Grizedale Hall, wondering why she seemed so familiar to him. As he got to the stables he realized who she looked like. It was a little girl he had seen in Phoebe Lowther's kitchen. Bella, was it?

He sighed. Mrs Lowther had not been so welcoming the second time he went to see her. In fact, she had put him off going altogether. And she had hinted that his mother's relatives wanted nothing to do with him, they simply weren't interested. He remembered again the desolate feeling when they had left him as a young boy and they disappeared from his life, leaving him to his father. He wondered again what he had done to deserve it, what sin he had committed that they should have cut him off so completely.

Sadly, Jonty stabled his pony and rubbed him down. There was no sign of his father's horse. Ralph Grizedale must be off on one of his jaunts to Darlington. Well, at least Jonty didn't have to deal with him for a while. He had enough to think about as it was, and was desperately aware that if things went on the way they were doing, the estate would be lost altogether. His trust money, when he got it, would come too late to do any good.

Sadly, he went indoors and climbed the stairs to his grandmother's room. He had to see that the old woman was comfortable. She was failing now, her joints crippled with arthritis so that she rarely left her room. She was dependent on him for everything.

Fifteen

It was autumn and the wind was blowing from the north and straight down the colliery rows as Meg walked slowly along to the end and turned right. She passed three rows, turning in when she came to the last but one. Pausing, she stared down the street, noting the washing strung across from one side to the other, for these rows had no gardens to string washing in. Only Pasture Row where she lived had gardens. Her inner turmoil was eased slightly by thinking of such inconsequential things.

She shivered. The wind was bitterly cold. It was only October but the north-easters were already bringing the taste of winter from the Arctic.

Meg's deep-down thoughts were as bitter as the wind. It took all her will-power to stop herself from turning round and going back home. But she could not. She pulled her shawl tighter round her shoulders and walked on down the row to number eleven. Here lived the Cornish family, Wesley and his widowed mother. Mrs Cornish had been widowed last year when her husband was killed in a fall of stone at the pit but they had kept the tenancy of the house by virtue of Wesley's position as a coal-hewer.

Her feet slowed as she approached number eleven and halted at the door. Meg was ready to turn and run; she was ready to face her father and brothers first and confess the pickle she had got herself into. They wouldn't turn her out, why no, they wouldn't, not like happened to some girls in the same position. They were a close family, even Da for all his withdrawn silences. But Auntie Phoebe's voice came back to her, ringing in her ears.

'There's only one thing you can do,' her aunt had said when she caught Meg being sick over the drain in the back yard, only yesterday morning. 'You'll have to tell the lad. Them that makes their bed has to lie on it. It'll be that Wesley Cornish, is it?'

Meg had nodded miserably.

'Aye, well, you wouldn't be told. You would go with him.'

Meg had leaned against the wall and wiped her mouth with a rag, the bitter taste of bile fresh in her mouth. She must have looked woebegone for Phoebe's tone softened.

'Never mind, lass, you're not the first this has happened to. It's the way of the world. He'll have to do the right thing by you. An' I know you haven't been seeing him lately. Was it just the once, like?'

Meg had nodded again, wordless.

'Hmm. Them that gets the puddin' doesn't always get the most gravy,' Phoebe commented sagely, though the remark was incomprehensible to Meg.

And now here she was, standing by the door of the Cornish house, not daring to knock. She glanced up and down the street but there was no one about, the doors tight closed against the wind which made the clothes flap and snap and wind themselves around the lines. Dully, she thought they would take a lot of ironing if someone didn't come out and see to them.

Meg hadn't seen Wesley Cornish since that fateful Sunday afternoon. She had returned home, feeling grubbily used, sure he would be boasting about his conquests to all the lads in the village and she would be named for a whore. Every day when Jack Boy or Miles

179

came in from the pit, she met them with a sick feeling rising in her gut, expecting them to show anger and contempt for her for bringing this shame on the family.

But it hadn't happened, everything was as normal. Evidently Wesley was not bandying her name about at all. Her heart had grown lighter with each passing day. She was going to get the chance to put it behind her. And then suddenly she had another worry, a bigger one, a much bigger one. What was she going to do?

Meg brought her thoughts back to the present. She had to lift her hand and knock on the door of number eleven. She had to, as Auntie Phoebe said. It was too late now to say she didn't want to marry Wesley Cornish. Bairns with no fathers just didn't happen in the closed society of the pit village. Or not often, they didn't, and when they did it was a blight on the whole family, not just the woman and her bairn.

Hadn't she heard a woman in Marsden once comment on it, when an unmarried girl and her child were laughing together on the beach?

'You'd think she'd keep him in the house, not make a show of him like that,' the woman had said. And Meg had looked at the child in surprise. He was an ordinary enough bairn, why should his mother have to keep him out of the way? She'd asked Mam, and Mam had told her some people thought like that because he had no da. But Meg still hadn't understood. Lots of children had no fathers. Men were killed in the pit or died of the cholera or their lungs rotted with the dust. Why was that one bairn different? But Mam would say no more.

The wind blew her hair in wisps about her face and Meg's hand dropped to her side almost of its own volition. She stared at the fading paint of the green batten door, the same green paint which adorned every door in the rows. She was just noting dully that the brass sneck could do with a bit of polish when it lifted and there, in the doorway was Wesley's mam.

'Er, good morning, Mrs Cornish.'

'Morning.'

Jane Cornish stared in astonishment at the girl standing on her doorstep which was newly scoured this morning with sandstone. She stood with the Brasso in one hand and a polishing cloth in the other, an enquiring expression on her face, obviously waiting for Meg to explain what she was doing there. Meg bit her lip.

'Did you want something, lass?' prompted Mrs Cornish. 'You're not tongue-tied, are you?'

Meg shook her head and smiled broadly. For some reason she had expected to see Wesley. After all, she knew he was off shift, that was why she was here. She didn't know what to say to his mother.

'Is your Wesley in?' she managed to utter at last.

Jane Cornish compressed her lips. She was a small, scraggy woman, everything about her meagre. Her thin hair was scraped back from her face and her narrow body dressed in a cheap black overall dress. From her five foot nothing she looked up at Meg, her gaze anything but friendly. This girl was a threat to her security and she knew it. Why else would a young lass come looking for a lad this early in the morning, before the jobs were done?

'He's in bed,' she snapped, and her tone implied she had no intention of disturbing him either.

'Oh.' Meg hadn't thought of that. She berated herself for not thinking of it. After all, he'd been on night shift, why wouldn't he still be in bed? 'Will you tell him I want to see him? Margaret Maddison, I am.'

'Indeed I will not,' snapped Mrs Cornish, openly aggressive now. 'Why should I disturb the lad? Why can't you wait?'

Meg faced her desperately. Oh, she didn't want to go

181

back home and have to come looking all over again, she didn't.

'Who's that, Mam?'

The annoyance on Jane's face deepened as Wesley came through from the back of the house, yawning widely, his feet bare and his braces hanging down by his sides. Obviously he had not been in bed, he came out of the kitchen.

'Meg!' he exclaimed.

Wesley's surprise was total. Since that summer day when they had taken their last walk in the fields he hadn't seen her. She had made it very plain then that she didn't want him yet here she was on his doorstep.

'Can I come in?'

Meg sounded tentative. Jane still held on to the door as though guarding the house against an enemy. Wesley simply stared. After a moment he spoke.

'Let her in, Mam.'

Reluctantly, Jane stood back from the door and allowed Meg to pass her, anything but welcoming.

Meg followed Wesley into a spotless kitchen. The table was scrubbed white and the brass rail below the mantelshelf gleamed in the light from the range. She felt that not a cinder would dare to fall on the white-washed hearth. The only concession to comfort in the room was a thin cushion on the wooden armchair pulled up before the fire.

Jane followed them into the room and stood on the clippie mat by the fender, arms folded over her skinny breast.

'Can I have a word with you, Wesley, on your own?'

Meg heard the tremor in her own voice and clamped her teeth together in an effort to get over her fit of nerves.

'There's nothing you can have to say to our Wesley that I don't have a right to know,' declared Jane.

'Mam!'

Wesley's exclamation seemed to have an effect on her for she nodded towards the passage.

'Go on then. You know where the front room is.'

Meg followed Wesley along to the front room. Once there and with the door firmly closed, she turned to face him. Wesley was smiling confidently and she could see he was thinking that if she'd sought him out, she must want to see him again.

'I knew you still liked me,' he said, 'lasses always have a soft spot for the first lad to take them.' He cocked his head on one side, a teasing light in his eyes. 'Well, I might think about it . . .'

'It's not that, not that at all. I had to come,' Meg said flatly.

'Oh?'

'I'm going to have a bairn.'

The confident grin was wiped from Wesley's face and his jaw dropped.

'A bairn?'

The door to the front room burst open and Jane Cornish catapulted into the room like a miniature whirlwind.

'A bairn, is it? An' you're trying to make out it's our Wesley's? Well, you can be ganning. Hadaway out of my house, you impittent little hussy.' She glared her contempt at Meg, her hands on her hips and her chin thrust forward aggressively. 'You don't think I'm going to let him be taken in by the oldest trick in the world, do you? Go on, I said, out of it, before I take my broom to you.'

'Mam. Stop it. You'll do nothing of the sort,' Wesley protested, but his voice sounded unconvincing and Meg's heart sank within her.

'I won't, will I not? I'll damn' well do what I like in my own house.' Jane's voice was rising. She advanced on

183

Meg, eyes flashing and her thin nose quivering with rage. For a minute Meg thought the older woman was going to hit her.

'How do we know who you've been with?' Jane went on. 'If you went with our Wesley you've likely been with a dozen more. I bet if I was to ask around the village I'd hear some right tales about you and your goings-on, you dirty little madam. I'm not one to gossip or I'd mebbe have—'

'Mam!' Wesley stepped forward and grabbed his mother's arm, propelling her towards the door. 'I think this is for me and Meg to talk about.'

'Why, man, you're a great soft ha'pporth. You know nowt, you'll believe anything she says. She'll take you in proper all right, that sort always does.'

Meg had had enough. If she had to listen to that woman screeching at her a minute longer she would knock her down herself, and where would that get her? She pushed past them and ran down the passage and out of the front door.

'Don't you worry, Mrs Cornish,' she flung over her shoulder, 'I'm all right, I don't need you or your precious son. We'll manage on our own, me and the bairn, you wait and see.'

Once outside in the cold fresh air, she set off at a run, quite oblivious of the neighbours who had suddenly found it necessary to test the dryness of the clothes hanging on their lines. The raised voices had been heard, of course, all across the street, the walls of the cottages in the row being only a single brick's thickness.

Vaguely, Meg heard Wesley calling after her as she turned into Pasture Row, but she took no notice. All she could think of was getting home and closing the door against the rest of the world. She had never been so ashamed in her life before.

'Meg!'

184

Wesley caught up with her before she reached her own gate. He took hold of her elbow and swung her round to face him.

'Meg, Meg, don't run away from me. Don't, pet. I'll marry you, I will. I just got a bit of a shock, that's all.'

Meg raised her face to his, flushed and tear-stained. She was ready to protest hotly, she wanted to tell him to go to hell, she didn't want him to marry her as a favour. No, she didn't.

Wesley saw the protest coming and forestalled it. 'Meg, I mean it, I want to marry you,' he said quickly.

'What about your mam?' she asked bitterly. 'You're underage. If she wants she can stop you.'

'Aye, but she won't. Any road, I'm twenty-one next month, she couldn't stop me then. But I'll speak to her, I'll tell her. Listen, Meg, I'll come back with you now and we'll make plans, eh? What do you say?'

'Da's off shift, he's in bed. A strange voice always wakes him up, we can't go there.'

'Well, we have to go somewhere. It's no good going back to our house, not with the mood Mam's in. Better take a chance on waking your da. I'll tell Mam when she's calmed down a bit.'

Wesley gazed earnestly at Meg. There was no hint of teasing or male arrogance in his face now. He just wanted to do right by her, she could see.

'Yes,' she conceded. 'We'll have to be quiet, though. We'll go through to the front room, Da sleeps over the kitchen.'

She led the way into the house and the front room, thankful that she had already put up the chiffonier bed and tidied the room so that there was no hint that it was also her bedroom. There was no fire in here and the air struck chill, icy draughts coming in through the ill-fitting door which led directly to the outside.

Meg didn't feel the cold now as she pulled up a chair

185

for Wesley and sat down opposite him. No, she felt all of a lather, hot and embarrassed now she actually had to talk about her trouble to him. She pondered where to begin.

'How far do you think you're on?' asked Wesley, and he too seemed awkward and shy. He leaned forward on his chair, looking at the floor and with his hands clasped before him. Then he sat back and looked out of the window, anywhere but at Meg.

'You know how far I'm on,' she said. What was he talking about?

'Oh, aye, you're right. It must be three or four months.'

They sat quietly and, through the wall, Meg could hear Bella, chattering on to Auntie Phoebe in her high, shrill voice. Wesley cleared his throat loudly and Meg looked apprehensively at the ceiling, listening for any signs of Da waking up.

'Whisht,' she whispered.

The silence lengthened until at last Wesley broke it, speaking in a low voice. 'We'll get married.'

'Aye,' said Meg, realizing he couldn't plan any further than that, it was up to her to see to arrangements. Wesley was of that breed of miners who had everything done for them by their mothers.

'When?' she prompted him.

'We shall have to book the chapel and the minister,' he said, pleased that he had thought of it.

'No, we will not!' Meg said in her normal voice, and this time it was Wesley who looked up at the ceiling and raised his hand warningly.

'No, we won't,' she whispered. 'I don't want to be wed in our chapel, not with a thick waist and everybody sniggering at me.'

'I'd soon stop anybody sniggering,' he snapped.

Meg glared at him. That was just like him, she thought,

a bully-boy. He thought everything could be settled with his fists.

'I'm not getting wed in chapel,' she reiterated. 'We'll have to go to the register office in Auckland.'

'The register office?' Wesley sat back, shocked. 'That's not a proper wedding, not in the register office.'

'Aye, it is.' Meg nodded her head. 'We'll be wed just as much as if we were wed in chapel.'

'Me Mam won't like it,' he said gloomily.

'She's not going to like it any road. Now, we have to decide when.'

'As soon as we can, I suppose.'

'Don't be soft, Wesley,' said Meg, surprising herself at the way she was taking charge now he had agreed to the marriage. 'We haven't got anywhere to live, have we? We can't get wed 'til we know what we're going to do after, can we?'

'We'll live with me mam,' he said. 'I can only have the one house from the colliery, we'll have to live with me mam.'

Meg's heart sank. Oh, no, she didn't want to live with Wesley's mam, she didn't! 'We can live here, we can have this room.' She looked around the front room. It would do for a start and then she would be handy to see to the place for her da.

It was Wesley's turn to look impatient. 'What about me mam? If I'm not living there they might take the house off her. Why, man, we have to live with me mam.'

'What are you doing here?'

Both Wesley and Meg started guiltily. They hadn't heard anyone come in and when the door opened and there stood Jack Boy, still in his pitclothes, they were at a loss what to say.

'Our Meg?'

'Eeh, Jack Boy, is it that time? You'll have to have a

187

bit of bacon for your dinner, I haven't done anything else.'

'Never mind me dinner. I said, what's he doing here? An' in here an' all, where your bed is?' Jack Boy was glaring at her, his voice tight with rage.

'The bed's up!' she cried. 'It's not like that at all. We just had to talk about something, that's why he's here.'

'I can speak for meself, Meg,' said Wesley. Now he was over his initial surprise at Jack Boy's sudden appearance, he faced the younger boy squarely.

'Me and your Meg, we're going to get wed.'

'Aye? And who says so?' Jack Boy demanded, thrusting his chin forward aggressively. 'Meg's only eighteen, me da might have something to say about that.'

'We have to, lad,' she said quietly, blushing to the roots of her hair. She felt her brother's bitter gaze on her and wanted to die with embarrassment.

'You hacky, dirty sod!'

'Jack!'

Meg looked at Jack Boy in astonishment. She had never heard him swear in her life before. But the men were ignoring her, squaring up to each other, her brother's face red with rage, and Wesley's too.

'Why couldn't you stick to the whores in Auckland? What did you have to go getting a decent lass like our Meg into trouble for? Come outside, I'll show you what—'

'Lads! Lads!' Auntie Phoebe came running in, puffing and panting with the exertion. 'They can hear you all over the rows.'

But Jack Boy was fairly dancing with rage. Though younger than Wesley and not up to his weight, he was ready to take him on and Wesley was willing to fight too, Meg could see the angry sparkle in his eyes.

'Wesley! Take no notice of him, man, he'll come round in a minute.' She caught hold of his arm and pleaded

188

with him. And just then Jack Maddison came downstairs, his trousers pulled on over his nightshirt, braces dangling and his feet bare.

'What the hell's going on here?' he said grimly. 'Can't a man have some quiet in his own house after he's been on shift down the pit?'

There was a sudden silence. The boys and Meg didn't know what to say so it was left to Auntie Phoebe.

'Meg and Wesley Cornish here, they're wanting to get wed,' she said flatly.

Jack Maddison said nothing. He walked into the kitchen, took his clay pipe from the high mantel and lit it, using a spill of paper from the brass pot at the side by the fire. He waited until the pipe was burning to his satisfaction before turning back to them.

'Well, she cannot. She's only a bairn as yet.'

Meg and Wesley looked at one another as Jack Boy gave a short laugh.

'Bairn or no, she's having a babby herself,' he blurted out.

Jack Maddison took the pipe out of his mouth and Meg hung her head as he looked at her. She had thought she would never see any real feeling in her father's eyes, he had carried that dead look with him for so long, but just at that moment a touch of real fire showed there.

'You've shamed your mother's memory,' he stated, and tears welled up in Meg's eyes.

'Da!'

'Don't you call me Da, I'm no father of thine. Get your things and get out.'

Meg couldn't believe she was hearing it. What was Da saying? He'd never throw her out, she knew he wouldn't, he was just angry, that was all it was. Getting woken up an' all.

'Da?' she said, incredulous. She must have not heard him right.

'Jack, man,' Auntie Phoebe put in. 'Jack, they're going to get wed. Calm down man, it'll be all right.' She bit her lip anxiously. None of them could believe that Jack Maddison meant what he was saying.

'You'd better be ganning or I'll put you out, and you can whistle for your clothes,' said Jack, ignoring the older woman as he stared grimly at Meg.

'Da – this is our Meg, you can't put her out,' Jack Boy stepped forward to plead for his sister.

'Oh, I can. An' I don't want you saying her name round here neither, or you can be off yourself.'

There was a chorus of gasps and Meg turned blindly to find the straw box to pack her clothes in before remembering that Alice had it, away in Lancashire. She would have to make a bundle with her shawl. Her fingers trembled. She dropped the ends of her shawl and couldn't tie the knot properly. It came undone the first time.

'Here, I'll do it.' Wesley spoke for the first time. He was white and strained, looking more like a chastened schoolboy than a young man about to be married.

'You get out of my house. Go on, you can wait outside if you still want her, or else be off with you,' snapped Jack, and Wesley went without a word so that it was Jack Boy who secured the bundle and took it to the door for her.

'I'll try to help you, Meg,' he whispered.

She stood in the doorway and looked round at her father. She still couldn't believe this was happening. He had sat down in the rocking-chair and was staring into the fire, puffing furiously on his pipe and deliberately not looking at her.

'Jack, man!' Auntie Phoebe said again, but she might as well have saved her breath, he didn't seem to hear her.

Meg walked slowly down the yard to the back gate.

Wesley was there, standing round the corner leaning against the wall of the coal house. He looked at her sheepishly.

'Where am I going to go?' she asked helplessly, and he flushed an even deeper red than before.

'I cannot take you home. First I'll have to go and tell me mam.'

Meg nodded. Up the row a pair of housewives were standing by a yard gate, arms folded and eyes avid with curiosity as they watched the young couple.

'Go on then,' she said, and put her bundle down on the dirt of the back lane. She was past caring about getting dirt on her clothes.

She was standing there, gazing unseeingly at the wall opposite, when Auntie Phoebe came out.

'What are you going to do, lass?'

'I don't know,' answered Meg. 'Wesley's gone to ask his mam, see if I can go there.'

Auntie Phoebe eyed the two women further up the street and her expression changed from concern to truculence.

'Have you nowt better to do than gawp at folks as is in trouble?' she shouted, and the women retreated behind their own walls. They knew better than to start an argument with Phoebe Lowther. She knew all the gossip about everyone in the row and wouldn't be slow in bringing it out in defence of her family, they were well aware of that.

'Howay, pet, come in with me. We'll wait in our house, away from that lot.'

Phoebe picked up the bundle and led Meg round to her kitchen door.

'Wesley won't know where I am, though,' she protested weakly.

'Aye, he will, I'll keep an eye out for him. Any road,

191

he's likely to be a long time yet persuading his mother. If I know owt about that Jane Cornish, that is.'

Meg was filled with dread. What was she going to do if Wesley weakened and didn't wed her? What if his mam changed his mind for him?

Sixteen

'Are you going to live with me and Auntie Phoebe and Uncle Tot now?'

Bella beamed at Meg, obviously delighted at the prospect, and she had to smile back even though she felt more like crying.

'Stop asking questions, that's a good lass,' said Auntie Phoebe. 'Howay now, Bella, help me make the tea. You can peel the potatoes for me. You like to do that, don't you?'

They had waited and waited and Wesley hadn't come back. Meg had just about given up any hope that he would.

'I'll do them for you, Auntie,' she offered. 'I could do with something to do.'

'Bella likes to do them. You sit still, Meg, you've had some shocks today.' Auntie Phoebe hadn't said anything about Wesley not coming back but Meg knew the subject was lying between them and her aunt must also think he wasn't coming back.

What was she going to do? She couldn't stay here, she knew she couldn't. If she stayed here Da wouldn't have Auntie Phoebe in the house either, and then how would he and the lads manage? They needed a woman to see to things. There was Jack Boy, for instance. He'd already come in from the pit and there was no dinner for him, and Miles would be in any minute now from back shift.

193

He'd be hungry an' all. Miles was a growing lad, he was always hungry.

Meg fretted on, her mind jumping from one worry to the next. If Alice was here now, it would be all right to leave the menfolk to her, Alice was a good little housekeeper. But she was in Manchester, wasn't she? Maybe she would come home ... I'll write to her, decided Meg, I'll tell her. But Da might come in any minute, might say it was all a mistake, he wanted his Meg to come home.

'Get that down you.'

Auntie Phoebe placed a mug of tea in front of Meg, adding a spoonful of condensed milk. She sat down at the table beside her, sighing.

'What are you going to do?' she asked. 'I don't think Wesley Cornish is coming back, he's been too long.'

The sound of the words spoken aloud, the words which had been running through Meg's head for the last hour or two, seemed to make them definite.

'Can I stay here the night, Auntie? Da'll likely have calmed down by the morning.'

Auntie Phoebe looked doubtful. 'You can stay an' welcome, pet. But I don't know how you da will take it.'

Just what Meg had been thinking herself but she didn't know what else to do. She stirred her tea in the mug, round and round, round and round. This day was a nightmare, a terrible nightmare. It was almost worse than the nightmare about the candyman. This nightmare wasn't going to end, that was the worst of it, she fretted. And just then, there was a knock at the door.

'I'll go, I'll go,' cried Bella, dropping a potato into the water with a splash which marked her clean pinny. Eagerly she ran to the door. Bella loved company.

'Is Meg here?'

Her heart leaped as she turned to face the door and saw Wesley stooping under the low lintel.

194

'Eeh, Wesley, lad, we thought you weren't coming back,' said Auntie Phoebe, relief shining in her smile.

'I said I would. You didn't think I'd run away, did you?'

Wesley was speaking to Auntie Phoebe but he was looking at Meg and watching the conflicting expressions chase across her face.

'You did! You thought I wouldn't come,' he accused her, but he sounded more amused than annoyed. 'You don't trust me yet, then, do you Meg?'

'Oh, I do,' she answered swiftly. 'We knew Wes would come, didn't we, Auntie?' She looked at her aunt, daring her to deny it.

'Well, what did your mam say?' demanded Phoebe impatiently, deliberately not looking at Meg. What they'd thought didn't matter now that Wesley had come. Besides, Tot would be in from the pit soon and she wanted this settled before he came.

'You've to come along of me,' said Wesley, smiling at Meg, pleased to be relieving one of her worries at least. He did not say his mother would be happy to welcome her and Meg was fairly sure he had spent all this time using his powers of persuasion on Jane Cornish. That would be the reason he was late coming back.

'Right now?' she asked, dreading the thought of facing his mother again.

'Aye, you might as well. I've to go to work in half an hour.'

Meg's heart sank. That meant she was going to be on her own with her future mother-in-law for the rest of the afternoon and evening. But there was nothing she could do, she had to go with Wesley now.

'Don't forget, Meg, if you need me at all, I'm here, you just have to ask,' Auntie Phoebe said softly as Meg and Wesley were leaving.

'I know, Auntie, don't think I'm not grateful either,'

195

Meg answered. But in her heart she knew that her aunt was pleased that she wasn't going to have to take her in and cause more friction with the Maddisons.

Meg followed Wesley up the row and round to his house, hardly noticing the curious eyes at every window. She was too full of sorrow at leaving the house in Pasture Row where she had worked so hard to raise her brothers and sisters. And now she had to leave the lads to fend for themselves. But she would write to Alice as soon as she could, she promised herself.

I'm sorry, Mam, she cried inside. I am, I'm that sorry. For Da was right. She had failed her mother and shamed her memory an' all.

Whatever it was her son had said to Jane Cornish, it had had an effect, for she held her tongue when Meg came into the house, keeping her remarks to the bare necessities. Meg was to have the front room where there was a chiffonier bed, the twin of the one in which she had slept at home. Wesley had quickly changed into his pitclothes and picked up his bait tin and water bottle and gone off to work, leaving his womenfolk to sort themselves out. This was when Meg expected Jane to turn nasty. She was all prepared for it, determined the older woman would not upset her any more than she already had been that day.

'Poor lad,' Jane remarked to the air somewhere over Meg's head, after the door closed behind Wesley. 'How's he supposed to get through a shift at the coal face after a day like the day, I don't know. He'll be needing pit props to hold his eyelids open.' But she spoke mildly enough as she took up her knitting and sat down before the fire in the kitchen, working furiously away on a woollen sock. Meg watched her for a minute or two then awkwardly sat down on a hard wooden chair at the table.

'We'll have a bite of tea just now,' said Jane casually,

not even looking up from her knitting. 'I've got a knuckle of bacon and some taties left off Wesley's dinner. I'll fry them up with a bit of onion.'

Meg could only blink her eyes in surprise at the change in Jane. What had Wesley said to his mother to cause this complete about face?

In the following days, spent in a kind of limbo as she waited for the wedding date to arrive, Meg began to realize that the change in her future mother-in-law was only on the surface. Jane didn't seem able to stop herself from letting the odd acid remark escape her lips, and sometimes Meg would turn unexpectedly and see a malevolent glare directed at her, swiftly veiled as she caught Meg's eye.

'What did you say to your mother to make her change her mind about me?' Meg ventured to Wesley one Sunday morning when Jane had gone to chapel.

Meg herself had not attended any chapel service since she'd left Pasture Row. Oh, she told herself she would go back as soon as she was decently married, but just now, no, she couldn't face the sly glances and whispers of the other girls.

'Nowt. Well, not much any road,' said Wesley. He was sitting in his shirt-sleeves, unshaven and collarless, his feet, clad only in a pair of the woollen socks knitted by his mother, stretched along the length of the steel fender. He saw Meg's disbelief and qualified his answer. 'Aye, all right, but I didn't say much.' He grinned impishly at her. 'Well, I did say I was getting wed no matter what she thought, and as I could only get one house from the colliery, where was she going to live if she wouldn't have you in the same house as her?'

Meg gasped at the cruelty of it and for the first time felt some sympathy for Wesley's widowed mother. No wonder she was bitter. But Wesley didn't appear to see

197

it like that at all, he seemed to be amused by his mother's discomfiture.

Meg thought of her own family, Da and Jack Boy and Miles. None of them had been to see her though every day she expected a message at least. She sent a note round by Auntie Phoebe when she saw her in the store, telling them the date of the wedding. But there was no answering word from them. There was a hole in her life now. She woke at midnight every night, the time when she should have been calling Jack Boy ready to go on fore shift. Every day she fretted about whether they were getting a proper dinner.

One Saturday morning she managed to catch Miles as he left the pit yard with his marras, and asked how Da was, and Jack Boy, and were they eating properly. But Miles was embarrassed in front of his mates and anxious to get away to his quoits game. The local collieries competed with each other on Saturday afternoons and Miles was emerging as a champion player.

'Aw, go on, our Meg, you didn't think we'd starve just 'cos you're not there, did you?' was all he would say.

She wrote to Alice in Salford, asking her to come home, and had a reply by the next post.

'I'm sick of it here any road,' wrote Alice, 'but I have to work a month's notice. Mrs Rutherford treats me like a skivvy and the lasses round here think they're something better than us from Durham just because they work in a mill. Dirty stinking places they are too! And Jane Thompson is walking out with a lad now, so I've no one to go out with on my afternoon off.'

Meg had not told Alice about the baby, just that she was getting married. Plenty of time for explanations when her sister came home, she thought.

It was with a full heart that Meg set out with Wesley and his friend for Bishop Auckland on the morning of her wedding. It was already December and the wind bitingly cold as they walked along the road leading into the little town, so that they turned off on to the path through Badger Wood which was a short cut to the west of the town, grateful for the relief the trees and bushes afforded them. Above them they could hear the wind soughing through the bare branches of the trees and the cold became damp and penetrating. Meg shivered.

'Cheer up, lass,' said Wesley. 'It's a wedding we're going to, not a funeral.' He winked at his best marra, Dick Adamson, who grinned back. Dick had been prevailed upon to 'stand up' for them at the register office. Jane had refused to come, making the excuse that she would have a bit of tea ready for them when they came back.

Wesley looked uncomfortable in his Sunday suit and a high white starched collar which cut into his neck. Every few steps he would poke a finger down the front of it and try to ease it away from the red mark which was appearing on his skin.

Meg was wearing a deep blue serge costume with a long jacket which buttoned up to the neck. Wesley had insisted on spending most of his meagre savings on it.

'It's a waste, Wesley,' she had protested when he had taken her into Auckland to buy the outfit. 'We'll need things for the baby more like.'

'Don't be daft, Meg. You want to look nice, don't you?' he had brushed aside her objections. Jane had sniffed and looked more miserable than ever.

'There'll be no luck for you both, not with him seeing the dress before the wedding day,' had been her only comment.

The loose jacket covered Meg's burgeoning pregnancy, though, and she was glad of that as she walked alongside Wesley and Dick.

As they left the wood and turned towards the Cockton

Hill end of town, Meg's depression deepened. They were getting closer and closer to the register office and panic began to rise in her.

Why was she marrying Wesley Cornish? She would have managed on her own once the baby was born. She was strong, she could work and look after it. And yet here she was, tying herself to a man she didn't love, a man who had forced her. For that was what he had done even though she had gone out for the walk with him willingly enough. She peeped up at him as he lifted his chin yet again and pulled his collar away from his neck with his forefinger. He was a stranger to her, even though she had known him for years. For a minute Meg considered turning tail and running as far away from him as she could. But just then the child inside her, perhaps responding to the unrest she was feeling, turned in her womb and kicked heavily at her lower ribs. A strong, lusty kick; a kick which reminded her that the baby was innocent, it was she who had got into this mess and she owed the child a decent start to life, no matter what.

'It'll likely snow soon,' observed Dick as they came over the railway bridge by the station and walked along the dirt road to the stone building which housed the register office. And as if in response a few white flakes fell on to the front of Meg's costume, gleaming against the deep blue. She watched them dumbly as they melted and the soft whiteness became simply damp black patches.

No one was waiting by the gate of the register office and no one was in the doorway either. Secretly, Meg had hoped that her brothers would come and maybe Auntie Phoebe would bring Bella. She desperately wanted some of her own family round her. Now her hopes were dashed. Of course, they wouldn't want to upset Da, that was it. With a feeling of inevitability she followed the men into the building, not even looking at the group huddled in the far corner of the entrance hall round a smoking fire.

'Why, Meg, are you not even going to speak to us?'

The voice, so like her own, made her jerk her head up in disbelief. Alice? And it was, it was Alice, looking older and thinner and with her hair up on top of her head and buttoned boots on her feet, but it was Alice all the same coming towards her with outstretched hands and a beaming smile on her face. And behind Alice there was Auntie Phoebe and Uncle Tot and Bella, with a bright pink ribbon in her hair. And Meg went forward and into Alice's arms and sobbed on her shoulder.

'Hey, man, our Meg, what are you blubbing for?' Alice was saying as she kissed her and held her away. 'Let's have a look at you then. Eeh, what a lovely costume. It suits you it does, Mag. Now, howay, pull yourself together, man, you don't want to get wed with your eyes all red, do you?'

And Bella was dancing up and down and laughing because of the success of their surprise, and Auntie Phoebe and Uncle Tot were crowding round her, and Uncle Tot offered his red spotted handkerchief for her to dry her eyes and Alice a comb to tidy her hair.

Wesley and Dick stood to one side watching. Wesley was frowning. But for the moment Meg had forgotten her bridegroom altogether. Until, that is, someone came to call them and they were ushered into the presence of the registrar.

The actual ceremony, brief and formal, was over in minutes. They made their vows, Wesley put the ring on her finger, and it was over. It almost seemed like an irrelevance to Meg as she found herself back outside clutching her certificate with the snow coming down in earnest now and already lying on the path to the gate and speckling the low hedge. A lone urchin was hanging

201

hopefully about outside the gate. He must have been the only one to notice them.

'Shabby wedding!' he called, and Uncle Tot threw him a penny. It was a poor parody of the traditional 'hoy out' of coppers to local children.

'We're hired a trap, Meg, are you coming back with us? All of you, I mean, Dick an' all?' asked Uncle Tot.

'Aye, I thought I'd do a few pies and things. You can't have a wedding without a bit of celebration,' said Auntie Phoebe. But Wesley stepped forward and took Meg's arm.

'Nay, I'm sorry, Mrs Lowther,' he said, drawing Meg away from the family group, 'me mam's made us a bite and we have to get back.'

'Wesley!'

She was shaken out of her happiness at seeing Alice again and talking to her own folk. But Wesley was firm.

'And there's not really room for us all on the trap, is there? No, me and Meg and Dick, we'll go back the way we came. Me mam'll be waiting.'

'But it's snowing, you'll get wet,' Uncle Tot objected. Wesley ignored him. His grip on Meg's arm was like steel. She was pulled away, leaving Auntie Phoebe and the others staring open-mouthed after them.

'I'll come and see you the morn,' Alice called after her, and Meg only had time to nod before she was swept round the corner and down on to the entrance of the path which led back to Badger Wood.

'What did you do that for?' she demanded. 'I want to go back with them, I wanted to have a talk with Alice . . .'

'You're wed to me, now,' said Wesley gruffly. 'I'm your family now. Didn't your da show you he didn't want you near?'

'But—'

'Now you're my wife, you'll have more pride than to go round there.'

202

Meg stopped protesting, she could see she was getting nowhere. Through her sudden tears, she saw Dick Adamson redden with embarrassment and slow down, letting them get well ahead of him on their walk home through the snow. He must think it was a queer sort of a wedding, she thought miserably.

It took them almost an hour to walk back to Winton Colliery. By the time they got to George Row the snow was falling fast, blanketing everything and swirling round their heads so that their ears and noses were blue with cold. Meg's skirt was drenched up to mid-thigh and the weight of it dragged against her every step. She would never be able to get it back into shape, she mused. She would be lucky if it didn't shrink.

The welcome inside the house was almost as cold as the weather outside. The kitchen fire was low, the kettle not singing on the hob, and there was no sign of any meal ready for their return.

'I was going to go up to the store and get something,' said Jane Cornish, 'but the weather was so bad, I knew you wouldn't want me to go out in it, son. And any road, Meg can soon make you something now, it's her place to.'

Seventeen

Meg eased herself out of the bed she shared with Wesley, her usually deft movements slowed and awkward because of her advanced pregnancy. Wesley moved restlessly and she paused, looking apprehensively at his bulk under the blankets. But he turned over on to his side and slept on, for which she was thankful. If he had woken he would have insisted that she got back into bed with him. Sometimes she thought his appetite for the sexual act was insatiable.

Quietly, she pulled on her clothes, shivering in the icy cold air of the bedroom. Picking up her boots, she tip-toed down the stairs to the kitchen before sitting down and putting them on. She grimaced slightly and gingerly felt her left breast, feeling the imprint of Wesley's fingers on a place which had already been sore.

He was on night shift, the shift which went down from three in the afternoon until twelve midnight, but he had gone for a beer with his marras afterwards and hadn't come home 'til three o'clock in the morning, falling heavily into bed beside her and demanding his rights.

'No, Wesley,' she had protested. 'The babby, man. It's almost due, you'll hurt it.'

'Hadaway wi' you,' was all that Wesley had answered. And the baby had kicked and turned as he climbed on top of her, almost as if it was fighting back.

Meg sighed as she thought of it. The baby was quiet now at least. She picked up the iron coal rake from the hearth and raked away at the ash in the grate, looking to see if there was any life left in the fire. One or two cinders glowed and sparked and she drew them to one side and laid thin shavings of wood on top of them. There were sticks chopped from the ends cut off pit props in the bottom of the oven drying out, and she criss-crossed these across the shavings. She soon had these alight, and after pulling down coal from the fire back, put up the tin blazer, standing back in satisfaction as the flames roared up the chimney.

Jane had come into the room as Meg was settling the kettle on the coals. She had a shawl wound tightly round her thin frame. Her bony shoulders jutted out through the wool.

'You're late with the tea this morning,' she grumbled by way of a greeting.

'It won't be a minute,' answered Meg, 'the kettle's singing already.' She moved away from the fire, giving place to her mother-in-law. Jane Cornish hadn't been well since Christmas. What had started off as a feverish cold had settled into a racking cough which plagued her day and night.

'How are you feeling the day?' Meg asked as she got out the loaf and cut slices from it.

'None the better for you asking,' snapped Jane peevishly, but Meg took no notice, she was used to it by now. She stuck a slice of bread on the end of a toasting fork and handed it to Jane to hold against the bars of the grate. But a sudden bout of coughing made the older woman shake so much, the bread fell from the fork into the still unemptied ash box.

Meg rushed to pick it out, but it was no good, it was smeared with coal dust beside ash. They could ill afford any waste, she thought distractedly, not since the pit was put on a four-day week last month and the hewers had to take a five per cent reduction in pay besides.

The thought was only fleeting, however, Jane's coughing fit was not easing at all. Meg put an arm round the painfully thin shoulders, holding her steady, supporting her as the spasms rocked her.

'I'll get the doctor today,' she said. 'You're not getting any better.'

'No,' gasped Jane, 'just get me a bottle from the chemist's. I'll be all right once I get a cup of tea.' And indeed the spasms were lessening as she struggled to control them.

Meg poured a cup for her and she grasped it in both hands, drinking it down hot and sweet. Sitting at the table, Meg ate her own slice of bread and dripping and sipped at her tea. She watched her mother-in-law surreptitiously. Jane definitely looked worse. There was a hectic flush of red on her cheeks, and a pulse in her neck throbbed plain to see. But the cough was quiet for the moment. Maybe the warm air which was now filling the kitchen was doing some good.

Meg's mind wandered back over the few months of her marriage. At the beginning she had thought that it was Jane she had to beware of, Jane who would make her life difficult. Wesley was the one who would defend her, watch out for her. The reality had been different.

Jane, as her illness progressed, had lost most of her former antagonism. Oh, sometimes she was waspish and flashes of her old self would show through, but on the whole she was pathetically dependent on Meg who had taken over all the housekeeping. Jane's sudden decline worried Meg who wished she could talk it over with someone. But there was only Wesley, and he'd soon lost interest in talking of his mother's ills.

All he was interested in were his marras and drinking beer. And bed. Oh, yes, when he did finally come home, he was always interested in mauling her in bed, and that's all it was, you couldn't call it love. Meg had got into the habit of trying to keep her mind free and independent of what was happening to her body when Wesley took it. It was a question of survival.

Meg moved uncomfortably. There was an ache in her lower back today which was steadily becoming more insistent. She sipped her tea, feeling the warmth of it coursing down her throat. Here it was almost the end of March and still there was snow in the hedgebacks and ice in the buckets. The tap on the end of the row was usually frozen up and it was midday before she could refill the buckets.

Alice now, Alice was her lifeline, calling in to see her on her way to the store, giving her news of Da and the lads. But she always had to come when Wesley was out of the way, either down the pit or safely asleep in bed. He didn't like Alice coming, had taken against all of Meg's family.

A spasm of coughing began to shake Jane and she leant forward and put her cup down on the fender, gasping and coughing and straining for air as badly as any pitman with the dust disease. The older woman was swaying in her chair and Meg jumped up in alarm just in time to catch her as she toppled forward, her mouth a gaping hole in her drawn blue face.

'Wesley! Wesley!' Meg shouted, feeling her arms were being torn out of their sockets by the unexpected dead weight of the unconscious Jane. She fought to get her over to the settle by the wall, dragging her along the floor, up the proddy mat and tripping over it herself so that it took a superhuman effort to save herself from going down with Jane. Meg screamed in despair. Was Wesley never going to hear?

'Eeh, what's the matter, Meg? Is it the babby?'

It was not Wesley who came but Mrs Bates, the young wife from next-door. A woman as skinny as Jane, nevertheless she sized up the situation at once and helped Meg lift her mother-in-law on to the settle, propping her up against the hard horsehair-covered end where she promptly slithered down again, head lolling and eyes wide open.

'Go and get Wesley, Meg,' Dolly Bates said quietly. 'I think she's gone, pet.'

Meg had to climb the stairs to the bedroom to rouse him. He had slept serenely on through all the commotion. She even had to shake his shoulder before he lifted his head, grumbling loudly.

'What the hell's the matter with you? Can you not leave a man alone when he has to go on shift in a few hours?'

'It's your mam, Wes, your mam. She's . . .' Meg halted, hardly knowing how to say it.

'Me mam's what? Have you two been fighting, like? Can you not hold your peace between the two of you?'

'She's passed out, Wes, I think she's dead,' Meg blurted. 'You'll have to get up and fetch the doctor.' She watched him jump out of bed and pull on his trousers, the ache in her back deepening to a cramping pain which travelled down her thighs and threatened to cut her in half. Gasping, she collapsed on to the bed so recently vacated by her husband.

'Dolly!' she cried.

'Pneumonia,' declared Doctor Brown, 'aggravated by malnutrition. Her heart failed too, couldn't stand the strain.'

'She was fed, there's food in the house.' Wesley glared at the doctor. How dare he say his mother hadn't had enough to eat?

'Hmm. Well, she hadn't been feeding herself properly then,' said Doctor Brown, and snapped his Gladstone bag firmly shut. 'If you come up to the surgery I'll give you the death certificate. You'll be wanting it for the insurance.' He did not ask why he had not been called earlier. He knew the answer. There was talk in the village of the miners clubbing together to pay a doctor to see to them and their families, but nothing had come of it yet. He looked hard at the young miner. On his own with his dead mother, Wesley looked very young and vulnerable, unsure what to do.

'You can see to the undertaker at the same time,' the doctor prompted, then gave a puzzled frown. 'Is there not a neighbour to come in to lay – to see to your mother?'

Wesley was spared the need to answer this as a piercing scream rang out from the bedroom upstairs. Doctor Brown lifted startled eyes to the floor above.

'The wife,' said Wesley, dully. 'She's started the bairn.'

'I'll go up and see her.' The doctor walked towards the staircase.

'Aw, no, you won't,' Wesley sprang in front of him, his vulnerable expression disappearing. 'She doesn't need a doctor. The midwife's coming and she has Dolly Bates up there with her.'

'If it's the money you're worried about, I won't send a bill,' protested Doctor Brown, sounding frustrated. 'You have enough to think about now, let me see to your wife.'

'No.' Wesley stuck out his chin. 'What does she want with a man there? I tell you, the midwife is coming and Dolly can manage 'til she does. Meg'll be fine.'

'But—'

'I've told you. What do you want to be messing about with women for? It's not decent. Well, you're not going to mess with my woman, I'm telling you. Now, I'll be up for the death certificate as soon as the babby comes.'

Doctor Brown had no choice but to leave, cursing the ignorance of the pitmen as he went, the cries from upstairs, though muffled now, ringing in his ears.

Thomas Cornish, named for his mother's Uncle Tot, was born two days later, 28 March 1893, after a long and protracted labour. The midwife, a superstitious old woman who was sure the trouble was caused because there was a corpse in the house, could do little to help. She had a long-standing feud with the doctor but even she had been about to give up and insist on his coming.

Not that she would have persuaded Wesley, Meg thought, when she was again capable of rational thinking. Wesley knew perfectly well that women didn't need doctors to have babies. He'd told her so. Hadn't they been born for centuries without doctors? Doctors were just carnal men who liked to get their hands on other men's women. Wesley confidently asserted this as fact. Hadn't other miners told him so?

In the end the baby came in a rush, bawling his defiance at being expelled from the warm security of the womb even before the midwife held him up by the heels to clear his lungs. She wrapped him in a bit of flannel and showed him to Meg who was lying so exhausted she could hardly open her eyes long enough to see him. She had a brief impression of a mop of coppery hair and a bloodstained face, twisted up in rage, before sinking into a deep, healing sleep.

'I told you Meg didn't need a doctor,' said Wesley smugly when Dolly showed him his son, freshly bathed and only his red face showing between his flannel cap and shawl. 'He's a bit little like, isn't he?'

'He's a grand bairn,' declared Dolly Bates. 'Now, I'll leave him in his cradle. You'll have to keep an eye to him and his mam, I've to go and see to me own.'

'Me?' Wesley was alarmed. 'I cannot do nothing, man, I don't know what to do. Any road, I'm going on shift soon.'

'You're not going on shift the day, Wes. It's a four-day week, man, you've finished for the week.'

He had the grace to look sheepish. 'Oh, aye, I forgot,' he muttered. 'Can you not take the bairn upstairs to Meg? She'll see to him.'

Dolly had no choice in the end, she had to do just that, and when she returned downstairs, Wesley had taken off. She shook her head. Well, she'd done her best. Now she had to get back to her own bairns, even if it did mean leaving Meg lying upstairs with the baby and that poor dead woman in the coffin in the front room. Maybe she would call in to see the wife in the door next but one. She was getting on a bit but she was a canny body, and would likely give a hand if she was asked.

'Meg?'

Dolly Bates smiled her relief as the door opened and there was Meg's sister. She wouldn't have to bother anybody else now.

'By, Alice, I'm that glad to see you,' she said. 'Did you not hear that Wesley's mother had gone and Meg's babby had come? It's been two days since it all started. I thought the news would be all over the rows long since. It's the funeral on Monday.'

Alice's mouth dropped open. 'Eeh, no, I didn't know about the baby, Mrs Bates. I've been washing and cleaning all day, I haven't seen a soul.'

'It's a wonder if that auntie of yours doesn't know about it,' commented Dolly, rather sharply. 'Phoebe Lowther's name for being the first with any news is being dented a bit here like, isn't it? And you would think that young lass upstairs would have her family looking out for her at a time like this an' all. Not that I mind lending a hand, but I have to see to my own now.'

'Aye, Mrs Bates, of course.' Alice bit her lip and blushed. 'Auntie Phoebe's badly like, she's in bed with a cold on her chest, and what with seeing to her an' all, you know what it's like. Is Meg upstairs then? You go on home, I'll check on her.'

'Aye, that's right. And don't forget her in the front room.'

Dolly nodded her head in the direction of the connecting door.

'No, I won't. Thank you, Mrs Bates. Thank you for all you've done.'

Alice was dying to ask where Wesley was. She had indeed heard that Jane Cornish had died but hadn't dared come over to George Row to see her sister. Wesley could be so nasty and she just knew he took it out on Meg afterwards if he knew she'd had any family round to see her. Usually the sisters met up at the store if he was about.

Mrs Bates finally got off home and Alice raced up the stairs.

'Eeh, Meg, I'm sorry, pet, I didn't know, I didn't. And with Auntie Phoebe being poorly . . .' She broke off when she saw Meg's usually rosy face so pale and wan on the pillow.

'Are you all right?' she asked tentatively. Alice was only fourteen and a half and was awed at the sight of her sister laid so low. A sharp cry came from the bundle in Meg's arms and Alice gave it an anxious glance.

Meg smiled. 'Aye, I'm fine, just a bit tired, you know? Howay, come and have a look at your new nephew.'

Alice moved over to the bed and gazed down at the baby's face. She didn't know what to say. It was red and angry-looking and one fist had escaped the flannel wrapping and was waving in the air furiously. He opened his eyes wide and his mouth even wider and bawled loud and long. Alice stepped back in surprise. She could remember Bella as a baby, but surely Bella hadn't made a noise like that?

'He's grand,' she said politely, gingerly pulling the shawl further down so that the baby's fist waved freely in the air. 'A bit noisy, like. Is he hungry?'

Meg laughed fondly. 'We'll have to find out, eh, Alice?'

She unbuttoned the front of her nightgown and offered the baby the breast. He groped about blindly, his mouth wide open, but with a little guidance from his mother finally managed to get the nipple into his mouth, and at last the crying stopped. Alice was fascinated. She came closer to see better.

'Eeh, Meg, what's that mark? Have you bumped it?'

Meg flushed and swiftly drew the sheet over the tell-tale mark on the side of her swollen breast. The finger marks from the night before had almost merged into one now purpling bruise.

'It's nothing,' she mumbled, 'I fell against the bed post.'

Alice looked puzzled but let it go at that. She watched mother and baby quietly for a while.

'He's a bit greedy, isn't he?'

'A good trencherman, like his da,' Meg answered. She was tiring again, her eyelids already drooping in sleep. 'I wonder where Wesley is?'

'He had to go out, Mrs Bates said. Do you want me to do anything, Meg? I can get some tea ready for Wesley, and when you've finished I'll settle Thomas in his cradle so you can get some sleep. I have time, Da's on shift and I've done the tea for the lads.'

'Could you, Alice? I'd be grateful. I did think I'd be all right with Wesley's mam living here, but now . . . Look, if you get it ready, I'm sure Dolly Bates will give it to him.'

Alice frowned. It was the funeral in a couple of days and that would be a lot of extra work and Meg should stay in bed. And it wasn't fair to expect Mrs Bates to do everything. But there was Da, and Wesley an' all, he didn't like her in the house. Still, she had to do something.

'I'll wait and see Wesley, Meg,' she said decisively, sounding more like an old woman than a young girl.

But Meg didn't answer. She had fallen asleep, the baby too. The nipple had slipped out of the baby's mouth and his little fist had stopped waving about in the air and was still. Carefully, Alice picked him up so as not to disturb her exhausted sister and placed him in his wooden rocking cradle.

'Thomas Tucker, that's who you are,' she whispered, before turning back to the bed and covering Meg. She began to tiptoe to the door and then thought again; turning back, she picked up the cradle and carried it down the stairs to the kitchen. If he woke up he was less likely to disturb Meg there.

Downstairs, Alice raked fresh coal on to the fire and filled the water buckets from the tap at the end of the row. Then she sorted through the provisions Meg had in the pantry. There was some stock from boiled bacon and a few scraps of meat on a bone. Soon she had a pan of broth thickened with vegetables bubbling on the fire.

The baby stirred, snuffling and opening his mouth ready to cry, but he quietened down when Alice gently rocked the cradle with her foot.

'Whisht, babby. Whisht, babby,' she crooned, as she had seen Meg do with Miles and Bella. Then she lit the lamp and sat down on the rocking-chair by the fire to wait for Wesley. Not once did she look at the connecting door between the kitchen and the front room wherein lay the body of Jane Cornish. It was getting dark and the row was quiet and Alice felt that if she resolutely refused to acknowledge there was a body there, no ghosts would walk.

'What the hell are you doing here?' demanded Wesley as he banged the outside door shut behind him. Truculently he strode across the kitchen and glared at

214

Alice. But she was not going to be intimidated, not this time.

'Somebody had to see to Meg and the bairn while you were gallivanting,' she replied with some spirit. The baby stirred and she put her foot back on the rocker, moving it up and down gently.

'Well, I never asked you to come, did I? Where's Dolly Bates, then?'

'She's her own family to see to, hasn't she?' Alice puffed her lips out in disgust as she caught a whiff of beery breath. 'Do you not want this broth then, since I made it?'

Wesley peered in the pan. 'We can't let good food go to waste,' he conceded, almost as if he were doing her a favour.

Alice took the pan from the fire and spooned some into the bowl she had ready. She brought the loaf from the pantry and cut a couple of slices. After a moment, Wesley sat at the table and began eating. She watched him, wondering how on earth Meg could have got mixed up with such a lad. Seeing her sister in this pickle was enough to put Alice off men for life. She would make sure it didn't happen to her, she surely would.

'Meg's sleeping now, she'll feel better after a good sleep,' Alice said dryly for a moment. 'I'm sure you must have been worried.'

'Eh?'

Wesley looked up in surprise, his spoon halfway to his mouth.

'Well, have you been up to see her yet?'

'I've been busy, haven't I?' He jerked his head in the direction of the front room. 'I had to see the minister.'

'Oh, aye,' said Alice, her tone a copy of Auntie Phoebe's when she was censoring a man. 'An' of course you had to pass the Black Boy on your way?'

215

'What business is it of yours what I do?' demanded Wesley, his face purpling.

'Somebody has to see to your wife and bairn,' retorted Alice, unintimidated.

For a minute she thought Wesley would get out of his chair and hit her. She even stepped back a pace. But though he gave her a ferocious look, he ate another spoonful of broth before he spoke.

'You're an impittent bit of a lass, aren't you? You want to watch your tongue, you do.'

'And another thing,' Alice was emboldened to say, 'You'll have to get someone in to help for a few days. I'll do what I can and so will Mrs Bates, I daresay, but you'll have to get someone else, especially on the day of the funeral. Now I'll have to leave you to it, I have the lads to see to.'

She wrapped her shawl round her shoulders and walked to the door. Wesley watched her, saying nothing. He couldn't think of anything to say. For the first time in his life he had to make domestic decisions himself and he just didn't know what to do.

In the cradle at his feet the baby stirred, whimpering softly at first but soon setting up such a screaming that Wesley was convinced there must be something seriously wrong. Gingerly, he bent down and picked up the cradle, placing it on the table by his supper things. He rocked it with one hand, peering under the blanket at the red face all twisted up with rage. With some hesitation, he caught hold of the tiny, tightly closed fist waving in the air.

'Now then, little 'un, what's up?' he mumbled, but the squalling continued unabated. Panic-stricken, Wesley moved the blanket and picked up the flannel-wrapped bundle. He felt stiff and awkward and didn't know what else to do when the baby went on crying. He was just

216

considering knocking on the wall for Mrs Bates when he heard Meg's voice, weakly calling down the stairs.

'Fetch him here to his mam, Alice,' she called, and with some relief Wesley made for the stairs with the decidedly damp and howling baby.

'You're back, then,' Meg commented as she held out her arms and took the child. She eased herself up against the pillows and proceeded to take off the wet clout wound round Thomas's bottom. 'Howay, then, fetch us a clean clout from the dresser.'

Wesley did as he was told and then stood silently by as Meg made the baby comfortable before opening her nightdress and offering him her breast. With the baby quiet now apart from an occasional snuffle, Meg looked up at her husband.

'How're you managing, lad?'

Wesley shuffled his feet. 'I'm all right. I've seen to the undertaker and the minister. Dolly's been good an' all.'

'Did she get you some tea?'

Wesley shuffled his feet. 'No, it was Alice. And an impittent bit she is an' all! She made us some broth, like.'

'She's all right, our Alice. It's a wonder she comes near after the way you speak to her. You want to think. I'll need somebody now your mam's gone, for a few days, any road.'

Wesley opened his mouth to argue but thought better of it and sat down on the bed beside her instead. He gazed at his son, so firmly attached to Meg's breast.

'He's a proper little Tommy Tucker, isn't he?' he said softly and grinned at Meg. She looked from him to the baby and back to Wesley, her eyes full of wonder and love. And for the first time in their short courtship and marriage, they were at one with each other. Wesley reached out one finger and stroked the baby's cheek. He nodded his head with satisfaction.

'I did well there, didn't I? he said. 'He's a grand babby.'

Eighteen

Meg glanced at her reflection in the overmantel mirror, smiling in satisfaction as she noted her waist, slim once again after so many months. Why, it was almost two years. She looked down at Tucker who was cautiously standing on her feet and hanging on to his mother's skirts to steady his perilous swaying. Bending down, she picked him up and swung him in the air, laughing and chuckling along with him.

'Mam, mam, mam,' he crowed, his hazel eyes, so like Wesley's, shining with excitement.

'Howay, me lad, we're off for a walk, and blow the work,' she said. The sun was streaming in the front room window, and though it was February there was an unseasonable warmth in the air, a touch of spring.

'Now,' said Meg, putting Tucker down on the clippie mat, 'you sit there, pet robin, while I get your little brother ready.' Tucker frowned and his bottom lip stuck out pettishly in his rosy, chubby face, but he didn't protest.

Meg lifted the new baby from the cot. He was not yet a month old but already she could see the difference in personality between her two sons. Robert cried little, slept most of the time, and didn't even protest when he was bathed.

The past few months had been tranquil enough for Meg, Robert's birth had been easy and swift, and even Wesley had been more considerate to her. She hummed as she changed the baby's clout and dressed him in the little woollen shawl Auntie Phoebe had knitted for him. Her aunt often came to see her now, and Alice too, though Meg's heart ached for Da and the lads who still kept away. Da didn't even want to see his grandsons. When Meg had met him by accident in the village one day, he had walked past her, not even looking at her or little Tucker who was with her. And that night, with Wesley away down the pit on shift so that she had the bed to herself, Meg had wept into her pillow for her father.

But today Wesley was on back shift, he would be out the whole day, and she was going to have a holiday while the weather was nice. Robert had been christened last Sunday and she herself had been churched, so at last she was considered fit to go out and about and into other people's houses. She and Alice and the babies were going to Bishop Auckland on the carrier's cart. It was Thursday, market day in Auckland, and even though they didn't have much money to spend, they could look round the stalls and walk in the Bishop's Park. It cost nothing to look any road, she thought.

Alice came at last, breathless and laughing, her fair hair tied back with a ribbon the same blue as her eyes and a large new shawl round her shoulders, the better to carry a baby.

'Are we ready then?'

Alice swung Tucker up in her arms and wrapped him in her shawl so that her shoulders took some of the weight from her arms. Tucker beamed. He was a little angel when things were going right for him, and he loved outings.

Trouble was, he was a little devil when he was thwarted, Meg thought ruefully as she watched him with his young aunt. She frowned for a moment. Alice was under five foot as yet, was Tucker too heavy for her? She reminded Meg of their mother. She resembled Hannah and was not so strong as Meg herself.

'Here, you take Robert, I'll take Tucker, I can manage him better,' said Meg.

219

'No, man, I'll be fine with Tucker. It's you who should be careful, I'm strong enough. We're not walking to Auckland, after all.' Alice was adamant and Meg let her have her way. After all, they could change over later if she got tired. They trooped out of the house and up to the end of the row, stopping at intervals for the neighbours to admire Robert.

Even though it was Thursday, a market day in Auckland but a working day all the same, the little town was bustling with people, most of them wending their way down to the market place. There were miners' wives, a few men who were off-shift, along with farmers and local townspeople. Meg and Alice wandered happily down Newgate Street, looking in shop windows and marvelling at the splendid new buildings being added on to the Bishop Auckland Cooperative Society headquarters.

After a while they exchanged babies to relieve the load on Alice's arms. A cool wind sprang up and was channelled by the tall buildings on either side of the street which ran straight as a die all the way to Cockton Hill, being built over an ancient Roman road. But Meg hardly felt the chill, she was so busy looking at everything around her: the goods in the shop windows and stacked on the pavement, the traffic on the road. There were carts and traps and men riding horses, and on the corner of Newgate Street and Bondgate, a horse bus in from Stanhope.

The two sisters enjoyed wandering round the market stalls. Meg bought some cod from a fishwife from Shields, a nice easy meal for Wesley's tea. But the clock on the castle gates was moving towards midday. They had to find somewhere to feed the babies. The morning was speeding by.

'Let's not go in the park, let's go down by the Wear,'

suggested Alice. So they bought tuppenny pies and a bottle of ginger beer and walked down Wear Chare to find a spot sheltered from the wind but still in the sun.

There was no one about, even Jock's Row looked deserted, and Meg could feed her babies and herself in peace.

'By, it's grand, isn't it?' she said, smiling as she watched Alice feeding Tucker with pieces of meat and pastry while he clamoured greedily for more. Gravy was running down his chin and Alice wiped it away with a bit of pastry before popping it into his mouth. He chewed noisily with the six teeth he had so far.

Robert was sucking comfortably with Meg's shawl drawn discreetly over him. Meg herself bit deep into a pie, relishing the rich meatiness of it. When Robert had had his fill, she took up Tucker and he finished his meal at her breast.

Alice laid Robert by his mother and stood up. 'I'll just have a walk along to Jock's Bridge,' she said, 'then I suppose we'll have to be going back to catch the carrier.'

'Aye, go on then,' said Meg, watching her sister strolling along by the river. The sun sparkled on the peaty brown water and the air was lovely and fresh after Winton Colliery where it was so often filled with fumes from the gas ovens. Little Tucker had fallen asleep at her breast and Meg gently moved him so that she could refasten her dress.

She looked down at the peaceful Robert. He was growing now. Soon she would have to wean Tucker, for Robert would need all her milk, she mused. It would be nice if there were a few months' breathing space before she had another baby, but there was nothing she could do about that short of locking Wesley out of her bedroom. And that wouldn't be an easy thing to do! She chuckled to herself at the thought.

'Look what I found – snowdrops!' cried Alice as she

221

came running back holding out a tiny bouquet. 'Aren't they bonny?'

'Oh, aye, they are.' Meg smiled in delight at the pure white flowers against the dark green of the leaves. 'They're real bonny, Alice.' But quick as a flash, Tucker had woken up and was grabbing at the flowers, crushing them in his tiny fists before Alice had a chance to draw them away from him.

'Tucker!' she cried, but it was too late. The flower heads lay bruised and broken on the grass. 'Tucker, you've spoilt them now, haven't you?'

'Ma-am!' he wailed. Seeing both his aunt and his mother annoyed with him, he stuck out his bottom lip and took a deep breath preparing to scream at the top of his lungs. The peace of the day was shattered. It took them ten minutes to pacify Tucker and then it was time to climb the steep bank into town to meet the carrier.

'Did you enjoy the look out?' asked Alice as they jogged along in the cart, both babies sleeping like cherubs.

'It was grand,' declared Meg, 'I wouldn't have got out but for you, Alice, and I'm grateful, I am.'

'I've enjoyed it an' all.'

Just then Meg's attention was caught by two men standing by a farm gate, one obviously a farmer. The other was tall and dark-haired. He wore shabby riding clothes but there was something in the set of his shoulders and the way the older man was talking to him which set him apart as a gentleman. He turned to watch the cart come trundling up and for a split second his eyes met Meg's, dark eyes they were, and then his gaze went from her to Alice and he took on a slightly puzzled look.

The cart lurched to a halt and the carrier spoke to the farmer.

'I'll be round this way tomorrow if you want anything special bringing, Farmer Teasdale.'

Meg had time to look properly at the farmer's companion. She couldn't think what it was about him, but she thought she had seen him before. He had a pleasant open face and lovely dark eyes. Surely if she had seen him before she would have remembered him? It was a puzzle . . .

'Gee up!'

The carrier was setting off again and Meg was still puzzling about it. She risked a backward glance and saw the young man staring after them. She almost felt like putting up a hand to wave to him, make some acknowledgement, at least. Daft! she said to herself, and turned to her sister.

'Did you know who that was?' she asked Alice, her question unheard by the carrier as the wheels rumbled on loudly.

'Who? Farmer Teasdale?'

'No, the other one, the man with him,' said Meg.

'I didn't notice,' answered Alice, surprising Meg who thought that any girl would have noticed the man with Farmer Teasdale. 'Why, like?'

'Oh, nothing, I just wondered,' Meg answered, and they said no more about it.

But she remembered the young man. And in bed that night, when Wesley took her for the first time since Robert was born, it was the stranger's face which swam before her eyes and she was ashamed afterwards so that she tried to be especially understanding with Wesley. Yet the memory lingered and she knew it was linked to another, more elusive one. She thought of it at different times during the day as she worked at the possing stick, thumping clothes through soapy water, or did the thousand and one other chores which made up her day.

But the happenings of the next few months kept all Meg's fanciful thoughts at bay. Fever was sweeping the colliery rows, scarlet fever which decimated the children and even took some of the adults. The Cornish babies both fell victim to the dread disease in July, but whereas Tucker returned from the fever hospital thinner and paler and more fractious, Robert did not return at all.

He was but six months old when he died of the fever and Meg four months pregnant with her third child. Wesley and Dick Adamson went to the fever hospital to bring the tiny coffin home for burial.

The funeral was quiet, there had been so many such for children in the last few weeks. Dolly Bates came, and Alice and Auntie Phoebe and Uncle Tot, but no one else apart from the parents and the minister.

Meg stood by the tiny grave and it was Alice who took her arm to support her. Wesley stood separate from them, his face hard and impassive as the coffin was lowered into the earth. And afterwards he strode away by himself.

Auntie Phoebe sniffed and lifted her chin in disapproval.

'Gone to meet his marras in the Black Boy, I reckon,' she said tartly.

'Whisht, Phoebe, the lad has a right to go for a drink if he wants,' said Uncle Tot. He took Meg's other arm. 'Howay, lass, let's get you home. You have to think of the bairn that's left now.' And Meg was glad of his strong arm as they turned away from the grave, and walked back to the rows.

So many little graves there were, she thought dumbly. Oh, God, what is it all for? Here she was, only just twenty-one, with a baby at home and one dead in the earth. And another on the way, a tiny tremor inside her womb reminded her.

Alice stayed with Meg until the clock struck ten. They sat on either side of the kitchen range, Alice in the

224

rocking-chair where she had nursed the still weak and fretful Tucker to sleep before taking him up to bed. Meg sat in the hard chair opposite, staring into the fire until it became quite dark. Alice watched her, her own young heart throbbing with pity at the sorrow of her sister. They spoke little, just sat there in companionable silence, until at last Alice stirred.

'I'd better be getting home now, Meg,' she said. 'Shall I light the lamp before I go?'

Meg looked up, startled out of her melancholy thoughts.

'Oh, Alice,' she said, 'I was going to make you some supper. The time's just run away with me tonight, I didn't realize it was so late.' She rose from the chair and lifted the kettle, testing its weight to see if there was enough water in it before putting it forward on to the coals.

'No, don't make any for me, I'll get some when I get home,' Alice said quickly. 'I'd better be on my way, Meg. There's bait to put up for Miles, he's on fore shift the night.' She picked up her shawl and put it round her shoulders before turning back. 'Shall I light the lamp, then?'

'No, don't, Alice. There's only me and I can see enough by the firelight. If I want to see anything better, I've a candle on the mantel shelf.' Meg sank down again into her chair and sighed, almost as though the effort of rising to her feet had been too much for her.

'I don't like leaving you on your own.' Alice's face was full of concern. 'I wonder if Wesley will be long?'

What Alice meant, Meg understood only too well, was that she didn't want to be here when he came home. For if he came home and had been drinking, he could be nasty with Meg because her sister was there and she'd had enough to deal with for one night. But, on the other hand, Alice didn't want her sister sitting on her own on the evening of her baby's funeral.

'You go, pet,' said Meg, 'I'll be fine. I'll go to bed myself as soon as Wes comes in.'

Alice hesitated but in the end left, walking home through rows which seemed strange to her with their alternating dark and shade for they had recently been illuminated with gas lamps which cast their eerie glow every few yards.

On her walk from George Row to Pasture Row, sorrow and sympathy for Meg formed a hard knot in her stomach which turned to anger the nearer to home she drew.

'I've lost all patience with them,' she said aloud, and her feet quickened as she turned into the back street of Pasture Row. 'I'll have it out with the lads first chance I get, I will.' The resolve hardened in her. She determined she was going to have her say about this even if it did get her into trouble.

The chance came almost at once. Miles and Jack Boy were sitting in the kitchen, Miles in his pit clothes ready for work and Jack Boy in his shirt sleeves, sitting at the table reading the *Auckland Chronicle*. Alice wasted no time in getting down to it.

'I think you two should be bloody well ashamed of yourselves,' she said flatly as she came through the door and hung her shawl up on the hook behind it.

Jack Boy and Miles looked up in surprise, shock even, at hearing a young lass like Alice swear.

'Our Alice!' Miles reproached.

'Why, man, it's enough to make a saint swear,' she snapped. 'There you two sit without a care in the world at all, and your sister just buried her babby. You haven't even the ments to go to the funeral.'

'Aw, Alice! You know Da wouldn't like it,' said Miles, but both he and Jack Boy went a bright red and Jack Boy looked quickly down at his paper, folding it in two and placing it carefully to one side.

'You're old enough to decide for yourselves, both of you. Da never notices what you do any road. An' you must know our Meg hasn't got it easy, not with that Wesley Cornish. Why, man, if it hadn't been for Uncle Tot, I don't know how she would have got back from the funeral. Two brothers and not one to support her at a time like this.'

'Why, where was Wes? Did he not go to his own bairn's funeral?' Jack Boy's eyes opened wide in surprise and a dawning anger.

'Oh, aye, he went to the funeral, but then he went straight out drinking with that Dick Adamson. I tell you, man, I've just come away from our Meg's and her useless man isn't back yet.'

Alice started banging about the kitchen, filling the kettle for tea and fetching out the bread and jam to make sandwiches for Miles's bait tin. All her movements showed her fury: the way she thrust the kettle on the coals, the way she almost threw the bait tin on the table. She looked a proper virago to the boys with her blazing eyes and tightly compressed lips.

'I think it's time you two did something for our Meg, after all she's done for you. An' it's about time you had a word with Da. Our Meg's married now. Who do you think's going to remember or even care how it was she came to get married? She was like a mother to you two an' all, she was. You're old enough to know how young she was herself when she had to take Mam's place.'

The brothers looked at one another, both of them feeling a trifle sheepish. It was true, everything Alice said, and they knew it.

'I'll call in the morn,' said Miles after a minute's embarrassed silence. 'On my way home from the pit I'll call in, tell her I'm sorry about the babby, like.'

Jack Boy cleared his throat. 'Aye,' he mumbled, 'me an' all.' He rose from the table and stretched his arms to

227

the ceiling, yawning hugely, his expression nonchalant. Almost, thought Alice, as though it was nothing unusual, just something he did most days. She couldn't believe how easy it had been to get them to cave in on this. She should try playing war with them more often.

'I'm off to bed,' said Jack Boy, moving towards the staircase. Then he halted and turned to face them both.

'An' another thing, our Alice,' he said, as though it had been him laying down the law a minute or two ago, 'another thing. You can call me Jackie from now on, like me marras do, I'm not a bairn any longer, I know when you mean me or Da.'

Alice nodded, unsmiling. It was true, he was no longer little Jack, he was a man now and beginning to face up to the real world.

Nineteen

It was twelve o'clock when Wesley came home and Meg by that time had fallen into an exhausted sleep in her chair by the fire. She woke with a start as he came in the door, lurching from side to side and wafting before him the stench of his beery breath, making her feel sick and ill, compounding her aching misery.

'You're pallatic drunk,' she said flatly, watching him as he flopped down in a chair.

'Aye, I am,' Wesley replied equably.

'On the day of your baby's funeral an' all, you should be ashamed!'

'Ashamed, is it? Me ashamed! You mind your tongue, lass, or I'll mind it for you.' Wesley glowered, his quick tember already rising. But Meg was past seeing any danger signals. She needed to vent her anger at Wesley and the world, needed to break through the ball of desolate misery which was threatening to choke her.

For while she was asleep she had dreamed of the day she had spent in Auckland. Not so long ago, though it seemed an age. She was with Alice and the babies, down on the river bank where the Gaunless flowed into the Wear. And she had woken still feeling the weight of little Robert in her arms, smiling down into his tiny face. And then Wesley had come in and spoilt it. She had to face the reality of the future with no baby Robert to hold in her arms. And she agonized about whether she should have weaned Tucker earlier. Had Robert succumbed to

229

the scarlet fever because he wasn't getting sufficient milk? Had she done something else wrong in her care of him?

'I have a perfect right to go for a drink, I've lost me babby and I had to get out for a drink,' Wesley stated, his face red with anger. 'Now, get me a bite of supper, woman, an' don't be so impittent. Who do you think you're talking to?'

Meg took the kettle and went into the pantry to fill it from the water bucket. Her hand shook as she lifted the dipper so that water splashed over on to the floor. She felt dizzy and sick and her head throbbed.

'You have to go to work in the morning, you're on back shift, you should have come home sooner,' she said, and bent over the fire to rake it together the better to boil the kettle.

The next moment she felt his fingers on her shoulder and he pulled her round so violently that the kettle went flying out of her hand to clatter against the wall and fall to the ground, leaving a wet, sooty stain on the lime-washed plaster.

'I should have, should I?' Wesley snarled, and lifting his fist he slammed it into the side of her face so that if he hadn't been holding her up she would have gone the way of the kettle.

'Wes!'

Meg's head rocked back and for a moment she was so dazed she hardly heard her own strangled cry. But it was enough to wake Tucker in his bed upstairs and he set up a frightened howling.

'Mam, mam, mam!'

Wesley brought his face close to hers, glaring at her, his eyes red-rimmed and his cheeks suffused with fury.

'I should have done that a long time since!' he shouted. 'What you need is a bit of stick, my lass. Mebbe if I'd done it sooner you wouldn't have neglected the babby, let him catch the fever. But, by, I've learned me lesson, I have, and from now on you'll have to watch your step or I'll take me belt to you.' He released his grip on her shoulder and flung her down on the floor, himself sitting back down at the table.

Meg lay for a minute or two, her ear ringing from the blow, unable even to think straight until Wesley pushed his foot roughly into her back.

'Get yourself up and see to the supper,' he said. 'Don't lie there sulking like you've been hurt, or by God I'm telling you, you will be hurt before I'm done with you.'

Upstairs, Tucker's terrified screaming grew louder and louder and Dolly Bates's husband knocked on the wall with the poker.

'What's going on in there?' he shouted. 'Can't a man have a bit of rest when he comes in from the pit?'

'Now look, you've gone and disturbed the neighbours,' said Wesley.

Shakily, Meg got to her feet. The kettle was boiling and she brewed Wesley a pot of tea and brought him the remains of a meat pie from the pantry. She worked like an automaton, going through the motions only, until the fog in her head gradually cleared and the throbbing lessened.

'I should think so an' all,' said Wesley smugly. 'Now get away up and see to the bairn. I'm telling you, Meg, if you let another bairn of mine go because you don't look after it properly, I'll swing for you, I surely will.'

She didn't answer, just climbed the stairs and lifted the hiccuping, shaking Tucker from his bed. Sitting down, she offered him her breast, though he had been weaned for a month or more now. But it was the only way she could think of to comfort him quickly. Tucker cuddled into her, holding himself tightly against her, and she crooned softly to him, rocking him gently backwards and forwards until at last he quietened, giving only an occasional sob. His tear-beaded eyelashes drooped and he fell asleep, comforted.

Meg was ironing on the kitchen table when the knock on the door came the following morning. She was surprised. It was early for Alice, only nine o'clock. Surely she would be busy this time of the morning? But her heart lightened as she took the flat iron back to the fire and scooped Tucker up in her arms, just in case. Now he was more steady on his feet he was like lightning, into everything before she could catch him usually.

'Morning, Meg.'

'Miles!' she gasped, holding on to Tucker with both hands as he struggled to be free.

'I thought . . . I thought I would just look in and see how you are like,' Miles mumbled, and even through the streaks of coal dirt on his cheeks she could see his face reddening.

'Miles, Miles. Howay in, lad, howay through to the kitchen.'

Meg stood back to let her younger brother into the house and led him through to the kitchen. Once there, he stood awkwardly before the range, not sure what to do. They gazed at each other for a long moment until Meg let Tucker, who had been fighting heroically to wriggle out of her arms, down on to the floor.

'Sit down, lad, sit down,' she said, beginning to smile until she suddenly thought of something. 'There's nothing wrong, is there, at home I mean? Nothing's happened, has it, not an accident at the pit?' Her eyes were beginning to widen in horror, for surely after all this time something drastic must have happened to bring Miles round to her door?

'No, no, nothing's up,' he said quickly. 'I thought I'd just call in on my way back from the pit, you know, tell you I was sorry about the bairn.'

'Oh, yes, little Robert.' Meg's smile dimmed for a moment as the sorrow threatened to overwhelm her again. She fought against it.

'Eeh, Miles, I'm that glad to see you, I am. Sit down, lad, sit down and I'll make some tea.'

'I'm in me pit clothes,' he objected, looking at the clean cushion on the chair.

'Aye, well, I'll put the cloth on the chair, the one I keep for when Wesley's black from the pit.' Meg rushed for the piece of old sheeting and spread it and saw him settled in the chair, then she removed the iron from the heat and put the kettle on for tea. She was so delighted, she hardly knew what to say, fairly flying into the pantry for the biscuit tin. Eeh, she thought, wasn't it lucky she'd made currant biscuits for the funeral yesterday? Miles always had had a sweet tooth.

'What happened to your face, Meg?'

She was brought up short. In the excitement of having her brother in the house for the first time, she had forgotten all about the large black and blue bruise which covered most of one half of her face.

'It's nothing, I fell down,' she said, and it was her turn to feel awkward. She tried to cover her confusion by chattering on.

'Mind you've grown, our Miles,' she said. 'Are you getting on all right then? By, it is lovely, it's grand, I'm so pleased you've come round. Go on, have one of these biscuits, they're lovely, I know you like them.'

Miles was looking hard at her. Though he was only fourteen, he had grown a lot since Meg left Pasture Row and was now quite tall for his age and already showing signs of developing the powerful shoulders and arms characteristic of the pitman. He was almost a man and it was as a man that he now regarded his sister.

'Did Wesley do that?' he demanded.

Meg dropped her eyes quickly and mumbled a denial but Miles was not to be fooled.

'He did, didn't he?'

'Miles, Miles, let's not talk about it now.' Meg, her emotions in a volatile state with grief and unhappiness, was terrified she would burst into tears and pour it all out to Miles, and that wouldn't be right, it would do no good at all. Stooping down so that her face was hidden, she picked up Tucker and sat him on her knee, bending her face over the child.

'Howay, Tucker, come and see your Uncle Miles.'

Tucker beamed and stretched out his hand to the untouched biscuit in Miles's hand, never one to miss the opportunity for extra food.

'Tucker! I'll give you one of your own,' exclaimed Meg.

'It's all right, he can have this one,' said Miles, and handed the biscuit to the little boy. 'I'll spoil my breakfast any road. Alice'll be having it ready.'

'Oh, you're not going, are you? I was going to ask you all sorts of things. How's Da? And Jack Boy? I do miss you all, you know, even if you did drive me mad sometimes.'

Miles grinned. He had obviously decided to respect Meg's wish not to talk about her Wesley or the bruise on her face, and she was glad he was adult and sensitive enough to respond to her appeal.

'I can stay a bit,' he said. 'As for Da, he's much the same, as I reckon Alice will have told you. And it's not Jack Boy. He's a man now, he says, and likes to be called Jackie. His marras call him that.'

'Da, da, da, da,' burbled Tucker. He had finished the biscuit and was trying to reach the plateful on the table, leaning over and pumping his legs up and down on Meg's lap.

234

Miles stood up and pulled on his cap. 'I'd better be on me way,' he said.

'Oh, Miles, do you have to go?' His visit had been so short, but at least he had come and would be back again, she told herself. 'Still, I suppose you're ready for your bed.' She went with him to the front door, carrying Tucker.

'I'll call in the morn.' Miles paused, his hand on the sneck of the front door, and half-turned to face his sister. 'Meg, I'm sorry. I'm sorry I didn't come sooner. I never thought like, and I should have. And I'm sorry about the babby.' He opened the door and stepped out into the street. Then he hesitated.

'Don't you be anxious, Meg. We'll help you, me and Jackie.' And before she could ask him what he meant he was away up the row and round the corner.

Meg went back to her ironing with a lighter heart, though she was somewhat puzzled by what he had meant by the last remark. What did he mean, he and Jackie would help her?

It was an hour or two later when Alice popped in, bringing with her Auntie Phoebe. They were on their way to the store but Alice, of course, was dying to see Meg after the visit from Miles. Her eager questions were forgotten, however, when she saw Meg's face.

'I'll murder him. I will, I'll kill him,' she said.

'Now wait on, Alice, I didn't say it was Wesley did it,' said Meg.

'No, but you didn't have to, did you? There's nobody else living in this house, is there? You didn't get that face from walking into a door, nor from any fall either, an' you with a baby on the way!'

'I told you he was a bad 'un,' put in Auntie Phoebe. 'I told you not to go with him. But no, you would do what you liked, and look what it's got you. Nowt but trouble since the day you married him.' The older woman folded her arms across her ample chest and turning her mouth down at the corners, shook her head, as if almost pleased to have been proved right.

'It wasn't all his fault,' Meg felt constrained to say. 'I lost my temper an' all.'

'Not his fault? Not his fault when he hits a lass half his size, a lass who's having his babby and has just lost another? By, if I had my way . . .'

'Leave it alone, Auntie Phoebe,' Meg said quickly, becoming alarmed. 'You won't go spreading this about the rows, will you? It's nobody's business but mine and Wesley's, I don't want you to say anything about it.'

'Don't be so daft, Meg,' said Alice. 'I daresay it's all about the place already. Nothing goes on here but everybody knows about it nearly before it happened.'

'Aye, well, but I don't want you to say anything.'

Meg could foresee that she wouldn't be able to hold her head up in the store for shame if this got about, let alone the chapel. She changed the subject.

'Have you been talking to Miles, Alice? Why, I got such a lovely surprise when he turned up on my doorstep. It was like a Christmas box in summer, it was.' She beamed at the memory, the lovely surprise it had been when Miles turned up.

Alice grinned. 'I told him, I did an' all, and our Jack Boy – pardon me, our Jackie. I gave them what for last night when I got home and caught them both in the kitchen. They went down like nine pins, they did.'

'Thank you, Alice. I'm ever so grateful.'

'We'd better be away to the store if we're to get anything more done today,' Auntie Phoebe reminded Alice. 'We'll get your messages, eh, Meg?' They all three knew she wouldn't be going out of doors until her bruises faded.

The afternoon flew by for Meg, comforted now by the

feeling that the rifts in her family were healing. She hardly thought of Wesley at all. He was simply there, part of her life, and she must put up with him. What little regard or feeling she had had for him was long gone. She couldn't imagine she had ever been fond of him at all.

She was just lifting the pot pie from the pan when Wesley came in from the pit, striding through the kitchen and stripping off his pit coat and cap and dropping them in a heap in the corner before sitting down and unlacing his pit boots. He didn't speak, in fact he didn't look at her at all.

Meg cut the pot pie, releasing a stream of gravy which ran over the suet crust in a dark, rich stream, taking a smaller portion for her and Tucker and putting the rest on to Wesley's plate. She spooned out potatoes and leeks and they sat down to eat and still they hadn't spoken. Meg occupied herself with feeding Tucker, trying to coax him to eat something else apart from the meat which was his favourite.

The meal was almost finished when a knock came on the front door. Hoisting a protesting Tucker on to her hip, Meg went to answer it and there on the doorstep stood her brothers, both wearing a look of determination.

'Good day, Meg, is Wesley in?' asked Miles.

'Why, yes, he is, he's having his tea,' said Meg, open-mouthed with astonishment. Jackie was still black from the pit, he could hardly have had time to eat anything since coming to bank. Yet here he was. He'd not been inside her house before, ever.

The two boys walked past her. These pit row houses were all laid out on the same pattern and they knew exactly where they would find Wesley.

'What the hell—'

Meg, following them into the kitchen, saw Wesley stand up from the table, his brow darkening into a scowl.

237

He pushed back his chair so that it fell with a clatter and Tucker jumped in her arms nervously.

'Take the bairn into the front room, our Meg,' said Jackie quietly.

'But, Jackie, what's up?' Meg hovered, uncertain what to do.

'Aye, what have you come barging in here for?' demanded Wesley.

'You can look at our sister's face, all puffed up and bruised like that, and still have the gall to ask us what we're here for?' Jackie strode up to Wesley, facing up to him with only a few inches between them, and even in that tense moment Meg had to marvel at the way he'd grown. Why, he was almost as tall as Wesley and equally as broad.

'Well, what do you think we're here for?' he said again before turning back to Meg. 'Go on, lass, take him out of the room.'

'You stay where you are in our own house,' snapped Wesley to her, 'you're my wife, not his.'

'Go on, Meg, man, you don't want to frighten the bairn,' said Miles softly, and Meg had perforce to go into the other room. But once in there she could hear every word that was said in the kitchen.

'You're going to take me on, both of you together, eh? Two against one, like? I reckon you're too feared to fight me one at a time. Pair of bloody cowards, that's what,' blustered Wesley.

'Oh, no, it wouldn't be fair, would it, Wesley Cornish? An' I suppose it's fair for a man to fight a woman, an' one that's carrying his bairn at that,' snapped Jackie. Miles and he were crowding Wesley 'til he had his back against the table, one on either side of him.

'She deserved what she got,' said Wesley. 'She neglected my bairn so that he caught the fever. Many a

238

man would have brayed her up before now, I'm telling you . . .'

'Aye, Wesley Cornish, and *we* are telling *you*. Lay one finger on our sister again and we'll lay a few on you. You'll be hounded out of the village an' all, and we'll see your name's dirt in the pit. How long will you last, do you think, if all your marras turn against you? And they will an' all when we've finished with you. You'll stink to high heaven, you will.'

Jackie paused and spat into the fire as a gesture of contempt.

'Hadaway, man, you can't do nowt like that, not in the pit,' jeered Wesley, though Miles could see he was half-believing.

Jackie laughed, a low, mirthless sound that made Meg, in the next room, shiver. Suddenly she jumped clean out of her chair as there was a loud crash from the kitchen. Leaving Tucker, who was playing on the clippie mat with the peg bag, she rushed back through the connecting door. Wesley was slumped in the corner, a bruise fast coming up on his face almost as big as the one she had herself. Jackie had bided his time, catching Wesley completely off guard and flooring him with one punch.

'Now, lad,' he said gently, helping his brother-in-law to his feet. 'Now I'm sure you can see what I mean, can't you? You mend your manners with our Meg, Wesley Cornish, and keep your fists to yourself in the house. Now howay and finish your supper.'

He nodded to Meg. 'I don't think you'll have any more bother, lass. Now, I'm away for me tea. I'm fair famished after all that exercise, an' after a shift on the coal face an' all.'

'Oh, Jackie, you didn't have to—' she began.

'Oh, aye, I did. You know us, Meg, us Maddisons will look after our own. And just you think on, like,' he added to Wesley, who had sat down in his chair again

239

and was feeling gingerly in his mouth where a tooth had come loose. 'You think on, Wesley Cornish, what I've said the day.' He turned back to his sister. 'Well, it was nice seeing you, Meg. I'll call again the morn, just to keep an eye on things, like. Howay, Miles, we'll be off now, leave them to their teas.'

Outside the two boys strode to the end of George Row and turned the corner before looking at each other and bursting into uproarious laughter.

'You made a good job of that, our Jackie, but you'd have had a job setting his marras against him,' chortled Miles. 'And I know you wouldn't start any trouble down the pit an' all. You were pulling it a bit there, lad. Why, you know it wouldn't be safe. If the owners got to hear of it, we'd all get the sack.'

'Aye,' said Jackie, sobering up and walking on his way, 'but if Wesley's fool enough to think I might . . . well, that's all we need, isn't it?'

'It was great the way you caught him like that.' Miles, still laughing, had almost to run to keep up with his brother. 'Thinking about going in for the bare-knuckle fighting when the show comes to Auckland, are you?'

Meg brought Tucker back from the front room, his face all covered in coal dust where he had found the coal pail and sucked on a large lump. She found a flannel and rubbed his face clean before sitting back down at the table, apprehensive about what Wesley would do next. He had his head bent over his half-eaten meal, his knuckles white as he grasped the edges of the table, the muscles in his arms standing out with tension.

Nervously, Meg picked up a spoon and began feeding Tucker again. The whole incident had taken only a few minutes and the meat and suet crust were still warm. She jumped when Wesley spoke.

'You go round crying to them brothers of yours, did you?'

Meg glanced over to him, quickly. The bruise on his face was coming up nicely now and it did indeed match hers. She picked up a morsel of meat and popped it into Tucker's mouth before answering.

'No, I didn't, Wesley. Our Miles came round this morning. He saw my face and must have guessed.'

'Oh, don't tell me your lies, he never comes round here, why would he suddenly come round now?'

Meg put the fork down and gave Tucker a drink from a cup of milk. Since he'd come back from the fever hospital, Meg had been buying milk for him from a farm just outside the village. She wiped his chin with the flannel and held him up to her shoulder where he lolled his head, already drowsy with sleep.

'Well, are you going to answer me?'

'I don't know why he came round,' she said at last. 'Maybe Auntie Phoebe or our Alice told him how you went and left us at Robert's funeral, he likely felt sorry for me losing the baby, there's many a reason. Maybe he's just growing up a bit now and realizes families have to stick together.' She rocked Tucker a little against her shoulder before staring levelly at Wesley. 'Any road, I'm right pleased he did come round. I only wish me da would come round an' all.'

'Oh, aye. You always did think more of your family than you did of me. Well, you can have them bloody Maddisons, thinking they're something better than anybody else.' He got to his feet and took down the clay pipe he had recently started smoking from the mantelshelf. Settling down in the rocking chair, he puffed away for a minute or two.

Meg laid the now sleeping Tucker on the settle and brought a dish of water from the pantry to wash him for bed. She was adding warm water from the kettle when

241

Wesley took the pipe out of his mouth and pointed it at her.

'When you've seen to the bairn, you can fetch in the bath. I'm off out early the night.'

Meg glanced at him. He didn't usually go out until much later. He was smiling maliciously at her. 'An' not to meet me marras either. If you can't act like a wife should, I might have to go somewhere else for it.'

Twenty

'Us women would all get along just fine without men,' said Alice. She and Meg were walking along the track to Old Pit, Tucker skipping along beside them and little Kit dawdling along the way and falling behind as he usually did. Kit, short for Christopher, was a pretty child with his mother's bright blue eyes and fair, curly hair. He was interested in everything around him. He stopped to watch a line of ants cross the track and disappear down a hole, and then a few yards further on there was the equally absorbing sight of a snail climbing up a thistle. He had to watch that, wondering all the time if it was going to get prickled.

'Kit! Howay now, don't lag behind,' called his mother, and he regretfully abandoned the snail and scampered to catch up.

The women waited for him, putting the bath tin full of clean washing down for a moment to ease the drag on their arms.

'What are you on about now, Alice?' asked Meg as they started on their way once again.

'Well, I mean,' she said, 'what good are they? Here am I, spending all my time housekeeping for three men who likely would be just as happy to be left in their muck and eat bought pies for their dinners every day. Unpaid skivvy, I am.'

Meg laughed indulgently. Alice was always going on about something these days.

243

'An' you don't have much cause to laugh,' said Alice. 'Look at you, saddled with a lad you hardly ever see, never mind anything else. When did he last come home?'

'Oh, not so long ago.'

In truth, Meg thought, Wesley had rarely been in the house in George Street since little Kit was born. She knew well enough where he spent his time all right, as did the rest of the colliery rows. Jackie and Miles had been to see her one night, soon after the baby was christened, and asked her if she wanted anything done about it.

'Does he give you any money, Meg?' Jackie had demanded.

'Oh, he does. Yes, he does,' she had answered, earnestly but untruthfully. 'Let it bide, Jackie, I don't want any trouble.'

'Well, I don't know how he can be paying that strumpet Sally Hawkins, and you an' all,' said Jackie.

'Let it bide, Jackie, let it bide.'

Meg was willing to work night and day to feed her boys herself. She was only too pleased when Wesley stayed away. It was worth slaving all day in other people's houses, seeing that there was a clean home and a meal ready for the men coming off shift when their own wives were lying in bed after a birth or illness. It was worth falling into bed aching from head to toe with weariness when she had that bed to herself.

At first Wesley had gone with Sally Hawkins in a spirit of defiance. He was getting his own back on Meg and she was well aware of it. But his visits to Sally had become more frequent, until now he was considered a rare visitor in his own home. An unwelcome visitor at that.

'Well,' Alice said now as the row of cottages by Old Pit came into sight, 'you've managed fine without him, haven't you?'

'I have,' Meg acknowledged, smiling. She had good reason to feel pleased with herself. Goodness knows, it was difficult for any woman on her own in a colliery village miles from nowhere to earn a living, but she was managing, just. She had started a little business, making home-made pies, born of a chance compliment, a remark from one of the new mothers she was 'helping out'.

'By, Meg, you make a tasty meat pie.'

So now every morning she was busy turning out pies: meat pies, tatie and leek pies, and bacon and egg pies. And doing nicely, an' all. But she still took in some washing, especially for the retired folk of Old Pit. It had been taken over by the union and now it housed aged miners and their wives, or else widows. She and Alice were bringing back the clean washing they had washed and ironed for the old people the day before.

Now they waited by the end of the row, looking back as they waited for Kit to catch up with them yet again.

'We can manage fine without men,' Alice reasserted, 'we'd be far better off.'

Meg bent and swung four-year-old Kit up in the air, round and round until he was chortling with glee.

'What, our two little men an' all?' she cried.

The grim expression on Alice's face relaxed and she bestowed a loving smile on Tucker, now rising eight, and tall and strong, always into trouble of one sort or another. She and Tucker had a special relationship. In her mind he was the child who took the place of any she might have had herself. For Alice was determined she would never marry. Would never, never, put herself at the mercy of any man.

'Mebbe not these two,' she said. 'Though I might change me mind one day if they don't behave themselves!'

Meg laughed and put Kit down. She lifted her end of the bath of clothes while Alice picked up the other. They walked up to the door of Mrs Dobbs' cottage. The old lady was still living there, seemingly no better and no worse than she was nine years before when Meg had first started to help her out.

'Play outside, Tucker, and watch out for Kit, see he doesn't wander too far away,' she said.

'Aw, Mam, he's such a babby,' Tucker protested. 'Walter's here, he's staying with his grandma, we were going to look for conkers.' Walter was Tucker's marra, the two boys had it all planned to leave school the same day and go down the pit together.

'You can take Kit with you then,' Meg insisted. 'Not far, mind, don't go out of earshot.' The boys scampered away.

The cottages had been spruced up for the aged miners. The roofs all showed patches of new slating and the broken windows had been repaired. Even the doors had a new coat of green paint, donated by the owners. And inside the walls had been lime-washed and the woodwork scrubbed by miners' wives, even the one where Mrs Dobbs was already living. Meg knocked at the door, and without waiting for an answer, lifted the sneck for her and Alice to enter the low-ceilinged kitchen.

'How are you today, Mrs Dobbs?' she asked, smiling at the old woman, still sitting in her chair by the black-leaded fireplace as she always was whenever Meg called. Only now there was a good fire in the grate, the coals from an allowance donated by working pitmen.

'I'm grand,' the old woman answered, 'in fine fettle, I am.'

Meg and Alice took out the old woman's clean linen and Meg put it away in the chest of drawers by the bed. Mrs Dobbs lived in one room now, couldn't negotiate the narrow, steep staircase.

She and Alice tidied round for her. 'While we're here,

like,' Meg said. They had just finished making the bed, spreading a clean, white bedspread over the blankets, when the door burst open and Tucker flew into the room.

'Mam! Mam!' he cried, his eyes wide and his normally rosy complexion white with shock.

'What? What's the matter?' Meg's heart jumped in her breast and began pumping painfully.

'Kit! Kit, he . . .' Tucker stopped, panting heavily, and edged back towards the doorway. 'It wasn't my fault, Mam,' he cried. 'Me and Walter, we were just gathering conkers from that tree by the old slag heap.'

Meg stared at him, not daring to ask. Oh, God, she thought, what had happened to Kit?

'Kit, tell us about Kit!' Alice ran to the boy and took hold of his upper arms. 'What's the matter, Tucker?'

'He – he fell down the old shaft, Auntie Alice. The wood was rotten and it gave way. It wasn't my fault.' Tucker was sobbing now, casting glances at his mother, more fearful of the trouble he was in than the fate of his younger brother.

But Tucker was left standing there forgotten as Alice and Meg ran out into the road and up by the small, weed-grown slap-heap to the old colliery workings, to the old shaft which was covered with rotten planks of wood. And there, at one side, was the evidence. Broken planks of worm-infested wood with a gaping hole just big enough for a small boy to fall through. Meg stared at it in horror, unable to comprehend what had happened. Then she began tearing at the planks which had been rotten when she was still a child. They came away bit by bit, the cover wholly disintegrated.

Walter stood beside her, shaking with fright. 'I heard him cry, Missus,' he said. 'He's not dead.'

'Dear God, no!' cried Alice, lending a hand to clear away the wood. But both women stopped abruptly when a large piece fell into the shaft. They listened for it to hit the bottom or else water, and it seemed a lifetime before they finally heard the soft 'plop' echoing up, a hollow, unnerving sound which only intensified their dread.

'Wait a minute, wait a minute,' a man's voice called out, and Meg and Alice turned to see a stranger dismounting from a sturdy Dales pony. Behind him a straggling line of retired miners were approaching, all of them bent and aged but all responding to the cries of distress from the women.

'Wait, I say,' said the stranger again. 'You don't want any more falling in, do you? It might hit the child. It's better if I do it. Stand back a bit.'

Meg and Alice fell back, instinctively responding to the note of authority in his voice. By this time three or four of the old men had reached the edge of the pit shaft.

'Best make a circle round the shaft,' suggested one, and the stranger nodded his agreement, quickly catching the old miner's plan and deferring to him. Miners were used to disasters, they were good at coping with them.

The men formed a circle round the ancient shaft, thankfully smaller than more modern ones. Squatting on their hunkers, a movement which would have been beyond most old men but not these who had spent their working lives mostly working in that position, each one took hold of a plank, their gnarled hands easing it away gently, carefully, until at last the old cover was completely gone and they could look down the deep hole.

There was nothing, no sign of Kit at all. Meg pushed forward, crying out in her anxiety: 'Kit! Kit!'

The stranger took hold of her, restraining her as she craned down into the depths, blinking her eyes rapidly, trying to sharpen her vision. Nothing. There was nothing. Even the water at the bottom couldn't be seen in the blackness. Only a rusting iron ladder, leading

248

down to the first platform, and from there the top of another, leading even further down.

'Hey, lads, you're not playing a game wi' us, are you?' An old man got to his feet and glared sternly at Walter and Tucker, standing close together behind the pitmen.

'Tucker?' said Meg in the wild hope that this was a game, a cruel game. Oh, she would forgive them willingly if it was a game and Kit was to pop his head round a bush and shout, 'Got you!'

'No, Mam,' said Tucker. 'He fell in. We saw him, didn't we, Walter?'

'Aye, we did,' Walter asserted. 'An' I heard him shout an' all.'

'When did you hear him shout?' asked the stranger. 'While he was falling, was it?'

'No, Mister, after. It was after. We saw him go down but we were up the track picking conkers. An' we ran up here, then Tucker went for his mam and I heard him shout. Well, he cried, really.'

'I'll go down,' said the stranger, and started to unbutton his coat and take off his hat. He rolled up his shirt-sleeves. 'We can't see properly from here.'

'Wait on, lad, it's no good going off at half cock,' an old man stepped forward and said. 'We'll get organized first, like. Tom, hadaway and fetch a rope. We'll have to secure this ladder from the top. A lantern an' all, he'll be wanting a light.'

'Aye, right, Bill.' The youngest-looking of the old miners set off for the colliery row, hurrying straight through a patch of nettles and rosebay willow herb in a bee line rather than going round by the path. Meg watched him, shivering now and cold without realizing it. A steady drizzle began to fall and the stranger picked up his coat and put it round her shoulders.

'Call down to him,' he suggested, 'he might answer you. What's his name?'

'Kit. Christopher,' Alice said quickly, for Meg had moved forward to the rim of the shaft again, the coat clutched round her. She knelt on the ground, then lay full length so that she got as close as possible.

'Kit! Kit, son, are you there?' she called.

'We'll all call,' the gentleman said, for vaguely in the back of her mind she recognized him as such. The miners and Alice all took up the cry, even Walter and Tucker joining in.

'Kit! Kit!'

They waited anxiously for an answer. Nothing, nothing at all. Bill, evidently the leader of the group of retired pitmen, shook his head.

'I doubt that . . .'

'Wait! Was there something?' Meg thought she had heard a sound. A whisper, a moan, something.

'Just the wind, I think,' Alice put in.

But by now Tom was back with a sturdy hempen rope and a Stephenson lamp, already lit and glowing behind the wire gauze. He also had a tallow candle.

'Here, Mister, stick this in your hat band,' he said, holding out the candle, and the gentleman took it and secured it to the front of his hat which had been lying discarded on the grass. He thrust the hat firmly on to his head and prepared to descend the ladder.

Bill had tied the rope to an iron ring in the ground which had been hidden from view by rank grass and nettles. The pitmen had known there had to be one there and only a second's search found it. He then tied the rope to the top rung of the iron ladder and was ready.

'Mind,' he said, 'this thing's fair flaked away wi' rust. I would gan down meself, but you'd stand a better chance. Me lungs have given out, I couldn't climb up again.' He formed the rope into a coil and tied it round the stranger's waist, tucking the coil into his belt.

'Pay it out as you go,' he advised, 'then if the ladder

gives out, you've got some back up. Now mind, this ladder only goes to the first platform. If he's not there, you'll have to go on to the next. I'll be honest, I don't know how many there are. But the ladders'll likely be better further down. Give us a shout any road. Now, gan canny, I don't want to have to climb down after you, like I said, I'd never get back up again. It's a young man's job is that.'

In his earnest wish to instruct the stranger in the best way he could, the old miner was talking to him as he would a marra. Now, belatedly, as he stepped back to allow access to the top of the ladder, he noticed the white shirt and riding breeches.

'Begging your pardon, like, Sir,' he mumbled, a bit red in the face.

The stranger smiled and paused with only his head showing above the rim of the shaft.

'Whatever for?' he asked.

Meg and Alice and the two boys huddled together, Alice with her arm around her sister. 'He'll be down there,' she whispered, trying to comfort her. 'You'll see. Walter said he heard him shout, didn't he?'

Meg nodded, clinging to the shred of hope flickering within her.

Steadily, step by cautious step, Jonty descended into the black hole of the shaft, paying out the rope as he went. The ladder had looked quite short from the top but he was beginning to realize that had been an optical illusion. The light wavered and almost went out. Rain was coming down steadily now. A good thing he had the Stephenson safety lamp, old though it was and dim the light it cast.

At last he reached the first platform and thankfully stepped off the ladder into the brick-lined recess in the wall. The candle flared away from the rain and he looked round him. The hole was not very big, not big enough to take a man above six feet tall, but it was two feet deep and capable of holding a small boy terrified out of his wits and unable to call out. But it did not.

'Anything there?'

He poked his head out of the hole and looked up at the square of light, so far above him. The shape of a man's head was silhouetted against the sky.

'No, nothing,' he said, and drew his head back in before the rain really did put out his candle. 'I'm going on down.'

'Watch yourself, lad.' The call came echoing eerily down to him as he wound the rope round the top rung of the second ladder and climbed on to the first rung.

Further and further he went, sure he would reach the second platform any time, incredulous that it was so far. And then his rope gave out. He peered down. Only a few yards more. He fastened the end of the rope to a rung.

'This is what they mean by being at the end of one's tether,' he murmured drily, feeling an urge to lighten the tension.

'Are you there yet?' came the call from above.

'Not yet,' he answered, and climbed down the last few yards unsecured. He stepped off on to the platform, desperately hoping the boy would be there. He didn't at all fancy going any further down. Nothing. There was nothing. He shone his candle all round the recess, but there was nothing but a decaying wicker basket, a corf, in the corner. He bent over it and touched it, and it crumbled in a puff of dust.

He got to his knees and peered over the edge of the platform. Surely the bottom couldn't be very far away? These old pits hadn't been so deep. Why, this place must have been built early in the century.

Faintly, in the distance, he saw a glimmer of light, the

reflection on water of the candle in his hat. And there were two more ladders to go before he got there. God knows how deep the water is, too, he thought. He looked up at the patch of sky, the black silhouettes of heads at its perimeter.

And then he heard it, a faint moaning, coming from somewhere below and to his right. Quickly he took off his hat and held the light in the direction of the sound. There was something against the grey stone, something black. He leaned perilously over, stretching as far as he could. A shelf of some kind was projecting from the wall. No, it was a timber, at least a foot across, set into the wall. For what purpose it had been put there by the original shaft-sinkers he couldn't begin to guess, but it was there, and crouched hard against the wall, with one leg stuck out at a very peculiar angle, was a small boy. With both hands he was clinging to the timber support, his head down and his hair glistening in the rain. He whimpered again, softly.

'Kit?'

The boy didn't move, except for a convulsive sob.

'I'll get you lad, just be a good boy and stay still.'

Kit raised his head and looked up, his eyes wide with fear.

'Don't move, lad. Hang on there. You're doing grand, just hold on to the wood. We'll get you out, I promise we will, just hang on.'

Kit clutched at the timber and stared upwards. 'My leg hurts. I want me mam,' he said, his voice scarcely above a whisper.

'Aye, she's waiting for you, lad, just you be brave.'

'I don't know you, I want me mam,' Kit repeated.

'I'm Jonty, a friend of your mother's. Now, I'll just have to go back up for a rope, and then I'll get you. Look, I'll leave the candle on the ledge. It'll be all right if you can see a light, won't it, lad? Kit?

'Aye.'

Jonty put his hat with the burning candle on the edge of the ledge where Kit could see it, praying it wouldn't go out before he got back. If it did the child might panic and goodness knows what might happen then. He climbed back up the ladders at a speed that paid tribute to his fitness, not even pausing for a rest at a platform.

'He's there,' he said. 'He's alive, though I think he's broken his leg. Now, I'll need a good thick plank and another rope. And something to tie his legs together, make sure we don't compound the damage.'

'Oh, thank God, thank God!' cried Meg, and promptly fainted clean away.

Twenty-One

'Kit? Kit? Are you there, son?'

Jonty stepped stiffly off the ladder on to the second platform, his movements hampered by the plank tied to his back. The candle had gone out. He had only the light from the Stephenson safety lamp swinging at his belt. Luckily, he had thought to bring lucifers down with him and he lit the candle again before peering down to the jutting piece of timber where he had left the young boy.

'Kit?' he said again, and wide eyes peered at him out of the gloom. The child sobbed, convulsively.

'I'm coming for you, son,' Jonty said swiftly. 'Just you be still now.'

This time he was better prepared. The rope securing him to the top of the shaft was knotted to another which took him all the way to the second platform with some to spare. Jonty had listened patiently to Bill's instructions on the best way to reach the lad and bring him up to the surface. Even though he had a fair idea himself what to do, he deferred to the old man's superior knowledge of situations such as these.

'Don't rush, Sir,' Bill had said, and the other aged miners nodded in agreement. 'More haste, less speed like. Don't make a move 'til you're sure it's the right one.'

Jonty, impatient to go back down to the boy, glanced across at the young mother, sitting on the grass now, supported by her sister.

'I won't do anything foolish,' he had reassured Bill, and climbed on to the rung of the top ladder.

Carefully, he took the plank in one hand and climbed down until he was on a level with Kit's timber. With a bit of manoeuvring he managed to support one end of the plank on a rung of the ladder and slide it over until the other end was resting beside Kit, thanking God that he had guessed the right size of plank he would need. It had taken a few precious minutes to find it but it had been worth it.

With the spare rope, he secured the plank to the rung and then was ready to crawl across. The operation was not quite so hazardous as it might have been because Jonty was still tied to the rope connecting him to the ladders.

'Good lad,' he said, trying to keep his voice confident and calm. If he frightened the boy now he might slip off his perch into the water below. But Kit, though he was not yet five, came of generations of miners. Instinctively, he stayed still and quiet, letting Jonty rope him to his back and take him over the temporary bridge, even though every movement gave him pain in his broken leg.

At the surface there were willing hands stretched out to haul them up over the rim of the shaft, and a crowd to take the boy from Jonty's back and lay him gently on the ground. Jonty sat down beside him, breathless and panting from the long climb up. The sense of relief at the success of the rescue was overwhelming, both to his tortured muscles and to his mind. People were milling round, patting him on the back and congratulating him, and there was the mother of the little lad, kneeling down and holding the child to her, tears coursing down her face.

'Mind now, watch his leg,' he warned her, and she turned to him, catching hold of his hand and sobbing out her thanks. And he looked hard at her, her fair, curling hair and blue eyes, he knew her, he felt sure he did. And the other girl, Alice, kneeling beside her sister and adding her thanks too. It had to be her sister for they were so alike.

'Dear God, Meg,' said the younger sister, 'it's a miracle the bairn wasn't killed, isn't it?'

Meg? thought Jonty. Meg. And it was like a thunderbolt. He knew now who the women reminded him of: it was his Auntie Hannah. They were both the spit of his Auntie Hannah. And Meg, this was his little cousin Meg. He opened his mouth to speak but just then the doctor bustled up. Someone had had the presence of mind to fetch him from Winton Colliery. He knelt by the boy and within minutes the damaged leg was in a temporary splint and someone had found an old door to carry him back home on.

'Take him out on the old waggon way,' suggested Bill. 'It's level, it'll be better than going up the path.'

The track was steep and rutted, Bill's suggestion made sense. So the lad was carried home along the waggon way which once, so long ago, had taken horse-drawn coal trucks from Old Pit.

'A mite tired, are you, lad?' asked Bill kindly as Jonty picked up his coat and pulled it on over aching shoulders. 'It's the ladders. Me father used to say, it wasn't the shift on the coal face that knocked you out, it was the walk to the shaft after it and the climb up the ladders to bank. By, it was a red letter day when they brought in the winding gear and cages.'

Jonty grinned at him. 'I reckon your father was dead to rights,' he said with feeling. 'By the way, can you tell me the family name of the lad?'

'Oh, aye,' Bill nodded. 'That was young Kit Cornish. His mother's a canny body, do anything for us old folk along here, she will. But the father now, that's a different tale altogether like. He's a wild one, all right. I only hope

257

poor Meg's lads don't go the same road as him. The scandal of the place he is, a wonder the village doesn't throw him out. I lived there meself 'til last year. Oh, aye. Wesley Cornish is a bad 'un all right. Flaunting a fancy woman, and doesn't care who knows. Couldn't give a damn about his own wife and bairns.'

Jonty could see Bill was working himself up into a righteous rage about Wesley Cornish. He butted in swiftly when the old man paused for breath.

'Do you happen to know where they live? I thought I would see how the boy is in a day or two.'

Bill paused, already gathering strength to continue his tirade. He looked at Jonty, remembering he was speaking to a gentleman. Maybe he had said too much.

'Aye, Sir, I do. Me daughter lives in the same street. George Row, that is.'

Jonty looked after Meg and her sister, just disappearing round a bend in the wagon way, following the men carrying Kit. He wanted to know how the boy got on, but at the same time he was determined to have a proper talk with Meg, find out if she remembered him and if she knew what had happened all those years ago when her parents abandoned him to his father. Thanking the old pitman, he mounted his horse and rode off in the opposite direction to Winton Colliery, making his way back to Grizedale Hall.

On his ride, memories flooded back to him. Hannah bathing him in the tin bath by the kitchen fire when he and Meg had covered themselves in mud; the day he and Meg had played in Grizedale Hall, the last day they had been together. And he remembered how he had found that cousin of the Maddisons, Mrs Lowther, and how hopeful he had been that she would lead him back to the Maddisons and there would be a simple explanation for what had happened. But he also remembered his bitter disappointment when they'd refused to see him. When he went to see Meg, in a few days, when she had got over the shock of Kit's near brush with death, he might not say who he was at first. He'd test the water first.

Meg started up in bed, her pulse hammering and sweat breaking out all over her body. It was barely morning. A dim grey light filtered through the thin, cotton curtains so it must be just after dawn.

She rubbed her forehead with the sleeve of her nightie, trying to collect her thoughts. She had had the nightmare again, the one which had plagued her from childhood. The gigantic man on the grey horse had been chasing after her and Mam. And she was a child again, stumbling and running up the old railway track, hanging onto Mam while the candyman was getting nearer and nearer. The candyman . . .

She hadn't thought of him for years. Vaguely, in the back of her mind, she knew his name. What was it? Her brow furrowed as she tried to recall the name.

'Mam?'

The candyman was forgotten as Kit said her name. Jumping out of bed, she pulled a shawl over her nightgown and hurred to him.

'What is it, son?'

Kit moistened his lips with his tongue. 'Can I have a drink, Mam?'

Meg filled a cup from the water jug, and putting her arm under his shoulders, lifted him while he drank thirstily. She looked at his leg, now immobilised properly in a splint of gutta percha. Nothing to worry about, a greenstick fracture that was all, the doctor had said. But she worried nevertheless. She felt Kit's forehead. It was a little hot, but nothing to get alarmed about.

There was a bruise on his shoulder and another on his chin but they would be gone in a few days. She couldn't bear to think of what could have happened, closed her

259

mind against a picture of him lying face down in murky water at the bottom of the shaft. She brushed her lips against the boy's cheek.

'I was just looking to see what was down there,' he whispered. 'I was being careful, honest, Mam, I was, I don't know how I fell in.'

'Whisht, petal,' she said. 'Try and get to sleep, you're not going to get into trouble.'

Kit would always be looking to see what was there, she thought with a wry smile. He had had a natural born curiosity since the day he first focused his eyes on his folded fist, staring at it for minutes at a time. She kept her arm under his shoulders and leaned back against his pillow.

'Go to sleep, hinny,' she said softly. 'I'll stay with you 'til morning now. Just go to sleep, stop thinking about it. It's over now.'

The boy drifted off to sleep but Meg herself stayed wide awake. It wouldn't be long before it was time to face the day, but for now she was content to lie there with her young son against her arm, letting her mind drift.

She had thought Wesley would come home last night. Surely he had heard about the accident? Didn't he care what happened to his son? Not that she cared whether he came or not, not now. They got along fine without him. Sally Hawkins was welcome to him. Meg didn't even care when the neighbours looked sideways at her though she knew they were speculating on what she had done to drive him away.

Her mind wandered back to the man who had rescued Kit from the old pit shaft. He'd been grand, he had, she would be grateful to him for ever, she thought, rubbing her thumb up and down the boy's arm. He'd been so sympathetic an' all, with such lovely eyes, like dark brown velvet. She'd seen eyes like that before.

260

Meg began to feel deliciously drowsy and her eyes closed of their own accord. She drifted back to sleep as the grey light at the window became brighter and in the rows the caller went on his rounds, rapping lightly at the windows to call the pitmen up for back shift. And the man of her dreams had changed from the frightening figure of the candyman. This one had the same dark hair and eyes, but instead of the eyes being hard like black bullets under frowning lids, they were soft and gentle and understanding.

Wesley came just after Tucker had gone to school, walking straight in the front door and through to the kitchen as though he still lived there instead of being an irregular visitor. He was black from the pit. Meg jumped in apprehension as she heard the metallic ring of his metal-studded pit boots on the boards.

'What's this then?' he asked, without bothering with any greeting. 'It's a fine thing when everybody in the pit knows my lad has had an accident except me.' He stood, legs astride and hands on hips, his pit cap pushed to the back of his head, and glared at Meg.

'If you'd been here you would have known, wouldn't you?' she pointed out.

Wesley scowled. 'You should have sent Tucker round to tell me, I have a right to know,' he snapped.

'I'm not sending Tucker round to your fancy woman's house,' Meg replied sturdily.

Wesley stepped forward, his eyes narrowing to slits. 'Sally's twice the woman you ever were to me, frozen little bitch that you are. I've a good mind to show you now how a proper woman should act with her man.'

Meg stood her ground. 'Oh, yes, that's what you came for, is it? I thought you hadn't come to see Kit. You don't care about the bairn. Why, you hardly know him. And when did we last see any of your pay to feed him? How do you think I manage?'

'You do all right, you don't deserve any money from me. Why, you're lucky I let you stay in my house.'

'*Your* house? Your house, is it? I always thought it was a pit house,' she taunted.

'You've got a sharp tongue, haven't you?' Wesley lifted his hand to threaten her and she laughed.

'Oh, aye, that's going to do your name the world of good, isn't it? Your marras'll cheer you on all right, living with that Sally Hawkins and only coming round here to knock your wife about. Any road, I thought you were bothered about Kit?'

'Mam! Mam!'

As if on cue, his frightened cry came from above their heads, calming Meg immediately.

'We've gone and upset the bairn, now,' she said more quietly as she hurried to the bottom of the stairs.

'It's all right, pet,' she called up, 'it's just your da come to see how you are.' She looked back into the kitchen at Wesley. 'Now, go on up and see the lad. And be nice to him. The doctor says he has to be kept quiet for a few days. He had a bad fall and a nasty shock. This is no time to be fighting, with a sick bairn in the house.'

Wesley had the grace to drop the quarrel. Sitting down in his old chair by the fire, he took off his boots and went upstairs in his stockinged feet.

Meg hovered around the bottom of the stairs, listening to him talking awkwardly to the son he hardly knew. He's only doing it so that he doesn't look bad to his marras, she thought bitterly. If he cared at all about the lads he'd do more for them. Her thoughts went back to baby Robert. Wesley had cared about him. He'd cared enough to take it as a personal insult when Robert took the fever and died.

Coming downstairs some minutes later, Wesley put

five shillings down on the kitchen table. Meg gazed at it, feeling like picking it up and throwing it back at him.

'What's that for?' she asked his retreating back.

'Buy the bairn something,' he called over his shoulder.

Meg picked up the two half crowns, staring at the silver in her hand, tempted to throw it on the fire back. But in the end she reached up and put it on the mantelshelf. Proud gestures would get her nowhere.

It was the following Saturday when the little house in George Street had another visitor. Meg had prevailed upon Tucker to stay at home and entertain his small brother while she did her messages at the store.

A horse and trap was standing outside her door when she got back, loosely tethered to the lamp post. She looked at it curiously. Someone had an unusual visitor but it couldn't be here, she didn't know anyone with a horse and trap. No one who would come to the house at least. She dismissed it from her mind as she opened her door.

'Tucker?' she called, a little apprehensively. She had been gone longer than she had expected, for the store had been crowded and she was well aware that Tucker might have got bored with his younger brother and gone out. As she walked through to the kitchen, taking off her hat as she went, a figure rose from the armchair and she started with surprise.

'Mrs Cornish?'

It was the gentleman who had brought Kit up from the old pit shaft, smiling at her as she put her shopping basket down on the table. She didn't have time to open her mouth before Tucker rushed into excited speech.

'It's Mr Dale, Mam. He's come to see if our Kit's better. An' he's brought him a present, Mam, an' me an' all.'

'A present?'

263

'Nothing much, just a token,' the man broke in. 'I was interested in knowing how the boy was.'

'Grand, he's doing grand.' Meg looked up into dark eyes, dark, velvety eyes, kind, concerned eyes, the nicest eyes she had ever seen, she thought distractedly.

'I took him up to see our Kit, Mam,' said Tucker. 'An' he's brought him a rocking-horse. A rocking-horse, Mam! Something to hurry up and get better for, like, so that our Kit can ride him. His name's Neddy.'

Tucker was so excited his words were falling over each other so that it was a moment or two before Meg understood what he was saying.

'A rocking-horse? Eeh, you shouldn't have done that, Sir. A rocking-horse must have cost a mint of money.' No wonder Tucker was excited. No other child in the rows had a rocking-horse, there just wasn't the money for toys as grand as that.

'Don't worry, Mrs Cornish,' Jonty assured her. 'It's just an old one from the nursery at Gr— at my home. It was nothing, I assure you. And I've stood it beside the boy's bed. He can look at it, it will encourage him to get well.'

'He brought me some toy soldiers, Mam,' cried Tucker, holding them up for her to see, and obligingly she looked at them. They were a bit battered it was true, but they were soldiers still and Tucker would have a fine time with them. His eyes were shining more than they had on Christmas morning last year, she saw. He was fair bubbling with excitement.

'They're real bonny, they are,' she said, his delight in the toys making her smile. Tucker ranged his soldiers on the table beside her basket. There were six of them in scarlet coats and tall black hats, resplendent still though in places the paint had rubbed down to the metal beneath.

'It's very kind of you, Sir. Mr Dale, did you say? Please sit down. I'll make some tea. Will you have some tea?'

'I don't want to impose,' said Jonty, but he sat down nevertheless and watched her as she put the kettle on the fire and brought the biscuit tin out from the pantry. Luckily, she had a set of nice china cups and saucers which Alice had cajoled her brothers into buying for Meg last Christmas. She'd have been mortified if she'd had to offer him tea in a pint pot.

'I'll never be able to thank you enough for what you did for Kit,' she said fervently as she handed him his tea and sat down facing him. Tucker was standing at the table, already deep in a battle with his loyal troop of soldiers, issuing commands to them in a low voice and the next moment lifting his arm in an arc and zooming in on them, knocking one down.

'Boom, boom,' he cried, imitating guns.

Meg glanced at him before turning back to Jonty. 'You are so very kind an' all,' she said softly.

He smiled. 'Well, they were just lying around the old nursery, there's no children to play with them now.'

He took a sip of tea and Meg was thankful that she'd had some real milk in the house to put in it, she'd bought it for Kit.

'Still, it was very good of you, Sir,' she insisted.

'Oh please, don't call me that, it makes me feel old,' he said. 'My name's John. Do call me John.'

'Well . . .' Meg was about to object to such familiarity but just then the front door opened and she heard her sister's footsteps.

'Auntie Alice! Auntie Alice!' Tucker broke off his game abruptly and ran to the door to meet her. 'Look what Mr Dale brought us.'

Alice halted in the doorway and stared at the man sitting in Meg's rocking-chair and drinking tea from a china cup.

'He brought us soldiers, Auntie Alice.' Tucker cried impatiently. She wasn't showing the interest in the soldiers he thought she should do.

'Yes, pet,' said Alice, and dropped her gaze to the toys. 'Grand, they are.'

'Oh, Mr Dale, this is my sister, Alice. You remember, she was there when—'

'Yes, of course.' Jonty rose to his feet and held out his hand to the young woman, who blushed with embarrassment as she hesitantly took it in hers.

'Miss Alice, er – ?' Jonty lifted an enquiring eyebrow at her.

'Maddison,' she mumbled, suddenly seeming to Meg very shy and overwhelmed for a girl who professed to be completely uninterested in men.

'Maddison, Miss Alice Maddison,' he murmured. 'Do sit down, Miss Maddison.' He pulled out a chair from the table and offered it to her.

Maddison, he thought, glancing at Meg. Of course it was Maddison, he had known it would be.

Twenty-Two

Jonty drove back to Grizedale Hall full of old longings and dreams and a wild determination not to lose sight of Meg now that he had found her. He had sat in her kitchen and talked to her and her sister Alice, and had been filled with a feeling of homecoming. Every gesture the sisters made, every expression on their faces, seemed familiar to him. It must be their mother, his Aunt Hannah, they reminded him of, he mused, even though he had only vague memories of her.

He had looked into Meg Cornish's eyes and his lost childhood had returned to him. He had been loth to leave the kitchen of the little cottage in the colliery rows and go back to the large, cold and decaying mansion which was his home.

'I'll call again,' he had said to Meg as he left, 'to see how the boy goes on, I mean.'

'You're very kind,' she had answered as conventions prescribed and watched as he turned the horse and trap round and drove away up the row. He had turned at the corner and she was still standing there and he had given her a salute with his whip and she had smiled and his heart sang as he went on his way.

His feelings of warm elation were soon doused as he opened the front door of the Hall. The sound of raised voices from the floor above came resounding down the wide staircase, his father's bullying tones the loudest.

'Don't you tell me what Father said, you mean old

267

bitch, God rot his soul in hell, and yours too. I've a good mind to throw you out on the streets, you—'

Ralph's words were slurred. Obviously he had been drinking again that morning.

'Ralph, Ralph, I know you don't mean it, son, you don't. It's the drink talking,' quavered the old woman.

Jonty took the stairs two at a time, his anger mounting as he heard a crash from his grandmother's bedroom. As he reached the door he saw that she was cowering down in bed with her son towering over her, his face suffused with rage. Beside him was an overturned chair, obviously the cause of the crash. Jonty strode into the room and thrust his father roughly to one side.

'Get out! Do you hear me? Get out. And don't you come in here again,' he cried.

'What the hell . . .?' Ralph blustered, but retreated nevertheless before Jonty's fury.

Ralph was not the man he used to be. Years of riotous living had taken their toll. He was stoop-shouldered and paunchy, his hands covered with liver spots and his face a map of red and purple veins.

'I have a right to come and see my own mother,' he shouted now, taking a little courage from the fact that Jonty had turned away from him. But his son ignored him for the moment.

'Are you all right, Grandmother?' he asked gently. 'Shall I get you some tea? Come now, let me help you to sit up, you know you can't breathe too well lying down.'

Mrs Grizedale gratefully let him lift her to a sitting position and plump up the pillows behind her. Jonty put an arm round her thin shoulders, feeling her trembling, almost shaking, with fright.

'You're not going out again, are you, Jonty?'

'No, Grandmother. I'll stay with you for a while,' he promised.

'That's right, Grandmother's little boy,' sneered Ralph

who was still standing in the doorway. 'The old witch always did think more of you than me, her own son. I was always the wicked one, the one who dared to enjoy life. Not like that sanctimonious old sod who was my father!'

Jonty gently covered his grandmother's shoulders with a woollen shawl, ignoring his father's taunts though he was well aware that every word was upsetting her more.

'Don't listen, Grandmother. He's drunk. I'll get you some tea to calm your nerves,' he said to her before striding to the door and confronting his father. 'Are you going to go or do I have to throw you out?' he asked quietly.

Ralph laughed. 'Oh, yes, throw me out of my own house, would you? That'd be a fine thing. A misbegotten son like you throwing a man out of his own house.'

Still he backed away before Jonty's threatening stance and started to descend the stairs.

'Don't worry, I'm going anyway, I'm not staying in this hole. I'm off for a bit of life.'

Ralph took his hat and coat from the hall stand and lurched out on to the drive. It was a long time since he had seriously stood up to his son.

Escape was his father's usual answer whenever he was thwarted, Jonty thought as he watched Ralph's erratic progress round to the stables, wondering for a moment if he ought to stop him. His father was in no condition to ride anywhere, let alone the ten miles or so to Darlington which was where his cronies hung out. But in the end he closed the front door and went into the kitchen to get a tray of tea and biscuits of his grandmother. The old lady came first.

'What did he want, Grandmother?' he asked as he poured her tea into a dainty china cup and handed it to her. 'Money, was it?'

She didn't answer, though a silent tear ran down her withered cheek.

Jonty sat down by the hearth, his thoughts bitter. Now his grandmother was upset, he wouldn't be able to go out again and he had work to do in the stables. It was so long since they had any proper help with the horses. Though if things went on the way they were, there would be none to look after soon. Sometimes he got so tired of trying to hold the estate together, if it wasn't for his grandmother he would have taken the money his grandfather had left him and emigrated to Canada, or Australia, or anywhere away from here. Instead the money he had come into on his twenty-first birthday was earning interest in a bank, well away from his father's clutches, and the interest was being used up fast in staving off the day when the estate finally went bankrupt. His grandmother had a tiny income left from railway shares and his father was always trying to get money out of her.

His thoughts returned to the little colliery house in Winton, the love he saw between the two sisters and the children. Where was the husband? he wondered. There was no evidence of a man living in the house, no smell of tobacco, no men's shirts hanging on the overhead airer along with the other washing. Was Meg a widow then?

Meg was wondering about Jonty that afternoon too as she rubbed lard into flour and cooked meat for pie fillings. Dreamily, she rolled out pastry, made pies and put them in the oven, her hands working automatically at the oft-repeated tasks but most of her mind was free to go wherever her wandering thoughts wanted.

She dreamed of dark, velvety eyes smiling at her and was filled with unfamiliar feelings, urges, such as she hadn't felt for years.

'Mam! Mam!'

Kit calling from the bedroom brought her down to earth with a crash. She wiped her hands and hurried upstairs to attend to him. She'd been building pie in the sky that day. It was the real kind she had to get on with, never mind dreaming about a dark-eyed gentleman who couldn't possibly be in the least interested in her. He'd only come to see Kit, she reminded herself. When the child recovered she would likely never see him again.

So when Jonty came calling again, a few days later, Meg insisted on calling him 'Sir' and was deferentially formal with him, fearing he might see in her eyes that she was attracted to him and be embarrassed, or worse amused.

But Jonty was not to be put off. He came no more to Winton Colliery but got into the habit of regularly riding past Old Pit Cottages where the aged miner, Bill, had told him Meg often came to help out. But it was some months before this strategy paid off.

'Mr Dale, how nice to see you,' exclaimed Meg, putting down the basket of bread and pies which she was taking to the cottages.

Jonty took off his hat and smiled in delight at finally seeing her. 'And you too, Mrs Cornish, how are you? And Kit, how is he? His leg is mended, I hope?'

'Oh, aye, thank you, he's grand,' said Meg. 'The lads are both at school now, so I'm on my own.'

'At least they won't be getting into mischief, then,' said Jonty, hardly knowing what he was saying, he was so busy watching the dimples in her cheeks below the bright blue eyes and the sun glinting on her corn-coloured hair.

'No,' she laughed. 'Well, they can still do that, the pair of them. But at least the old shaft is fenced in now.'

'Yes.'

They stood for a moment, looking over to the old

271

workings, now fenced in by the Winton Colliery joiner. The owners had even supplied a new cover for the shaft, made of strong new wood.

Meg thought about that awful day, the nightmare of terror when Kit had fallen down the shaft. She would never forget it, nor the courage of this man who had brought the child out, miraculously alive. She shivered.

'Cold?' asked Jonty, surprised.

'No, I was thinking of what might have happened if you hadn't been there that day,' she answered.

'Oh, someone would have gone down, I didn't do so much,' he murmured.

Meg smiled her disbelief. 'Aye, but you did, and I'll always bless your for it, Sir.'

'John. My name's John,' he insisted.

'John,' she said softly, her resolve weakening as she looked up at him. By, he was a grand man, she thought dreamily, so kind and good, not giving himself any airs like some gentlemen did.

Jonty indicated the basket. 'Can I help you with that?' he asked.

'I-I was just taking it to the miners' houses,' she replied. 'Leftovers from yesterday. I let them have the pies at cost.'

'I'll walk along with you, then.'

Jonty picked up the basket in one hand, leading his horse with the other, walked along to Old Pit Cottages with her and waited for her to deliver the pies.

'Wot cheor, Sir.' A couple of the old men, one of them Bill, were idling on the end of the row, sitting on their hunkers and smoking clay pipes. Jonty acknowledged the greeting courteously. They watched curiously as he stood there, the reins of his horse hanging loosely to allow his horse to graze on the new grass springing by the roadside.

They watched without comment as Meg came out

again and joined Jonty, and the two of them walked along the track back to the road. Then Bill took his pipe out of his mouth and pointed it after them.

'Likely he's just been asking after the lad like,' he said, and frowned heavily beneath bushy eyebrows at his companion, daring him to suggest there was anything more to it.

'Aye,' answered his companion, gazing peaceably into the distance. Bill's unspoken warning was not needed. If any gossip was going to get out about that canny lass, Meg Cornish, why, it wouldn't be him that started it. The lass had enough to put up with, what with that man of hers. And Wesley Cornish had a lot to answer for any road. By, he was the scandal of the place since he took up with that Sally Hawkins, a lass no better than she should be even before she started carrying on with poor Meg's man. The old man took his pipe out of his mouth and spat on the ground at the thought of the brazen hussy.

'You live on your own with the two boys?' asked Jonty.

'Aye.'

'You're a widow, then?' he probed, hoping she might answer in the affirmative.

No,' Meg blushed painfully. 'Wesley doesn't live with us. He's my husband, like.'

'Oh.' Jonty was sorry he had brought it up, it had created a moment of embarrassment between them.

'He lives with another woman,' she said baldly.

Jonty's eyes widened. It was the new century and things were changing in the modern world, but this was something unusual in a pit village, he was sure.

He's wondering what I did to drive my man off, Meg thought miserably. He must be scandalized. They walked on in silence until they came to the junction where the track joined the road back to Winton Colliery and here

273

they halted and looked at each other. Meg's cheeks were still rosy and she looked quickly down at her basket, biting her lip.

'I didn't mean to pry,' he said gently, taking her hand.

'It doesn't matter,' she said, her voice low and throaty, hardly above a whisper.

He looked down at her hand, red and work-roughened and so small in his own. He drank in the scent of her, fresh and female and smelling faintly of lye soap. He marvelled at the way her hair sprang, so thick and abundant, in a straight line above her white forehead. And he did not want to let her go.

'I have to get back for the bairns,' she murmured.

'Yes,' he said, lifting her hand to his lips. 'Will you be back this way soon?'

'Probably on Tuesday.'

'I may see you then.'

Meg set off down the road, knowing he was still standing by the path, watching her go. Her hand felt warm where he had kissed it, the first time anyone had ever kissed it. She lifted it up to her own mouth, touching the spot which he had kissed with her own lips. By, he was a grand man, she thought, a lovely man, so fine and handsome and bonny. Even his slight limp was attractive to her, romantic, and at the same time making her feel slightly protective.

The following Tuesday, Jonty was at the junction of the road and the overgrown track to Old Pit early, just in case. And even though he knew it was illogical, he felt a pang of disappointment that there was no sign of her. Somehow he had expected Meg to feel the same eagerness as he did. He opened the gate and took his horse through so that it could graze in the field, the reins tied loosely on to the saddle, then climbed the gate and settled down on the top bar to wait. It was May, and though the wind was still blowing cold, the sun was warm on his back.

Jonty whistled idly as he waited. And waited and waited. Still Meg didn't come. He took his watch from his waistcoat pocket. It was already one-thirty. They would have no time together if she didn't come soon. Not if she had things to take to Old Pit Cottages and also had to be back for the children coming in from school.

'Good day, John.'

The soft voice came from behind him. With a quick smile, he jumped down from the gate and turned to her, the gladness he felt showing in a sudden brightness of his eyes.

'I thought you weren't coming,' he said, the first thing that came into his head.

Meg smiled, 'I was early, I've already been to the cottages.'

In fact, she had been afraid he wouldn't turn up. After she'd got home the week before, she had gone over and over their last meeting in her mind. How he had looked, what he had said, the feel of his lips on the back of her hand. And now she was seeing him again she found the reality was even better than her imagination.

'We can take a walk then,' said Jonty, offering her his arm. Meg hesitated, unsure what to do. Wesley had never walked arm in arm with her, never even offered her his arm. Tentatively, she put her hand out, feeling a touch of embarrassment at how red and rough it looked against the fawn sleeve of his jacket. It was so very strange to be walking along the path, his horse following them without being bidden.

At the place where the track forked, one branch leading to Old Eldon and one to Old Pit, she hesitated.

'We'll go this way, shall we?' he asked, leading her away from Old Pit.

'Er, I saved two pies for us,' she ventured. 'That is, if you haven't had your dinner yet?'

She walked on, not daring to look at him after she had said it, and there was a moment's silence which seemed to her to stretch on and on. It was a mistake, she thought wretchedly, he doesn't want to eat with me, of course he doesn't.

But Jonty was simply looking around, seeking a good place for a picnic, and soon he found one. A stand of ash trees shading a grassy bank lay a few yards from the path. There they would be sheltered from the wind yet still warmed by the sun.

'Course, if you're in a hurry—' she began.

'Meg, I'd love to share a picnic with you,' he said. 'Over there's a good place, don't you think?' He took her basket and led the way to the bank where they settled on the dry grass.

They ate tatie and leek pie and meat and onion pastie, and drank water from the bottle Meg had brought with her, just in case. And they talked and talked, about anything and everything except what was really on their minds, their wild, blind attraction to each other.

'There's to be a procession in the village on Saturday,' she told him. 'Because of the relief of Mafeking, like. The colliery band will be leading off.'

'Your boys will like that,' said Jonty, smiling. 'I suppose they'll be marching too?'

'Not Kit.'

'Oh? I thought his leg was better now?'

'It is,' she assured him. 'But, you know, Kit's a funny lad. He'd rather be out roaming the countryside than marching in a procession. Tucker now, Tucker wants to be soldier.' She laughed indulgently.

'I might see you there,' said Jonty.

'Oh, I don't know . . .' Meg looked alarmed. Wesley might not want her for himself but she didn't know how he would react if he thought anyone else was interested in her, especially someone like John. In her position she had to be careful. She couldn't afford to let pit folk turn against her, she depended on them for her living, not just with the baking but also the extra she earned attending to women lying in.

'I didn't mean – well, I meant I might go along to watch, perhaps take my grandmother if she's feeling well enough,' Jonty said quickly.

For Mrs Grizedale was responding to the better weather, her aches and pains had eased and she often was well enough to be brought downstairs for tea. A fine day in the open air might be good for her.

They parted reluctantly when the time came for Meg to go back and both looked forward to Saturday when they would see each other again, even though they could not acknowledge each other in the village.

The intervening days were busy ones for Meg as she made up for lost time, but it was worth it. She worked with a new energy and vibrancy.

'There's going to be crackers, Mam, fireworks, the minute it's dark,' cried Tucker, his round face bright with excitement. 'Eeh, it'll be grand, won't it?'

'If you don't stand still, we won't be there to see the procession, never mind the crackers,' said Meg. She was putting the finishing touches to a bright red soldier's tunic she had made for him out of an old sheet dyed the appropriate colour. She had tried to persuade Kit to have one too but when he'd showed opposition to joining the procession she'd let it go, though insisting he go with her to watch the fun.

'You'll have a grand time, lad,' she'd urged, 'and there'll be a penny each for you to spend. And we'll go to the Lantern Show after, there'll be pictures of Africa, lions and tigers an' all.'

This had been enough to sway Kit. Now he sat patiently on the settle, waiting for his mother to finish dressing Tucker in his soldier's uniform.

They went out to the street and joined the throng of other families, the adults dressed in their Sunday best and the children in fancy dress, some of them making very peculiar-looking soldiers indeed. They were laughing and chattering, making the most of the carnival atmosphere. It was already late-afternoon for the men had had to work in the morning, but the sun still shone.

The procession formed up at the head of Pasture Row, there being some delay as the children sorted themselves out behind a troop of real soldiers from the Durham Light Infantry, there to boost recruitment for the war in Africa. But at last they were ready and the colliery band led them off, along the top of rows made gay with bunting strung across from one to the other, then on up the road to the old village, the main street and the shops.

The band played and the children whooped as they marched along and the onlookers cheered enthusiastically. Walter and Tucker marched proudly side by side, and Meg and Alice, who had by then joined her, gave them an extra loud cheer.

'Look, Meg, there's Mr Dale,' said Alice, pointing over to a governess trap with a man and a woman sitting in it, watching the fun. The woman looked very old and frail, thought Meg, but John now, he looked grand. Her heart swelled with pride that so handsome a man should take notice of her, should actually be interested in a lass from a pit village like her.

'He looks nice, doesn't he, Meg?' whispered Alice. 'Howay, let's go across, mebbe he'll have a word with us.'

'Oh, Alice, I don't know,' Meg objected, panicking. If anyone saw them together, and she actually had to speak to him and listen to his answer, she was sure it would be obvious how she felt about him. She couldn't disguise it, her feelings were too strong.

'What the heck's the matter with you, Meg? Don't be so fond,' said Alice impatiently. 'What's the harm in saying hello?'

Just then, Jonty bent down to the old lady and spoke a few words and she nodded her head. He picked up the reins and prepared to go, carefully keeping his horse to a walk to avoid the milling crowds.

'Now look,' said Alice, 'we're too late. I don't know, our Meg, you're so backwards at coming forwards sometimes.'

But Meg had caught his quick glance in their direction, the way he half-smiled and lifted one eyebrow in secret salute to her. And her heart warmed within her.

'Would you just look at that!'

The sisters glanced round at the sound of Auntie Pheobe's voice. She and Uncle Tot were standing on the kerb looking over to their right. They followed her gaze.

It was Wesley, Wesley and Sally Hawkins standing together as bold as brass, Wesley with an arm around the girl's shoulders.

Alice let out her breath in a hiss, eyes glittering at the thought of the public humiliation the sight of them must give to Meg.

'Brazen hussy,' she exclaimed.

Meg looked quickly away. She didn't want to watch them, didn't want to see the triumphant smirk on Sally's face which would surely be there if she thought Meg was looking.

'She's having a bairn,' Auntie Phoebe's eyes widened as she took in the shape of Sally's belly. 'Eeh, our Alice, have you ever seen the like? Standing there proud as punch, she is, a proper little trollop.'

'There's me da,' said Kit, glowering, his normally pleasant face transformed darkly. As he spoke, Wesley bent down and gave a boy of about ten years old a copper. Of course, they all knew who the boy was: Ralph Hawkins. Sally had had him with her when she came home in disgrace from a place as a housemaid. She and the boy had lived in a broken-down cottage in the village with her mother until the older woman died and Wesley moved in permanently.

'Got money for her by-blow but not for his own bairns,' sniffed Auntie Phoebe.

'Let it be, woman, don't spoil the day,' urged Uncle Tot. He saw Kit's face and, drawing the wrong conclusion, took a penny out of his own pocket.

'Dinna take any notice, lad,' he said. 'I'll give you a penny, and one for Tucker an' all.'

Kit still glowered darkly, though he took the coppers and thanked Uncle Tot nicely.

'That Ralphy Hawkins,' he said, 'he's always picking on our Tucker. Says he's not our da now, but Ralphy's. He says our mam's no good to anybody.'

Meg looked at him in dismay. Oh God, she thought, what is it all doing to my lads?

In the evening, she took Tucker and Kit to see the Magic Lantern Show, gazing blindly at the pictures of the wicked Boers who had dared to rebel against the Queen, and black boys who were not black from coal dust yet grinned cheekily at the camera much the same as her own boys would have done. There was a great noise in the hall as the audience cheered and booed, according to whatever was on the screen, but Meg sat silently, in a turmoil of conflicting emotions. But guilt was not one of them. Any remnants of loyalty she might have felt towards Wesley were destroyed now. And in the dark hall she admitted to herself how deep was her love for John Dale.

Twenty-Three

'Meg, I have a confession to make,' said Jonty.

'A confession?'

Meg looked up from repacking her basket with the bottle and cups and pie dishes. They had got into the habit, that summer of 1900, of meeting every Tuesday when the weather was fine and sharing a picnic on the grassy knoll by the stand of ash trees. And it had been a good summer, a fine summer, there had been only one Tuesday when it had rained.

'Yes.' Jonty hesitated, not sure how to begin. But it was long past the time when he should have told Meg the truth about who he was, he wanted there to be no secrets between them. He took her hand and she lifted questioning eyes to his.

'My name is not John,' he began. 'Well, it is, but I'm generally known as something else. Jonty.'

'Jonty?'

'Yes, Jonty. Jonty Grizedale.'

'Jonty Grizedale?'

Meg suddenly realized she was repeating everything he said. She was a bit taken aback. They had talked and talked this afternoon as they did every time they met and she had thought she knew him so well, yet here he was telling her he had been lying to her all this while.

Then the significance of the name dawned on her. He was saying he was Jonty, her childhood friend, the son of her Aunt Nell and Ralph Grizedale, the candyman.

Memories crowded in on her: her mother wondering aloud how Jonty was getting on, her father's short replies. But she had to make sure.

'Jonty, my Jonty, Auntie Nell's son?' she asked and he nodded.

'Do you hate me, Meg?' He had moved closer to her and was searching her face for a sign or for her reaction to his revelation, his dark eyes anxious. She gave an involuntary movement of denial. How could she hate him?

'How could I hate you?' she said, and silently she was saying: I love you, I love you. Then an awful thought came to her.

'But – you're my cousin then, aren't you? Close kin? Does that mean . . .'

'No, no, Meg, no! Not that close. There is no reason at all why we shouldn't love each other, being cousins doesn't matter.'

She relaxed. Silently she folded the tea cloth which they had used as a tablecloth and laid it over the things in the basket. Having something to do with her hands gave her time to think. For apart from anything else, this was the first time Jonty had put into words their feelings for each other.

'But why, why didn't you say?' she said at last.

'Oh, Meg, I thought you must hate me. I thought all of you must hate me. Why else did your mother and father go away like that and leave me to a man such as my father? I must have done something terribly wrong for that to happen. I agonized about it all the time I was growing up. And then, when I found your aunt a few years ago, none of them would have anything to do with me. Why was that? What did I do to you all?'

Meg looked helplessly at him now. In his moment of distress she could see the little boy in him, the Jonty she

282

had loved so long ago, the Jonty of her dreams when she was younger.

'Oh, Jonty, no, you didn't do anything!' she cried. And out tumbled that old, terrible memory, the one which had haunted her nightmares for so long. The day the candyman had come and put the railway families out of their houses. Jonty's father sitting there on his great horse, seeming larger than life and twice as powerful. And how they'd had to go away, find work and shelter elsewhere.

And he told her of how it had been for him, in that great house with no mother and not even Auntie Hannah to run to when his father whipped him. He told her about the time he found the cottages boarded up and empty, and how abandoned he had felt.

Meg, in her turn, told him of her girlhood dream that he would come riding up like a knight in armour and rescue her from a life of unhappiness and drudgery, and they would go away together and live happily ever after. And he told her of his gentle grandmother and how he stayed at the Hall and tried to keep things going for her sake.

They were very close together by this time, arms around each other, comforting each other for old wounds which had never healed, her fair head nestling on his broad shoulder, his hand in hers. And what came next was as natural as life itself as they made love in the grass, screened from any prying passerby on the track by the fall of the ground and the stand of trees.

Meg couldn't believe it. Here she was, a mother of three children, two living, and she hadn't known what making love was. She was well acquainted with sex. Oh, yes, she had had too much of that in the short time Wesley had lived with her, but this was different altogether to that aggressive, and for her painful, act which she had gone through with him.

Jonty was gentle yet passionate. Instinctively he knew how to raise her dormant sexuality, arouse feelings of an intensity that she had never suspected she was capable of, until at last they reached the height together and collapsed, lying heart to heart, as they slowly descended from the apex. And Meg had a wild hope that she had conceived. She wanted Jonty's baby more than anything in the world. Oh, she wanted it, even though she was well aware of the difficulties it would cause her. But it didn't matter, the world didn't matter, all that mattered was Jonty and the baby she might already be carrying in her belly. And her boys, of course, her lads.

Meg sat up abruptly. It must be getting late. The boys would be coming home from school and here she was. She would never get back to the house in time for them.

'What is it?' Jonty was lying on his back, looking up at her. He held out his arms to her. 'Come back, Meg. Don't go, not yet, please.'

'The lads will be home from school long since, I'll have to run.'

She rose to her feet and hurriedly brushed the dried grass from her clothes, tidied her hair, pulled her bodice into position and fastened it back up to the neck.

'Oh, Lord, yes.' Jonty scrambled to his feet and dusted himself down, then stopped and looked at Meg. 'You can come tomorrow? Oh, Meg, my love, we have so much to talk about, so much time to catch up on.' He caught hold of her hand and drew her to him, gathering her in his arms and kissing her tenderly – her lips, her eyes, the nape of her neck.

'Meg,' he groaned, 'how can I let you go, now I've found you?'

'I'll try to come tomorrow,' she said doubtfully. She had so much to do, had already taken this afternoon away from her work. She had to work to live, it was a hard fact of life. 'I must run now,' she said regretfully.

'I'll put you up in front of me, we'll ride to the road,' he suggested. And that was another first in her life when she was lifted before him on to the horse and held in his strong arms as he cantered along the track. She felt his chest at her back, his legs against hers. The wind was in her hair and her eyes shone with excitement so that when they reached the junction and he lifted her down, she sparkled with delight.

'By, it was grand,' she cried, and quickly reaching up to give him a farewell kiss, was away down the road, breaking into a run as she neared the colliery rows.

Jonty stood by the gate, watching her until she was out of sight, his heart soaring within him. She was his love and he would have her, he told himself, no matter what obstacles they had to overcome.

He rode back to the hall, his head full of her, his normally observant gaze not seeing his father's horse galloping across the field jumping the hedge and blowing heavily as Ralph flogged it on.

Ralph was standing idly in the stable yard when Jonty cantered in. He was leaning against the stable wall, his bloodshot eyes gleaming maliciously, the horse, still saddled, panting beside him.

Jonty dismounted and unsaddled his mount, ignoring his father. Ralph had obviously been off with his cronies again and drink had given him Dutch courage. Just as well I got here before he could pester Grandmother, Jonty thought wearily. He moved to lead his horse past his father to the stable but Ralph blocked the stable door, one hand on his hip and the other on the door jamb; he grinned evilly.

'Gadding about with a pitman's woman, now, eh? Not such a saint as you'd have us think, are you? Whatever will your grandmother have to say when I tell her?'

Jonty halted and stared at his father, stepping back a

pace as the stink of whisky-laden breath hit him. Ralph misunderstood the gesture altogether and laughed aloud.

'That shook you, didn't it? I saw you, you prating hypocrite, with that woman. Wasn't that the lass you were so hoity-toity about a few years ago? What was that you said. The pitmen look after their own? We have to live in this community, you said. All bloody cant.' He sneered. 'Well, I suppose it shows you are a man, any way, I was beginning to doubt it.'

'Get out of my way, Father,' said Jonty, feeling sick to his stomach.

Ralph made an exaggerated gesture out of moving aside and bowing to his son.

'By all means, lad, I'll get out of your way. I have other things to do than stand here blathering to you. I'm off to have a word with your grandmother.'

'You stay away from her, you hear me?' Jonty barked. 'If you say anything to her, tell her any of your lies, upset her in any way, I'll – I'll—'

'You'll what, lad? Nay, I don't think you will. The old witch needs to be told about her precious grandson carrying on with a pit wife. I don't think she should be deluded any longer, do you? It's for her own good, after all.'

Ralph remained standing by the door though, making no move to go into the house and carry out his threat and Jonty realized his father thought he could blackmail him over this.

'What do you want, Father?'

'That's better,' said Ralph, his grin turning into a smile of satisfaction. 'Now, I shall have to think about that for a minute.'

Grimly, Jonty led his horse past, put him in his stall and shook hay down for him. He went back and did the same for his father's horse, without even looking at

Ralph, then began to rub down both horses. He waited for Ralph to set out his conditions but wouldn't give him the satisfaction of knowing it meant much to him.

His grandmother's health was precarious to say the least, she had to be protected from any unpleasantness. There was Meg, too. Ralph could make trouble in the village for her and her children. Whatever his father wanted, Jonty would have to go along with him, at least so far as he could. He finished rubbing down his own horse and began to see to his father's before Ralph came in to the stable, triumph gleaming in his eyes.

'Well?' said Jonty, straightening up and giving Ralph a level stare.

'I've decided I might not trouble the old witch,' said Ralph. 'Of course, one good turn deserves another, as they say. What are you prepared to do for me?'

'I already do everything around here,' snapped Jonty. 'Come to the point, Father, what do you want?'

'I want you to tell her to sign her shares over to me,' said Ralph, getting down to business. 'What does an old woman want with railway shares, anyway? She's just being dog in the manger about them, I can put them to much better use.'

'Oh, yes, like selling them and drinking the money,' Jonty said bitterly.

'Watch how you speak to me, you young lout, or I might change my mind and tell her anyway,' snarled Ralph.

'She can't give you the source of her only income,' protested Jonty.

'No? Well, you know the alternative.' Ralph scented victory. He crossed his arms over his paunch and grinned.

Jonty thought about it, absently rubbing down the horses as he did so. He had to do something. There was only one thing for it if he was to save his grandmother from his father.

'I'll tell you what, I'll give you ten pounds a week if you leave grandmother alone and swear not to mention anything about this to anybody else,' he offered.

Ralph threw back his head and laughed uproariously, his hands on his hips and his belly shaking with mirth.

'And where the hell are *you* going to get ten pounds a week?'

'I can get it,' said Jonty.

Ralph stopped laughing and looked closely at him, slowly beginning to believe that it might be true.

'How will you get it? You're not saying you have money, are you?'

'I can get it, I told you,' Jonty repeated.

'Aye. And I'm not going to believe you until I see the money for myself.'

'Wait here.'

Jonty went into the house and climbed the wide staircase, desperately trying to work out the best way to handle his father.

'Is that you, Jonty?' his grandmother called and he poked his head round her door.

'Yes, Grandmother. I won't be a minute, I have something to do, then I'll be up to see you and we'll have a chat. You're feeling all right, still?'

'Yes, thank you, I'm fine,' she answered. 'You're so good to me, Jonty, such a good boy. What would I do without you?'

He smiled and hurried on to the old nursery. In the toy box, under the few remaining toys, he had hidden his money box. The nursery was one place he was fairly sure his father would not think of looking. Taking the key from his waistcoat pocket, he unlocked the box and took out twenty pounds before hiding the box carefully away again.

The money was all that was left of his last dividend and it had been earmarked for repairs at Home Farm. Now the repairs would have to wait.

Back in the yard, Jonty showed his father the four-five pound notes, being careful to keep them out of his reach.

'Ten now, and ten next week,' he said.

Ralph's eyes widened, his scepticism turning to anger. He stepped forward aggressively, demanding to know where the money came from.

'A bequest,' said Jonty. 'Now, do you agree or don't you?'

'A bequest?' sneered Ralph. 'Who in hell would leave you anything? Not your mother's family, that's a safe bet. Those pitmen haven't a penny to scratch their arses with.'

For the moment, Jonty had to ignore the insult to his dead mother's kin. He had the living to protect now.

'It was Grandfather,' he admitted.

Ralph laughed aloud. 'Are you trying to say I wouldn't know if you had been left anything in the old man's will? Don't be bloody daft, man, I heard it read myself.'

'Not in his will, no,' answered Jonty. 'He put it in trust for me when I was born. He kept it from you because he knew you wouldn't rest 'til you had it. Now, I assure you I can pay you ten pounds a week. It will be worth it to keep you away from Grandmother.'

'Keep me away from her? Why, that sly old bitch must have known about it all this time! Conspiring against me, they were, their only son. All for the low-born get of a miner's daughter. I've a good mind to go up and tell her now, I have.'

'But you won't,' said Jonty. 'Oh no, you won't. If you do you will not get a penny from me.'

'How much have you got?' Ralph changed his tack. 'How much did the old man rob me of?'

'He robbed you of nothing. And I have no intention

of telling you how much I have,' Jonty said firmly. He could see that his father was wavering, dying to get his hands on the money in Jonty's hand.

'Ten pounds isn't enough. If you're offering me ten pounds, it must mean you can afford to give me twenty. Twenty's not too much to give for your beloved grandmother, is it?' Ralph looked cunning, he thought he could bargain with his son.

Jonty put the money in his waistcoat pocket, deciding to chance all on a last bluff.

'Right then, Father,' he said. 'Go on, tell her. Do what you like, I'm sick of it all. I'm going to take my money and emigrate, make a new life for myself in Canada.'

'And what about your whore?' asked Ralph with a sneer, but he looked somewhat uncertain now, as he saw the money disappear from view.

'I won't care what you tell people, not if I'm not here to face them,' said Jonty, his expression bland, though his heart beat painfully at the thought of the humiliation Meg would endure if their affair was bruited about the village. I won't let it happen, Meg, he vowed, silently, as he turned on his heel and walked away.

'Wait a minute, wait a minute, I didn't say I didn't agree,' cried Ralph, running after him.

Jonty halted, forcing himself to keep calm as he faced his father again.

'Go on, I'll take the ten pounds,' said Ralph. 'I'll say nothing, keep my mouth shut.' After all, ten pounds a week would buy a fair ration of whisky. With ten pounds in his pocket he could afford to go off to Darlington more often. There was a barmaid in The Hole in the Wall he had his eye on, young and full-breasted and happy to make a little extra to supplement her wages. Girls these days weren't so keen to go with him without payment in advance.

'You'll keep away from Grandmother?' Jonty insisted.

'What do I want with a snivelling old—'

'That's enough,' snapped Jonty, pressing home his advantage. 'She has the right to expect some respect from you.' He took the money out of his pocket and handed over two crisp five-pound notes.

Ralph smiled his satisfaction as he took them. Life was definitely taking a turn for the better he thought. He was off to Darlington, as fast as his horse could take him.

What a sot he is, thought Jonty as his father rode out of the yard. He went indoors and tidied himself up before going upstairs to his grandmother's room. At least one good thing had come out of it, they were unlikely to see much of his father until the money had run out.

'I'm sorry I've been so long, Grandmother,' he said lightly, dropping a kiss on the old lady's cheek. 'I had things to attend to.'

Twenty-Four

Meg was happily preparing the picnic basket one day the following week when the midday quiet of the colliery rows was shattered by the sound that was dreaded by everyone there, from the oldest down to the youngest school child. The piercing racket sounded over the rows, shrieking loudly before settling into an undulating wail like some tone-deaf monster. It was the call for the rescue men.

Dear God, she prayed, the happy anticipation which she had felt all the morning dropping from her and leaving in its place a dreadful fear. She was running to the back door for her old shawl in a split second, desperately going over in her mind which miners were down the pit at that time. Was Da? Or Jackie, or Miles? Miles, of course, Miles was there, and Da. Jackie was on night shift, he would be home, thank the Lord.

Maybe it was a false alarm, she told herself, maybe it was just a small fall of stone, someone injured. But as she joined the crowd of women hurrying from the rows to the pit head, she knew the siren would have stopped sooner if that were so. No, this was something more.

The women half-ran, ashen-faced, not talking to one another, not even looking at one another. And Meg knew they were thinking as she was herself, Let it not be my man, my lad. Let it be someone else, please God, let it be someone else. And were ashamed of wishing it to be so though still they wished it.

Alice joined Meg by the entrance of the pit yard and the sisters huddled together, united in their fear.

'A fall of stone.'

The whisper came back to them through the thong. The cage had come to bank and the viewer, the colliery manager, was stepping in with the undermanager.

Alice and Meg looked at each other. A small fall of stone wasn't always so bad. It would be localized. Da and Miles could have been a mile away, working another seam. The faces of all the women had lightened slightly. Not a major disaster, then.

The men were coming up, the rest of the shift, the ones not needed for rescue work. The women watched anxiously, hoping to see their own men among them. There were thankful murmurings going on all around Meg and Alice as wives found their husbands and mothers their sons. But there was no sign of Miles or Da.

'They'll be in the next lot up,' said Alice, not looking at her sister.

'Aye, they will,' said Meg.

They waited, watching the winding wheel spinning round and round as the cage went up and down, anxiously peering at the men who emerged from the pit. An ambulance drawn by two sturdy galloways pulled into the yard. The women drew to one side to let it pass. The ambulance was a fairly new acquisition by the union. Before that the injured were often taken away in flat carts. Now only the dead were. The ambulance had a red cross painted on the side in brave new paint and the crowd looked at it nervously.

One or two of the younger boys who had come out of the pit and were standing around looking solemn, fingered their collars.

'Touch collar, never follow, don't come to my door,' they chanted quietly.

293

'It's taking a long time,' said Alice, and Meg nodded her agreement.

Jackie came running into the pit yard. He had been away up the fields when the siren went and had had to run all the way back. He had changed into his pitclothes ready to go down if he was needed.

'The face is a distance in bye,' he said. 'It will take a while.' He had caught Alice's remark and answered it as he went past his sisters. 'I'll see if I can find anything out,' he promised, going off to join the knot of miners preparing to go down with a second rescue team. But he did not return with any news. He glanced over to Meg and Alice and then he was stooping to step into the cage and was gone. And they waited and waited.

'You go back for the bairns coming in from school,' said Alice.

Meg shook her head. 'No, no, they'll be all right, they're old enough to wait. I can't go 'til I know.'

Alice left it at that. Meg was right about the boys, they were miner's children. They would wait quietly, along with a lot of other children in the rows.

And then the whistle blew and the great wheel began whirring again and a shout went up.

'They've got one lad! He's alive.'

They were manoeuvring a stretcher with a man strapped to it out of the cage. The man screamed. Only it wasn't a man, it was a lad, a boy of twelve or thirteen, and his body was lying at a strange angle, his head right back on his shoulder blades, and he was screaming.

'It's Owen Thomas,' someone said and they watched as he was put into the ambulance and the colliery doctor climbed in beside him. After a few minutes, the screaming stopped, become a low whimpering as the doctor gave him something to ease his pain. And the driver turned his horse and drove out of the pit yard.

The wheel was moving again. It was a full-grown man this time, he fairly filled the stretcher.

'Who is it?' Meg ran forward and caught hold of the sleeve of one of the men. 'Who is it?'

It was Wesley who stepped forward. He had been a member of the first rescue team and had helped to carry the injured boy.

'Come away, Meg, come away,' he said, the first soft words he had had for her in years. 'You can't do anything. It's Miles. Don't look, Meg, it's his head. Howay, lass, don't look.'

Meg pulled her arm away from Wesley. It wasn't true, it couldn't be true, he was just trying to torment her, she thought wildly. But Alice was standing with tears streaming down her face and Auntie Phoebe came and put an arm around each girl and drew them away.

'Hold up now, you have to hold up. There's your da yet.'

'What?'

Meg stared stupidly at her, what was she saying? She turned to Wesley, unable to put the question into words, but she didn't have to. He was nodding sombrely.

'He's under the stone, Meg, we haven't got him out yet.'

Da under the stone. Da who had always been terrified of being in confined spaces, who had surprised everyone when he went down the pit to earn enough to keep his family. And now he was buried.

'We still could get him out alive,' said Wesley. 'He wasn't working directly under where the stone fell, he could be in a pocket of air. He might be fine, Meg.'

Fine? Da, buried alive and still fine? Dear God, she prayed, let him be dead. He was a railway man, not a pitman. Why had he stayed in the pits when his family had grown? Her thoughts were racing round and round, jumping wildly from one thing to another.

'Howay, lass, there's nothing you can do. It could be a while yet before they get to him. You and Alice, you have to go home and see to things for Miles,' said Auntie Phoebe. 'I'll ask Dolly Bates to keep an eye on your lads.'

So Alice and Meg, with Auntie Phoebe and Uncle Tot, followed the flat cart to Pasture Row, the cart which held the body of their young brother Miles, twenty years old that week.

The rescue team with his son among them got Jack Maddison out alive, hardly a scratch on him. They had been sure he was dead. Every few minutes they had jowled on the coal with a stone and listened for an answering jowl from the trapped man, but none had come.

'Did you not hear us, Da?' Jackie had cried, but his father had withdrawn into himself. He sat passively on the cracket he had used to lean on so he could swing his pick in the confined space, the pick in his hand still. He made no move to follow them out of the hole they'd made in the fall of stone. Jackie and his marra had to lead him, bit by bit, forcing his hand open to release the pick first to make it easier for them to get him out. There was hardly a scratch on him.

A miracle, they called it in the rows. There should have been a gang of them working the face in the narrow seam but the others had moved out to the loftier entrance passage to eat their bait when it happened. Jack Maddison, as he did so often, worked on alone, not bothering to break for food.

His son pieced the story together and told it to his family that night, with Miles lying in the front room and his father insisting on staying in the back yard so that Alice took him out a chair and gently sat him in it.

'The stone didn't kill Miles, nor hurt young Thomas

either,' said Jackie. 'Not directly, that is. Miles was killed by a tub. There's an incline just there, the seam is in a dip, you know. The putter lad had just started work again and the galloway was having a job getting started up the incline. The pony was pulling and Owen was pushing but they were making no headway so Miles left his bait and went to give a hand. They got the tub going and Miles stood back but when the tub was halfway up the galloway stopped dead. His ears pricked, like they do when something's up, and then the weight of the truck pulled him back and it rolled down the rails and knocked the putter lad down.'

Meg and Alice looked at him, puzzled. How had that killed Miles and buried Da? But Jackie wasn't finished.

'The tub came off the rails, like,' he continued. 'And then the stone fell, right behind it, blocking off the entrance to the seam. The other lads saw it all. That was what put the wind up the pony, he knew it was coming. The lad was hurt bad, they thought he was dead, but they couldn't get him out 'til they got the pony and tub out of the way. Miles was frantic, they said, what with Da under the stone an' all.

'They had to unload some of the coal and manhandle the tub back on the rails to get it out of the way but the air was thick with dust and Miles bent down to try to see if they'd got it right. And it fell on his head.'

There was silence in the kitchen as they pictured the scene in their minds, the frantic haste to get the boy out, one disaster falling on top of another. It was broken by Auntie Phoebe coming into the kitchen.

'I've brought you a pan of broth,' she said, carrying the heavy pan in and putting it down on the brass-handled bar hooked over the grate. 'I know you likely don't feel like eating, but you have to keep your strength up to get over the next few days.'

Meg rose to her feet. 'I'll have to get back to the bairns,' she said dully.

'No you don't, not at all,' Auntie Phoebe said firmly. 'Tot went round there earlier on. He's brought them round to our house. They're in bed this minute, they've had their suppers and they're tucked up in my back bedroom.'

Meg sat down again. The shock of the day's happenings had got to her and her legs felt as though they were made of jelly.

'Thank you, Auntie Phoebe,' she said. 'Dolly Bates was going to see to them, but I couldn't expect her to have them all night.'

'Aye.' Auntie Phoebe nodded her head in the direction of the already darkening yard. 'We'll have to do something about your da an' all,' she said grimly.

Meg looked at her brother and sister. 'Maybe you'd better try, Alice,' she said. 'He might not take kindly to me, like.'

'Nay, lass,' Auntie Phoebe shook her head. 'I don't think he knows who it is talking to him at all. He just sits there, staring at the wall.'

'We'll all go,' suggested Jackie, and they trooped out into the back yard.

'Da?' said Jackie. 'Howay, Da, you can't stay out here, man. Howay in and sit by the fire, it's getting cold out here. Dark an' all.'

Their father gave no sign of having heard them.

'We'll try to help him up,' decided Meg. 'Come on, Jackie, you take one side and I'll take the other.'

She stood by her father's side and slipped one arm under his armpit and Jackie did the same at his other side.

'Now, one, two, three, heave,' she said, and after an initial resistance, Da was on his feet.

'I'll come behind,' said Alice.

It was weird urging Da to walk forward, Alice pushing gently from behind. Puffs of coal dust came from him for they had not yet succeeded in getting him to change his clothes or bathe. But he walked, albeit slowly, until they reached the door, when he came to an abrupt halt.

'Come on, man, Da,' urged Jackie.

'We'll leave the door open for you,' said Alice.

'Aye, we won't close the door,' said Jackie, and pulling and pushing, they at last managed to get their father inside and over to the hearth and into his chair.

'His hands are like ice,' whispered Meg, distressed. 'Let's try to get him cleaned up and some hot broth inside him. He'll come round, he will, it's the shock. That's all. He'll come round when he gets over the shock.'

The tin bath was filled with hot water and Da sat there unresisting as Jackie and Meg stripped him of his pitclothes down to his pit hoggers, the short cotton under trousers worn down the pit. They washed him and dried him as if he were a child and dressed him in a clean shirt and trousers.

'Stand up now, Da,' they said, and he stood up obediently. 'Sit down now, Da,' they said and he sat down. Meg brought him a bowl of broth and put the spoon into his hand and he took the spoon but didn't use it. She took the spoon from him and tried feeding him with the hot soup but he closed his mouth firmly and turned his head away.

'Leave him be,' advised Auntie Phoebe. 'Likely he'll be better tomorrow.'

The next day, Da was no better. He still sat in the chair and stared ahead of him. Neighbours and friends came in to pay their respects to the family and offered him their condolences, and he sat without speaking so that they were at a loss what to say next.

The kitchen became filled with a terrible smell for he

was incontinent and the sisters were obliged to close the room off to visitors, receiving them only in the front room where Miles lay in his coffin. A closed coffin, because nothing could be done to make Miles's head anywhere near presentable for viewing.

The colliery doctor came and went and returned with another. A mind doctor, the pit folk whispered, one from the asylum at Sedgefield. He asked that they be left alone with Da, and Alice and Meg and Jackie went into the front room where Miles lay and listened to the murmur of voices from the kitchen. Then the doctors came out and talked to the family.

'He'll be better off in hospital,' said the colliery doctor. So Da was taken away in a green van to the asylum, the day before his youngest son was to be buried. The folk in the pit rows watched as he was driven away.

The funeral was held on a Friday morning bright with sunshine which glinted off the steel toecaps of the men who followed the family to the graveyard, Miles's marras and others who were off shift. There were flowers. The union had sent a wreath and the owners another, beautiful exotic flowers brought in from the south, dwarfing the family wreath of garden flowers, roses and lilies. Overhead the birds still sang in the distance, the wheel of the winding engine still turned and the collier whistle blew. Afterwards the men lined up to to pay their respects but no one mentioned Da.

Meg and her two boys followed Alice and Jackie home for the funeral tea, wishing fervently that it was over. She didn't know how they were going to get through the afternoon. But she did, as did Alice and Jackie. The hours went by and at last it was evening and everyone had gone. Meg put the boys to bed in Auntie Phoebe's house, in a spare bed in Bella's room, and left her to mind them. Then she went slowly round to sit with Alice.

For Jackie was on night shift, he had to go back to the pit, and it was unthinkable to leave Alice on her own in the silent house.

A horse was tethered by the tap at the end of the row. Jonty's horse. Meg's pace quickened and she ran up the yard and burst into the kitchen and into Jonty's arms, holding him to her, feeling the solid strength of him, drinking in the scent of him. And she wept, tears rolling down her cheeks, great sobs wracking her body.

Alice watched, wondering, and the attraction Jonty had held for her withered and looked a very poor thing in comparison to the passion between her sister and him.

Twenty-Five

Jonty had not heard of the accident until he was on his way back to the Hall that day. He had waited and waited for Meg, sitting on the grassy knoll. While he waited he made plans for the future, what they would do, he and Meg and her boys, when he was free to go away and take her with him. Dreamily, he stuck a stalk of grass between his teeth and chewed on it idly.

Canada, that was the place. There were lots of opportunities in Canada, he mused. They would go to Canada and buy a farm. He could make a go of it, he knew he could. No one would know they weren't married to each other. The boys would soon forget their early life. He would be a father to them, he would train them in farming. They would have a much better life, better prospects. Farming in Canada offered so much more than a life in the mines of County Durham.

He took his watch out of his waistcoat pocket, noticing with surprise that it was already two o'clock. Meg must have been delayed by something. He would wait another hour.

Jonty smiled as he looked at the watch. It had been his grandfather's. Grandmother had saved it for him until he was twenty-one and put it in his hands on his birthday.

'He would have wanted it to come to you,' she had said. It was an old watch with a cover and when the cover was opened it played a tinkly tune: 'Bobby Shafto'.

The wonder was that she had managed to save it from being sold by his father, he mused. Carefully he replaced the watch in his waistcoat pocket and got to his feet, walking to the path and looking up and down the length of it. There was no sign of Meg, but Bill, from the miners' row, was limping up the path with the aid of a stick, a whippet looking as old as his master walking along beside him.

'Good day, Sir,' said Bill, looking stern. The gentleman was seen loitering there far too often nowadays. It would not be long before others beside him and his marra began to wonder who it was he came to see.

'Afternoon, Bill,' said Jonty. 'Nice dog you've got there.' He smiled and bent to pat the dog but it backed away, growling.

'He doesn't like strangers coming round here,' said Bill shortly, and went on his way.

Jonty stared after him, puzzled. Bill had been so friendly at other times. He went back to the stand of trees and waited half an hour longer. She wasn't coming, he realized, the disappointment heavy on him. Disconsolate, he mounted his horse and rode away. He might as well visit Farmer Teasdale, he thought. He still had to explain why the repairs to his barn would be delayed until next month though how he was going to do this he had no idea. He could hardly say he had given the money to his father to spend on whisky and women.

Jonty was riding along the road when he heard the ambulance coming up behind him, the bell clanking to warn of its approach. Hastily, he pulled over to let it go past, thinking, There must have been an accident in some local mine or other. It was not the fever ambulance, it had to be the new one bought by the Durham miners' union only recently. He followed it on 'til he came to the entrance to Teasdale's place, seeing the farmer just coming out of the barn.

'There's been an accident, I think,' said Jonty.

'Aye, Winton Colliery it was,' Farmer Teasdale answered, shaking his head in solemn sympathy for the pit community. 'My lad told me when he came back from his dinner. He lives in the village with his mother, travels back and forth on his bike.'

'A bad one, did he say?' asked Jonty. He was filled with concern for Meg. Was any of her family involved?

'One killed,' the lad said. 'One with his back broke an' all. They've taken him to the County Hospital in Durham.'

'That must have been the ambulance I saw a minute since,' said Jonty.

'Aye.'

'He didn't happen to know who was killed, did he?'

Farmer Teasdale turned away and called up the yard. 'Ted! Ted!' A stocky youth came out of the byre and looked over to them.

'Aye?'

'Who was it killed, like, did you hear owt about it?'

Ted walked down to them, wiping his hands on his sacking apron.

'It was Miley Maddison as was killed,' he said. 'An' young Owen Thomas had his back broke. An Miley's da, he's trapped under the stone.'

Jonty's first instinct was to gallup to Winton Colliery. In fact he was already on his horse and turning him round when the farmer spoke.

'Are you going already?' he asked, his eyebrows lifting.

'I've just remembered something. I'll see you later,' Jonty mumbled, suddenly remembering the need not to betray his love for Meg.

304

The next few days he agonized over Meg and her family, desperately wanting to go and comfort her. But she was a married woman, he told himself, he had to be careful.

And then he thought of something else. Why he hadn't thought of it before he couldn't imagine. He was kin, wasn't he? He could go to ask after them quite legitimately. He would go to see Mrs Lowther, test the water, so to speak. No one could object to that.

He wasted no time in following the thought through. Within the hour he was riding along the road to Winton Colliery, going along the top of the rows to Pasture Row and tethering his horse by the end house. It was already evening, but he could not wait until the next day. He felt if he did not see Meg tonight he would go mad.

'Eeh, hello, it's Jonty isn't it?'

Auntie Phoebe was at the gate of the second house, the house he knew was that of Meg's father. He stepped forward and held out his hand.

'I thought I would come, offer my condolences,' he said.

'Why, come away in, there's only Alice there. Meg's putting the bairns to bed and Jackie's at the pit, but you'll be more than welcome.'

Jonty hesitated, remembering how unwelcome he had been made the last time he was here. Auntie Phoebe shook her head.

'It's different now,' she said. 'Poor Jack, they took him away.'

'Took him away?'

'Howay in, lad, we can talk inside. I'm telling you, no one will say you nay.'

Alice was inside, tidying up after the funeral tea. She looked worn and tired and her eyes were red with weeping.

'Look who I've brought to see you,' announced Auntie Phoebe triumphantly. 'It's your cousin Jonty.'

305

Alice stared at him in disbelief. What was Auntie Phoebe on about now? This was Mr Dale, the man who had rescued Kit from the shaft at Old Pit.

'Mr Dale?'

'Please forgive me, Alice,' he said. 'I know I said my name was Dale. It's not, it's Grizedale. And it is true, I am your cousin. I thought you wouldn't want anything to do with me if you knew who I was.'

'It was Jack who took against you,' Auntie Phoebe declared. 'And the poor man's not here, they took him off to Sedgefield.'

Jonty was horrified when he heard the full story of what had happened during the last few days, and blamed himself for not being there to support Meg and her sister through it all. What did it matter what people said? But he had no time to ask any questions for just then the door burst open and there was Meg, his darling Meg.

'Well, I cannot believe it!'

Both Meg and Jonty heard Auntie Phoebe's exclamation, but it was Jonty who found the strength of will to take hold of Meg's arms and put her from him. He pulled his handkerchief from his pocket and gave it to her, anxiously trying to help her control herself. He glanced over to the older woman who was staring, open-mouthed.

'We know each other,' he explained. 'We met the day Kit fell into the shaft at Old Pit. I've met her since, we sometimes talk.'

Even in his own ears his explanation sounded weak but Alice, the quick-witted Alice, jumped in and backed him up.

'Yes, Auntie Phoebe, that's right. Oh, he was so good that day, going down the shaft after little Kit and bringing him up. And he came over to see how Kit got

306

on an' all, I was there when he came, he brought Kit a rocking-horse.'

'Well,' said Auntie Phoebe, looking from Meg to Alice and back to Jonty. 'You didn't say it was Jonty. That's right though, you were telling Alice why you didn't give your proper name before. I never knew you were so well acquainted with our Meg, though.'

Shakily, she dried her eyes and stuffed Jonty's handkerchief in her apron pocket. She made a desperate attempt to cover up for herself and Jonty, embarrassed for him more than she was for herself.

'Auntie Phoebe, is Bella all right on her own? It's getting dark. You know she doesn't like the dark.'

Her aunt forgot all about Jonty at the mention of her beloved Bella. She jumped to her feet and made for the door.

'Aye,' she said, 'I don't want the lass to be getting her nightmares again. She's had them ever since Miley went, poor lad. I'll see you again, Jonty, don't keep away now, will you?'

The house seemed quiet. Alice rose to her feet and drew the thin curtains over the window and lit the lamp above the table. She turned back to the other two and bit her lip as she saw the way they were looking at one another. Meg was heading for a lot of trouble and heartache if she went on like this, she thought sadly.

But, 'I'll make some tea,' was all she said.

Jonty jumped to his feet. 'No, not for me, I must get home. I'll have to go round by the road as it is. There's no moon tonight, it's not safe to ride over the fields, can't see the rabbit holes in the dark.'

'Yes, of course. Well, it was nice of you to come,' Alice said formally.

'I'll go to the gate with you,' Meg said quickly, too quickly. It was all too painfully obvious to Alice that her sister wanted desperately to hang on to him for a few

307

seconds more. She watched as they went out of the door and even though they did not touch, it was as though they were joined together somehow. Her sister who had always been so sturdy and strong, both physically and mentally, had an air of fragility about her, and the man with her was bending irresistibly towards her, concern and support flowing from him to her. Alice felt foreboding rise within her as she saw it.

'I'll come to see you tomorrow,' Jonty whispered. He stood in the shadows just inside the gate, holding Meg's hand in his. She gripped the warm fingers and put them to her cheek in a gesture of love, holding them there. From the street, the horse nickered softly, restless.

'I must go,' said Jonty, and drawing her further into the shadows, he kissed her, a tender, loving kiss, a comforting kiss.

She watched him mount and ride away before going back into the house, closing the door behind her and slipping the bolt.

'A fine mess, isn't it?'

Alice, arms folded across her chest, was standing before the range. Meg looked at her uncertainly.

'What is?' she asked.

'You know fine what I mean,' said her sister. 'You've said nothing to me about getting so friendly with Mr Dale, or Jonty Grizedale as he says he is.'

'We were raised together as bairns,' said Meg, on the defensive.

'Oh, aye?' Alice was scornful. ''Till the ripe old age of four, wasn't it? Or was it five?'

Meg didn't answer. She felt so wrung out emotionally with all that had happened, she couldn't face her sister's censure. She sat down heavily in the rocking-chair and stared into the fire.

'Why Meg, man,' said Alice, in a gentler tone, 'I don't want you to be making any daft mistakes. I know

Wesley's no man to you, but you're still married to him, aren't you? An' this Jonty, you don't really know him, do you? Maybe he thinks it safer to go with a married woman. You're not likely to trick him into getting wed, are you?'

'He loves me!' cried Meg. 'It's not like that at all.'

'Aye. I dare say.'

Alice looked at her sister's downcast face, seeing the dark shadows under eyes still haunted by tragedy.

'Goodness knows, you deserve some happiness,' she remarked. 'But are you sure he'll stand by you if anything happens? I mean, if you fall wrong, Wesley's not going to let you pretend the babby's his, is he now? He's not been near you, has he?'

'I love Jonty, Alice,' Meg said simply, looking up with tears in her eyes.

'Aye, a blind man can see that.'

She knelt on the clippie mat before Meg and took the work-roughened hands in hers. Her heart ached for her sister. Men! she thought savagely, and not for the first time, it was men caused all the pain and trouble in this world.

'Howay, lass,' she said, drawing Meg to her feet. 'Come to bed, things'll likely look better come the morn. It's no good thrashing it all out now, the both of us are over weary.'

Next morning, Jackie was sitting in his shirt-sleeves in the kitchen when a knock came on the door. Alice and Meg were out, gone together for the messages from the store, so Jackie had to get to his feet to answer the knock. When he saw who it was, his brow darkened. Wesley Cornish stood there, dressed respectably in a clean shirt and suit.

'What do you want?' asked Jackie, making no move to ask the visitor in. 'You hadn't the ments to come to

309

the funeral yesterday. You should think shame on it an' all. But then, you never did think of nowt but yourself, did you?'

'I don't want to fight with you, Jackie,' said Wesley. 'Can I come in, like?'

'What for?'

'I want to see our lass.'

'Your lass?' Jackie laughed his derision. 'Our Meg, do you mean? It's a long time since you treated her like any lass of yours.'

'Let us in, Jackie,' said Wesley, ignoring the jibe. 'We don't want the whole row to know our business, do we?'

'Our Meg's not in, and even if she was, I don't think we want a shite like you in the house, any road,' said Jackie, looking down his nose at his brother-in-law. 'Now, hadaway with you, before I do something worse to you than swearing. I don't want to mucky me hands with the likes of you.'

Wesley bristled, an angry gleam coming into his eye. He clenched his fists and raised them in fighting stance, but thought better of it and let them fall to his sides.

Jackie looked speculative. It wasn't like Wesley to let insults pass without a fight.

'I have to see her, man,' said Wesley.

'Aye. Well. You can wait for her in the back row if you like. I'm telling you, you're not getting in here.'

Jackie closed the door in Wesley's face. His blood was up. By, he thought to himself, I'd have liked to belt him one. He sat down before the fire again, one hand rubbing the knuckles of the other as he imagined what it would have been like to bray Wesley's face to a pulp. He might yet do it, if the man said anything to Meg.

He was dead tired. Going back down the pit with the night shift had been the hardest thing he had done in his life. He didn't know which was worst: the quiet expressions of sympathy from his marras, or the way some of them looked away, creating an uncomfortable silence which was hard to break. They just didn't know what to say, he knew that, but still, it was hard.

Wesley was lounging against the yard wall when Meg and Alice came back with their baskets of shopping. He straightened up as he saw them turn into the row, waiting for them to draw closer.

'What are you after?'

Alice halted close to her sister and glared at him uncompromisingly. Meg stood quietly, holding her basket in front of her like a shield.

'I want to talk to Meg,' he said. 'Your Jackie said I couldn't go in, I had to wait out here.'

'Quite right an' all,' snorted Alice.

'Can I come in, Meg?' he asked.

'Our Jackie's the gaffer in the house now,' snapped Alice. 'If he says you can't come in, you can't.' Her eyes glinted like chips of blue ice as she nodded to give emphasis to her words.

'I have to talk to you, Meg,' he insisted. 'We can't let everybody in the row know our business, can we?'

'Do you think they don't, like?' Alice asked with a hard laugh.

'Alice,' Meg at last found her tongue, 'go in now. Tell our Jack I want to fetch him in.'

'Meg! Don't be so soft, man, he just wants something from you. You don't think he's come to pay for his bairns' keep, do you?'

'Go on, Alice,' Meg said quietly, and her sister exploded, turning to Wesley and letting rip.

'By, Wesley Cornish,' she yelled, losing control altogether. 'If you were my man you wouldn't have done to me what you've done to Meg. She's been a saint to you, and you carrying on with that Sally Hawkins like

311

that, even before Kit was born. Aye, you wouldn't have done it to me, I'm telling you. I'd have knifed you first!'

Wesley looked at her, her cheeks red with anger and her eyes snapping and flashing and he was unable to suppress a spark of admiration for her.

'Nay, lass,' he said with a wry smile. 'Nay, if I was your man, I'd have used a knife on meself.'

Meg decided it was time she intervened. She was beginning to be afraid that Alice, in her fury, would attack Wesley physically and that would be a mistake. Woman or no woman, Wesley would knock her down for it.

'Go on, Alice,' she urged. 'Go on, ask Jackie, I don't want any trouble in the row.'

Reluctantly, after a final glare at Wesley, Alice marched inside the house, coming out a minute later.

'Jackie says you can come in.'

Once inside the kitchen, Wesley glanced nervously at Jackie and Alice before speaking to Meg.

'Private, like,' he insisted.

'You can say what you have to say here,' snapped Jackie. By his side his fists were clenching and unclenching; his lips were compressed so tightly they had a thin white line round them.

'No, Jackie,' said Meg, 'we'll go in the room.' She led the way through the connecting door and sat down on the settle, indicating for Wesley to sit opposite her. She shuddered slightly, deliberately not looking to the side where Miles's coffin had stood. It would be a while before she stopped seeing it in her mind's eye whenever she looked that way.

'What do you want?' she asked.

'I heard they took your da away. I'm sorry, Meg.'

She studied him, well aware that he had not come to see her just to offer his sympathy. Though not yet thirty, already his paunch bulged out below his chest and broken veins littered his face. His hazel eyes were bloodshot, she noticed, and unbidden came the thought of clear dark eyes – Jonty's eyes.

'Aye,' she said flatly.

'Er . . . I was thinking, Meg,' Wesley said awkwardly, looking down at his hands. 'There'll only be your Jackie and Alice living in the house now?'

'Say what you've come to say.'

Wearily, she got to her feet and walked to the window, staring out at the garden.

'Well, I mean, like, there's plenty of room for you and the lads here, isn't there?' Wesley blurted out.

Bitterness welled up in Meg. 'You mean you want to take my house away from me?' she demanded.

'Aw, Meg, look at it from my side,' he pleaded. 'Sally's cottage is falling to bits and what with the pay cuts an' all, we could do without paying the rent. I need the house more than you.'

Meg stared at him. He was actually going to take her house from her. She couldn't believe it.

'You can live here, you know you can, man,' argued Wesley. 'Now your da's not here, you and the lads can have his bedroom.'

'Da will be coming home. What then?' she asked evenly.

'Aw, no he won't, he's gone crazed, everybody knows that, or why would they take him to Sedgefield?'

'He's not crazed! It was just the accident, he'll be coming back!' cried Meg.

'Hadaway, man, he's a loony. Always has been . . .'

The door from the kitchen burst open and Jackie stormed in, glowering at Wesley. He looked so menacing that Wesley stepped back from him and cut off what he had been going to say.

'Get out of here, Wesley Cornish, get out of our house, or I'll put you out meself,' Jackie shouted.

313

'Hey! Who do you think you're talking to, like?' blustered Wesley, but nevertheless he was moving to the door, whilst keeping a wary eye on Jackie.

'I'm not going to fight you, man, not now, I'll go. This is a bad time for you, too soon after your trouble, like.'

He walked to the back door before turning and speaking directly to Meg.

'I want the house, Meg, I want it for me and Sally. She's my lass and it's me has the house through the colliery, I have a right to it.'

'Get out!' Jackie exploded in a fury and ran to the door after him, but Wesley was gone, down the yard and away up the row before any neighbours thought to join in the argument. For Wesley had felt the cold disapproval of his fellow pit folk, intensified this last week since tragedy had hit the Maddisons. He knew it wouldn't take much for the whole row to turn on him and help Jackie throw him out of the village, let alone the house. But still, Sally would be waiting for him in the tumbledown house in the old part of the village, the part which had been a hamlet in the days before coal reigned in the county.

Twenty-Six

'Well, what did she say?'

Sally, a new baby on her knee, was sitting by the fire in the dirty kitchen. Ashes had spilled over from the ash box on the hearth and some even on to the filthy proddie mat under her chair. There was a strange smell in the air, a sickly smell which permeated the whole house. Bed bugs, Sally said it was, they couldn't get rid of them. They were embedded in the crumbling plaster, coming out to plague them at night.

'I'll have to go back, later on like. Mebbe it's a bit soon,' he said, excusing his lack of success.

'You get away back there, Wesley Cornish! I want that house,' yelled Sally, jumping to her feet and waking the baby who began screaming in fright. Wesley was saved for the moment by the pit whistle, the fore shift men were coming to bank.

'I will in the morn, I have to go to work now,' he reasoned with her, beginning to take off his clothes and change into the pile of pitclothes by the hearth, still lying where he had left them the day before.

'Some bloody man you are!' snarled Sally with cutting contempt.

Wesley bent his head without replying, concentrating on getting dressed for the pit and out of the house away from her scorn.

'Could you not have dashed me pitclothes against the yard wall, Sally?' he said, careful to speak softly. If she

315

thought he was complaining she wouldn't make him any dinner to come back to. 'Get rid of the coal dust, like?'

'Don't you tell me what I should have done. An' me just out of childbed!' bawled Sally.

'No, no, I'm not.' Placatingly he dropped a kiss on her cheek and went out to work.

'Are you going to let him have the house?' enquired Alice. She was pinning on her hat before the overmantel mirror for she was going out tonight. She had started going to classes in Bishop Auckland a few weeks before, determined to educate herself, get a certificate so that she could start some vocational training. She wasn't quite sure what she wanted to do but she was sure she didn't want to stay in the village and be kept by her brother, taking on other women's housework and washing in the way Meg had had to do for a bit of extra money. Plenty of time to decide what she was going to do the next year, when she finished her course.

'What else can I do?' asked Meg.

Alice picked up her exercise book. She would have to be going if she was to walk to Auckland and still get there in time. There was a horse bus now, running from Winton Colliery to the station, but it cost a penny each way and she could only afford to use it for the return journey.

'Well, for a start, I think you should go back into your own house. If you stay here any longer, Wesley will say you don't need it.'

'Yes, you're right,' said Meg. 'I might go over tomorrow. I have to make some sort of a fight. Any road, our Jackie will likely be getting wed soon, he'll want the house then, won't he?'

'Getting wed? He's never said anything about a lass to me,' exclaimed Alice.

'No, I know, but you know how he is, he doesn't tell us

316

much about anything. He could meet somebody and decide to get wed all in a hurry, couldn't he?'

Alice went to the door. 'That's a fact, then it'll be me an' all who'll be in the way. Well, I'm off.'

Next morning, Meg sent the boys off to school and went round to George Row. The house seemed very quiet as she let herself in, the fire dead long since in the grate and the iron range beginning to show signs of needing a polish with black lead before the rust took over. Well, she thought, a bit of hard work would keep her occupied. Besides, she needed to get the oven hot. Her money had run out and she would have to start up her baking business again.

She got out her box of cleaning materials and soon was brushing rhythmically, burnishing the range 'til it shone. Without washing the black lead from her hands, for to do that she needed hot water and hot water wasn't to be got until she had the fire lit and the boiler heated up, she laid the fire with sticks and cinders and a shovelful of good round coal on top and put a lucifer to it. Then she put the tin blazer in position and leaned back on her heels, watching the sticks catch alight through the bars and hearing the chimney roar as the blazer did its work.

A knock at the front door made her get to her feet and hurry to answer it, rubbing her hands across her forehead as she did so. It must be Dolly, she thought, she would have heard her working through the thin wall which separated the two kitchens. But it was not Dolly, it was Jonty.

'Oh!' Meg looked at him and lifted the sacking apron she wore to do the range so that she could hide her grimy hands in it.

Jonty smiled. 'Can I come in?'

Wordlessly, she stood back so that he could enter,

blushing with embarrassment that he should have caught her looking such a sight.

'I was just cleaning up,' she mumbled, closing the door behind him.

'So I see,' Jonty said gently. He touched her brow where her hand had left a sooty streak, and his touch was a caress.

'You shouldn't have come here,' Meg whispered.

'I had to see you. Your aunt told me you were here.'

'Oh Lord,' sighed Meg. He had been to Pasture Row and now here he was in George Row. Everyone would know.

'I am your cousin, Meg,' he pointed out. 'Isn't it perfectly natural to come to see my cousin at a time like this?'

Meg nodded, not convinced. She led the way into the kitchen and took down the blazer and a lovely warmth spread into the room immediately.

'I'll have to wash my hands, I'll put the kettle on.' But as she turned to the kettle on the hearth, Jonty took her into his arms and held her tightly to him, caring nothing about the state of her hands or her apron.

'Jonty! You'll get black lead all over you,' she protested, but it was a half-hearted protest to say the least. Her emotions, still so raw after all that had happened, were easily roused. She clung to him, eyes closing as he brought his mouth down to hers and she was caught up in a sea of feeling which threatened to drown her.

Jonty held her for a few moments then he sat down on the chair by the fire and took her on his knee.

'You shouldn't have come, folks'll talk,' she murmured in his ear.

'Shh, my love.' He rocked her to him and Meg felt the waves of comfort and love coming from him to her, and could no more have put him away from her than fly to the moon.

'Well! I've never seen anything like it.'

They were brought out of their private world by a voice at the window, the voice of a woman shocked to the core. Meg jumped to her feet and stared at the kitchen window, at the woman standing outside, a baby in her arms.

'Sally Hawkins!' gasped Jonty, and the woman nodded her head triumphantly.

'Aye, it's me, Master Jonty,' she said. 'How's your da, then?'

'You know Sally?' asked Meg, eyes widening in surprise as she looked from Sally to Jonty.

'I do,' he said grimly. 'She was a housemaid at the Hall until my father threw her out when she got pregnant. Grandmother gave her five pounds to see her through.'

Meg was about to ask him why his grandmother should do that, but Sally was hammering on the back door by now. Meg opened the door and let her in.

'What do you want, Sally?' she asked, her brow wrinkling as she got a whiff of sour milk and strong body odour.

'Aye,' sneered Sally. 'You can speak to me now I've found you out, eh? An' you, Master Jonty. Not too high and mighty now, are you? As bad as your da, aren't you? Except at least he wasn't messing about with a married woman. You wait 'til my Wesley gets home, he'll show you what for an' all. Pretending you're better than us when all the time you've been rutting . . .'

'Shut your dirty mouth, you slut,' Meg snapped, and Sally turned on her.

'Slut, is it? And what about you, eh, carrying on with a fancy man in Wesley's house? Aye, well, it'll be my house now, see if it isn't.'

The baby in her arms began a fretful crying and Sally

319

sat down in the chair recently vacated by Jonty and bared her breast to suckle him, not bothering to cover up in front of Jonty. She looked around the room, taking note of the furniture, the clean mats on the floor and the fresh curtains hanging at the window.

'Aye,' she said with a satisfied air, 'I reckon I'll be moving in tomorrow. And don't you go taking anything away, mind. It was Wesley's money bought this stuff and it belongs to him. You have no right to nothing, you haven't.'

Jonty glanced at Meg, seeing the angry glint in her eye at the thought of losing her house. He felt helpless. What could he do to stop this girl, his father's ex-mistress, from blackening Meg's reputation? Oh, it was all his fault. He cursed himself for being too weak to keep away from his Meg. He desperately wanted to take her and her boys and ride away with them, away from this dreadful slattern of a woman, away from her brute of a husband.

'I'll give you money,' he said.

'No! No, you won't, Jonty,' cried Meg. 'You can't go that road, there'll be no end to it, man.'

'How much money?'

Sally had a sudden gleam to her eye as she pulled one breast away from the baby and put him to the other. Milk spurted out of the breast, wetting her bodice where there was already a large patch stiffened with sour milk.

'Five pounds,' said Jonty, trying to remember how much he had left of this month's dividend. What with his father and now Sally, he would have nothing over, he thought.

'Ten,' said Sally quickly.

'I haven't got ten.'

Meg had by this time pulled herself together. She saw clearly that one payment, no matter how much, would never satisfy Sally.

320

'Have you finished feeding the bairn?' she asked in a deceptively quiet voice.

'Aye,' said Sally, wrapping the baby up in his filthy shawl and holding him against her shoulder.

'Right, then, out you go!'

Meg took hold of Sally's shoulders and pulled her up from the chair, pushing her unceremoniously out of the door.

'Hey! Watch what you're doing, will you? You'll hurt the babby,' Sally shouted, but Meg had her outside and the door bolted firmly against her in a trice.

'You'll be sorry, Meg Cornish, you see if you're not. I'll put Wesley on to you, I will, as soon as he comes in from the pit.' Then Sally stood at the back window and screamed abuse.

'You shouldn't have done that, Meg,' said Jonty. 'The whole village will know about us now, your life will be hell.'

'The whole place'll know all right, these walls are paper thin,' said Meg. 'And if they don't know now, they soon will. You don't think they would have kept their mouths shut, do you, Wesley and Sally? I don't care how much you paid them.' She drew the curtains to shut out the sight of Sally and after a minute they heard her go off down the yard, still shouting insults over her shoulder.

Jonty looked gravely at Meg. 'I'm sorry. I never meant to get you into trouble like this. Do you want me to stay here? If she comes back with Wesley it could get very nasty.'

Meg sighed. 'No, love, best not,' she said. 'I think I'll just go back to Da's house. Wesley can have this lot.' She was dispirited. One disaster seemed to be following another. She considered telling Jonty about the other thing which was on her mind, but decided against it. Not today. She couldn't bear to pile more trouble on to him and nor could she take any more emotional scenes herself. She might be wrong, any road, she told herself, what with Miles's accident and Da and all, it could just have been that which had upset her rhythm.

'You'd better go, love.' She lifted her face to his for his kiss, feeling incredibly tired.

'How can I go, leaving you to face all this?'

'Go on, Jonty. I'll meet you tomorrow, if you like.'

'You're sure you'll be all right? Will Jackie be at home? Promise me you'll go to your aunt's place if he's not. I don't want you facing those two on your own.'

Meg smiled gently, knowing she was better equipped to face Wesley and Sally than he was. Jonty was such a gentleman, a gentleman born, she thought fondly. He wanted to protect her.

'Go on, love. It'll be better if you're not here, really it will. If Jackie's not in I'll go to Auntie Phoebe's. Uncle Tot is off shift, I know.' She looked thoughtfully up at him. She had just realized why his grandmother might have paid Sally Hawkins off.

'Jonty, do you mean Sally's lad, the older one . . .'

'I do. He's my half-brother, yes,' said Jonty, his lips tightening into a straight line.

Meg shook her head. 'And the baby is half-brother to Tucker and Kit,' she commented. 'Queer world, isn't it?'

Gathering up her few personal belongings into a bundle, Meg looked round the house in George Row, checking to see if she had missed anything. The rocking-horse . . . Jackie would have to come over for that. Kit would be heart-broken if it was left. The toy soldiers which Jonty had given Tucker were already gone. Tucker couldn't bear to be parted from them.

The house had never been a real home to her, she mused as she locked the front door and trudged home to Pasture Row with the bundle over her arm. She would much rather live in Da's house. But there was the nagging worry that it would soon be Jackie's house if her father didn't come home. The owners had a strict rule that tenants had to work in the pit.

Her mind wandered back to Jonty, as it always did nowadays. He had been so reluctant to leave her, making her promise faithfully to be at the grassy knoll by the stand of trees at one o'clock sharp tomorrow. She walked up the row, nodding to the women standing in their doorways. They nodded back, faces alive with curiosity. No doubt they knew more about her and Jonty than she knew herself, she thought wryly. But there was no condemnation in their faces. The whole place was aware of the life Meg had led with Wesley. But how would they react if a new baby came?

Twenty-Seven

Next morning broke wet and windy. The first cool days of autumn had come at last. Meg walked out of the village on her way to meet Jonty, her thoughts going over the last few months.

What a summer it had been! All highs and lows. She seemed to have done more living in the short time between May and September than in all the years since she got wed. She remembered the terror of Kit's near fatal accident, and how it had led to her meeting Jonty. The lovely hours with him, her delight in his every gesture, the feel of his hands on her. She even loved the way he walked with that slight bias to one side, not quite a limp. She smiled dreamily as she left the road and took to the track, going past Old Pit and taking the fork which passed by the grassy knoll. Her pulse quickened as she dwelt on the thought of seeing him again, as it always did.

Poor lad, when he fell in love with her he hadn't bargained for the trouble it might bring. He had led a sheltered life, she mused, unaware of how mistaken she was in this surmise. She felt a protective love for him. He couldn't know anything of the harsh realities of life as lived in a pit village.

Wesley had come round to Pasture Row the day before, but thankfully Jackie had been off shift and saw to him. Her brother had sent Wesley off all right, flinging the key of the house in George Row at him and swearing that if he ever came near Meg again he would regret the day. But Wesley had been so relieved to get the key to take back to the demanding Sally, he had soon gone off, not prepared to face up to Jackie.

'Don't you worry, neither,' he had blustered as he picked the key up from the brick-paved yard, 'I wouldn't touch her. Not after—'

He hadn't got to finish the sentence for Jackie was on him and Wesley was off like a hare racing for safety. At least Jackie had been able to get the rocking-horse out of the house for Kit before handing the key over.

Meg sighed. Jackie had said nothing as she haltingly explained why she was giving in to Wesley so easily. He had simply looked at her, a world of disillusionment in his eyes, and Meg had flushed. He had carried on eating his dinner and afterwards lit his pipe at the fire before speaking.

'This is still Da's house,' he had said. 'You know he wouldn't want a Grizedale to be anywhere near it. Don't bring him here, Meg, you owe that to Da.'

'Jonty's not like his father,' Meg had protested.

'No, mebbe he's not. An' I know you and Mam thought the world of him when he was a bairn. I've heard you say often enough. But what sort of a man would cause such trouble for a lass like you?'

'He didn't! He—'

'Leave it be, Meg,' Alice had advised. She had been sitting quietly on the settle listening to them. Alice could see both her brother's and her sister's point of view, but knew they could not agree on this. So she had let it be, too emotionally strung out to argue further anyway.

Meg walked down the track 'till she reached the place where she had spent her happiest times that summer. The grass was brown and wet and slippery with the rain. The leaves from the ash trees were already beginning to turn brown and fall. She sheltered under the largest tree, achieving only limited protection from the rain which was coming down harder now.

The nightmare had returned last night, she remembered. The awful nightmare which had plagued her since her childhood. The one about the candyman. She had woken up panting and sweating hard, as though she had in reality been running up the black road of the old permanent way. Her reactions were physical as well as psychological. The sense of foreboding which always followed the nightmare was still lingering in her thoughts.

It must be past one, she thought, shivering slightly and hugging her arms together under her shawl. Where was Jonty? He was not usually late. Where was he now? Surely the weather hadn't put him off? Meg smiled at the absurdity of the thought as she huddled under the tree. Jonty loved her, didn't he? Nothing so trivial as bad weather would put him off. She lost herself in dreams of him: how it felt when he touched her or gazed at her with that intimate, dark-eyed look of love.

Jonty was just leaving the Hall. When he had risen that morning, he had been disturbed by the dry, hacking cough coming from his grandmother's bedroom. He had found her lying in bed, flushed with fever, her thin body wracked with coughing. His morning had been taken up in fetching the doctor from Shildon to her and arranging for Emma Teasdale, Farmer Teasdale's daughter, to sit with her and keep the fire up and the room warm. Thankfully Ralph was absent. He had not been near his home since he'd received his ten pounds last week. Otherwise, Farmer Teasdale might have objected to his daughter's going to the Hall.

'A feverish chill, nothing worse,' the doctor had pronounced. 'Keep her warm in bed and give her hot nourishing drinks. I'll be back tomorrow.' He had looked from Jonty to his grandmother and back again before drawing Jonty out of the room. 'Of course, you know this can only have an adverse effect on the old lady's general health, with her rheumatism and considering her age. The winter ahead of us, too.'

The rain was coming down steadily as Jonty rode off to his meeting with Meg. He glanced at his watch anxiously. She must have been waiting some time now, she would be soaked to the skin. He urged his horse into a brisk canter as he crossed the field to the track.

'Meg! Are you all right?'

Jonty jumped to the ground and threw the reins over the saddle as she stepped out from behind the tree. He took her in his arms, feeling her shiver through the sodden wool of her shawl.

'Oh, my love, you shouldn't have come, you'll catch your death,' he said, full of concern. 'I would have understood. I'd have ridden down to Winton.'

'That's just it,' she said, 'you can't, not any more. Jackie doesn't want you to come.'

Jonty looked quickly at her. He had to get her out of the rain, find out what this was all about. There was only one thing to do.

'We'll go back to the Hall,' he said, and anticipating her objections, 'Surely Alice is at home? She will see to your boys just this once. We have to have a proper talk, Meg, we can't go on the way we are.' He gestured at the rain. 'The winter is drawing on, snow will soon be coming. Come on, Meg, back with me.'

She was still hesitating, thinking of Ralph Grizedale, that menacing though shadowy figure, her own private bogeyman.

'Your father?' she asked anxiously.

'Oh, he's not there, Meg. He's away in Darlington or

somewhere with his cronies. I don't expect to see him for another day at least.' About the time when his money usually runs out, he thought silently.

Meg allowed him to take her up before him and they rode off to Grizedale Hall, even though her sense of foreboding had intensified.

When they at last came out of the field and crossed to the drive leading up to the Hall, she stared at it, awed by the size and stone-built solidity of its walls, the large imposing windows. It was somehow familiar to her. She felt she would know what the back of the house would be like as they cantered up the drive and turned to go round to the stables. Sheep were grazing on the lawns and the flowerbeds were unkempt and devoid of flowers but for a few forlorn Michaelmas daisies, much afflicted with mould and bent away from the walls by the wind and rain.

There should be rose beds there, she thought suddenly, with daffodils round them in the spring and sweet william in the summer. But the only rose bush she saw was withered and brown back to the ground.

'What happened to the gardens?' she asked.

'No money for a gardener,' said Jonty. 'I haven't time to do it all. Sheep keep the grass down though.'

He dismounted and lifted her down, drawing her into the warmth of the stable before bringing in his horse.

'Take off that wet shawl,' he advised. 'I won't be long attending to my horse, then we can go inside and I'll make a fire. You'll have to dry out before you can go back.' He paused and looked curiously at her.

'You remember the gardens?'

'Not very well,' she admitted. 'But I remember the flowers. I loved the flowers.'

The inside of the Hall she didn't remember at all. There was an air of neglect about the place, she saw. Dust lay on the furniture and the carpets were shabby

328

and threadbare. But it was still opulent enough to awe Meg: the rich dark wood of the stairs and wainscoting round the entrance hall, the lofty embossed ceilings and high windows, though the velvet drapes at these were faded and dirty.

Even though Jonty had assured her that his father was not in the house, she looked round fearfully, praying he had not returned and was waiting to pounce on her. Daft fool, she told herself crossly. She wasn't a little girl now, she could well take care of herself. Besides, she had Jonty. He would never let the candyman hurt her. She was acting like a bit of a bairn. She shivered nevertheless, whether from cold or nervousness she didn't know. But Jonty was concerned and, as ever, conscious of her fears.

'Come away up to my room,' he said, keeping his voice low. 'You'll be out of the way there should my father return and I can light the fire for you to dry yourself.'

He took her hand and led her up the stairs and along the passage to a door at the end, letting her in and closing the door firmly behind them. Meg breathed easier. He lit the fire and she watched his strong capable hands setting the sticks and piling coal carefully on top. It was the first time she had ever seen a man light a fire, for to a pitman that was woman's work.

'Take your dress off, it will dry quicker by the fire,' he murmured quietly. And noticing her hesitation, he added, 'I'll find something of Grandmother's for you.'

Of course the dress he brought back was far too small for a sturdy girl such as Meg. In the end he took the worn eiderdown from the bed and wrapped it round her.

'Sit quietly, my love,' he said, kissing her on the cheek. 'I have to see to Grandmother first and then I'll bring some tea and we can talk.'

Meg sank to the hearth rug before the fire. Worn though it was, it was still soft and infinitely superior to a proddy mat made from old clothes. The eiderdown too, its satin cover faded and threadbare, was luxuriously warm and cosy, so that with its warmth and the heat from the fire, a heavenly relaxing feeling was spreading through her body. She leaned back against the arm of a leather armchair and took off her boots, stretching her bare feet to the blaze. By, she thought dreamily, it's grand. Her eyelids drooped and gradually closed. She felt warm and cosseted all over. Her toes tingled from the heat and she drew them back and under her, and in a minute she was asleep as her exhausted mind and body took a break from the strains and stresses of recent events.

'Is everything all right, Emma?' asked Jonty as he entered his grandmother's bedroom. Emma Teasdale was sitting by the bed feeding the old lady from a dish of chicken broth. She put the tray down on the bedside table and smiled at him.

'She's a little better, I think,' she said. 'She's had a little broth and earlier I made her a dish of boily.' Boily was a concoction of bread and warmed milk often given to invalids, Jonty knew.

'Hello, Grandmother,' he said as he approached the bed. 'How are you?'

The old lady smiled at him and he saw that she did indeed look somewhat improved, her breathing was easier and her face a better colour.

'I'm fine, Jonty,' she replied. 'Emma has been looking after me very well.'

'You can get off home now, Emma, before it gets dark,' he said to the girl. 'I know you usually help out with the milking. Thank you so much for coming at such short notice.'

'A pleasure,' smiled Emma, blushing a little. She was just seventeen and a plain girl, though capable-looking with the strong hands and arms of a milkmaid. She was very much attracted to Jonty, though he was unaware of it. But it was obvious to Mrs Grizedale and she smiled kindly at her and added her thanks to Jonty's.

'She likes you, Jonty,' said Mrs Grizedale as the door closed behind Emma. 'She's a nice girl, too, you could do worse.'

'Grandmother! You're talking nonsense,' he replied. 'I'm sure she doesn't even think of me once she's out of the house.'

The old lady sank down on her pillow, still smiling. 'It's been nice having her here,' she said softly. 'I miss having a girl in the house. Oh, not necessarily a maid, though I miss having one of those too, but another woman, so to speak.'

Jonty gave her a troubled look. She should have a maid, he was well aware of it. She needed a maid. But there had been so many disastrous experiences with young girls in the house, his father was not to be trusted at all. Goodness knows, he thought, a girl costs very little, a few pounds a year and her keep and one would make life so much easier for him too. The time was coming when he would have to look for someone who was willing to come and look after the old lady full-time. Maybe an older woman, a widow? Someone who wouldn't attract the amorous attentions of his father.

He thought of Meg and was furious with himself. He couldn't possibly bring her into the house on such a basis, it would be a dishonourable thing to do. In any case, Meg was so beautiful she would never be safe with his father.

His grandmother fell asleep and Jonty watched her fondly. She was so little and delicate, yet there must be something tough about her. She had had so much to put up with these last few years from his father. His jaw hardened at the thought of what she had had to endure from her own son. Even if it took all he had left, he decided, he would find a woman to look after her. He would go searching in Shildon tomorrow.

He built up the fire and placed a guard around it, then drew the curtains though it was not yet dark. Sleep was the best thing for her, he thought, and crept out of the bedroom, closing the door quietly behind him.

Before going back to Meg, Jonty went down to the kitchen and made some tea. He was quite a while about it, having to use bellows on the dying fire for there to be enough heat to boil the kettle.

The clock in the hall chimed five and it startled him. He hadn't realized it was so late. If he wanted that talk with Meg he would have to hurry up. She would have to get back to her boys soon.

He was crossing the hall towards the stair, tea tray in hand, when the front door burst open and Ralph tumbled rather than walked in, shouting and cursing as he tripped over a piece of worn carpet and almost measured his length on the floor. When he recovered he looked up at his son who was standing on the bottom stair.

'What the hell are you looking at?' he demanded, frowning, 'Anyone would think I hadn't a right to come into my own house.' His words were slurred and he lurched into his study without waiting for Jonty to reply.

His heart sank. How was he going to get Meg out of the house now? Before she was seen by his father and had to face the undoubted insults he would throw at her.

Meg woke as Jonty came into the room and put the tea tray down. She felt deliciously warm and happy, permitting herself to dream about what it would be like if she was married to him and they shared this bedroom. She smiled lazily at him and stretched out her bare feet to the fire, toasting her toes.

Jonty poured her tea and handed it to her before

sitting down in the armchair against which she was leaning and putting a hand down to stroke her hair. He considered telling her that his father had returned then decided against it. In the drunken state Ralph was in, he had probably fallen into a stupor in his study and would be asleep for hours.

'We have to talk, Meg,' he said quietly. Here at the end of the house it was unlikely that his grandmother or father would hear them, but it was best to be careful.

'Aye.'

Meg leaned her head back against his hand. Somehow her fears for the future had all gone, dispelled by the feeling of security and peace which being with him brought. She didn't really want to talk about anything at all, she just wanted to stay there, away from the world with Jonty.

'Why has your brother said I cannot come to see you, Meg?'

She sighed. It was such a difficult story to tell him. Her thoughts ranged back over the years since she had been old enough to understand how her parents had suffered because of Jonty's father.

'It's Dad,' she began at last. 'He's so bitter about your father. Da said that it was him who swayed the board of the railway company and had us all evicted. The whole street, even though it was just us Maddisons he wanted out. Da couldn't get work round here then, he was blacked and we had to go away. And in the end Da had to go down the pit, there wasn't any other work. He was always so frightened of being shut in anywhere, and it was because of your father that he had to go down the pit.'

Meg paused, thinking of her father. Did they keep him locked in that asylum at Sedgefield? she wondered. Did he even know if they did? The silence lengthened and the room grew darker, only the firelight casting a glow upon the two sitting there. Meg's happiness had dimmed as she remembered her father, her sense of foreboding returned.

'I never knew why you went, I always thought it was my fault,' Jonty murmured. He rose to his feet and went to the chest of drawers by the wall. Opening the top drawer, he took out what looked to be a bundle of rags. He returned to his seat and showed it to Meg. It was an old peg dolly. She took it, puzzled, not knowing what the significance of it was.

'A peg doll?' she asked.

'Your peg doll, Meg. I went back to your street and there was nothing there, the houses all boarded up and empty. There was only that peg doll, lying in the road. So I brought it home with me.'

She turned to face him, full of compassion for the little boy he had been. He must have felt truly deserted by her and her mother, she realised. She took his face between her hands and kissed him tenderly, the eiderdown slipping from her white shoulders and breast. Love and passion leapt between them once again and old ills were forgotten and somehow healed as they clung to each other. And Jonty picked her up and carried her to the bed where they made love, deep satisfying love which gripped the whole of their love-starved bodies and carried them to heights they had never dreamed existed. And afterwards they slept, a deep, trouble-free sleep.

Meg woke slowly, almost in continuation of a dream she was having, a delightful, happy dream though she couldn't remember what it had been about. The room was pitch black. The fire had gone out. She felt Jonty's arm around her, his knee thrown over hers, and listened to his deep steady breathing. Putting up her hand, she felt the shape of his face and ran her fingers through his hair. Oh, he was her lovely man. She almost sang the words to herself. Somehow she knew that whatever happened she would not be parted from him, not ever again. Hadn't she always known that Jonty would come looking for her? Jonty, her shining knight.

But waking brought her everyday cares back to her. Alice would be worried about her, she thought suddenly, and instantly slid out of Jonty's arms and from the bed. He murmured slightly but slept on. Her eyes were becoming accustomed to the gloom now. She went to the window and held the curtain back to peer out at the sky.

The rain had stopped. Small clouds were rushing across the full moon. She watched it, still under the spell of the enchantment which Jonty had brought to her. There was a ring round the moon, it was beautiful; a ring round the moon meant a frost, she mused.

'Meg?'

She dropped the curtain and turned back to the bed.

'What are you doing?' he asked, holding out his arms to her. 'Come back to bed, you'll catch your death.'

'I have to go,' she answered. 'Alice will be worried about me. And Kit and Tucker will be wanting me.'

Jonty didn't argue. He got out of bed and lit the candle on the ornamental mantelshelf as Meg pulled on her clothes. Her dress was quite dry now but the shawl was still sodden with the rain. She bit her lip. It would be cold without her shawl, if the frost ring round the moon was anything to go by. But Jonty had already thought of that. He found her a coat of his own to pull on over her dress. It was too big, of course, the sleeves dangling over her hands, but who was to see it at that time of night?

'What time is it?' she asked, and he opened his watch.

'Ten o'clock.'

Meg was relieved. At least it wasn't already the middle of the night.

'I'll saddle up,' he said, finishing tying his boot laces

335

and taking her hand to lead her from the room. They crept down the stairs and into the hall. There was no light coming from under the door of Ralph's study and no sound until, just as they opened the front door, there came a tremendous snore and a clatter. He must have moved in his sleep and knocked something to the floor.

'Jonty!' Meg froze for a second but his arm was around her and he was sweeping her out of the door. It was but a moment later when he led out his horse and they were away, cantering down the drive to the road.

They were approaching Winton Colliery when the whistle blew. Meg's heart sank. It must be time to change shifts. The night shift was coming to bank and the fore shift would be going down. There would be men walking from all over the village and a man and a woman on a horse would set tongues rattling all right. Besides, she didn't want to go against her brother's decree.

'Put me down here, Jonty,' she whispered urgently, and he brought his horse to a halt but didn't loose his hold on her waist.

'I'll take you as far as the house, Meg,' he protested. 'It's too late at night for you to be out on your own.'

'I'll be fine,' she insisted. 'There'll be men about, there's nothing to fear.'

Reluctantly, Jonty dismounted and lifted her down.

'You'll come in the morning?' he asked.

Meg hesitated, thinking of his father and berating herself for being silly. How could the candyman hurt her now? She had Jonty, hadn't she?

'I'll come,' she said.

'What time? I'll meet you on the track.'

'Ten, I'll be there at ten o'clock,' said Meg, and sped away the short distance to the house.

'Mind, it's nice of you to come home,' Alice said grimly. There was no sign of Jackie, he must already have gone out to work. Alice was banking up the fire for the night, the lamp already out and the candle lit on the table.

Meg bit her lip. She had no excuse, she knew she hadn't.

'I got wet, I went somewhere to dry out and I fell asleep,' she offered.

Alice gave a short laugh. 'A bit lame, that one is for an excuse,' she snapped. 'Kit was wanting you, and Tucker an' all. They'd both had a bad time at school today.'

'At school? Why?' Meg looked her surprise.

'Oh, why do you think, man? The other bairns were jeering at them all playtime.'

'Jeering?' Meg still didn't follow, why would the others jeer at Tucker and Kit? 'What for?'

'Because of Da,' Alice said flatly. 'Kit was crying his eyes out. Said they were dancing round him singing his granda was a loony and his Auntie Bella an' all. They said we were all loonys. And that lad of Sally Hawkins, he was leading them on. And Tucker heard them and laid into them and *he* came home with a bloody nose.'

Guilt flooded over Meg. There she had been, happy as a larrikin with Jonty, and all the time her lads had needed her. She'd let them down. She stared at Alice, not knowing what to say, and Jonty's coat fell from her shoulders and on to the clippie mat. Alice looked pointedly at it but said nothing.

'I'm sorry, Alice,' Meg said at last. 'Are they in bed now, did they go to sleep?'

'Oh, yes, they're asleep. It took me 'til now to settle them. Jackie was all for going up to the school that instant and having a word with the master. But I thought it wouldn't help. Best just let it die down. It never does any good, interfering with the bairns.'

Alice picked up the candle from the table and moved towards the stairs and Meg picked up Jonty's coat and followed her. The sisters shared the back bedroom now with the two boys.

By the flickering light of the candle, Meg looked down at Kit's tear-stained face. The child hiccuped softly and turned away from the light and Meg's heart ached for him. She moved the light so that she could look at Tucker, lying with his back to Kit, only his nose showing above the blanket. She moved the blanket down a little to inspect his face. There was a trace of blood still on his nose and his upper lip was split open.

'Hurry up and put out that candle,' Alice whispered hoarsely, from her narrow bed in the corner of the room.

'Sorry,' said Meg, and blew out the light and undressed in the pale moonlight which filtered through the thin curtains. She climbed into bed, being careful not to disturb the boys, and lay on her back, thinking. Something would have to be done, she knew that. She would have to find somewhere else for herself and her boys, but where? Jonty would try to help her, but she knew something now of his circumstances at home, his feeling of obligation to and love for his grandmother, the need to protect her from his father.

Maybe he could find her a cottage in Shildon? She could keep herself and her children. All she needed was a home for them, a place where she could bring the boys up away from Winton Colliery.

I'll meet him tomorrow, she thought, he'll help me, he will. She had to get away before it became apparent to the whole village that she was having another baby, a baby Wesley was certain to deny was his.

Twenty-Eight

Next morning the sun shone from a blue sky and the air was warm in a north-eastern version of an Indian summer. It would probably last no longer than a day or two, but the children were determined to make the most of it. When Meg woke up she could hear girls' voices as they played at hitchy stones in the back row, and under her window Tucker was talking earnestly to someone.

'I showed them lot, didn't I?' he boasted, and a boy's voice answered.

Saturday! It was Saturday. How could she go to meet Jonty when it was Saturday? Jackie usually worked back at the pit on a Saturday morning after fore shift, if he could. And Alice went to Auckland to a class. So she couldn't leave Tucker and Kit. Surely Jonty would understand?

Meg got out of bed, washed in cold water at the wash stand and put on her clothes. She had slept late, she realized. Alice's bed was already made. She must already be preparing to go out. Downstairs, the wall clock was striking nine. Meg blinked. She had never slept so late before. Alice was already gone. But the kettle was simmering on the brass-handled bar and the kitchen had been swept and dusted. Meg combed her hair and put it up before the overmantel mirror, pinning it securely with hairpins. Then she went to the back door.

Tucker and Kit was playing there, and Meg was

pleased to see that Walter was with them. At least Tucker's best friend hadn't turned against him. She was about to call to them when she was struck by the game they were playing.

The large iron mangle stood in the yard and the boys had the tin bath propped against it, forming a sort of tunnel. Tucker had appropriated the cracket from the kitchen and was leaning against the small stool with the piece of sandstone which Alice used to scour the steps in his hand. The other two boys sat on their hunkers, each with their hands full of small stones from the road. They were watching him gravely as he tapped the stone against the tin of the bath, making a sharp, hollow sound. He tapped twice and held his ear with one hand in a parody of listening, then repeated the action, intoning in a sing-song voice as he did so:

Jowl, jowl and listen, lads,
And hear the coal face working,
There's many a marra missing, lads,
Because he wouldn't listen, lads.

As he finished the old jingle, repeated over generations by old pitmen to the young, he began to scramble out from under the bath. But the other two boys were quicker. They jumped up and showered it with stones, and when that didn't prove satisfactory, knocked the bath down over Tucker, laughing uproariously.

'We won, we won,' shouted Walter. 'It's my turn now.'

'Tucker! Kit! What are you doing?' Meg cried.

Tucker pushed over the tin bath and got to his feet, mystified as to why his mother was so upset. All three boys stared at her, laughter gone now.

'We were only playing, Mam,' Tucker mumbled at last. 'We're going to be pitmen when we leave school.'

340

'I'm not,' asserted Kit, 'I'm going to be a farmer.'

'A farmer? What do you want to be a farmer for?' demanded Walter. 'Any road, how can you be a farmer? You haven't got a farm.'

'It's only cissies as is farmers, any road,' Tucker said, full of scorn for such an idea. 'Proper men go down the pit.'

They began a heated discussion of the relative merits of farming and coal-mining until Meg intervened, cutting it short.

'Never mind that now, get this mess cleaned up, I'll have to swill the yard after you. And Auntie Alice just did it yesterday. Then you can have some bread and jam. Anyway, Tucker, I thought you were going to be a soldier?'

'No, I'm not. A pitman's the best.' He nodded his head to emphasize the words.

Meg grinned and went inside. She made herself a cup of tea and got out the loaf and jam. Tucker was right to some extent in that all lads went down the pits here, following their fathers usually. But if Kit wanted to work on the land then he would. He would never have to go down the pit if he didn't want to and she could do anything about it. Not like poor Da.

She cut bread and spread it with jam for the three boys and sat down to eat herself. But she had only taken a few mouthfuls when she felt sick and had to rush out into the yard and bend over the drain, retching miserably, throwing up what little she had eaten. She leaned against the wall and wiped her mouth with the back of her hand.

'Are you badly, Mam?'

She looked down at Kit's anxious little face, his mouth besmeared with plum jam, and smiled wanly.

'No lad, I'm fine, I am. Something went down the wrong way, that's all.'

341

Kit looked relieved and she took his hand and went back into the house with him. That settled it. She had been nauseous the first few months in all her pregnancies so she was sure now. She had no choice but to ask Jonty to help her.

Can we go up the bunny banks, Mam?' asked Tucker, breaking into her thoughts. 'Me and Walter? We'll get some brambles for a pudding.'

'I want to come! I want to come!' Kit danced up and down before his brother.

'Aw, man, I have you trailing after us all the time,' said Tucker, disgusted. Kit tried Walter. Sometimes Walter let him go with them on their expeditions, he was a kind-hearted lad. And so it proved this time.

'Howay, then,' Walter said. 'Mind, you'll have to keep up wi' us, and don't fall down no holes neither.'

'I don't know,' Meg said doubtfully, reminded of that terrible day when Kit fell down the old shaft.

'Aw, Mam, all the lads go, there's nothing to hurt,' argued Tucker. And it was true, the children of the rows usually wandered around the countryside and no harm came to them. Maybe she was being overprotective because of Kit's accident?

'Well, you watch the little 'un,' she admonished, and they went whooping up the yard and along the rows, scattering the girls' hitchy stones as they went.

I could go to meet Jonty, Meg told herself after they had gone. She glanced at the clock. It was half-past nine. If she hurried she could be there not too long after ten and still be home to give the boys their dinner, she reasoned. Oh, she wanted to go, she wanted to go so badly. But Tucker and Kit, what if they should need her in the meanwhile? Last night she had failed them, staying with Jonty when she should have been home when they needed her. And the time Kit fell down the pit shaft, if

342

she had kept a better watch on them maybe it wouldn't have happened. The weight of her inadequacies as a mother lay heavily on her.

In the end, Meg decided she could not go. On the other hand, she could not wait another day before seeking Jonty out. Her mind was full of uncertainties, fears and hopes she hardly dared to express even to herself. The morning dragged on. She had thought that Alice would be back by one o'clock, but she must have missed the horse bus from Bishop Auckland. At ten past one there was no sign of her sister.

Her brother Jackie came in and she took his dinner of pan hagglety from the oven and served it to him. As she spooned out the layers of potato and onion and bacon, covered with bubbling cheese, she considered asking him to keep an eye out for the boys. But one look at his weary face convinced her she couldn't do that. Jack needed his bed. He was working so hard in the pit, and at the same time working for his deputy's ticket. That was the reason he had stayed on at the pit that morning.

Meg brought in the tin bath and filled it from the boiler on one side of the range with the ladling tin before sitting down and pouring herself some tea. She felt she couldn't eat a bite herself. Jack ate silently, hungrily. After all, he had had nothing but his bait of bread and jam since the night before. After he finished his meal he lit his pipe and sat a few minutes before the fire before stripping to the waist and bathing the upper half of his body.

'Wash my back, Meg,' were the first words he had spoken since greeting her as he came in the house. Jackie didn't understand about her and Jonty, she thought miserably. She knew how hard it could be for a man if there was talk about his sister, and she and Wesley had already provided enough of that. She soaped the proffered flannel and rubbed away at the coal dust and dried sweat.

It was time the bairns were back, she thought, suddenly beset with anxiety. Jack took himself off to bed and she went to the end of the row, looking along the road for any sign of them. There was none but Alice was walking along from the stile where the shortcut to Bishop Auckland came out on the road, swinging her basket by her side.

'I had to walk back,' she said. 'The lecture went on and on, you would think the teacher had no home to go to.'

The sisters went into the house and Meg served Alice her pan hagglety.

'You saw to Jack, then,' she commented, giving her sister a level stare. 'I thought you might have gone off again, leaving him to get his own dinner.'

Meg flushed, remembering how she almost had gone to meet Jonty.

'Please, Alice,' she asked, 'try to understand.'

Whatever Alice was going to say was forgotten as Tucker and Kit came running into the kitchen, eyes shining and faces purple with blackberry juice. Tucker had his cap in his hand and it was filled to the brim with large and luscious fruit.

'Look, Mam. Look, Auntie Alice, see what we got,' shouted Kit. 'We got pounds and pounds of brambles.'

'I did, you mean, me and Walter,' said Tucker, crushingly. '*You* only picked red ones. You don't know the difference between black and red.'

'I do, I do,' shouted Kit, turning on his brother furiously.

'Never mind, never mind, don't fight,' Alice intervened. 'I'm sure Kit did his best, Tucker. Now, won't we have a lovely pudding for supper tonight?'

Meg emptied the berries into a bowl, looking ruefully

at the purple-stained lining of the cap. She'd have a job getting that clean. She should have thought and given the boys a bag, they had said they were going brambling.

She gave the boys the rest of the pan hagglety and took the dish into the pantry to soak in cold water. Alice and the boys had fallen silent as they tucked into the meal. Should she ask Alice to mind them? she wondered. If she did she could go to Grizedale Hall this afternoon and seek out Jonty.

'Alice, are you doing anything this afternoon?' she asked as she came out of the pantry. Alice looked up, unsmiling.

'Why?'

'Oh, nothing, I just wondered,' answered Meg, feeling intimidated by her manner.

It would be a waste of time asking Alice, she decided. If she was going to see Jonty she would have to take the boys with her. Which was not a bad idea at all, she realized, they would have to know about him sometime.

'Eat up,' she said to Tucker and Kit, though they were already eating as though it was their first meal for a week. 'We're going out.'

'Out?' queried Alice, frowning.

'Yes.' Meg smiled at her. 'Don't worry, Alice, everything's going to work out, I know it.'

'I wish I felt the same,' her sister replied tartly, but she said no more.

Meg and the boys walked to the grassy knoll first, just in case Jonty was still there, though it was already late afternoon and it was a forlorn hope. In fact, no hope at all, Meg realized as she stood watching Tucker and Kit swooping round and round the ash trees, shouting and laughing.

'Be careful,' she called, for they had on their Sunday suits and the ground was very slippery. Too late. Kit tripped over a tree root and was rolling on the wet ground, amid dead leaves and loamy soil. He got to his feet and rubbed dirt from his trousers with his hand and then wiped his face with the same hand, leaving a dark smudge across his cheek.

'Oh, Kit,' she said helplessly, but he looked so like a grubby little cherub that she couldn't be really angry with him.

'Howay, now, we have to get along,' she said, taking each boy by the hand and leading them on.

'Where are we going, Mam?' they clamoured.

'Wait and see.'

They left the track and crossed over meadows to the drive of Grizedale Hall. Her heart quailed as she thought of maybe meeting Ralph Grizedale but she took a firmer grip on the boys' hands and quickened her step. This was no time to be faint-hearted.

'Eeh, Mam,' exclaimed Tucker, as the Hall came into sight round the bend in the drive. 'It's grand, isn't it? Is this where the Queen lives?'

The question made Meg laugh and this relaxed her. What had she to be afraid of anyway? She marched up to the house and hesitated, deciding after all to go round to the back. She had to leave the boys somewhere safe until she made sure that Ralph was not in. She wasn't going to let him frighten them. It was a problem though, she didn't know what to do.

A nickering from the stable made her go in there and close the door behind her. She and the boys stood looking round them, even Tucker overawed by the smell of straw and horses and leather. Kit's eyes shone as a horse put its head over a half-door and whinnied.

'Mam! Mam, look, it's Mr Dale's horse,' he cried, running to it and reaching up to stroke its nose.

So Jonty must be in then, thought Meg with a sigh of relief. It seemed to be the only horse in the stable so there was a good chance that Ralph Grizedale was away somewhere.

'Be good boys and stay here a few minutes,' she said. 'I won't be long, I just have to see someone.'

'Is it Mr Dale?' asked Tucker shrewdly. Had he heard something? she wondered.

'Never mind. Just you wait here. Stay on this side of the door mind. And watch that horse doesn't bite.'

'Aw, Mam, he won't bite,' said Kit with disgust. 'He likes us, see?' He rubbed the horse's nose, quite enchanted with it.

'Well, be careful any road,' she said, and left them. It wouldn't be for long, she told herself.

Meg went round to the front of the house and knocked at the door. There was no reply, no sound at all, though she knocked again and waited. Tentatively, she tried the huge knob and the door swung open on to the large, square hall with its curving staircase at the far end. There was no sign of life.

'Jonty?' she called softly, but no welcome answering call came. All was quiet.

Well, she thought, she wasn't going to give up now, not when she'd come this far. She stepped into the house and looked around. All the doors leading off the hall were shut so she walked to the bottom of the stairs, debating whether to risk going up. Jonty might not have heard her call if he was upstairs with his grandmother.

She was still hesitating when a muffled crash followed by a curse came from behind one of the closed doors and she raced up the stairs and along the passage to the room at the end, Jonty's room, bolting inside and closing the door. It was blind instinct which made her run for the voice had filled her with dread.

Twenty-Nine

'Bloody hell!' the voice had said, and it had been Ralph Grizedale who had said it. The voice resounded over and over in Meg's head, reducing her to a shivering panic.

'The candyman!' she breathed. All the dread of her nightmares was beginning to swamp her, paralyzing mind and body.

Dear God, she thought, her heart racing and threatening to choke her as she leaned against the closed door. It was Ralph who was home, not Jonty, even though she had been sure the horse in the stable was Jonty's. She cowered behind the door, all her old fears returning to her. The terror she felt was as strong as that she'd felt as a child when the candyman came and chased her and Mam and little Jack up the old line.

Where are you, Jonty? she cried in her heart. I need you, I need you now! She tried to imagine where he could be. If she could picture him well enough and cried to him he would come, she knew he would. She closed her eyes tightly and concentrated. She never knew how long she crouched there, behind the bedroom door. It could have been hours or just a few minutes.

Her eyes flew open as she heard someone on the stairs, heavy footfalls coming nearer and nearer. It had to be the candyman. He had reached the head of the stairs and was coming along the passage and Meg's heart pounded with every step. Did he know she was there? The footsteps stopped. Was he just playing with her, dragging out the thrill of the hunt as long as he could? Ralph Grizedale was a huntsman. Meg remembered the story Auntie Phoebe had told them when she was a child of how cruel he was in the chase. Oh, how she could identify with the hunted fox now, she could.

But no, he was moving again, going into another room. She breathed again before a new fear came to torment her.

The boys! She had to get back to the stables before Ralph found them there. He could go downstairs any minute. She couldn't let him get to her boys. The new fear was paramount, overcoming all others. Her limbs unfroze themselves, her brain began to work again.

What a ninny she was, she berated herself, full of self-contempt. Here she was hiding from Ralph Grizedale, and all the time her boys were in danger. Bracing herself, she opened the door a little and peered down the corridor. No sign of anyone. Taking off her boots and hanging them round her neck by the laces, she tiptoed out of the room, freezing to a halt as she heard Ralph say something. She could hardly hear what he said from here but she thought she caught the word 'Mother'. He was asking his mother something. It must be her room he was in and the door stood open. Now, if she could only get past the old lady's bedroom without attracting attention, she could reach her boys . . .

Meg forced herself to stay still until she had got her breathing under control. It was essential Ralph did not hear her.

Mrs Grizedale was saying something, her voice so thin and weak that Meg couldn't catch what it was. But she heard Ralph's reply, savage and threatening as it was.

'You bloody old witch,' he shouted. 'I'll put paid to you, I will. I'll get those shares one way or another, I'm telling you.'

Sweat broke out on Meg's forehead as she listened and heard the black menace in his tone. She had to get past the door, she had to get to her boys and take them away from here, yet she was paralyzed with fright once again, a fright summoned up by that long remembered terror of the candyman.

But Mrs Grizedale was saying something now. Her voice was stronger and more firm than it had been earlier so that Meg could hear clearly.

'Ralph, please don't speak to me like that. I have no intention of giving you anything more, so you may as well stop threatening me. I know you wouldn't hurt me. I'm your mother, after all.'

'You will give me those shares,' he said savagely. 'One way or another, I'll get them out of you.'

'Ralph, I'll tell you something I've kept from you before. But now I am almost at the end of my life. Oh, Ralph, I always thought you would realize how much you hurt me and Jonty. If your father knew, how he would grieve for you . . .'

'Sod my father, I tell you, I got the better of him and I'll get the better of you. Believe me, old woman, I will.'

Mrs Grizedale sighed. 'Well, Ralph, maybe you will. But I could not go and leave John Thomas with nothing, my conscience would not let me. What I have is left to him, there is no way you can get at it. But, my dear, Jonty would never let you starve, he will look after—'

She stopped talking as Ralph howled with rage, startling Meg in her hiding place in the passage so that she began to shake uncontrollably.

'Ralph, Ralph—'

The pleading cry was barely above a whisper and was cut off abruptly but it was enough to cut through Meg's terror. What in the name of Heaven was Ralph Grizedale doing to his mother? She stepped forward and looked into the room.

350

He was standing over the great four-poster bed, a pillow in his hands, pressing down with it on the tiny figure in the bed, the veins standing out on his forehead and his eyes glittering with rage. He was trying to smother her! Even as Meg flung herself into the room and raced for the bed, the thought flashed through her mind that she had witnessed this scene before. But instinct and action had taken the place of thought. She launched herself at him, the surprise of her attack catching him off balance so that he fell to the ground.

He was down for only a few seconds. Howling and screaming with rage he clambered to his feet, his red-rimmed eyes glaring at her. But before he could do more, she was at him, tearing at his face with her nails, kicking, scratching, riving at him so that he gave ground, grunting in shock.

Meg was screaming at the top of her voice without realizing she was. The scream seemed to come from a long way away.

'Candyman! Candyman!'

It was the old scream of fear and warning she had first heard as a child in the back street of the old railway houses, a scream which had haunted her all her life. But now she was doing something about it. She could fight back, and fight back she did.

She was not simply defending his mother, she was kicking him in the shins, kneeing him in the groin, she was paying him in kind for all he had done to her family, her father. Her hair had come down over her face and as she put up an impatient hand to brush it away she caught hold of a boot, still strung round her neck. Steel toecaps it had, a strong leather boot, heavy and hard-wearing and with a new steel heel plate put on by the cobbler only the week before. She drew her arm back and with all her strength she swung the boot, catching Ralph Grizedale on the side of the head with the heel.

For a moment she thought it had had no effect on him for he took hold of her shoulder and held her away from him, and lifting one hand high, brought it down on her head with a force which knocked her to the ground.

Meg lay there, winded, her hair falling back from her face. The room was going round and round, darkening and then lightening again, and in the centre of her vision was the violet-hued face of the candyman, and he was talking, saying something, what was it he was saying? She tried to shrink away as he fell to his knees and lifted her head. And a great cut opened up on the side of his face and blood began to flow, falling faster and faster on to her dress, her face, her hair.

'Hannah! Oh, Hannah!'

In the distance, she heard him call her mother's name. He was bending over her, crying and slobbering, lifting her head and kissing her on the lips, and she was powerless to stop him.

'Hannah, Hannah, I didn't mean to do it. Hannah, you made me do it. Hannah, Hannah, my love, I wouldn't hurt you, I could not. Hannah, Hannah, why did you not have me, why did you make me chase you away? But now you've come back to me, I knew you would come back to me. Oh, Hannah, my love . . .' His voice faded as he was drawn abruptly out of her vision and Meg blinked.

Fighting to regain control of her senses, she struggled up to a sitting position, only to fall back as the room swirled once more and her eyelids drooped. But someone had caught her and was holding her close, murmuring her name over and over. Her name, not her mother's. And Meg relaxed, slumping against him, for it was Jonty. Her Jonty had come at last. She opened her eyes and looked up at him, her lovely, lovely man, and she smiled.

'I knew you would come,' she murmured. And at that

moment she saw behind Jonty's head the face of Ralph, black and bloody, coming down on top of them, eyes fixed in a terrible stare. And then there was a great weight on her and she descended into the dark.

Meg woke tasting the salt of blood in her mouth. She moved her tongue around gingerly, feeling her teeth. They were sore but not loose. There was a gash on the inside of her cheek. She winced as the tip of her tongue found the place. Wesley must have really laid into her that time, she thought groggily.

'Meg! Meg, my love.'

Jonty, it was Jonty. What was he doing here? Alarmed, she opened her eyes. Had Wesley gone? Jonty was lifting her up in his arms. She looked around the room and remembered.

'Jonty! Jonty, is she all right? The candyman was trying to smother your grandmother. Where's he gone? Jonty, he's evil, he'll kill us both, he will.'

'No, no, it's all right, Meg, it is. He's gone now.' Jonty lifted her up and on to the *chaise longue* by the window. The room gradually settled as she clung to him, her panic lessening as she found herself safe in his arms.

'Gone? Gone where? The boys! Jonty, the boys, they're in the stable—'

How had she forgotten her boys? Ralph could be down there this minute. He would find Tucker and Kit in the stable and God knows what he would do to them. She scrambled to her feet and stood swaying, fighting to regain her balance. Jonty too sprang to his feet and held her.

'We'll go and get the boys, Meg, in a minute, when you feel better. It's all right, he won't hurt them. He won't hurt anybody ever again. He's dead, Meg.'

'Dead?'

She looked around the room, at the old lady on the

353

bed, lying back on her pillow, very white but still definitely alive as the bright, interested eyes showed.

'So you are Hannah's girl, are you? You look like your mother, my dear.' The old lady's voice was soft and frail, barely more than a whisper.

'This is Meg, Grandmother. My Meg. I love her.'

'Yes, dear, I know. Meg was everything to you when you were children. Just as Hannah was to Ralph.'

Meg looked away, hardly able to stop herself denying that Ralph's feeling for her mother could possibly have been anything like Jonty's feelings for herself. She couldn't even bear to hear Ralph's and her mother's names mentioned in the same breath. And then she saw him, lying by the door. She started, poised for flight. For a split second she thought he had moved, but Jonty had seen her reaction and came to her and put his arm around her shoulders, drawing her away, holding her face to his chest as they skirted the body and left the room.

'Come now, Meg, it's over. We'll go and get the boys,' he said softly, before turning to the old lady. 'You will be all right for a few minutes, will you, Grandmother?' And when she nodded her assent they went along the corridor and down the stairs and out the back way to the stables.

'Mam, mam, where've you been, Mam?' Tucker came running towards them but Kit was standing holding the reins of Jonty's horse and was not about to give up his proud position so easily. He hopped from foot to foot, his face bright and happy, and the horse put down its head and nuzzled him on the shoulder.

'I'm going to be a horseman when I grow up,' he cried.

Meg helped Mrs Grizedale sit up in bed and handed her a cup of tea.

'Thank you, my dear,' said the old lady.

Meg mumbled, hardly able to look at her. For now she realized what she had done. She had killed Ralph Grizedale and this was his mother. How could she look her in the eye? She took up her own cup and drank nervously.

'I'm very sorry, Mrs Grizedale,' she said. 'I'm sorry he's dead, I didn't mean to kill him.'

'Oh, my dear, don't ever say that! You didn't kill him. Why, it was an accident. I know it was an accident, didn't I see it myself? Ralph fell and hit his head on that sharp corner of the bedpost. Can't you see the mark?'

Surprised, Meg looked at the bedpost. There was a mark on it. Dried blood and a few matted hairs.

'But—'

'Now, dear, no more of it. It is true you had to hit him, but Ralph was not himself, poor boy. He was a slave to drink. Couldn't help himself, you know.'

Meg gazed at her. She was such a tiny thing, lost in the great bed, but though her face was white and her eyes full of unshed tears, her voice was firm.

'Do you think the police will believe us?' asked Meg.

'Of course. Why should they not?' Mrs Grizedale managed to sound outraged at the idea that the police should not take her word. 'Now go and see to your children, my dear. Two fine boys they are, you must be very proud of them. I shall be just fine now I've had my tea.'

So Meg went up the flight of stairs which led to the second storey and the nursery, to where the boys were playing with some old toys they had found in a box. Fervently, she hoped Mrs Grizedale was right.

Thirty

'I think you should stay here tonight,' said Jonty. He and Meg and the two boys were sitting round the table in the large old kitchen of Grizedale Hall, eating scrambled eggs on toast. The kitchen was a great, bare barn of a place, the range neglected and rusty in parts and the walls stained and brown. Yet somehow, in the soft light from the lamp hanging over the centre of the table, it looked a cosy scene. Almost like any other family gathered round for a meal, Meg mused. She looked across Kit's head at Jonty. He seemed tired and sad and worn, and her heart ached for him. She couldn't just leave him on his own tonight, not after all that had happened. Besides, there was his grandmother. She could have a delayed reaction to her son's death and then Meg would be needed to help her.

'I'll have to let Alice and Jackie know,' she said doubtfully, wondering how this was to be done.

'I'll ride over to Winton Colliery,' said Jonty. 'I'll be back in an hour.'

Meg didn't demur, though she knew what an ordeal it would be for him, trying to explain what had happened to her brother and sister.

The doctor had been, and so had the police, and the body of Jonty's father had been taken away for post mortem. For a panicky minute Meg had thought the police would not believe their story of how he had died, but Ralph had an evil reputation while Jonty was known as an upright, honest man. And, of course, the fact that Mrs Grizedale had witnessed his death counted for something. In the end, Jonty was just told that as his father had a head injury, he should hold himself available to answer any questions which might arise when the results of the post mortem were known. If the police had thought that it was strange for Meg to be in the house, they hadn't said so. Perhaps they simply thought she was working as a maid in the Hall, she didn't know.

She had told her story of how she had found Ralph Grizedale in the bedroom, drunk and threatening his mother. And how she had tried to stop him, how she had fought. Her bruised face had been enough proof for them to think she was telling the truth. But Mrs Grizedale had insisted it was later, after her son had calmed down, that he had fallen, hitting his head on the bedpost. She told her story so convincingly that Meg almost believed it herself. Could she have dreamt her own part in Ralph's death?

Mrs Grizedale was asleep now, exhausted by the day's events. The doctor had given her a bromide to help her sleep. Poor old lady, thought Meg. It must be a truly terrible thing to have a son like Ralph. Yet even so she would grieve for him. She had loved him for all his faults, Meg was sure of that.

Picking up her cup, she sipped her tea, wincing as the hot liquid got into the cut on the inside of her cheek.

'Shall I take the boys back with me to stay with Alice?' asked Jonty, finishing his meal and sitting back in his chair.

So far, the boys were blithely unaware of what had happened. While Meg had waited for the doctor and the police, Jonty had taken them down to Home Farm and Farmer Teasdale had, after a word or two of explanation from Jonty, taken them in without asking any more questions. The farmer had brought them back half an hour ago, both of them full of excitement at what they had seen on the farm and with Kit once more determined he wanted to be a farmer when he grew up. 'A horse farmer,' he said.

Now he paused, fork in the air, as he heard Jonty's question.

'Aw, Mam, I want to stay with you,' he said, his lower lip trembling. And Meg was aware that though he didn't know what had happened, he was well aware that his mother and his friend, Mr Dale, were very disturbed.

'I'll keep them here,' decided Meg, seeing this. 'We'll stay together, all of us.'

The boys had to know sometime about her and Jonty, she thought, for she and Jonty were together now, for the rest of their lives. Not that he had said anything as yet, but he didn't need to, she was sure of it.

When Jonty had gone, waving to the boys as they stood with her at the front door of the Hall, she took them back into the house and closed the door. The entrance was dimly lit by the lamp she held in her hand, the furniture loomed large and dark and shadowy, and Kit moved closer to her, taking hold of her skirt.

'You're afeared, our Kit!' jeered Tucker, but in truth his own eyes were wide open and round, and he looked about before running for the newly familiar kitchen.

'I'm not,' asserted Kit, but he clung to Meg with a trembling hand as they followed Tucker, looking relieved as she closed the green baize door firmly behind them and they were shut into the relatively light and warm kitchen.

'Aye, you are, feardy cat, feardy cat!' cried Tucker, dancing round his little brother.

'Tucker! Behave yourself,' said Meg sharply, and he subsided into a chair.

She cleared the dirty plates from the table and took them over to the brownstone sink by the window. A brass tap was over it and she tried it experimentally, marvelling at the convenience of having a tap in the house instead of on the end of the row. By, it was a grand thing to have, it was. She looked at the range, searching for a hot water boiler or a set pot and was surprised to find none. She would have to boil the kettle then. The colliery house did have some advantages, she thought drily.

The boys were very quiet as she finished the dishes and hung up the dish cloth before turning to see what they were up to.

Tucker was sitting on the chair, his head lolling to one side, in imminent danger of sliding to the flagged floor and on to Kit, who was curled up at his feet, his thumb stuck firmly in his mouth.

Their mother scooped Tucker up with one arm and Kit with the other, sitting down on the broad wooden chair and holding them to her. They stirred a little but slept on, and after a while her head drooped on to Tucker's and she slept too.

This was the picture which Jonty saw as he let himself quietly into the house and walked through to the kitchen. He stook for a moment, watching them, his heart filled with love for all three.

He remembered how he had waited for Meg by the grassy knoll that morning. Such a lot had happened in the few hours since then. Everything had changed. Though he grieved at the pain his grandmother must be feeling be feeling at the death of his father, he could not help the feeling of happiness which the sight of Meg and her children brought to him. It was so right for them to be there, in his house, under his protection. He walked softly nearer to them and looked down at the three heads, all with thick fair hair though Tucker's had a darker, reddish cast to it.

Jonty thought of his anxiety when Meg hadn't come to meet him that morning. He had waited and waited and in the end had decided he would go to Winton Colliery and find out if there was anything wrong. He must have just missed her on the road, he thought. Then his horse had cast a shoe and he had had to take time to go to the blacksmith a mile out of his way.

Meg woke and saw him watching her and they smiled at each other, an intimate smile which meant more than words.

'Jonty,' she breathed.

Later, when they had put the boys to bed in the room next to his so that he and Meg would hear if they woke during the night, he told her how he had gone looking for her that afternoon.

'I was almost to the village when something seemed to call me back,' he said. 'I don't know what it was, I just knew I had to get back to the Hall. I felt you were there and you needed me.'

'I tried to reach you in my mind,' she said. 'I knew you would come.'

They climbed the stairs together, hand in hand and walked along the corridor to the children's room, peeping in on Tucker and Kit before going on to the bedroom at the end. There were still a lot of things they had to talk about, but not tonight. Tonight it was enough to sleep in each other's arms.

Meg awoke to the shrill piping of the boys' voices sounding through the wall. Tucker was shouting with boisterous excitement and Kit giggling, he was always the quieter of the two. She reached out a hand for Jonty but there was only the warm place where he had lain and the dent in the pillow where his head had been. But the sound of his deeper tones was coming through the

360

wall. He must have heard the boys before she did and got up to see to them.

Rising from bed, Meg hurriedly pulled on her clothes and went into the next bedroom, to be greeted by the sight of Jonty swinging Tucker in the air and bouncing him on the bed. Tucker was giggling helplessly, filled with glee.

'My turn! my turn!' shouted Kit, and Jonty obligingly picked him up and swung him round before pretending to fall and they both landed on the bed beside Tucker. Tucker scrambled on top of Jonty, holding his arms down, and Jonty shrank back in mock submission.

'Skinch! Skinch!' he cried. 'I give in.'

'That bed will collapse in a minute,' observed Meg.

All three of them sat up and gazed at her, their faces flushed and eyes sparkling.

'Mam, Mam, Jonty says I can have a ride on his horse,' cried Kit.

'Yes. Well, for now, how about having a wash and getting dressed so that we can all have some breakfast?'

'Aw, Mam,' wailed Tucker. 'What do we have to wash all the time for?'

'Come on, lads,' put in Jonty, before the rebellion could go further, 'I'll race you to the bathroom.'

'Bathroom?' asked Kit mystified. Curiosity was enough to make them forget their aversion to soap and water. They had never seen a room kept solely for bathing in and neither had their mother. She made the beds and tidied the rooms before following the sound of splashing water and excited cries.

'Eeh, it's grand, Jonty.'

She gazed round the bathroom, at the hot water geyser on the wall, the boys sitting in the large iron tub, half-filled with hot soapy water. By the wall was an ornate basin with two brass taps. And Jonty, standing before the basin just like any ordinary father, watching his children while he shaved.

'We've saved you some hot water, Mam,' said Tucker virtuously. 'By, isn't it grand?'

'Don't splash so much about,' she said calmly, for all the world as though the sight of her boys in the huge bath was an everyday thing. 'I don't want to be wiping up after you.' But her eyes met Jonty's in the mirror and her smile was full of love. They were cocooned in a cosy little world here, she and Jonty and Tucker and Kit. Of course it could not last forever, they had to face the outside world sometime. But at least they had a little while to help each other recover from the shocks and traumas which had affected them in the last few weeks.

'I'll see to your grandmother's breakfast,' she said, and hurried along to the old lady's room where she found her already awake.

'Good morning, Meg,' Mrs Grizedale greeted her. 'Oh, my dear, I'm so glad you decided to stay for a while. Jonty needs you, you know.'

As Meg tidied her bed and helped her wash and comb her hair, she wondered if Mrs Grizedale would be quite so happy if she was aware that Meg had spent the night with her grandson.

'What did Alice say when you saw her, Jonty?'

They were sitting at the table drinking an extra cup of tea. The boys had found a ball in the old nursery and were off in the stable yard, kicking it about. Their whoops and cries could be heard through the kitchen window, the sound happy and excited.

Meg looked apprehensively at him, remembering her sister's disapproval of their relationship, but Jonty smiled.

'Oh, Alice said she understood. I told her my

362

grandmother was ill and you were helping out for a day or two. Well, it wasn't a real lie, was it?'

'And she didn't mind?' Meg was astonished.

'Well, she was full of her own plans to try for a scholarship. She hopes to get into Durham University. St Mary's College, she said. And evidently her teacher thinks she stands a good chance.'

'She didn't say anything about that to me,' commented Meg, feeling sad that her sister hadn't confided in her. But then, she thought, she had been so full of her own troubles, perhaps Alice had thought she wouldn't be interested.

'Maybe she was waiting until she had something definite to tell you,' suggested Jonty, ever sensitive to Meg's feelings.

'Yes,' she said, and rose to her feet. 'Well, I think I'll go and get Mrs Grizedale's tray and see what she needs in the way of help.'

'I'll come with you,' he said. 'The boys will be fine in the yard for now.'

The old lady was sitting up in bed, looking a little stronger. She watched as Jonty and Meg came into the room, seeing how close they were, even when standing on opposite sides of her bed. There was such a bond between them, she mused, they belonged together.

'You're looking better, Grandmother,' Jonty said as he bent over her and kissed her cheek.

'I am, I think,' she replied, before turning to Meg. 'I must know, there was something you were saying yesterday when you were struggling with my poor misguided Ralph—' She faltered for a moment.

'Please don't distress yourself, Grandmother,' Jonty put in swiftly.

'No, I'm all right, I think it's better to talk about it,' she answered, her voice strengthening. 'Candyman, that's what it was. Candyman, you were saying. Now why would you call him a candyman?'

Meg sat down suddenly on a chair by the bedside and clasped her hands tightly in her lap.

'Yes, candyman. I always thought of him as the candyman, ever since I was small,' she said, her voice low. And she recounted the story of the evictions from the railway cottages, how Ralph Grizedale had watched the candymen doing their work, sitting there on his great horse as she and her mother and little Jack were chased up the line by the candymen. And how ever since she had thought of Ralph Grizedale as 'the biggest candyman of them all', as she heard someone say.

'Well,' said Mrs Grizedale, sounding suddenly very old and weak, 'I'm sorry, my dear. If only I'd been able to do something. He always loved your mother, you know. Poor Nell was always second best for him.'

'Please don't upset yourself,' Meg begged, going to the bed and taking the old lady's hand. 'None of it was your fault, none of it. And it was so long ago.'

But in her heart she denied that Ralph could ever have loved her mother. If he had done, how could he have hounded them as he had?

The funeral of Ralph Grizedale took place the following week, after the post mortem had revealed he had died from natural causes after suffering a cerebral haemorrhage. The blow to his temple was attributed to his striking it on the bedpost, as his mother had testified.

'What difference does it make now?' Jonty said privately to Meg when the verdict was known. At least it meant that the inquest was straightforward and they could put it all behind them and start a new life.

They and Jonty's solicitor were the only mourners at the funeral, though afterwards there were many who came to the Hall to see if Jonty was going to honour his father's debts. He vowed he would pay them all in full.

But the debts were higher than he had reckoned on. Much higher.

'Grizedale will have to go,' he said sombrely, when he and Meg were at last on their own one evening some time later. Jonty had been in Bishop Auckland all that day, clearing up his father's affairs. 'We were already carrying a heavy mortgage, you know,' he added.

'Oh, Jonty, I'm sorry. It's been your home for so long, it's a shame you have to leave it,' sighed Meg. 'But what about your grandmother? She will miss it so terribly.'

She looked round the shabby drawing-room, still showing signs of its former splendour. She sat on the edge of a well-stuffed sofa, the brocade cover worn and threadbare, looking and feeling uncomfortable. She didn't like this room, she reflected. The chairs were too soft and the furnishings much too ornate. She preferred sitting in the kitchen on a hard chair before the range. No, she wouldn't miss Grizedale Hall, but her heart ached for Jonty and Mrs Grizedale. She was sure they would.

'Will you mind?' asked Jonty.

'No,' she admitted. 'I would rather have a smaller house, one I can keep nice myself. Mind, the boys will miss the bathroom.' They laughed together. Both Kit and Tucker were still enchanted with the bathroom, taking a bath every day without a murmur of protest. Jonty looked relieved. He had thought that Meg might want to live in the Hall and he knew it had to go.

He was sitting at a small occasional table, working on the estate books. After all his father's creditors were paid off there would be nothing left of his own inheritance. But if he could sell the Hall and Home Farm, well then, he would still have enough to stock a small rented farm somewhere, a place where he could

365

earn a living for his newly acquired family. Farming was all he knew and he owed that knowledge to Farmer Teasdale. He would offer the farmer the chance to buy Home Farm, he thought. It was the least he could do for him.

'Do you think you would like to move away from here, Meg? Could you be a farmer's wife?'

'Move away?' Oh, she thought, how she would like to move away and leave all her unhappy memories behind.

'We could go abroad, emigrate?' suggested Jonty.

'Or maybe just get a place by the sea?' Could we find a place by the sea, Jonty? Oh, I loved the sea, and you would love it too. Up Marsden way, maybe?' Meg looked up at him eagerly and in an instant Jonty dropped any idea of emigrating.

'We'll see,' he said, closing his account book and going over to the sofa. He sat down by her side and took her hand in his and they lapsed into silence for a while, simply happy to sit there together.

'Jonty, I have something else to tell you,' she said, not without a flutter of anxiety. He had enough troubles at the moment without her adding to them, she thought. Yet he had to be told, she had put it off long enough.

'I'm going to have a baby.'

She heard the words echoing round the room and bent her gaze to her lap, biting her lip. But the next moment she was gathered up in his arms and he was kissing her joyously and her apprehension dropped away as though it had never been.

'We'll get married,' he stated, very positive about it.

'But Jonty, how can we?'

'You can get a divorce.'

Divorce? What was he talking about? Divorces cost money, no one in the coal field got divorced, it was unheard of. Meg's brow furrowed as she looked up at him.

'Don't worry, my love, of course you can get a divorce.' Jonty was a new man. He was sure he could make everything all right for them now. 'I may not have much left, but I can afford to pay for a solicitor, and pay Wesley off too if need be. But you have grounds for a divorce. Hasn't he lived with Sally Hawkins all these years? I'm sure Sally would like to be married, don't you think so?'

Meg had to agree. Sally would love to be married. And there was no doubt as to who wore the trousers in that household!

Her thoughts went back to the awful day when *it* happened, remembering the rage and horror she had felt as she saw Ralph with the pillow in his hand as he stood over his mother. And somehow it stirred another, older memory, something that happened so long ago she thought perhaps her memory was playing tricks on her.

But no, she had seen Ralph holding a pillow in just the same way, and in just the same place. When was it? It must have been before she and her family left the railway cottages, she was sure she had not been to the Hall after that. She probed the elusive memory in her mind, almost like probing an aching tooth for the source of the pain. And suddenly it clicked into place.

'Jonty?'

'Yes, dear?'

'Jonty, I think I know why your father took you away from us and blackballed Da so that we had to leave the district. Thinking of your poor grandmother, I remembered.'

Slowly, haltingly, frowning in concentration, Meg told him of the day they had been playing hide-and-seek upstairs in the Hall.

'Do you remember, we were hiding in some sort of cupboard?'

But Jonty shook his head, he couldn't remember at all.

367

'We were, though,' Meg insisted, 'and your grandfather was in bed. Your father came in and he picked up the pillow and he . . . he put it over his father's face.'

Meg stopped. Had she really seen that happen all those years ago and not realized what Ralph Grizedale was doing? Or was it just in her imagination?

'Go on.'

'We fell out of the cupboard, Jonty, and we ran and ran, we were so frightened.'

'Oh, yes, I think I do remember,' he cried. He had always been frightened of his father, he could remember that well enough. He had feared his father's hard hand, his scathing contempt. The fear had been a hard, physical reality, a deep pain in the gut.

They sat stunned by the horror of that old, shared memory.

'It was my fault,' Meg whispered, and Jonty put his arm around her.

'Oh, Meg, how could it have been your fault?'

'No. It was because of me that your father hounded us away. If I hadn't been there that day, Da would still be working on the railway, and me and you, Jonty, we would never have lost each other.' She felt a great sadness at the thought of what might have been, but Jonty soon drew her out of it.

'Oh, Meg, Meg, we're together now, we love each other, we have the boys. And soon we'll have another, will we not?' And once more he drew her into his arms and they were lost to the world.

Thirty-One

Mrs Grizedale passed away peacefully in her sleep a few weeks later. She did not live to see Grizedale Hall sold. She was happy in those last few weeks, though, she and Meg becoming firm friends, and without the worry of what her son might do next her health seemed to improve. But she was an old lady and in the end her heart gave out.

Meg was sad to see her go. She had herself become genuinely fond of Jonty's grandmother and grieved with him.

'She was all the mother I knew,' commented Jonty sadly on the evening after the funeral. 'But I'm glad she didn't have to face the upheaval of moving away from here. And it was right for her to be buried alongside Grandfather in Shildon.'

Meg took his hand in hers and lifted it to her cheek. She did not need to say anything, the empathy between her and Jonty grew stronger every day. Within her, she felt the first trembling movement of the baby. She waited, not even breathing, and there it was again.

'What is it?' asked Jonty.

'The baby . . . the baby moved,' she whispered, and held his hand over her stomach. But of course the movement was not yet strong enough for him to feel. Meg lapsed into a dreaming half-consciousness. Oh, she was happy, so happy. The divorce proceedings were already started. It had been as Jonty had said it would be. Though Wesley blustered at first, Sally soon put him right about whether he was willing to let Meg divorce him.

'You'll make me an honest woman, Wesley Cornish,' she had shrilled, and he had caved in immediately. Jonty had given them a hundred pounds on condition Wesley waived any claim to the boys.

'And only right an' all,' Sally had declared, 'after the way you and Meg were carrying on.'

She had shut up abruptly when she saw the expression on Jonty's face, but he was glad Meg had not come with him to see Wesley and his mistress. She might not have been content with giving Sally a withering look.

'It's a pity we can't get married before the baby is born, though,' Jonty said now.

'We are married. We are as married as we'll ever be,' Meg said stoutly. 'Any road, what will it matter in the end? We won't be living here, no one will know us, wherever we're going.'

Epilogue

Meg walked along the sandy shore, her fair hair blowing loose from its pins and her dress dragging against her legs in the stiff north-easter coming in off the sea. She paused to watch a string of colliers ploughing slowly along past Marsden Rock to the mouth of the Tyne, where they would pick up their load of coal, bound for the south of England. They were ugly, squat, little vessels, but they always caught her imagination. They went up and down the coast, stopping only to load and unload, the pit ponies of the sea.

Oh, how she loved the sea, she thought. The cries of the seabirds, the tall cliffs with Marsden Colliery village perched on the top and the Souter lighthouse alongside. She thought of the steps inside the lighthouse, how she had scrubbed them as a child, how proud she had been to take her pay home to her mam.

'Mam! Mam! See what I've found.'

Meg turned at the sound of her daughter's voice, high and squeaky with excitement as she held out her shrimping pail to show her mother half a dozen shrimps in the bottom.

'They're grand, Hope, I'll cook them for your tea,' Meg said, smiling down at Hope's flushed face, the dark eyes so like Jonty's, yet her hair as fair and abundantly curly as Meg's own.

'No, for Daddy's tea, I've got them for Daddy.'

'For Daddy then,' Meg agreed. 'Now we must get back, or we'll be too late to cook them for tea.'

She took Hope's hand to help her up the steep cliff path which led up to Whitworth village and on towards their farm. But Hope shook herself free.

'I can get up myself, Mam,' she said decisively.

'Well, be careful, you don't want to drop your pail,' answered Meg. Hope, ever since she had been old enough to sit up and demand what she wanted, had ruled not only Jonty but Kit and Tucker, both of whom were her willing slaves. It was Meg who had to discipline her for she was the only one who could resist the charm of those dark eyes.

But Hope was not a bad child, she had a healthy sense of fair play and was not given to tantrums, Meg thought to herself as she followed her daughter up the cliff. She remembered the day when Hope was born, three years ago now. They had decided on the name for not only was it the maiden name of Meg's and Jonty's common grandmother, but somehow the coming of the child symbolized their own hopes for the future.

And they had done well, thought Meg, pausing to catch her breath as they got to the top of the cliff. Seagulls were swirling and swooping about the sky before going to roost for the night in the crevices of the cliffs, calling raucously to one another as they did so. The money from Mrs Grizedale's railway shares had enabled them to buy the farm and Jonty had worked hard to improve it. Now they were earning a comfortable living.

'Come on, Mam, I'm hungry,' said Hope, looking back impatiently at her mother.

'I'm coming,' said Meg, and they hurried to the gate of the farmyard, where Kit was leading a horse across to the stable for the night after a day spent ploughing. He whistled as he went. Though he was only just gone ten, he was proud of his skill with horses and liked to show his mother he could do a man's work.

Inside the house, Tucker was standing before the range in the kitchen waiting for them. He was just fourteen but already almost six feet tall, his shoulders broad and powerful.

He's so like Wesley, Meg thought. It could almost have been him standing there. Wesley at fourteen, proud and strong. But Tucker was not wild, he had a lot of his mother in him too. He was hard-working and considerate and fond of little Hope.

It was as the family sat round the table for tea that he dropped his bombshell.

'Da,' he said, addressing Jonty. Both boys had called Jonty Da for years now. 'I'm going down the pit. You've got Granda to help now and Kit's big enough to help you an' all and I want to be a pitman.'

'Tucker!'

Meg was horrified. How could Tucker want to be a pitman when he had a good job on the farm, in the open air? When he had seen what the pits did to his grandfather? She glanced across to the doorway where her own father was sitting with a tray on his knees, eating his tea.

They had got Jack Maddison out of Sedgefield only last year. He was very much better in that he was rational and continent in his habits, though still liked to stay by the door, no matter what the weather. But even in the short time he had been on the farm, Meg could see how the open air life was working on him, bringing him back to his former self.

Jonty put a hand over hers. 'If that's what the boy wants, Meg,' he said.

'I do, I want to be a miner,' asserted Tucker. 'An' they're wanting putters at Horden, I could start on Monday.'

So it wasn't a whim, Tucker had really thought this out. Meg felt sad. He was growing up. Jonty was right, the boy had a right to decide for himself. And hadn't his father and grandfather been pitmen?

'Don't be hasty, our Tucker,' said a crisp voice from the doorway and the family looked across at Alice, just coming in with her Gladstone bag in her hand. Alice was wearing a severely tailored costume and had her hair drawn back tightly in a bun. But she could do nothing about the curly tendrils which escaped to frame her white forehead above the piercing blue eyes. Now she walked into the kitchen and threw her bag into a corner.

'Have you left me some tea?'

Hope rushed at her and flung herself into her arms, laughing and talking excitedly.

'Have you come for a holiday, Auntie Alice? Our Tucker wants to go down the pit, did you hear?'

'No, I'm just here for the weekend. I have to be back at University on Monday. And, yes, I did hear Tucker,' Alice said calmly. She sat down at the table and Meg poured her tea, smiling proudly at the young sister who had managed against all the odds to win a bursary to Durham to study English. Oh, she had done well, Meg thought, she had. And Jackie had too for he was now working for his under-manager's ticket.

'I'm not being hasty,' said Tucker, picking up Alice's remark.

'Well, you haven't thought it out, have you?' she demanded. 'You've got brains in your head, why don't you use them? If you must go down the pit, you could study surveying or even mining engineering, do the job properly.'

'I want to start now,' insisted Tucker, and Alice began to reason with him, using her now considerable debating skills to try to change his mind.

Meg listened. Alice stood a much better chance of

changing Tucker's mind than she did. He had always been especially fond of Alice. But Tucker was adamant.

'I want to go down Horden, I'm going to start as a putter,' he said stubbornly.

Later, in the privacy of their own bedroom, Jonty took Meg in his arms.

'Don't worry, Meg,' he whispered. 'Tucker will be fine.'

'But—'

'Meg, Meg,' said Jonty. 'We each have our own lives. My grandfather made a fortune when the railway came. He rose from humble farmer to gentleman and built Grizedale Hall. And Father threw it all away, and here am I, a humble farmer again. But we're happy, Meg. We are, aren't we?'

She put her arms around his neck and held his face against hers, the depth of her love welling up in her. She thought of Jonty's da, the candyman of her nightmares. She hadn't thought of him for a long time. And she thought of her own da, at last achieving some sort of peace in his old age. They had won in the end, she and her da, the candyman was defeated. She looked down at the broad wedding band on her finger, still shiny and new after only a year of wear.

'I'm happy, Jonty,' she said.